"I SHALL NOT WANT"

ƁR

BLOOMSBURY READER

Discover books by Norman Collins published by
Bloomsbury Reader at
www.bloomsbury.com/NormanCollins

"I SHALL NOT WANT"

NORMAN COLLINS

BR

BLOOMSBURY READER

LONDON · NEW DELHI · NEW YORK · SYDNEY

This electronic edition published in 2012 by Bloomsbury Reader

Bloomsbury Reader is a division of Bloomsbury Publishing Plc,

50 Bedford Square, London WC1B 3DP

ISBN: 978 1 4482 0080 1
eISBN: 978 1 4482 0212 6

Visit www.bloomsburyreader.com to find out more about our authors and their books
You will find extracts, author interviews, author events and you can sign up for
newsletters to be the first to hear about our latest releases and special offers
Printed and bound by CPI Group (UK) Ltd, Croydon, CR0 4YY

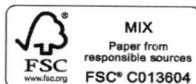

MIX
Paper from
responsible sources
FSC
www.fsc.org   FSC® C013604

To
Henrie and Peter

Contents

Author's Note

All the characters and incidents described in this novel are, like the sect of Amosite Baptists to which most of the characters in the story belong, entirely fictitious and have no originals in life. No kind of reference is intended to any living person or to any existing shop, firm, or religious body.

N.C.

Book I

The Fall

Chapter I

The Amos Immersionist Tabernacle imposed itself upon the whole thoroughfare. There it stood, a defiant citadel of righteousness looming over the insignificant abodes of men: it dominated. Its façade of twin, stucco columns and chocolate-coloured pilasters dwarfed everything around it, making the terrace of inferior shops and shabby, old-fashioned villas on either side seem like so many dolls' houses set up against something serious and life-size.

Across the front of the Tabernacle ran a row of spiked, green-painted railings; and behind the railings there mounted a steep flight of steel-tread concrete steps. These steps, however, served another and more important purpose than to be walked up: they provided a high place from which to announce the Message. And in the twelve-inch letters, behind thick plate-glass, the Word was exhibited in a series of notice-boards. It was a strange, disjunctive Message which emerged: GOD IS LOVE the first board announced. Above it, in still larger letters, were the words I CAME NOT TO SEND PEACE, BUT A SWORD. Over to the right, a pasted notice, THE RIGHTEOUS SHALL REJOICE WHEN HE SEETH THE VENGEANCE: HE

SHALL WASH HIS FEET IN THE BLOOD OF THE WICKED, caught the eye. And down almost on the pavement level was the printed advice, now a little soiled and yellow at the corners with age and exposure, SALUTE ONE ANOTHER WITH AN HOLY KISS.

Above all was another notice board, set back a little and lettered in gold. This gave the style and title of the chapel, the times of the services, and the name and address of the verger; and, in the second line from the top, bolder and more freshly gilded than the rest, were the words: *Prebend and Minister: the Reverend Eliud Tuke, B.D., Surrogate for Marriages.*

To-night the Tabernacle was lit up in almost pagan splendour. Every gas-jet in the place was hissing and, through its four long windows, it glowed. There was, even for one of West London's leading fortresses of nonconformity, an unusual stir of activity. Ever since six o'clock the devout had been arriving. They had passed up the concrete steps in their multitudes, and in batch after batch the big Tabernacle had swallowed them. Behind those studded, panelled doors between five and six hundred people were now seated in their pews.

It was bleak enough outside, with a threat of sleet or snow in the air, but the heat inside was terrific. Eight steep steps up from the roadway it was tropical. Already, before the important business of the evening, the baptisms, had started, two of the sisterhood had fainted. With waxen frightened faces, on which the beads of sweat stood out like raindrops, they had been carried off to the vestry and been revived on the long benches that were used for Zenana soirées and Missionary Teas. On Baptism Nights a deaconess of the Order was permanently stationed in the vestry: it was her duty to revive the fragile, one after another, as they were brought in. Smelling salts, a bottle of lavender water

4

and the tea-urn from the basement comprised the whole of her equipment. As soon as the women—and there were always some men among the fainters as well—were breathing again, they were packed off into the body of the chapel once more to see the sights and be edified.

There was certainly something tremendous to see. On these immersionist nights the Tabernacle resembled an arena more than a temple. Only the plain altar, the Table of the Lord, in the eastern wall broke the symmetry of the seats. And from the central dais where Mr. Tuke stood, it Was like being submerged in a vast well of gleaming faces, so that no matter in what direction he looked there were still those endless batteries of peering, fascinated eyes. From Mr. Tuke's standpoint it was even more alarming when the congregation began a hymn; it was as though he were being swallowed. Those pink layers upon layers of faces would suddenly open, and what he would see would be not eyes but the dark cavities of six hundred throats. Then with the intoning of the Amen the whole hall would go pink again.

One point of variety in the encircling panorama of the Tabernacle was that the men were separated from the women. On the north side of the central aisle was a sea of bosoms and feather-boas and veiled faces; to the south, it was all beards and watch-chains and deep bass voices. To balance the altar, stood the organ. Controversy had raged round this instrument, and its erection had once been a matter not merely of vestry politics but of heresy; the unwitting donor, long since deceased, had been the cause of a schism which had divided the entire Synod of Amosite Elders. In the first place, it had been suggested that the foundations were not strong enough for such a monster. But objections of this kind were no more than subterfuge: the Amos Tabernacle was clearly strong enough for *anything*. Then the question of propriety had arisen and the real row had begun. On one side it was felt that the presence of a box of pipes of this nature was so dangerously High as to be almost Roman, and on the other there was an equally determined move not to deprive themselves of anything costing the colossal sum of nearly four hundred pounds. In the end, it was the acquisitive who won; and, after suitable safeguards had been laid down as to the nature of the music that was to be played, the gift had been accepted. It now stood against the west wall, a towering mass of cylindrical metal, with a little red velvet curtain in front of it, behind which the organist sat in his own private asylum of ivory keys, stops, swell-pedal and spy-mirror. The blower, a brother-in-law of the verger, had to stand right out in the passage, heaving away at the great wooden arm like a pump-handle during all the musical moments of divine service.

But it was not at the organ that anyone was looking to-night; after seven years' installation it had become as orthodox and unexceptionable as the gas-lighting. It was the Jordan Tank which was the focus of everyone's attention. It stood, a great zinc bath more than six feet square, let into the very centre of the auditorium. Five wooden steps, which flattened out deceptively under the surface of the water, led down into the tank on one side and a duplicate set led out on the other. The heating apparatus ran right underneath it.

It was only twice yearly that the tank was used, and it was at these bi-annual immersions that Amosites declared their faith to the world. There was a kind of raucous majesty about the occasion. The adult choir, again divided into male and female, was augmented by choristers from other Amosite chapels; and there was a cornet player a strained, melancholy-looking little man— who brought his instrument all the way from Croydon. Nor was

6

this all: a large banner ran right across the hall, and on this in giant, embroidered letters ran the words: WITH THE BAPTISM THAT I AM BAPTIZED WITHAL SHALL YE BE BAPTIZED.

Mr. Tuke, in the simple surplice of his Order, was standing right beneath his banner. The singing had just stopped and there was an atmosphere of impatient expectancy throughout the hall. But it was not yet time for the immersions. There was the psalm first and Mr. Tuke, holding his surplice up with one hand so that he should not trip, mounted the two steps to the lectern. He was a large man, so large in fact that he made the sprawling Bible on the shelf in front of him seem almost small and trivial. And his voice was powerful and resonant; it had a thousand rich modulations in it. He used words slowly and gloatingly as though he were fingering them.

His large pink face—he always looked as though he had just emerged from the hot towels of a barber—began to crease and fall in folds about his mouth as he swung the heavy volume back onto the marker. Already at the thought of those words, his mouth was watering. He took a quick glance round the galleries (it was as though invisible wires of sympathy were radiating from him) and began. *"The Lord is my Shepherd; I shall not want."* The voice softened for a moment and it became like a woman speaking. *"He maketh me to lie down in green pastures: he leadeth me beside the still waters."* The womanliness vanished and a hint of brass and kettle-drum crept in. *"He restoreth my soul: he leadeth me in the paths of righteousness for his name's sake. Yea, though I walk through the valley of the shadow of death (pp.) I will fear no evil: for thou art with me (ff.) Thy rod and Thy staff they comfort me."* Mr. Tuke's expression changed subtly, and he spread out his hands towards the congregation, as though thanking them. *"Thou preparest a table before me in the presence of mine enemies: thou annointest my head with oil: my cup runneth over."* Then his face changed again and he magically cast off forty years of his life and was a little boy again: *"Surely goodness and mercy shall follow me all the days of my life: and I will dwell in the house of the Lord for ever."*

He became a mighty, all-powerful man again as he finished, a man capable of surviving without a tremor the ordeal of standing for over half-an-hour in lukewarm water up to his waist.

And the reading of the Psalm over, he offered up a prayer. It was the Amosite prayer which invoked God in the name of his servant Amos, to be present while these of the faithful dedicated themselves in His name. ". . . as in Jordan of old," Mr. Tuke magnificently intoned, "so do we, Thy mean and wretched disciples, ask of Thee the abundant and glorious blessings which Thou alone canst give."

With that he rose from his knees and walked towards the tank. His surplice, specially weighted at the edges to prevent it from billowing up round him like a parachute as he entered the water, hung round him in sullen, dejected folds. Behind him, in rows, sat the new disciples, the un-baptized. There were thirty-four of them in all; fourteen men and twenty women. They sat pale-faced and apprehensive, like victims ready for sacrifice. Even their dress was sacrificial: it was white from head to foot, a long, white clinging garment that buttoned up at the back and was gathered in closely at the wrists. Beneath this dress the Amosite initiate could wear whatever he or she chose; the men, for the most part, wore very little else, and the women only sufficient to ensure that when they climbed up the steps again after the dipping the garment should not cling to them too revealingly. On the advice of the deaconess in the disrobing-room below, many of the women had wound a bath towel round themselves before putting on the vestment; and, in the result, they sat in muffled, mysterious shapes that disguised everything about them except the fact that they were women and that they had disguised themselves. They were really doubly disguised for they wore a close white handkerchief around their heads; the men of course were bare-headed.

Mr. Tuke shuddered as his left foot touched the water even though, under the surplice, he was wearing waders like a fisherman. It was ten degrees colder than it should have been, and the contact sent a shiver running along the length of his spine. He registered a decision to speak to the verger about it as soon as the service was over—he had told the man when he came in that his duty to-night lay down in the stoke-hold—and, pursing up his lips as the icy water took his breath away, he went resolutely down the steps. Once actually in the tank he felt a powerful desire to duck his head under and be done with it; but he controlled himself. Instead, holding his little slip of paper with the names of Baptists-elect in one hand and the silver cup with which he was to anoint their heads in the other, he stood waist-deep in the water and called out their names.

"Brother Freeman."

A large man who moved importantly like a shop-walker, rose from the extreme right of the front bench and came forward. He stalked along as though intending to enter the water with dignity but, as soon as his ankle was covered, he drew back and muttered an involuntary "Ah!" Mr. Tuke frowned at him: he had no patience with people who made a fuss over less than a minute of it while he, in his fifty-second year, would have to remain there in the bath for nearly three-quarters of an hour. Brother Freeman observed the rebuke. Holding his breath, he almost ran down the five steps and presented himself before his Minister and Baptist.

Mr. Tuke placed his hand on the man's shoulder and his voice rang out like an organ note as he prayed over him; there was not a quaver in his throat . . . "now shall he sit," he chanted, "at the table of the Most Holy. Among the elect ones shall he sit down." With that, he filled the little silver cup—it held about half-a-pint—and emptied it over the new disciple. The man's astonished gasp—he had not expected the douching quite so soon—was audible throughout the chapel, and those who had themselves suffered a chilly baptism shifted uncomfortably in their seats. Then, Brother Freeman, urged on by a nudge from Mr. Tuke, shuffled through the water in his felt slippers and clambered up the other side. He was visibly shivering by now, and his air of importance had vanished. He was simply a big man in uncomfortable clothes drenched to the skin and without his glasses. He disappeared out of sight down a staircase on the left, leaving a water trail behind him as Mr. Tuke's voice was heard again.

"Brother Buckley," he said; and the next man arose.

There was a pause when all the male benches had been emptied, and the indeterminate forms in the female half could be seen stirring with foreboding. There was also a noticeable restlessness in the body of the temple itself at the prospect of the feminine immersions; they excited everyone—even the women—as no amount of male immersions could ever do.

In particular, there was one man seated to the left of the gangway immediately below the tank who was leaning forward with every muscle strained. He had not taken his eyes off the women's benches from the moment the service began. Even when the whole congregation had been kneeling in prayer, he had still, through clasped fingers, contrived to keep one of the white, shrouded figures in sight. The fact that she was swathed in so much material did not dismay him: he knew by heart the shape of her head, the way the slim neck mounted to support it, the heavy coil of hair that rested there. And under the uncomely coif the pale face was still the same. Once or twice the girl had become aware that she was being watched and had turned towards him. But each time it was her eyes which had dropped first and she had fixed her gaze modestly on the white, billowing back of the woman in front of her.

The young man who was so transfixed was John Marco. Within his Church he was regarded as a model Amosite. He was still young—not yet thirty-four—but there was a consciousness of purpose about him that counted for more than mere age. In his seriousness towards life, he seemed indeed a middle-aged man already; and he was respected as middle-aged men are respected. He was a pew-opener in the Tabernacle and taught the children of the Elders in Sunday School. In his business, too, he was respected; an aura of promotion surrounded him. In God's good time, he had often told himself, the reward would come; and he would have earned himself a place on earth as well as in Heaven. But the reward, the gift for which he had been waiting, still seemed as far away as ever, even though in the Silk and Cotton department of Morgan and Roberts where he worked he now had three young lady assistants.

The coldness and determination of his nature had left their mark upon his face. It was a calculating, close-lipped face. Only the breadth of the forehead gave it strength. And the eyes. These were deep-set and penetrating. In most lights they were almost black, and they held the gaze longer than was comfortable. They were the eyes of a man who would spare no one, least of all himself.

11

He looked towards the girl on the baptismal bench and the lines of his face softened for a moment. It was remarkable that her beauty should have such power over him. But there was no disputing it. It was there. In her presence he became meek and humble. Somewhere within the limits of her smile his ambition vanished.

It was only lately that he had known her. She had been shy and diffident at first, as though reluctant to let herself be loved. She had avoided him. In Sunday school where they both taught she had treated him like a stranger, not speaking to him, not noticing him. Not *showing* that she noticed him, at least. For it was impossible for her not to know. There were so many little things he did which betrayed him; he would be the first to hand her a hymn book at prayers; he would come into her class-room during sessions on odd excuses to borrow a wall-map of the Holy Land or an oleograph of the infant Moses among the rushes; he would arrive so early that he was waiting there in the prim, oak-panelled common-room when she came in to take off her gloves; he would time his lessons so that he contrived to meet her in the corridor; he would hang about after school was over so that he could say good night to her as she passed through the gate.

The first time he had ever walked home with her had been little more than a month ago. The memory was vividly imprinted on his mind for two reasons: he had seen her with rain on her hair—and he had committed a sin; he had stolen. The sight of her with the raindrops on her face and on the soft waves of hair that escaped from underneath her hat had affected him strangely; when he had seen that her cheeks were wet, he had been as much moved as if she had been crying. But after he had left her and he had come to his senses again, it was the sin, his sin, that troubled him. It frightened him. It showed that deep within him he was weak and frail and not to be trusted; it wiped out in a single moment the careful portrait of himself that he had been painting in his own mind through all the years.

In the manner of most temptations it had been enticingly simple, even innocent-looking, at the onset. At three-fifty-five on that melancholy Sunday afternoon in November he had still been whole; and by five minutes past he had succumbed. His Bible class had passed off smoothly enough and the lesson on the fruits of faith in the fathers of old time had been absorbed by the thirty ten-year old children of the Amosite parish. Then, as John Marco, his Bible under his arm, had walked in the direction of the common-room the rain had started. It had not been ordinary rain; it was as though the original flood-gates-of-the-deluge had reopened. On the corrugated-iron-roof of the chapel Sunday school it had drummed and battered. "A sound of abundance of rain," John Marco had thought. "The heaven was black with clouds and wind, and there was a great rain." When he had reached the common-room, Miss Kent was already there. She was standing at the window looking out into the small asphalt yard in which the raindrops were bouncing. He had seen her profile as he came in, lit by the yellow glow of the single gas mantle. It was pale and beautiful. The fair hair curled upwards over the temples and, under her hat, ran smoothly across her head into the thick coil behind. She was just drawing on her veil as he approached her.

"The rain's come on very suddenly," he had said.

"I know," she had answered. "And I didn't bring an umbrella. I didn't think I should need one."

He had paused. He had not brought his own umbrella either: his bowler-hat and his neat Sunday overcoat with the deep velvet collar were going to suffer. But as he stood there he had seen Mr. Tuke's umbrella in the corner, a stout, well-set-up umbrella, with a silver band which ran round the cherry wood handle. His throat had contracted and his mouth suddenly gone dry as he looked at it. Admittedly, it was not his; but it could be.

"May I offer you mine as far as your home?" he had asked.

Mary Kent had turned and looked at him, hesitating and awkward as he stood there before her. She could not help noticing that in his way he was a handsome man, virile and wide-shouldered and erect; and in his present awkwardness he looked somehow younger. She had dropped her eyes.

"Thank you," she had said.

It was only ten minutes' walk to the private entrance of the shop where Miss Kent lived, and they had not talked much on the way. John Marco had been aware only of one thing—that beside him, so close that his elbow almost touched her, was Miss Kent. And had he shielded her gallantly as he walked; his own bowler and the velvet collar had got no protection at all. And even so, the rain, which was blowing in gusts up every side road they passed, found its way to her. He kept glancing sideways at her, noticing as he passed each lamp how young she looked and how pure. It seemed incredible that in London where even the flowers are dirty there should be such a face straight out of Eden.

When they said good-bye he had held her hand for the first time. It was smaller than he would have believed: his own hand engulfed it. But it was very firm and alive. He tingled at the touch of it. Then with a wild, muttered remark about hoping that one evening he might call on her, he had turned away, without waiting for the answer and, still hot from the excitement of having been so close to her, had gone striding back through the gloom of the evening to return what he had stolen.

"Sister Kent."

Mr. Tuke's words startled John Marco. He had been lost within himself, not noticing the succession of muffled female figures who had padded their way down the narrow wooden steps into the water and up out of the tank on the other side.

His eyes had been fixed on Mary Kent and everything that went on around her seemed misty and unreal. Now that he looked about him again he was surprised to see how unchanged and ordinary everything in the Chapel now looked. There were the same tiers of faces, the same batteries of eyes, even the same heavy breathing of the exhausted Amosites. There was Mr. Tuke, too, as roseate and commanding as ever, standing in the middle of the Jordan Tank. Actually, he was moving a little from side to side, shifting from one foot to the other. He was both uncomfortable and apprehensive. The verger, after seeing to the supply of towels in the men's disrobing room, had remembered his Minister's injunction about the fire. He had stoked furiously. In the result, mysterious Gulf streams of heat now circulated about Mr. Tuke's feet: he began to wonder if, after having been so nearly frozen to death, he had been preserved only to be boiled alive.

Mary Kent, John Marco noticed, moved with a grace of her own, despite the thick folds of stuff around her. She still looked a woman as she walked. Her head in its white turban was bowed, and she looked young and virginal. He felt his heart hammering as she descended into the water and stood there, chaste and obedient, in front of Mr. Tuke.

She would stand just that way, he told himself, when somehow and against what odds he knew not, he would be there beside her at another and a greater sacrament.

About this time, a shabby, little woman in a rusty overcoat, an attenuated feather-boa round her neck, was endeavouring to push her way into the Tabernacle. It was not easy. The sidesman who met her in the porch tried to dissuade her. It was useless, he said, to hope for a seat even in the gallery; they had been assembling there ever since six o'clock when the door opened.

But it was not a seat that the woman wanted: it was Mr. Tuke himself. She had some urgent private mission of her own, she said; some purpose so secret that it might be confided only to the Minister in person. The sidesman, however, was adamant. His instructions had been to close the doors, and he was not disposed to re-open them. He knew, too, from experience that strange things could happen on Immersion Nights; the occasion affected some people—women especially—very queerly. There were hysterical outbreaks sometimes; confessions, public acts of contrition, importunings of the Almighty. And the woman, now that he came to study her more closely, certainly looked distraught. She was flushed—evidently she had been running—and she was breathing in quick gasps. Her hair, which was grey and untidy anyhow, had come loose, and now fell about her face in ugly, straggling wisps. He would not have been surprised if there had been drink on her breath as well.

But distraught or not, she was clearly in earnest. There was no stopping her. Every time he stepped in her path to intercept her, she sidled by him like a dog which is difficult to catch. And when he laid his hand on her arm for a moment to reason with her, she threw it off violently, as if the touch had burnt her. It was then that the sickening realisation came to him that, if he were to prevent her at all, he would have to use force; for Mr. Tuke's sake he would have to indulge in a scuffle with a strange woman in the Chapel porch. With that in mind he stepped in front of her for the last time and, with his back up against the green baize door that led into the Tabernacle, planted both feet firmly on the ground and faced her.

The effect was immediate and alarming. The woman eyed him for a moment with an expression of exasperated hatred, and then, raising her umbrella, came straight at him. The sidesman instinctively raised his arm to protect himself; in that instant he really feared that he was going to be struck. But it was not in him that she was interested. Instead, the appalling creature hammered with her umbrella handle on the panel of the door. It was a strong panel, strong but thin. Under the blows, it resounded like a drum. It shook. Everyone in the chapel heard it. Six hundred pairs of eyes were wrenched for a moment from the white figures in the tank, and were directed towards the door; even Mr. Tuke paused for a moment at the words, "among the elect ones shall she sit down," and looked up, angry and resentful, to see from what direction this rival commotion was coming.

The blows, moreover, had their effect. One of the sidesmen within the body of the hall got hurriedly to his feet and marched towards the door. He was a large man who had always seen himself as someone who is vital and reliable in an emergency. When, therefore, he found that the door would not budge forward, and when the fusillade of blows was suddenly repeated from outside, he did not hesitate: he wrenched the door open towards him. The result was disastrous. The sidesman outside who had been leaning against the door fell backwards into the arms of his brother from within, and the shabby little woman, her umbrella held across her breast like a sceptre, pushed her way past them both and started to walk up the aisle.

The disturbance by now was complete. No one at all was looking at Mr. Tuke, and everyone was staring at the rusty black back of the intruder. Everyone that is except John Marco. His eyes were still fixed on Mary Kent. As Mr. Tuke raised the cup to anoint her, John Marco closed his eyes for a moment: he was suddenly aware of being present at something that was too sacred to watch, something which belonged alone with God in the innermost Holy.

As for the woman she did not hesitate: she walked straight in the direction of the Jordan Tank. She was thus upon John Marco before he was properly aware of what was happening. She touched his sleeve, and he started.

"I've got to speak to Mr. Tuke," she said.

"Mr. Tuke?" he repeated.

"Tell him that I've got to speak to him now," the woman answered. "Tell him that Mr. Trackett says it's urgent."

John Marco looked at her coldly.

"No one can speak to Mr. Tuke now," he said. "The Minister is officiating."

"I've got to speak to him," she answered. "There's someone dying."

"Who?"

"It's Mr. Trackett."

It was then that John Marco became aware that everyone in the chapel was staring at them *both;* simply by pulling at his sleeve, the frowsty old harridan had somehow identified him with her cause. It was almost as though he, John Marco, were holding up the service himself. But the mention of a fellow human being who was dying gave her a kind of over-riding authority; it was impossible to ignore the woman.

"Do you know he's dying?" he asked. "Did you call a doctor?"

"He's dying all right," the woman answered. "And he's got something he wants to give the gentleman."

John Marco hesitated. Then, at the cost of making himself even more conspicuous, he did the only possible thing. He stepped over the brass chain and went to the very edge of the tank. The tank was empty of initiates for the moment. And Mr. Tuke, an expression of angry bewilderment on his face, came wading across the tank towards him like a resentful Triton.

"What does our Sister want?" he asked.

"She's been sent by Mr. Trackett," John Marco explained in a carrying whisper. "He's dying."

"Mr. Trackett's been an invalid for a long time," Mr. Tuke said dubiously.

"She says that he's got something for you," John Marco continued.

"What is it?"

"She wouldn't tell me," he answered. "It's something private."

Mr. Tuke glanced at the eight muffled figures on the baptismal bench. Then he glanced at the clock opposite the pulpit. It showed seven-thirty-five; there was almost another fifty-five minutes of divine service. He couldn't go now. It was unheard of for a Minister to suspend an Immersion night in this way. Besides, it was a sin that he would not have cared to have on his conscience to withhold the Sacrament of baptism from eight of the Sisterhood who, having properly prepared themselves for it, had now waited so long.

"You must go in my stead, Mr. Marco," he said. "Comfort Mr. Trackett. Console him. Tell him that I am detained on the Lord's business."

John Marco straightened his back.

"I'll go, sir," he said.

He turned and stepped over the brass chain again. As he did so, he heard Mr. Tuke, magnificently master of the situation, calling upon the next disciple, a Sister Bowen, to come forward. Mr. Tuke uttered the name as though nothing untoward had happened, as though it were the commonest of experiences at adult baptisms for the Minister to be called to the side of the tank like a swimming instructor.

But the magic had gone from the evening. Somewhere during those few seconds of turmoil followed by this remarkable incursion, the spell had been broken; and it was not at the swathed figure of the latest initiate that everyone was looking, but at John Marco and the woman in black.

While Sister Bowen was, so to speak, being baptized privately and without excitement to anyone, John Marco and Mr. Trackett's sluttish messenger became wonderland figures of speculation and mystery. Six hundred people exchanged glances and congratulated themselves on having been present on this unforgettable night when the door of the Amosite Tabernacle had been battered down, when one sidesman had flung himself upon another, when Mr. Tuke had been treated with contempt, and when one of their own Sunday schoolmasters had been whisked away from their midst by a drab.

Chapter II

It was Gold outside the Chapel, so cold that John Marco turned up the collar of his overcoat and shuddered. The rain, which had been holding off earlier, was now coming down in slanting, icy streams and every gas-lamp in the street cast a smudged, primrose-coloured path of light across the roadway. Chapel Walk, indeed, had more the appearance of a river than of a road; it flowed, gleaming and sinister, through the narrow stucco chasm that connected the western limits of Paddington with the northern fringe of Bayswater.

The woman at his elbow was talking to herself, he noticed. At first he could not catch the words. She had put up her gaping umbrella and was huddled nearly double as she walked; her head was pressed down on to her chest and her arms were raised almost as though she were trying to press the rain aside by sheer force. Only occasional syllables of what she was saying reached him. But these were enough.

"Got to get back in time," she was repeating. "Got to get back in time."

She turned up Flaxman Parade as though she had forgotten that he was with her. The rain was driving against their backs by now and she straightened herself a little. But she still kept her arms clasped in front of her and her chin crushed down into the collar of her coat. She was walking faster by now.

"Is it far?" John Marco asked.

The words had a strange effect on his companion. She began to run. Not a brisk, vigorous run, but a halting, limping movement, which made it appear as if she were skipping.

"Clarence Gardens: it's a good ten minutes," she said over her shoulder.

John Marco found now that to keep up with her he had almost to run himself. He could remain level with this prancing, jumping creature beside him only by proceeding with great, striding steps. The absurdity of the spectacle which they both must be making troubled him; to any onlooker they would have seemed to be competing in a fantastic race.

The tired *clop* of a cruising hansom met his ears. It was something which until that moment had not occurred to him. He had never taken a hansom in his life before; it was the kind of extravagance which he had despised in other men. But to-night it was different. It was not extravagance to reach the bedside of a dying man while he still had some life left in him.

"We'll take a cab," he said.

But the suggestion seemed almost to shock his companion.

"Oh no," she said. "Don't do that. He wouldn't expect it. He wouldn't like it."

"Why not?" John Marco asked.

He had nine shillings in his pocket and not to spend one of them seemed somehow to be treating death with less respect than it deserved.

The woman shook her head, however.

"Waste," she said. "Sinful waste."

22

It was then that John Marco remembered the reputation of Ephraim Trackett. It was not a pretty one. Even in those strict Amosite circles where everything that was not frugal was suspect, he was a bye-word for meanness and parsimony. Until a year ago when his illness had imprisoned him, Mr. Trackett had been a regular attendant at chapel. In a shiny, frock coat that was worn bare at the elbows and had been refaced, and again refaced, he had, every Sunday, glorified God and given a single penny to the collection. There was, John Marco recalled, a pale, dejected girl of about thirty—his niece—as shabbily dressed as himself, who used to accompany him. She had a sullen, bitter face. He had seen her looking round during the Sermon, eyeing the Amosite men on the far side of the aisle as though envious of other women whose lot allowed them to know such creatures.

They had reached the house by now and the woman beside him was fumbling for her key. They went up the steps together and stood sheltering in the Palladian entrance-porch. It was a large house, altogether different from John Marco's scale of things; it was the kind of house that hinted at wealth no matter how it might have decayed. The woman swung the heavy front door open and John Marco found himself in a dim entrance hall shrouded with palms and hangings and dense lace curtains. His companion pulled a chair up and tugged at one of the hanging-chains from the gas-burner—apparently there were no other servants in the house. When the mantle had lit itself she got down and told John Marco to wait.

It was not pleasant, waiting. The house was silent; very silent and very cold. It seemed to be composed of shut-up rooms and empty grates; it was like a house from which everyone had suddenly gone away. There was a peculiar, chilling atmosphere—an odour almost—of dissolution. It was as though

23

everything in the house—the stair carpet, the velvet pall at the foot of the stairs, the lace curtains at the windows—had withered and dried up; as though a gust of wind blowing through the house would have carried everything before it like dust.

John Marco had not long to wait, however. The woman—she had her hat off by now and her hair streamed across her head more wildly than ever—came down the stairs and beckoned to him to follow. She led him up to the first landing and, without knocking, flung open the door which faced him.

John Marco stood in the doorway without moving; the smell in the room was too much for him; it was the sour, human smell of a sick-room that has been occupied too long. The room itself was almost in darkness. The gas was not alight and a solitary oil lamp, turned very low, burned on the dressing-table.

John Marco peered into the design of shadows in front of him. First of all, he made out the bed. It was a lavish, brass-railed affair; at the head and foot were thick bars of metal that gleamed in the surrounding darkness. Altogether, it was like a cage from which the sides had been removed. And in it, amid a litter of bed-clothes, was the propped-up body of a small white-haired man.

His neck, which showed miserably thin like a chicken's over the top of his nightshirt, was stretched to its uttermost as he bent forward to catch sight of his visitor.

It was then that John Marco noticed that the old man was not alone. There was a dark head on the counterpane beside him. It was the head of a woman who was kneeling on the floor with her face resting in her two hands. When at last she moved, John Marco became aware of a white face with two sunken, staring eyes.

John Marco was about to say something when the figure in

the bed interrupted him. There was a rattling intake of breath, and he spoke.

"You're not Mr. Tuke," he said. "Someone's playing tricks on me again."

"No one's playing tricks on you," John Marco answered. "Mr. Tuke couldn't come."

But the old man wouldn't listen to him.

"Who are you?" he asked. "What are you doing here?"

John Marco took a step into the bedroom and faced him.

"I'm John Marco," he said. "Mr. Tuke is at Service. He asked me to take his place until he could get here."

Mr. Trackett bared his teeth; the lined, yellow face suddenly wrinkled up and revealed them.

"You can't deceive me," he said. "They've tried it too long. All of them."

"I've got nothing to deceive you about," John Marco replied. "If I can be of no service to you I shall go."

He felt angry within himself as he said it. Ever since the touch of the woman in the Chapel he had felt himself being drawn deeper and deeper into the affair of Mr. Trackett and his confidential message. It was a secret that he had not asked to share; it had been forced upon him against his will. He wanted to turn his back on them all and walk out of the house forever.

His words, however, had roused the woman by the bed. She had got quickly to her feet and was moving in the direction of the door as though to cut him off.

"No, don't go, Mr. Marco," she said. "Please don't leave me here alone again."

He turned and stared at her. It was that hard, impersonal stare of his. But she did not flinch under it. Her own dark eyes returned it, unwaveringly. He could recognise now the down-trodden creature who used to accompany Mr. Trackett to Sunday Chapel. But she no longer looked suppressed. In her attitude as she stood there, the palms of her hands pressed flat against the door behind her almost as though they were nailed to it, there was something of desperation about her. She was colourless and sallow-skinned, but a single spot of red burned in the centre of each cheek.

John Marco paused.

"I'll stay if Mr. Trackett wants me," he said.

"Who told you my name?" the old man asked.

"The woman you sent to the chapel," John Marco told him.

"*You* sent her," said Mr. Trackett, bitterly, turning to the girl again. "You told her—to bring—this man."

He dragged the words out of himself with difficulty; they came in quick, jerky rushes. And in between them was the painful, clumsy breathing. It was as though having once got the air inside him, his lungs no longer knew what to do with it.

"Then send for Emmy yourself and ask her." The girl passed her hand wearily across her forehead. "Send for her and stop accusing me."

"It's no use," Mr. Trackett answered in a low voice, almost as though he were talking to himself. "It's no use sending for anyone. You've got them all in your power. They're afraid of you."

He lay back against the pillows and began gasping. He was gulping at the air as though trying to eat it. His hands which were spread out on the bed-clothes, kept clenching and unclenching. John Marco could see the miserable little body under the counterpane writhing under the strain of keeping itself alive.

The girl regarded him for a moment without moving and then crossed over to the small table beside the bed. There was a dark bottle standing there. She poured some of the mixture from the bottle into a medicine phial and held it to Mr. Trackett's lips. But the old man only shook his head and kept his mouth pursed closely together. He was shaking all over. As soon as the spasm subsided he pushed his phial away altogether. The gesture was so violent that some of the dark drops were splashed onto the sheet.

"I won't touch it," he said in a whisper. "You're poisoning me."

John Marco then did what he believed Mr. Tuke would have had him do; what Mr. Tuke himself might have done if he had been there. He went over to the side of the bed and bent over the sick man.

"Mr. Trackett," he said. "We are in God's presence. He overhears every word we say. You would not do well to meet Him with those words on your lips."

The speech seemed to have a sobering effect on the invalid. He did not attempt to answer. He lay back, without speaking. His eyes, too, closed for a moment as though even sight were becoming too much of an effort for him. When he opened his eyes again he no longer looked on John Marco as an enemy.

"Are you a minister?" he asked.

John Marco shook his head.

"I'm a lay teacher," he answered.

"Help me to pray," said the old man, "I'm dying."

John Marco looked doubtfully at the girl for a moment; he wondered what kind of a prayer was expected of him.

But the girl merely nodded her head.

"Start any prayer you like," she said. "It's his only comfort."

John Marco prayed extempore; he prayed as he had heard other Amosites pray. Kneeling at the table beside the bed, with the huddle of bottles and the old man's spectacles upon it, he put his hand over his eyes.

"O Lord," he began, "now that the darkness is closing around our brother be Thou a light to guide him, a hand for his support. Help him to throw off all earthly thoughts like raiment, so that he stands before you naked like a little child. Be Thou beside him at this bed and, at the other side, waiting for him before the gates. Empty his heart of all unkindness and fill it with Thy divine love. And in Thine infinite mercy let the last awful moment be gentle as a kiss."

The spirit no longer moved him and he rose, blinking into the darkness around him. The girl rose at the same moment from the other side of the bed. They both looked down at the old man they had prayed over. But he was past noticing. His jaw had dropped and he was asleep. He was lolling there, oblivious. It was not a pretty sleep, however. Each breath that he took still shook him.

"You pray beautifully," said the girl. "Beautifully."

"I was moved," said John Marco simply.

They did not speak again for some minutes. John Marco walked across the room and sat himself down in a chair to wait for Mr. Tuke. It was a rocking chair. It tossed him gently to and fro with an idiotic peacefulness of its own. The room was very quiet now except for the sound of Mr. Trackett's breathing, and John Marco's thoughts began to wander idly back through the events of the evening. He saw Mary Kent again with her fair head bent under the anointing cup of Mr. Baptist Tuke; he heard the words of the Psalm: "I shall not want . . . Surely goodness and mercy shall follow me all the days of my life: and I will dwell in the house of the Lord for ever"; he felt the touch of the drab-bish servant on his arm in the Tabernacle; he entered the house

28

again, and came into the sick-room for a second time.

There was a movement from the bed and John Marco turned. The girl beside the bed was staring at him, her hot, devouring eyes fixed full on him. But she, too, turned away and bent over to hear what the old man was saying.

At first, the words were jammed inside him. Then Mr. Trackett managed to force them out of himself.

"Why doesn't—anyone—get—me—something to eat?" he asked. "They're starving me."

The girl crossed to the mantelpiece and pulled at the bell handle: there was a creaking of wires and somewhere down in the basement a bell jangled.

"He's very difficult," she said. "He probably won't touch it when it comes."

"Give me food," said the old man. "I'm dying."

"He's been like this for weeks," said the girl. "Earlier this evening I really thought he was passing."

"I won't touch it unless you eat some, too," said Mr. Trackett suspiciously. "Eat it where I can see you."

The heavy footsteps of the servant came up the stairs and stopped outside the door. There was a bump as she thrust her knee against the door; she was evidently carrying something.

"I've brought him his gruel," she said.

There was a weariness in her voice as she said it, a kind of dull, familiar disappointment. John Marco guessed how many times she must have climbed those stairs carrying up a tray to someone who was as difficult as a sick child. She turned and dragged her feet out of the room again as sullenly as she had entered.

The girl put the bowl of gruel in front of the fire and began propping the old man up. The effect on him was remarkable: he kept twisting his head round to see the gruel. There he was in his seventy-sixth year becoming as excited about food as a baby. His mouth began to water.

John Marco looked at his watch. There was still another quarter of an hour before Mr. Tuke could be along, another fifteen minutes of this suffocating sick-room. The girl was staring at him again, sitting quietly in her chair not taking her eyes off him.

The crash as old Mr. Trackett dropped his spoon startled them both. The spoon simply slipped out of his fingers and his hand fell with it. The fingers closed themselves and would not open again. Mr. Trackett turned his eyes down and regarded that withered, twisted fist that would no longer obey him.

His two eyes were all that he could move. His head was now fixed immovably on his shoulders. He tried to tell them that it was a stroke, that one side of his body was dead already; but, though his mouth was open, no words would come.

The girl slipped the pillows away from under him and laid him back on the bed. He was quite stiff to move; it was like handling a dummy. In a way it even seemed rather absurd to be tucking him up so carefully. The paralysed arm lay rigid and useless across the counterpane. Only the eyes continued to be alive. They were casting desperately around the room, peering after the vanished gruel.

"I think it's come at last," said the girl. "It's what we were expecting."

"Send out for the doctor," said John Marco. "There may still be some hope."

The girl shook her head.

"It's no use," she said.

"You can't let him lie there like that."

The girl looked first at Mr. Trackett and then at John Marco.

"There's no one can help him but himself," she said. "He's finished."

But before she had finished uttering the words they both knew that she was wrong. There were still waves of life passing through the object on the bed. The dummy managed at last to move its tongue; and with the tip of it proceeded very slowly to moisten its lips. It was evidently preparing to say something.

Mr. Trackett whispered the word when he did say it, as though speech were not a thing on which the breath of living could be wasted; they had both to bend over him to catch what the one word was. And as he stood there John Marco was suddenly aware that even though the girl's head was bent forward like his own she was still regarding him. He kept his own eyes deliberately averted.

"Doctor!"

It was difficult to say whether Mr. Trackett had actually spoken at all; it was rather as though he had moved his lips and had imprinted the pattern of the word on the air.

"Doctor!" he said again just as noiselessly.

The girl went over to the mantel and rang the bell again. There was the same scraping of wires, the same peal, the same interval and the servant appeared in the same weary fashion.

"Go and get Dr. Preece," said the girl. "Mr. Trackett wants him."

The servant paused and dropped her voice.

"The doctor said not to bring him again until the old gentleman was unconscious," she said.

"Go and get him," said the girl. "Bring him here at once."

There was a suggestion of temper concealed somewhere within her as she said it.

The woman shrugged her shoulders.

"Very well," she said. "But he won't like paying for it."

She went out of the room still complaining, and the girl turned to John Marco.

"He's been like this for months," she said by way of explanation.

John Marco made no answer. He pulled out his watch. It showed eight-thirty. No Immersion service ever went on much longer than that. Allowing time for Mr. Tuke to rub down and dress and drink a cup of the Mission tea, prepared by the deaconess, and get round here, he ought not to be more than about another twenty minutes. The doctor would be there, too, by then, and John Marco could slip quietly away, leaving Mr. Tuke to walk, bland and imperturbable, through this particular valley of the shadow.

But the figure on the bed was endeavouring to speak again. The tongue and the lips were both moving. John Marco and the girl bent low over him for the second time.

It was a name this time that he uttered as silently as before.

But the girl shook her head.

"You don't need him," she said. "To-morrow will do."

The eyes in the stiff face flickered for a moment; they hardened and then grew pleading again.

"Now," he said.

The girl looked at him grimly and dispassionately.

"Now," the lips soundlessly repeated.

"What does he want?" John Marco asked.

"It's his lawyer," the girl explained. "He wants him."

"Shall I go for him?" John Marco asked.

"No," the girl replied hastily. "You stop here in case anything happens."

The lips repeated the same name again; the eyes seemed to be giving the message, too.

"I'll go myself," the girl said angrily. "There'll be no peace till we bring him here."

John Marco half rose to his feet as she said it.

"You mean me to stay here with him?" he asked.

The idea suddenly frightened him; he was not used to death, at least not used to it so close that he could feel the breath of it on his brow. There was something terrifying in the thought of staying there and seeing the life choked slowly out of that desiccated little idol in the bed in front of him.

But the girl did not seem to notice his hesitation.

"I've only got to go as far as Sussex Villas," she said. "He'll be no trouble to you. He can't move." She spoke with the callousness that comes of close association with a long illness. "Let Mr. Tuke in if he comes," she added. "I'll leave the door open so that you can hear him. There's a book on the table if you want to read."

John Marco drew himself up; he remembered whose deputy he was.

"I shall pray," he said. "I shall pray for God's mercy towards contrite sinners."

"He'd like it better if you prayed out loud," the girl answered.

She picked up her coat, which was lying thrown across a chair, and put it on. Then she found her hat. It was an old, slatternly affair with half the ribbon torn and hanging down over the brim. There was a bunch of flowers on it that had been bright once; now they were torn and dirty. They were like flowers that might have been picked up in the roadway. But the girl put on this objectionable hat with the finicky grace of a cocotte. She even arranged for a sweep of her dark, lustreless hair to come down across her forehead and break the hard line of the brow. Then she stood in front of John Marco almost as though asking him to admire her.

"I shan't be long," she said. "You start praying."

John Marco waited while she went downstairs. He heard her footsteps descending and then there was the slam of the heavy front door. He crossed over to the table beside the bed and went down on his knees again. The house seemed unnaturally silent. Great blankets of stillness wrapped up everything in it; a clock ticking away on the mantelshelf seemed like an intruder from a noisier world. John Marco did not pray aloud at once; instead, he addressed himself privately to God and waited for the spirit to move him for a second time. He was still kneeling there in prayer when he felt a touch on the back of his neck, a touch as cold and damp as death itself, and as unexpected.

He sprang back on to his feet, trembling all over. It was then that he saw that Mr. Trackett had edged himself inch by inch towards him; he had crawled across that expanse of tumbled bedclothes as noiselessly as a snail. And, having arrived within striking distance, he had jerked out his useless arm like a stick and touched John Marco.

"What do you want?" John Marco asked. "Speak to me."

Mr. Trackett drew up his living arm, the arm that still belonged to him, and beckoned. The crooked forefinger motioned John Marco towards him. John Marco regarded him for a moment with repugnance and then bent over him. He could feel the stale, sickly breath of the old man on his face.

"What is it?" he repeated. "What do you want?"

Mr. Trackett's lips still moved with difficulty. They seemed to become rubbery and unreliable. The words slurred into each other and became continuous. But he could speak again. And apparently there was something desperate and urgent

34

that he wanted to say.

"It's the box under the bed," he said. "The black metal box."

"Do you want it?" John Marco asked.

The old man nodded. There was impatience in his face as he lay there; it was as though whatever this thing was that he wanted to do he was afraid that he would not be given time to finish it.

John Marco paused for a moment. Then he went down on all fours and raised the overhang of the counterpane. The box faced him. It was a large, battered tin box of the kind in which lawyers keep their documents; a holy of holies with the grime of years upon it. As he dragged it out onto the carpet he felt the old man in the bed begin to stir in anticipation.

"Open it," Mr. Trackett gasped.

He began fumbling inside the collar of his nightshirt and disclosed a soiled noose of tape that was about his neck. On the end of it was a key.

He tried to lean forward and John Marco removed the noose from his neck. As he did so his fingers touched the withered flesh and he shuddered. But the dying man's impatience was urging him on again.

The lid of the box squeaked on its hinges as he opened it. It was so stiff that he had to force it open with both hands.

"Prop me up," said the old man.

The box was full of small packages of paper, little sheaves tied together with string or cotton or even pieces of something that might once have been ribbon. They were mouldy, those papers; an odour of mildew and decay rose from them.

But the effect on the old man as he saw them was remarkable. The colour which had gone from his cheeks ever since he dropped the spoon, came back again. He breathed faster and his eyes lit up. As his gaze wandered over them he seemed to derive a strange, disordered joy.

It was only then that John Marco saw what they were. They were bank notes, pile upon pile of ancient, discoloured Bank of England notes. In that box was more money than he had ever seen; it was as much money as Mr. Morgan took over his counter in a month; enough money for him to marry Mary Kent at once and set up house in the style of house that he wanted to give her. There, inside that battered tin chest, was wealth and everything it stood for; power and a wife and a position in the world.

The old man was speaking again.

"It's my gift to the Chapel," he said. "It's Mr. Tuke's."

John Marco looked at his watch. Mr. Tuke should be there at any moment now; he was probably walking down Clarence Gardens already.

But the old man had apparently given up all hope of him. "It's in your keeping," he said. "All of it. It belongs to the Chapel." He paused for a moment, and dropped his voice still lower. "Don't show it to the others," he said. "They don't know I've got all that. They'd try and stop me. They'd steal it."

He had twisted himself so far forward off the bed that his arms were inside the box as he said it. Suddenly he began to scoop out armfuls of the notes, holding them to him like a child and crooning over them. He held them against his face so that he could feel the smooth surface of the paper on his skin; he tried to stuff them into the open collar of his nightshirt. He spread them out on the sheets and doted on them. He raised one bundle to his lips.

John Marco stood looking at him, without moving. His disgust was threatening at any moment to become master of him. He wanted to tear Mr. Trackett from his heap of dirty paper and remind him that he was a human being with a soul. But it was no use addressing the old man. He was living already in an insane

36

Paradise of his own. Every moment he was snatching up fresh bundles of the notes; they now lay beside him in a great heap.

And as John Marco looked, Mr. Trackett heaved himself up in bed almost onto his knees and plunged his head and shoulders into the box. Having done so, he remained fixed there for a moment, his back bent into a high, unnatural arc. Then, quite slowly he began to roll over onto his side and fell backwards onto the bed with his feet in their massive pink bed-socks up on the pillow.

He did not move again and the bundle of notes in his arms slipped one by one out of his grasp and left him there, clasping nothing.

John Marco drew back a pace when he saw what had happened; he was afraid to approach any nearer. He wished that Mr. Tuke would come; Mr. Tuke was used to the dark places. The armour of Mr. Tuke's faith was inviolable. Then his eyes again caught sight of that great pile of money on the bed. It was as though he had seen it for the first time, however; for he saw it now as though it were his. Everything that men struggle for a life-time to obtain was there, spread out in front of him; it was the future thrust into his open hands. It was the very stuff of life.

His heart began suddenly to storm with the excitement and the rush of blood within him made him feel faint and dizzy. He was helpless and possessed. His sweat—he must have started sweating in that instant when he first *saw* the money—was already congealing icily upon him. He felt sick and ill. But already he was slowly moving towards the bed.

When he reached it he paused. He was in a mood of exaltation he had never known before. He was intoxicated with this new madness that had taken hold of him. He prayed—wild snatches of words that came to him from nowhere. "The Lord is my shepherd," he kept saying. "I shall not want." He uttered Mary Kent's name several times aloud. And all the time his heart was drumming inside him, sending the blood thundering past his ear drums. Then averting his eyes from the dead man's face he began to gather up the notes. He had three bundles—there must be ten notes in each, he calculated—already in his hand, when the clamour of the front door-bell rang through the whole house. To John Marco's ears at that moment it was like a peal sounding through all the halls of hell.

The next few seconds were swift and desperate. He was mad no longer. He was terribly and wickedly sane. He was cautious, too. He filled his pockets carefully so that the mass of paper that was in them should not betray him. When the front door-bell rang again, longer and more frantically than before, he was ready. The rest of the notes he flung higgledy-piggledy back into the box and turned the key. Then, pulling down the flaps of his pockets as he walked, he went down the stairs to let in Mr. Tuke.

Mr. Tuke, calm and majestic as he was, started when he saw the dead man. John Marco had warned him that he would not find Mr. Trackett alive, but he was not prepared for this huddled, twisted figure with one arm stuck out like a scarecrow's and his feet in the gay, pink bed-socks where his head should have been.

"Horrible," he said. "Horrible."

"He had a stroke," said John Marco quietly. "I didn't move him."

At that moment John Marco was calmer than his minister.

Mr. Tuke looked wonderingly towards the large black box. John Marco followed the direction of his eyes.

38

"That is yours now," he said in the same flat voice. "It's Mr. Trackett's bequest. He left you everything."

Mr. Tuke did not move. He appeared reluctant to approach the disordered death-bed.

"Give it to me," he said. "What's in it?"

"He told me that it was money," said John Marco slowly. "Money that he had saved for God."

They moved Mr. Trackett between them and, when he was decently on his back again, Mr. Tuke passed his hand across his forehead.

"You poor boy," he said. "What you must have endured. What you must have been through."

Then he bent over the box and opened it like one who is in authority. And when he had seen what was inside—one of the bands had sprung open and the box seemed to be full almost to the brim with the cascade of notes—he turned to John Marco again.

"Jehovah is bountiful," he said, raising his hands above his head. "Glory be to Jehovah."

Chapter III

Punctually at Eight-Thirty next morning, John Marco was present behind his counter. He was there even before the young lady assistants; when they arrived, they found the dust sheets off and the top row of display brackets already arranged— it was an understood rule of the house that the *man* in charge of each department should arrange any goods which were set out so high that it necessitated standing on a chair to arrange them. So long as Mr. Morgan had supervised the retail side of his establishment, no young woman had ever publicly stood upon a chair.

The three young lady assistants, dressed most respectably in black, walked through to the ladies' retiring-room leaving no trace of perfume or emotion behind them. They were workers; and they knew it. Mr. Morgan engaged only that sort. It was left to the more fashionable customers to introduce the scent and the excitement. Those—the fashionable ones—arrived during the afternoon. They were helped down from their carriages by the doorman, they swept into the shop with a kind of proprietary grace, bought half-a-yard of lace or a pair of twelve-and-eleven-penny gloves, had it put down to their account and swept out again, leaving the assistants with a sense of enlarged horizons and vicarious intimacy with wealth—Messrs. Morgan and Roberts were in the very best quarter of Bayswater.

After the three young ladies had filed past him and he had nodded good-morning, John Marco resumed his work of counter-dressing. It was moiré ribbon that he was arranging. He was expertly letting the flat roll uncoil between his fingers so that an elegant spiral was formed between the brass rail above and the counter. This done, he inserted a price ticket into the roll and stepped back. He swayed a little as he did so.

It was the first time he had ever arrived at work having had no sleep at all on the night before.

It had still been early when he had left Mr. Tuke in Mr. Trackett's bedroom; Mr. Tuke had been comforting the niece by then; he had refused to believe that she was not broken-hearted. And he had not seemed to notice John Marco's departure at all.

He had tiptoed out of the room, his heart still hammering. At that moment it had been the girl that he was afraid of. He did not want to pass under those eyes of hers a second time. They were such steady, inquisitive eyes; far steadier than his could ever be again. And as he had closed the door behind him, he had become aware of a strange feeling of isolation. The John Marco who began, slowly and sedately, to go downstairs again was a man of unchallengeable probity, a draper and a Sunday School teacher. But because of this thing that he had done, because of something that he would not have believed possible, he could never be the same as other men again. He was conscious as he went down the broad, twisting staircase that for the rest of his life he would have to walk alone; and the prospect frightened him. However often in the future he might stray back onto the path of virtue he knew now that he would never really belong there.

He had nearly reached the bottom of the stairs when he heard his name called out behind him. He started. But he steadied himself immediately, and told himself that above all things he must not act guiltily. There must be nothing in his manner or in his bearing which could betray him.

"You called me?" he asked.

The girl came down the stairs towards him. There was no emotion in her face, no sign of tears or agitation; simply those unsmiling dark eyes that seemed to be calculating everything about him. And when she spoke, it was still the same flat, unrevealing voice.

"I wanted to thank you," she said. "There was no one else that I could have left. He trusted you."

At the words John Marco started again. He raised his eyes to hers. But there was nothing concealed there; she knew nothing, suspected nothing. He smiled involuntarily at the relief, and then checked himself. Already he was behaving foolishly; people with free minds do not smile in the face of death.

"Good-night," he said. "I shall pray for you."

Then buttoning his coat around him—it felt tight and grotesque with those heavy wads of money beneath it—he crossed over to the front door and pulled it to after him.

He was conscious as he went down the steps of an enormous feeling of release. In escaping from that house it was as though for the moment he had escaped from himself as well. But the feeling passed off as suddenly as it had come. There was *no* escape for him: he knew that. Even though he was walking so fast that his lungs were hurting him, he wasn't getting away from it. It was there—his private and neatly executed sin—lodged securely inside him for ever.

42

His mind now began playing strange tricks with him. He felt hunted, and kept glancing over his shoulder to see if he were being followed. But the road behind him was vague and empty. There was no threat in that long perspective of yellow street lamps that dwindled away, like lights seen in a double mirror, into the respectability of Bayswater. The feeling of pursuit remained, however. He could feel those hard wads of money pressing into him as he walked, and a sudden wave of terror hit him at the thought that he might be arrested as he was, his pockets loaded with his guilt. He would be the Ishmaelite then, the accursed one, the Baptist who had robbed the dead; because of that one moment of temptation which he had not resisted, he would become a legendary figure of iniquity, something with horns that the Amos Tabernacle would never be able to forget. He started trembling again and took an oath with himself that if once he got home undetected he would destroy the money utterly, burn the whole fortune into powder and unaccusing ashes; then mite by mite in the future he would pay back to God what he had stolen from Him.

The house was in darkness when he got there. He looked up and down Chapel Villas to see if he were observed—this fantasy of people watching him still remained—and went inside. As the door closed behind him he felt his strength go from him; he simply sagged up against the panel, holding onto the handle. The relief of knowing that he was safe, that as soon as he had destroyed the money he would be a free man again, overcame him.

When he had recovered he walked upstairs, silently and with caution, not pausing even to light the candle that old Mrs. Marco had left for him. And when he reached his room he locked the door, and drew the curtains closely together, pressing them into

43

the window-frame at the corners, so that not a chink was left. There might be eyes anywhere, he told himself; the whole night was full of them. Then he lit the gas—the match jumped about in his hand, jabbing dangerously at the mantle as he held it—and pulled the money out of his pocket. The three thick wads stared up at him. He tore open the string that bound them and began to count. The notes filled his hands. He made little piles of them and went on counting. As his fingers ran across the surface of the paper, the same unaccountable exhilaration rose within him that he had ever known when he had first seen money. He began breathing deeper again. There was £150 of it; enough for a man to buy himself a place in the world, to be independent, to marry. And as he stood there, looking down on it and trembling, he knew in his heart that he had not the strength to destroy the money; knew that the vow which he had just made was broken already.

Already, he even knew minutely and exactly how to dispose of the money until it should be safe for him to spend: he would deposit the sum not in one bank but in several, and there would then be nothing to connect those humble, scattered accounts with the fortune that accused him.

"Your hair, Mr. Marco, is all brushed up at the back."

It was Mr. Morgan who had spoken. He was standing in front of his assistant, regarding him with a pained, dis-esteeming eye. So far as he could remember, this was the first occasion on which he had ever had to speak to the young man about his appearance.

"I'm sorry, sir."

John Marco flushed as he said it. He was conscious of what the rebuke meant and was only glad that the young ladies had not emerged from their retiring-room to hear it. But he was aware also of a new emotion: he found himself despising Mr. Morgan instead of respecting him. There now seemed something contemptible about the idiotic narrowness of his life, its senseless regularity. There Mr. Morgan was in the presence of someone who had risked everything; someone who had chosen with his eyes open to walk a tight-rope slung between hell and heaven—and looked even like getting to the further side; and all that Mr. Morgan could think of to say to this astonishing person was that his hair was brushed up the wrong way.

But he went obediently and tidied himself in the cold, back lavatory. When he emerged he was the copper-plate assistant again. His paleness rather added to his appearance. And he was as attentive and efficient in his work as ever. He reprimanded one of the young ladies for her roughness in drawing a pair of the thin suede gloves over the fingers of a wax hand that stood on the counter (he had told her before that the pressure should be on the side of the fingers and not on the front where the wear would subsequently come); and he was inspired in the presence of a difficult customer who had already had half the shop turned out without seeing what she wanted. From a shelf in the stock room marked "Discards" he had got down a roll of dubious sateen that Mr. Morgan had reluctantly regarded as unsaleable, and sold the customer the whole length. Mr. Morgan, who overheard the whole transaction, almost apologised for having criticised his star assistant.

But at seven o'clock when the shop closed, John Marco was already fainting with fatigue. When he had covered everything on the counter with the enshrouding dust-sheets he said goodnight to Mr. Morgan who stood at the door like a benign and white-haired sentinel, waiting to pounce on any one of the minutiae of the business that had been left unattended to, and stepped out into the coldness of the street. The sharpness of the air braced him. He walked home briskly and steadily. A new feeling of calm had descended on him. He saw now that London, despite his crime, was going on very much as before. It was unaware of him. But when he got inside his own front door he found Mr. Tuke sitting by the empty grate in the parlour. He had been there ever since half past six, waiting for John Macro's return.

The air of suspense was heavy in the room when he entered it. His mother was there, covered up in shawls and dangling all over with jet and tippets, assiduously endeavouring to entertain Mr. Tuke. She was doing her best. In her high strained voice— she was so deaf that it was years since she herself had heard it—she was telling Mr. Tuke what a model son she had.

"But he didn't seem himself this morning," John Marco heard her saying as he stood in the doorway. "He said someone had died. I couldn't find out who."

"It was Mr. Trackett," Mr. Tuke said loudly.

Mrs. Marco looked surprised.

"What about him?" she said. "You keep on mentioning his name. I don't know him."

But Mr. Tuke had already seen John Marco. He got up, towering impressively.

"I have something to say to you," he said.

John Marco's heart betrayed him for a moment, and he wondered if he had gone pale. But he took the large, pink hand that Mr. Tuke held out to him, and tried to look his Minister in the eyes.

"I'm sorry to have kept you waiting," he said.

Then Mrs. Marco saw her son.

"You didn't tell me where you'd been last night," she

46

complained. "I sat up for you until I went to sleep."

"I went to see Mr. Trackett," he said. "I told you."

"I thought you were going to the Immersion," she said.

"Mr. Trackett was taken ill," John Marco explained. "He died."

Mrs. Marco paused, her mouth working.

"Everybody seems to have died," she said. "It wasn't always like this."

Mr. Tuke and John Marco exchanged glances; Mr. Tuke had had his fill of that kind of conversation.

"I wanted to speak to you about last night," he said.

John Marco made no reply: he waited with tight lips for whatever it was that Mr. Tuke had to say.

The words, when they came, were reassuring, however; to his relief Mr. Tuke was purring over him.

"You did well," he was saying. "Very well. You came to man's estate."

"There was nothing that I could do," John Marco replied quietly. He was careful to let his voice disclose no hint of emotion.

"You did a great deal," Mr. Tuke corrected him. "You took the burden off a woman's shoulders."

"She didn't know that he was going to die," John Marco answered. "No one knew."

"Perhaps Mr. Trackett knew," Mr. Tuke suggested. "The last hours are sometimes very clear." He came over and put his hand on John Marco's shoulder. "Miss Trackett is very grateful," he said. "She thanks you."

At the touch of Mr. Tuke's hand John Marco instinctively stepped back. Mr. Tuke seemed surprised; he took a pace forward and placed it there again.

"She wants to reward you," he said.

47

"There's no call to do that," John Marco replied. He paused and added under his breath, as though ashamed of the words, "I only did my duty."

"It is not a reward as the world knows it," Mr. Tuke explained, looking hard at John Marco. "It is not money or riches. It is a privilege, a hard and painful privilege that she is offering."

"What is it?" John Marco asked.

"She wants you to be a bearer," Mr. Tuke replied. "She honours you by asking you to be among those who carry our brother to the grave."

John Marco stepped back again, this time right out of reach of Mr. Tuke's patronising hand.

"She wants me to do that," he said.

His heart failed him at the words; he felt the past reaching out into the present and drawing him back again just as he was certain that he had escaped from it all. He wanted to have nothing more to do with the memory of Mr. Trackett or with that girl with the steady, bewildering eyes. They were something that belonged to a single dark page, almost a paragraph in brackets, of his life's clean history; it was not a page that he wanted ever to go back to and re-read.

But Mr. Tuke was a man of authority: he assumed acquiescence.

"And I know that you won't disappoint her," he said. "It's not for her alone that you will be doing it," he said. "It will be for me. *I* ask you."

"What's that he's asking you?" Mrs. Marco enquired suddenly. "Why aren't I told anything about it?"

She got up and came towards them, her head thrust forward in an endeavour to catch some hint of what was going on around her. With her deafness she was as much cut off as if she had been alone. To her, it seemed that she was living in a world of sinister and malevolent conspiracy; even when she went shopping, the tradesmen with whom she had dealt for years whispered things that she could not hear.

"It's Mr. Trackett's funeral," Mr. Tuke explained. "Your son has been asked to be a bearer."

Mrs. Marco drew back her head like a tortoise.

"It's all deaths and funerals to-night," she complained. "I don't like it."

"You will do it, then?" Mr. Tuke asked, smiling on John Marco like the sun.

John Marco bowed his head.

"I will," he answered.

"Excellent." Mr. Tuke uttered the contented sigh of a man who has got his own way against difficulties. "Remember," he went on, "you're one of the lucky ones. You have a home—a mother who loves you. This unfortunate young lady has no one."

John Marco did not reply, and after a moment, Mr. Tuke resumed.

"Think of her sometimes," he said. "Think of her when you are seated at your own fireside. Our brother had few friends. She will be very lonely."

"I . . . I'll think of her," John Marco promised.

"Excellent," said Mr. Tuke again. "Excellent."

He began buttoning up his coat and started to move towards the door, when he suddenly stopped himself.

"I was forgetting," he said. "I have something that I want you to sign."

John Marco was aware of his heart again, as Mr. Tuke spoke the words. He was suddenly afraid that it might be a confession that Mr. Tuke would put before him.

But it was only a piece of paper bearing the words in Mr. Tuke's finely pointed hand: "*This is to certify that the sum of money entrusted to my keeping by Mr. Ephraim Trackett on behalf of the Paddington Amos Immersionist Tabernacle and given by me to the Reverend Eliud Tuke amounted to £875.*"

John Marco read the form and handed it back to Mr. Tuke.

"I can't sign it," he said.

Mr. Tuke seemed surprised.

"Why not?" he asked.

"I didn't count the money."

"That's most regrettable," said Mr. Tuke. "It's very awkward. It leaves me so unprotected if any questions should be asked. I'm only a steward remember. You don't think . . .?"

"If I signed that paper," John Marco interrupted him, his lips drawn tightly back as he spoke, "I should be putting my name to a falsehood."

"Quite so," said Mr. Tuke sadly. "In that case it only remains for *me* to *give you* a receipt," he said. He sat down at the circular table in the centre of the room, pushed the ornamental pot of maidenhair fern to one side and began to write.

When he had completed the chit, he handed it to John Marco with a little bow.

"That's all we can do for the present," he said. "Perhaps the young lady will know how much was in the box. One can't be too careful with God's money. . . ."

Chapter IV

The Amosite Literary, Scientific and Debating Society met at seven-thirty on Tuesday evenings during the winter session. There were fourteen lectures in all, every one of them in its way uplifting, inspiring and instructive. To-night's was the fifth. The subject "Holy Places in the Holy Land," was a tried favourite; the Reverend Mr. Shuttleworth, the lecturer, had delivered it more than two hundred times, and knew at any point throughout the fifty-five minutes of it just where to wait for the murmurs of appreciation. It was a lantern lecture—and lantern lectures always filled the Tabernacle. For people who had been in offices or at home all day, there was something strangely exciting and out-of-the-ordinary about sitting in Stygian darkness, reeking with the fumes of scorching enamel and hot metal-work, while a pale ray, like Hope, emanated from the oven-like box of the magic lantern and established a snap-shot of Rachel's Tomb upon the screen.

John Marco had not intended to go; this was another of those gatherings in which, until his conscience had worn a little cleaner, until the smirch was less noticeable, he felt he had no place. But when Tuesday evening came, he realised suddenly that by stopping away he would be doing the very thing he wanted to avoid—he would be making himself conspicuous. It was essential that in this as well as in everything else he should show no alteration; he must continue to go as freely as ever into the house which he had robbed if only to show that he still felt himself at home there.

And he had another reason for going. He would see Mary Kent; and he felt that he could no longer live without sight of her. The whole Kent family usually attended these lectures. It was the one night in the week when Mr. Kent left his business, took his watchmaker's glass out of his eye, put down his tweezers and screw-driver and enjoyed himself. John Marco had often seen the three of them sitting there—Mr. Kent, small and fidgety and as wiry as a watch-spring himself, Mrs. Kent, large and faded and rather stupid-looking—and between them, Mary, the miraculous offspring of this uninspiring marriage. Ever since the day when he had first noticed her, he had been waiting for the time when he would be there by right, sitting beside her in the Tabernacle.

But as he went up the steep front steps of the Tabernacle, the memory of his sin suddenly descended; it extinguished him. He asked himself what point there was in dragging himself through the endless avenues of the future when, because of this one folly, he would be carrying his shackles about with him forever. He even, for a moment, thought of throwing himself on the mercy of the astonished Mr. Tuke and confessing everything. But as soon as he was inside, the mood passed; his fears fell from him. He wedged himself in the corner of his seat—the seats he had discovered from long experience, could be made as comfortable as a drawing-room chair provided the sitter's arms were kept folded so that the shoulder blades did not actually come into contact with the hard back of the seat—and marvelled at his previous panic.

Under the glare of the lights, among all these people, listening to the strains of the presentation organ, he was now inclined to laugh at himself. No one here suspected anything, no one guessed that he was changed in any way from the unblemished and respectable John Marco who had always attended. And how was he changed? As he got to his feet to allow a mother and her two plain daughters to crush into the pew beside him, he told himself that there was nothing about him that was different from his fellows. How could it have been a sin that he had committed, if he didn't feel like a sinner? And as he sat there he realised that this sin was something that the years would reduce to its right proportion, something that would weaken and eventually die inside his conscience when, in the fulness of time, he had made his pile and paid back a hundredfold, this little he had borrowed, this paltry sum that no living being knew about and so could ever miss.

At seven-twenty-five with the body of the Tabernacle already over three-quarters full, the Kent family had still not arrived; there was no Mary. John Marco became impatient. Then the impatience cleared away and was succeeded by a strange sense of punishment. Perhaps he wasn't going to be *allowed* to see her after all, perhaps to be denied the sight of her was the first step in the retribution that he now no longer doubted was somewhere already being prepared for him. And then at seven-thirty, just as the black figure of Mr. Shuttleworth appeared in front the white screen and his assistant began fiddling with the acetylene flare inside the lantern, Mary Kent came in. She was alone. John Marco's spirits rose at the first glimpse of her. But there was no time even to catch her eye. She went quickly up the aisle—he caught a swift impression of the pale, lovely face, and the gleaming coil of her hair as she passed—and sat down in the Kents' family pew. Then the lights were lowered and Mr. Shuttleworth's experienced voice began.

"My first," he said, "shows the most famous city in the world—Jerusalem. Note the Temple area, now occupied by the Dome of the Rock"—here he seized hold of a long pointer, like a billiard cue, and began stroking the screen with it—"and at the back, on the left, the Mount of Olives itself. . . ." He paused and banged twice on the platform with the butt of his pointer: the assistant dexterously inserted another slide, and the show proceeded. "We are now looking," said Mr. Shuttleworth, "at the Sea of Galilee, with the summit of Mount Hermon in the distance. I want you to observe on the left the feathery branches of the date-palm. In case any of you should not be clear which is your left and which is your right I should explain that *this* is the date palm and that *this* is your lecturer in native dress."

Mr. Shuttleworth dropped his voice impishly for a moment and then passed on to the next slide. "Here," he said, "we have the Salt, or Dead, Sea and away in the distance we see the peaks of the Mountains of Moab. . . ."

To-night, however, John Marco was a bad listener. His thoughts wandered. He felt a contempt for the stale, familiar stuff of Mr. Shuttleworth's address; if Mary Kent had not been there, he would have found an excuse to slide from his pew and leave while the lights were still down. But as it was, he sat on, waiting for it all to be over. He saw the site of Nineveh, and the Ishtar Gate of Babylon, the Golden Calf and a portion of a Roman Road in Syria. But it was of none of these that he was thinking. He was wondering how he should approach Mary Kent and ask if he might walk home with her.

It proved to be quite easy, astonishingly easy in fact. As she passed through the porch, there was John Marco waiting for her. He held his hat in one hand and a mission appeal that he had just been given in the other.

"If you're alone," he said with a little bow, "might I have the pleasure of walking home with you?"

The question amused him as he asked it, and this amusement gave him confidence. After what he had done already for her sake, it seemed so slight and innocent, this new thing that he was asking.

And Mary Kent seemed pleased by his attention.

"Thank you," she said. And after a pause as they walked along together, she added by way of making conversation: "My father isn't well to-night. My mother is looking after him."

"Nothing serious, I trust," John Marco replied with proper formality.

"It's a carbuncle," Mary Kent answered.

"They can be very painful," John Marco replied seriously. And for the moment as he spoke he almost felt concerned about it.

They walked on side by side through the shadowy, gas-lit streets. John Marco was most punctilious and attentive. He took up a position gallantly on the outside, changing over rather ostentatiously when they turned the corner, and allowed himself to take Mary Kent lightly by the arm when they crossed the road. Even so he was careful to drop her arm again as soon as she had safely reached the pavement. It could not possibly have been said of him, he reflected, that he was being cheap or famil-iar; so far as Mary Kent was concerned, he wished his conduct to be entirely and gracefully beyond reproach.

The little family business was closed when they got there;

closed and shuttered. The only evidence of its nature was a round hole in the shutter through which a solitary clock face, inscribed with the words "Alexander Kent, Clock-Maker and Jeweller," was visible. Mary Kent stood aside and did not attempt to hold out her hand. Instead she spoke the words that he had always hoped he would hear.

"Won't you come inside for a moment, Mr. Marco?" she asked. "It's really quite early."

"Thank you," said John Marco simply. "I'd like to."

Mary Kent had her own key; it had been given to her so that she should not disturb her mother in the process of attending to the suffering Mr. Kent. She opened the door that gave onto a steep flight of stairs, and John Marco followed her up. A feeling of excitement came over him as he did so. It was his moment of victory. He was in her home at last. But there was something deeper than the mere sensation of victory, something deeper and far sweeter: she had asked him herself.

Mrs. Kent, however, did not seem at all pleased to see him; she made it clear that in her opinion Mary Kent had acted gauchely and impetuously in admitting him at all.

"You shouldn't have brought Mr. Marco up like this, dear," she said quite frankly. "It isn't fair. If we'd known he was coming we'd have been prepared."

She began making little swooping excursions round the room as she was speaking, snatching up a work basket, a pile of mending, a plate with a knife across it.

"Please don't trouble on my account," John Marco began. "I shan't be stopping. It was only that I showed Miss Kent home."

But Mrs. Kent was now equally emphatic that he should stay. It was evident that she felt that somehow her daughter had contrived to bring the hospitality of the Kents into disrepute,

56

and she wanted to restore their reputation in Mr. Marco's eyes.

"You can't go until you've had a cup of tea," she said. "You can't really."

As she said it she went over to the corner cabinet where the best china was kept and began removing the milk-jug with the fancy crinkled edge, the square pedestal tea-cups, the urn-like sugar bowl. John Marco remained politely standing. He was rather amused by her agitation. It was the first acknowledgement that he had ever received that he was someone of importance. It gratified him, too, to find so obviously that he was the first man whom Mary Kent had ever invited into her house. He looked across at her where she was sitting—she had just taken her hat off and the brightness of her hair was showing—and they smiled at each other.

Mrs. Kent asked if he would move while she got the biscuit barrel. . . .

It remained a tense and rather difficult interlude. Mr. Kent lay in the next room, too ill to join them, too well-bred to cry out. But John Marco had forgotten about him: his eyes were fixed on Mary. She was pouring out tea for her mother and, as he looked at her, he realised that never before had he seen anyone cock her finger so enchantingly as she poured.

As the minutes passed, Mrs. Kent's agitation increased. She glanced from the clock—there were four clocks in that room alone—to John Marco, and back at the clock again. Finally, she put two more lumps of sugar into her tea and sat stirring them, trying to appear as though she were a woman without a duty or a worry in the world.

But Mary Kent was not to be deceived.

"If you want to go and do anything for father," she said, "I'll look after Mr. Marco."

"No, please," said John Marco. "Please don't let me stop you. I was just going."

He half-rose as she said it. But Mary motioned him down again.

"You don't have to go," she said, "just because Mother's got something she wants to do."

The firmness of her tone surprised both of them. Mrs. Kent looked from one to the other, debated with herself the propriety of leaving them alone together, and finally decided that her daughter had meant what she said. She got up in a tangle of apologies about how the doctor had said that she ought to attend to Mr. Kent at nine o'clock for certain, and went out into the kitchen, leaving the door open after her. John Marco regarded Mary Kent with fresh admiration. To-night was the turning point in her career—he could see that. He was savouring the glorious sensation of the lover who for the first time finds himself being preferred to the family.

There was a long awkward pause during which John Marco did not take his eyes off Mary Kent. He just sat there gazing. She could feel his eyes on her, passing all over her. It was a new sensation for her to be looked at by a man in this way; and she found, to her surprise, that she liked it. But she had to say something, something to break the silence.

"Did you enjoy the lecture?" she asked.

John Marco was bold. In this, the intimacy of her own home, he felt that he could tell her that he loved her.

"I wasn't thinking of the lecture," he said.

Mary Kent dropped her gaze.

"I wish," she said, "that we could have that lantern for the Sunday School. It would make the Scriptures so much more interesting for the children."

But John Marco was not to be put off so easily.

"I told you I wasn't thinking about the lecture," he repeated. "I was thinking about . . ."

It was Mrs. Kent who interrupted him. She emerged from the kitchen wearing the air of self-conscious importance that descends on all amateurs about to execute a professional operation for which they are not qualified. In her hand she was holding a massive quart bottle—she had been forced very humiliatingly to borrow it: being Amosites, the Kents were not a drinking family—wrapped up in a bath towel. She had just been boiling the bottle, and it was now so hot that it could not be held. In a few minutes the bottle was going to be applied by Mrs. Kent, neck downwards, onto the unfortunate man's carbuncle. It was the doctor's idea that the bottle should then be held there until, as it cooled, the vacuum inside it had sucked out the core of the inflammation. The whole scheme hinted somewhat of the torture chamber; it was medical practice at its most simple, most painful and most effective.

The peculiar nature of the operation appeared to embarrass Mrs. Kent.

"Whatever will Mr. Marco think?" she said, "me coming through like this?"

She covered up the neck of the bottle with the corner of the bath towel as she spoke, making the whole bundle appear like a swathed and probably smothered baby, and passed through into the bedroom. A few minutes later a groan indicated that she had interrupted the sufferer in a doze into which he had just dropped off.

John Marco turned to Mary Kent again. He was blushing.

"I was thinking about you," he said.

"Were you?" said Mary Kent.

She was looking straight at him now, a smile half timid, half happy, playing across her face.

"Do . . . do you mind?" John Marco asked.

"I'm glad," she said.

She spoke so softly that John Marco scarcely heard the words. He got up and came over to her. He was trembling: his knees felt so weak that they might let him down.

"May I . . . may I call you Mary?" he asked.

She held out her hand and took hold of his. She could feel then how nervous, how frightened of her, he was; and it moved her far more than any show of strength, of self-possession, could have done. She felt happy and excited to think that she could reduce this hard, fine man, with his black, piercing eyes, to such a pass. She had an idiotic fear that he—not she—might be going to cry.

"Do you want to?" she asked.

He came closer to her until he was touching her; he was gripping her hand by now so hard that it hurt. Her head with its bright sweep of hair was against him. He could trust himself no longer and closed his eyes in the sheer happiness of the moment.

"Mary, I love you," he said. "I loved you from the first moment I saw you."

She did not answer for a moment, and he could feel that she was trembling.

"I like you too," she answered.

"That's not enough," he said quietly. "You've got to love me. Say that you love me."

"I . . . think I do," she replied. "But I hadn't expected anything like this to happen."

"Then you do love me!" John Marco repeated. "You do!"

He went down on his knees beside her and his face was now close to hers.

"Kiss me," he said.

Her lips were parted, and he could see that her eyes were smiling; smiling and still a little startled. Putting his arm round her he pulled her to him. She began stroking his hair; it was the first time that she had ever touched a man's hair and it felt firm and crisp beneath her fingers. She kissed him, conscious of a strange new excitement within her. Then when they had kissed, John Marco began speaking to her; his voice was now low and rapid.

"Promise to marry me," he said. "Swear that no matter what happens you'll marry me. Don't let anything stop us."

She was frightened now and drew back from him, but he raised himself on his knees until his face was close to hers again. Those black, intense eyes of his were staring into her.

"Whatever happens—do you hear me?" he was saying. "You've got to marry me. You're never to leave me."

"Stop," she said. "Please stop."

John Marco paused and passed his hand across her forehead. He spoke gently now as though apologising.

"It's only because I love you so," he said, "that I can't bear . . ."

But he was never able to finish the sentence. At that moment there was a sudden scream from the adjoining room, a scream followed by the sound, confused but unmistakable, of bare, running feet.

It was Mr. Kent. Never spartan in the endurance of pain, and with the reserves of his courage sapped by the shootings of the carbuncle, he had found Mrs. Kent's hot bottle too much for him. At one moment, he was lying on his face with his handkerchief stuffed into his mouth, ready for anything that his wife might do to him; and, at the next, as he felt the white hot pain go plunging into him, he had let out a shriek and was scrambling out of bed and across the bedroom.

He paused for a moment, his narrow chest heaving, holding onto the wash-stand. Then, at the sight of Mrs. Kent, advancing towards him, the torturing bottle still held in the bath-towel in her hands, his nerve finally left him. With another little squeal of terror he tore open the door and ran into the safety of the living-room.

In his long flannel night-shirt that buttoned up at the wrists and fell below his ankles, and with his tufts of greying hair erect upon his head, he made an astonishing and terrifying figure; and also, now that he saw there was a stranger in the room talking to his daughter, a very shame-faced one. He muttered something that might have been an apology and turned back towards the bedroom. But not in time. The face of Mrs. Kent, scarlet at this fresh humiliation, appeared round the door. She got hold of her husband by the back of his night-shirt and gave a jerk. Mr. Kent was a small man and Mrs. Kent was a powerful woman. Mr. Kent seemed suddenly to sail through the air like a ballet dancer on a wire. The bedroom door slammed and all was silence again.

John Marco went over and took up his hat and coat. He was the respectable lay-teacher again.

"I oughtn't to have come to-night," he said. "I'm sorry."

"I'm sorry, too," Mary answered.

They stood in front of each other like strangers.

"I'm afraid I invited myself at a rather awkward moment."

"Oh no. It was my fault. It was really. I asked you to come in."

And then suddenly they both laughed and John Marco went over and kissed her for the second time.

"When may I come again?" he asked. "Say when I may come."

Mary avoided his eyes.

"You'll have to ask my father, when he's better," she said. "You'll have to ask him if we may see each other."

"May I ask him?" he said.

And Mary nodded her head.

"Yes," she answered.

Then because it was late and because she felt that she ought to be there in the sick-room, she said good-bye to him and they went into the dim, opaque-looking hall together. At the foot of the stairs he stopped.

"But when may I see you?" he asked.

She paused and in the half-darkness he could see that she was smiling at him.

"I shall be at the school on Sunday," she said.

With that she pulled open the front door for him and he stepped into the street. It had been raining since he had gone inside and the pavements under the shine of the lamps now gleamed ahead of him like gold.

It was nearly ten-o'clock when he swung open the gate of his mother's tiny house in Chapel Villas. The gate squealed at him on its hinges as it always did: it was a clear octave of rust that had greeted him every night as far back as he could remember.

To his surprise there was a light in his mother's room as he passed it. She called out to him. It was strange how despite her deafness, she could always hear any sound that she had set her mind on. Evidently she had been lying awake, waiting for him.

He went in and kissed her. She was sitting up in a confusion of shawls and bed-jackets—so that she appeared not little and frail, but vast and boundless—her Bible open on her knees. Her hair brushed out in plaits for the night hung in two wisps no lower than her shoulders. Because her sight was bad and the room was lit only by a candle she held a heavy reading glass in her hand.

"Where have you been?" she asked.

And then before he could tell her, she went on to explain why she had lain awake for him.

"There's been a young lady here asking for you," she said. "She came twice. She said she was Mr. Trackett's niece."

Chapter V

They were all gathered together in Mr. Tuke's drawing-room—even the organist, who had discovered an empty seat in the mourning carriage and had insisted on coming back with them.

Not that it could be called a large party. There was Mr. Tuke, smooth and rubicund as usual, but with a purple woollen comforter round his neck because of the cold. Circulating round him like a planet was Mrs. Tuke. She was the most meagre of women, a mere fleshless and bloodless backbone in black satin; if Mr. Tuke had been a vampire and Mrs. Tuke his victim, she could not have looked more depleted and anaemic and he more full-veined and nourished. On the chair over by the fireplace Mr. Trackett's niece, Hesther Croome, was sitting. Her hands were crossed on her lap and she was silent. Only her eyes gave an indication of any life within her: and they were straying perpetually. From the way she kept glancing at John Marco it was almost as though she were sizing him up, sizing and weighing him, so that if it ever came to a difference between them she would know which of the two was the stronger. For his part, John Marco had tried all the afternoon to appear indifferent to her. He had himself looked in her direction more than once; but he had been careful each time to look away again before their eyes could meet. Even so he had not failed to be conscious of her perpetual scrutiny. He sat there awkward and uncommunicative, his shoulder still aching from the sharp edge of Mr. Trackett's coffin.

The funeral, Mr. Tuke confessed to himself, had not been a success. The sparseness of it had shocked and disappointed him; he liked to preside over a forest of black veils and bared heads, not over six mutes—one of them an amateur dragged in against his will—a domestic servant, and one relative. At the graveside they had looked more like a group of people waiting for a bus than an assembled company of mourners; they had, Mr. Tuke felt, made him look ridiculous in the eyes of the resident Anglican chaplain. But there it was; it was the comment of the world upon Mr. Trackett. For fifty-three years Mr. Trackett had schemed and laboured to grow rich: he had worked ceaselessly, guarding every penny. And, in the result, even in a country where people enjoy funerals, not so much as one friend or acquaintance had come forward to pay his respects at the end. It was as though the whole of London had united in principle to boycott this final episode in a life at once so strict, so sterile and so anti-social.

It was not that alone, however, that had ruined the funeral. It was the weather. The morning had been so densely foggy that the funeral horses clopping along towards the Harrow Road had seemed not like ordinary horses at all, but like legendary and heraldic beasts prancing and gavotting through the mist. To the occupants of the carriage all that was to be seen through the inferior, rattling square of window was a pageant of swirling yellow nothingness that swept past, without cessation and without variety, so that only the sound of shunting trains served to distinguish the metropolitan activity of Westbourne Bridge from the semi-surburban deathliness of Kensal Rise Approach.

The cemetery itself, had nothing to commend it, shrouded in the encompassing blanket of fog. Its outlines and dimensions were vague and uncertain and, in a way, alarming. For, though all that one could see was a near-by huddle of plunging marble doves and truncated columns and wax-flowers under glass domes, there was a suggestion that this wilderness of death extended through the fog for miles and miles. It was as though, once having ventured through the high iron gates and past the late-Gothic chapel, one was then on a gravel highway that led right into the heart of those limitless prairies of grave-stones amid which a man might walk endlessly in circles until he dropped trying to find his way back to the living world of Acton or West Hampstead.

But worst of all was the fact that Mr. Tuke's voice had gone. Despite his garglings and his lozenges and his throat sprays, the aphonia had persisted. What had begun as a common cold had suddenly developed into a sinister ailment attacking Mr. Tuke's chief instrument of livelihood. In the chapel and at the grave-side, instead of declaiming the great Biblical truths about the dust and ashes, he had been forced to whisper them to the tiny circle around him as though they were all a kind of indelicate secret. And throughout the whole time he was reciting, he was wondering what was going to be the effect on a man of his age who, already suffering from his chest, was forced to stand about on a great heap of dank, London clay in a fog. That was why, safe at home again at his own fireside, he was now drinking down scalding tea with an almost feverish abandon. He had just taken his fourth cup when he noticed that Miss Croome was eating nothing.

"What can I press you to?" he asked.

But Miss Croome shook her head.

"A little more," Mr. Tuke said. "Just a little more to keep us company."

Miss Croome, however still refused. And for a moment Mr. Tuke laid his hand on her shoulder.

"I understand," he said. "Times like these. I feel for you."

He stirred up his own tea as he spoke and drank it off at a mouthful. The room then became silent again. Mrs. Tuke took the cup from him and automatically filled it up again. The organist pulled out his handkerchief and brushed a few crumbs off the arm of his chair. Miss Croome's eyes rested on John Marco. John Marco crossed his arms and stared into the fire.

For the first time he found himself beginning to feel sorry for this girl. Compared with Mr. Tuke and the rest of them she was living in a world of private desolation of her own. To Mr. Tuke and the organist one funeral was very like another; they met death on equal and professional terms. To Mrs. Tuke, Mr. Trackett's decease had meant no more than the setting out of another teacup. But to Miss Croome it represented something different; as she had followed the massive oak box with its beaded edges and its ornamental handles out of the house, she must have been thinking all the time that she would be going back to a home that could hold for her nothing but loneliness and the bleak face of life.

He wondered vaguely what would become of the girl. She was probably thirty already, he reflected, and he could not picture any man wanting to devote his life to her. At the thought, he glanced towards her pityingly—and their eyes met. Somewhere inside the black depths of hers she seemed to be smiling at him.

The organist was getting up to go; he was bending very low

over Mrs. Tuke's hand and thanking her for her hospitality.

Mr. Tuke turned towards Miss Croome who was stirring.

"Please don't feel that you ought to go," he said. "You can stay with us as long as you like. You must think of this as another home now."

His invitation was interrupted, however, by Mrs. Tuke, who had come back into the room from seeing the organist off. She approached Mr. Tuke like a foster-mother.

"We're going to get you straight off to bed as soon as every-one's gone," she said briskly. "We're going to rub your chest and give you a hot rum and milk."

"Not rum," said Mr. Tuke hurriedly. "Not rum. Hot milk, perhaps. But not rum."

Mrs. Tuke caught her breath and flushed. She had, she realised, been guilty of a major indiscretion. The rum that she and Mr. Tuke took when they had a cold was a secret between the two of them, something that had to be smuggled past the Amosite conscience. For a minister of Mr. Tuke's standing to admit to toping in the privacy of his own bedroom was tanta-mount to ecclesiastical suicide.

But Mr. Tuke was already covering up the blunder.

"In any case," he said, in his husky, unfamiliar voice, "I cannot go to bed now, ill as I am. I have just invited these two young people to stay."

John Marco left the mantelpiece where he had been standing.

"No, Mr. Tuke," he said. "You've done enough for to-day. You took a risk in being there at all. You mustn't neglect yourself."

Mrs. Tuke looked at John Marco gratefully; he struck her as being an unusually agreeable young man. And Miss Croome, too, made it plain that she was not stopping.

"Thank you," she said, "for everything you've done for me. I shall never forget it. I must go back now. I'm very tired."

Mr. Tuke turned to John Marco: he was not quite able to disguise his sense of relief.

"Then you perhaps will see Miss Croome to her home?" he said. "She ought not to be allowed to go back alone."

John Marco drew in his breath sharply; it meant going back to the house that he wanted to forget. He glanced quickly towards Miss Croome as Mr. Tuke said it. He thought that in her face he saw that fleeting smile again.

"That would be very kind of Mr. Marco," she said. "I shan't take him far out of his way."

Mrs. Tuke smiled kindly and led Miss Croome upstairs to get her coat; it had been left folded upon the bed in Mrs. Tuke's bedroom. The bed itself was a double one; it had as much brass work about it as a marine engine. Under the white counterpane it looked chaste and un-connubial. The whole room, indeed, looked unconnubial. Over the mantelpiece hung a large coloured photograph of the Rev. Levi Sturger, founder of the Amosite dissension; his bearded, pug-like face was set in a frown that seemed ready at any moment to deepen into anger at the first glimpse of the carnal and voluptuous. Perhaps that was why the Tuke's had been blessed with no off-spring; perhaps every time at the magical and tantalising moment, the bearded image on the wall shining in the light from the street lamp outside had caught their eye and prevented them.

Miss Croome went over to Mrs. Tuke's dressing-table and began re-setting her hair; there was a furtive vanity about the gesture. She was deliberately loosening and pulling down those two thick strands of hair again so that they should show underneath the hat band. The whole posture—the body leaning towards the mirror and the hand raised to the hair—seemed out of keeping with the black dress, the black woollen stockings and heavy, low-heeled shoes. But Mrs. Tuke saw nothing to object to; she was always ready to condone any amount of prinking in a plain woman that she would not for a moment have excused in a pretty one.

Downstairs in the hall John Marco was waiting. It was not a hospitable hall to wait in. The walls were covered with a shiny, oiled paper and the pictures were all either of the Holy Land or of Mr. Tuke. The furniture was limited to a pair of high-back chairs with curving ramifications like the seven branched candlesticks, and an umbrella-stand with a black-enamelled pan underneath to catch the drips. Down the centre ran a long strip of patternless oil-cloth. And when Miss Croome had joined them in her black coat and veil, her new black hand-bag clasped in her black-gloved hand, the natural gloom of the hall seemed suddenly to burst into flower.

But Miss Croome herself seemed to have outgrown her gloom. She was a little red-eyed and her face was still swollen from crying at the graveside. But those signs were the only witnesses to what she had been through. Her present mood had no place for them. She thanked Mrs. Tuke for her kindness and said that she hoped Mr. Tuke would be no worse for having taken the service. Mr. Tuke replied with the kind of smile that can be worn only by men who know that dying for duty is not death at all.

On the walk back, Miss Croome became quite communicative. She spoke of the occasion as though it had been a most ordinary one. It was in a way, as though she were outside it all and looking on.

"When you come to think of it," she said quietly, "it's strange that you should have been my uncle's coffin bearer. You really scarcely knew him."

"I'd never even spoken to him until the night he died," said John Marco pointedly.

"That's what I meant," Miss Croome continued. "It can't have been an accident that you were sent to him. These things have a meaning."

John Marco did not reply, and a moment later, Miss Croome spoke again.

"An hour before the end he had never met you," she said almost as though talking to herself, "yet in the face of death he trusted you with everything."

The memory of John Marco's crime came back to him. He felt his heart pause for an instant and hesitate; then it recovered and resumed its regular beating. Only a faint flush that in the darkness could not be noticed served to show that her remark had affected him.

But Miss Croome had not finished.

"It was his death-bed that brought us together," she was saying. "We must always remember that."

John Marco glanced sideways at her as she spoke. But she was apparently taking no notice of him; her face was hidden under the brim of the veiled black hat.

"I'm the only one left," she said after a pause. "I'm the last."

"Are . . . are you going to stop here?" John Marco asked.

They had arrived at the faded stucco house as he spoke and John Marco already felt his mind beginning to lighten to think that he would soon be away from it again. He had made this last remark with a note of deliberate unconcern in his voice as though he did not care whether or not he even received the answer.

But Miss Croome's reply was not casual: it suggested a careful and insidious calculation.

"I shall stop here for the present," she said. "I'm going to stay in the house until I see what happens."

"What happens?" John Marco repeated.

He pushed open the iron gate and stood back on the pavement for Miss Croome to pass.

"Yes," said Miss Croome in the same flat, unrevealing voice. "Until I see what happens."

She saw that John Marco was still standing on the pavement, not attempting to follow her, and she paused where she was.

"I know that it's difficult now that I'm alone," she said, "but I wondered if you would come in. I thought perhaps that you might care to sit with me for a moment."

"It's too late," he answered. "You must be tired. You need all the rest you can get."

"But I can't sleep," Miss Croome answered. "Not after what's happened." Then she stopped herself suddenly and held out her hand. "Good-night, Mr. Marco," she said. "I mustn't keep you. We shall meet some other time."

John Marco turned and left her as soon as they had shaken hands. He was shivering; even through her new black kid gloves he had disliked touching her. She and the house, even the road, too, that it stood in, all served to remind him too strongly.

There was a feeling about the whole place that at any moment he might come face to face with Mr. Trackett again; Mr. Trackett searching for what had been his.

Chapter VI

At twenty past twelve they all filed out again; the morning service had lasted from eleven, and the worshippers now emerged, blinking, into the sunlight. They wore the frowning, rather owl-like expression of an audience coming out after a matinée; it was as though they were surprised and a little shame-faced after such high mysteries to discover that ordinary everyday life had been going on outside all the time.

John Marco was among them. He had sidled out of his pew and had contrived to remain there standing in the aisle until Mary Kent and her mother reached him. Then, innocently, as though he had been waiting for no one in particular, he had turned and walked out beside them.

When they reached the porch where Mr. Tuke was standing (hot milk with nearly half a wine glass of rum in it had done its work and his voice was in magnificent timbre again) Mrs. Kent turned to him. Her daughter's hand was on her arm prompting her.

"We wondered," she said, "if you'd like to take tea with us to-day. Everything was so upset the last time you came."

John Marco blushed. He looked hurriedly in Mary Kent's

direction and saw that she was smiling at him.

"Thank you," he said. "I'll walk back with your daughter after Sunday School if I may. It's very kind of you."

"Mr. Kent really asked me to apologise," Mrs. Kent went on. "He was very ashamed over what happened. Only it wasn't his fault you know. A carbuncle is so very painful."

But John Marco was not listening to Mrs. Kent; he was looking at her daughter instead. He did not notice that someone was standing just behind him. Mr. Rumcorn, one of the Elders, drew his attention to the fact.

"Mind yourself, Mr. Marco," he said, "you're getting in the young lady's way."

John Marco stepped back and saw that it was Miss Croome who was standing there. Her dark eyes swept over him, then on to Mary Kent and back to him again. There was something faintly amused and contemptuous about her expression. But she merely apologised for disturbing them and passed on down the steps.

"That's Mr. Trackett's niece," John Marco explained.

Mrs. Kent peered after her with renewed interest: in her deep mourning she looked conspicuously alone amid the rest of the congregation that was filing out and going away home in two's and families.

"They say she's got money coming to her," Mrs. Kent remarked. "She'll need it too. She's certainly plain enough."

And she gave the happy laugh of a mother who has a pretty daughter.

They were already walking down the chapel steps as she spoke. Mary Kent was quite close beside him, and for a moment he dared to let his hand rest in hers. It was a quick, furtive gesture, something that it would not have done for the rest of the worshippers to have seen. But even so it succeeded. For an instant he felt the pressure of her fingers upon his. And then they were both walking down the steps again, sedately and properly, as though they were casual acquaintances who had met by chance. But John Marco's fingers still seemed alive and tingling from the touch when they reached the bottom and he raised his hat to bid Mrs. Kent and her daughter good-morning.

Old Mrs. Marco was dressed all ready for Sunday lunch when he got back. She had set a widow's cap on her head and pinned a large cameo brooch on her bosom. This dressing-up was her ritual, her reply and challenge to the road they lived in. When Mr. Marco had been alive and the little maid, flushed from the heat of the kitchen, had carried in the beef and the vegetables, Mrs. Marco had always been sitting there like that at her own table, her hair smoothed down and a brooch in her bosom. And now, even though she had to cook the meal herself, pottering shakily about that dark back kitchen, she was a lady again by the time she came to eat it.

The moment John Marco had hung his bowler and overcoat upon the hat-peg, Mrs. Marco's Sunday examination began: she wanted to know about the service. Ever since the cords of arthritis which bound her had been drawn tighter and still tighter, the journey to the Tabernacle had been too much for her. And this method of question and answer, was now, next to her Bible, the chief spiritual consolation of her life.

"What were the lessons?" she asked.

"An angel opposeth Balaam," and "The centurion's servant healed," he told her.

She went straight to her Bible—it was the size of a small suitcase and significantly locked against enquiry—and opened it. She found the place with the effortless precision of a scholar.

". . . And when the ass saw the angel of the Lord, she fell

under Balaam: and Balaam's anger was kindled, and he smote the ass with a staff.

"And the Lord opened the mouth of the ass, and she said unto Balaam, What have I done unto thee, that thou hast smitten me these three times?

"And Balaam said unto the ass, Because thou hast mocked me: I would there were a sword in mine hand, for now would I kill thee.

"And the ass said unto Balaam, *Am* not I thine ass, upon which thou hast ridden ever since I *was* thine unto this day? was I ever wont to do so unto thee? And he said, Nay.

"Then the Lord opened the eyes of Balaam, and he saw the angel of the Lord standing in the way, and his sword drawn in his hand: and he bowed down his head, and fell flat on his face. . . ."

It was, taken at its face value, a somewhat obscure and puzzling extract from the Scriptures, this lesson of the short-tempered rider and the talking donkey. But it was not the moral of the piece that was exercising Mrs. Marco: it was the words. They ran over her tongue like beads of honey, these rich, thick syllables which came straight out of her infancy. It was always the same: as soon as she began to read the Scriptures, the present, with all its miseries and privations, disappeared; and in its place was left the happy landscape of childhood. As she read about Balaam meeting Balak in the city of Moab she was a young girl seated in the Amosite Meeting House in Dalston; she had only to close her eyes to hear again, though faint and ghost-like after all these years, the loved accents of the Rev. Mr. Cluddock who had taught her.

"Did you see that Mr. Trackett of yours?" she asked suddenly; she still resented that her child should have friends that she had not chosen for him.

"Mr. Trackett's dead," he told her.

She nodded her head.

"I remember now," she said. "Mr. Tuke said something about it."

There was a pause: then John Marco spoke to her.

"I'm going out to tea this afternoon," he said.

Mrs. Marco paused; she suddenly saw the whole of her Sunday destroyed by her son's heartlessness in deserting her.

"Who with?" she asked.

"I'm going to have tea with the Kents," he said.

"Who?"

"The Kents."

"You mean the watch-maker?"

John Marco nodded.

"What are you going *there* for?"

She did not conceal the anxiety that lay behind the question; it seemed to her that her model son was suddenly throwing her over for a host of strange acquaintances of his own.

"I said what are you going there for?" she repeated.

"They asked me," John Marco replied.

She turned and stared at him: she had not known him like this before, secretive and non-committal. But it was not John Marco she saw. It was his father, John Augustus Marco whom she saw standing there. In his time he had been the larger man, thick-set and florid. But the line of the shoulders was the same—it was something that had been passed on—and the aggressive angle of the chin. It was all there. And now this duplicity, this deceitfulness, as well; during all the years of her marriage she had never been quite sure of him. Mrs. Marco got up and took hold of the back of her chair to steady herself and came over and peered into his face.

"Is there a *Miss* Kent?" she asked.

"There is," he answered.

"What's she like?" Mrs. Marco pestered him. "How old is she?"

John Marco looked steadily at his mother, his strong eyes meeting her weak upturned ones.

"I shall bring her here sometime," he said. "You shall meet her."

Mrs. Marco did not reply for a moment.

"What about the other young woman?" she asked. "What did she want with you?" She caught hold of him by the arm and stood there peering up into his face. "Have you been getting yourself into trouble?" she suddenly asked. "Have you done something you're ashamed of?"

John Marco felt a shudder of coldness run along his spine. He stepped back a pace so that old Mrs. Marco, her support gone, almost stumbled forward.

"I've got myself into no sort of trouble," he said. "I've done nothing I'm ashamed of."

The sound of the words frightened him as he uttered them; they were too brave. He wondered, in one of those little fits of terror which were now mercifully becoming less frequent and less severe, how long it would be before the whole of Paddington would learn the falseness of them.

But old Mrs. Marco was not thinking of him any longer. She was already on her way back to the kitchen from which was coming the unmistakable and disgraceful smell of good food left too long in the cooking.

ii

He began to get ready half-an-hour before it was time to go out.

Upstairs in his bedroom he dressed himself carefully and fastidiously. When he finally left the house he looked more like a young masher idly making his way towards Piccadilly than an Amosite Sunday School teacher on his path to the Tabernacle. Only the book that he was carrying betrayed him: it was the Rev. Samuel Wood's *Bible Questions and Bible Answers*.

Despite the book, however, his lesson that afternoon was a bad one. It wandered. Fourteen young Amosites of both sexes who had been sent by their parents to learn all about the marriage in Cana came away knowing no more than when they came in. For John Marco's mind was not on his task. When he should have been thinking about the miracle before Capernaum, his thoughts instead were fastened upon a small front drawing-room over a watchmaker's shop in which he would soon be sitting. And he was still further distracted by a Temperance banner that hung on the wall facing him. The banner was a bold, outspoken piece of work; it announced simply and without fear of contradiction: LIQUOR DISPLEASETH THE LORD. The words, printed in letters nearly a foot high, bore down on him: they overpowered him. Before he was halfway through the lesson, he found himself explaining the miracle of the marriage feast away as though it had not really happened.

Mary Kent's own lesson with the little ones had been almost as disjointed. She was not as intent as she should have been upon Pharaoh's daughter and the priest of Midian. Ever since that night when John Marco had said that he loved her she had thought of nothing else; he had absorbed her; she now accepted quite naturally the fact that in some obscure way she belonged to him already. Weddings in the Amosite dispensation are rarely the break-neck climax to a whirl-wind engagement; the affair is left to mature slowly, and the banns are read usually nine months

to a year after the couple has become betrothed. She knew therefore that there would be a long, seemingly endless, ordeal of
waiting before that night when at last, worn-out with waiting,
she could lay her fair head down on the same pillow that
supported his dark one. But for a whole week now it had seemed
to be the one moment in life worth waiting for.

All the same, his impetuousness, the lack of reticence in his
behaviour, rather surprised her. He was actually waiting there
ready for her, outside the infants' room door. For the sake of an
extra thirty-seconds of her company he had not gone along to
the common room where the teachers, all five of them, left their
hats and coats on chairs round the room and Mr. Tuke left his,
importantly, on the table. She felt foolish and a little flattered by
it all as she went into the common-room beside John Marco and
knew that the eyes of the other teachers, Mr. Chirkwell (who was
also the organist), Miss Mold, and Mrs. Birdlip were upon them.

And the walk back to the shop with his elbow up against hers
had the same quality of delicious unreality about it. She felt so
happy that she wondered if the other people they met would
notice it; happiness of that kind seemed impossible to conceal.
And John Marco himself was different, too. He looked younger.
His colour was higher than usual and his eyes were brighter. At
Chapel that morning he had looked pale; she had been worried
about him. Now, with his jet-black bowler and his neat silk tie he
looked as if he could take all earth and heaven in his stride.

It was obvious from the moment they got inside the flat that
Mrs. Kent had put herself out for them. She was wearing a
brown velvet dress with a high lace collar, supported all round
with little props of whalebone. It gave her a rich, ceremonial,
presence, like a latter-day Queen Elizabeth. Even Mr. Kent had
been made to get up and dress. In his blue serge suit with the

high butterfly collar which showed how pathetically thin and wrinkled his neck was, he was striving to make himself a fit consort for Mrs. Kent's magnificence. It was only the plaster in the middle of his back that thwarted him. When he rose to shake John Marco by the hand he walked with a curious crab-like motion, endeavouring to keep the waist-band of his trousers from rubbing up against the plaster.

The tea was a lavish, rather splendid meal—very different *from* the hasty, improvised snack that Mrs. Kent had knocked together last time. They all sat round the table for it. And they sat there for some time. It was not the sort of thing that could be hurried through; it opened with sardines and it closed with meringues and sweet biscuits. To John Marco, used to the close catering of old Mrs. Marco, there seemed an eye-opening extravagance about such a spread. He kept imagining a successful future in which there would be whole vistas of such meals, only with Mary Kent instead of her mother, seated at the head of the table, with one white finger engagingly cocked as she poured from the silver tea-pot.

But a sudden misgiving came to him and he wondered whether he could ever give her this security, this sense of a heaped fire in the winter and plenty to eat in the larder, that she had always known. He wondered even whether he had any right to ask her father to let her share the thin days of a linen-draper who was still only an assistant. Then he caught her eyes, grey and quiet and smiling, and knew that he would have to ask.

When tea was over, Mrs. Kent and Mary cleared away. They left with trays loaded with the spoiled dishes and did not return immediately. John Marco found himself alone with Mr. Kent. Mr. Kent took out his meerschaum pipe, the bowl of which with careful devoted smoking had become mellowed into a deep honeyed, coffee-colour, and told John Marco that Mrs. Kent did not object to the gentlemen smoking once tea was over. When John Marco told him that he did not smoke at all, Mr. Kent seemed surprised, and also, for some obscure reason, rather pleased. He stood himself in front of the fireplace and smoked on in silence. But he did not seem somehow to be altogether at his ease. It was as though he were waiting all the time to say something—or hoping that John Marco would say it for him. John Marco could not help noticing that Mr. Kent was not looking in his direction at all: he was staring with a fixed, self-conscious expression at the door. John Marco turned: Mrs. Kent was standing there behind him, making little signalling gestures to her husband. When she saw that she was observed she withdrew hurriedly, and the two men were left together again.

Mr. Kent took the pipe from his mouth and gave a dry, nervous cough.

"That was my wife," he said. "She wants me to ask you something."

John Marco drew himself up. But Mr. Kent was not at first able to express himself.

"Mrs. Kent and I . . ." he began, and stopped. "If you don't mind my asking," he began again, "we wondered, Mrs. Kent and me, whether . . ." he was in difficulties once more, however: the words would not shape themselves. He took out his handkerchief and blew his nose loudly as though to give himself confidence.

But John Marco interrupted him.

"I love Mary," he said simply. "I want your permission to marry her."

The words seemed at first to reassure Mr. Kent: it was all that he wanted to know. He liked the look of the young man, and he was ready to trust him. But there was Mrs. Kent as well. She had prepared a long catechism for him to memorise. He started to go through with it.

"Are your . . . your prospects good enough to marry on?" he asked.

The question as he put it sounded strangely different from the version that Mrs. Kent had dinned into him. As he said it, it was shy and diffident; there was a note of implied apology in his voice for having asked the question at all.

"I shan't ask her to marry me," John Marco replied, surprised at the moment at his own calmness in the face of Mr. Kent's perturbation, "until I can give her everything she needs. It may mean one year or it may even mean two. I can only say that in Morgan and Roberts' I'm well thought of. I have reason to believe that I shall be made manager one day."

"Have . . . have you saved any capital?" Mr. Kent enquired.

John Marco paused; he drew in his lips for a moment. The image of his trivial savings transformed last week at a single stroke into something solid and substantial rose before him.

"I have nearly two hundred pounds," he said quietly.

"So," said Mr. Kent respectfully. "So."

They were model answers. Mr. Kent let out a deep sigh at the relief of them. There was good money there already; and even so he was to be spared at least another twelve months, possibly another twenty-four, of his daughter's company. And only the proprietor of a one-man shop everlastingly struggling to keep a good face to the world on an income of sixpences for new watch glasses and five shillingses for as many hours' work, could know how desirable the managership of a flourishing draper's business sounded. Mr. Kent allowed himself to sit down and relax.

"You see," he said, "Mary's only twenty. It's nothing of an

age. I don't hold with young marriages; the girl hasn't had time to know her own mind yet. We shouldn't want anything to happen until she's twenty-one. And then only if those prospects of yours have turned out all right. She's still a child remember."

He was smoking peacefully again when Mrs. Kent and Mary came back into the room. The two men rose and the group reassembled itself round the fire. But Mrs. Kent was restless: she wanted to learn the result of Mr. Kent's cross-examination. And she knew that she would have to ask him for it. It was the greatest of her grievances against him that in the twenty-four years in which they had been married that he had never been known to do anything until she had badgered him to do so; and even then she had to bully him still further to get his assurance that the thing had been done. At this very moment, he was sitting back complacently pulling at his pipe as though what had transpired was not of the slightest importance to either of them.

But she caught his eye eventually and Mr. Kent rose obediently.

"Come along, Alexander," she said. "It's your medicine time."

John Marco waited for the door to be shut upon them and then he went over and took Mary's two hands in his.

"I've spoken to your father," he said. "He understands."

"He's given his consent then?"

John Marco did not reply. He pulled her towards him until she was facing him and her pure, grey eyes were on the level with his dark ones.

"Kiss me, Mary," he said.

They kissed lip to lip like lovers, with his arms round her. When he released her, her colour had mounted and she was breathing fast. She went up to the mirror on the over mantel and began re-arranging her hair.

John Marco stood regarding her. His eyes ran up and down her longingly, lingering on the slim waist, the small feet under the hem of her plain dress, the white hands raised to her hair. He could afford to watch; one day he would be possessed of all that beauty. She would be his entirely.

When she came away from the mirror, he put his arm round her shoulders, but gently this time as though to comfort her.

"We shall have to wait," he said. "We shall have to be patient. But every day now will bring it nearer."

"I shall wait," she said, "as long as you ask me to."

"But we shall see each other every day," he went on. "There won't ever be those weeks again when I used to see you only on Sundays."

"Did you mind so much?" she asked.

"Oh, Mary."

They were interrupted at this point by the return of the parents. They entered tactfully, leaving a pause between turning the handle of the door and actually stepping into the room. As for Mrs. Kent, she seemed to have been crying; she kept dabbing at her eyes and her nose with a screwed-up handkerchief which she held stuffed in her hand. But even so, Mrs. Kent was not a Woman to surrender her only daughter quietly and without a struggle.

"Alexander's just told me," she said. "It's come as a great shock."

"Mother . . ." Mary Kent began. But Mrs. Kent stopped her.

"I don't say I'm not pleased," she went on, "but I can't quite get used to the idea. I still think of Mary as such a little girl." She paused. "And I don't want to think of her making herself unhappy by doing anything silly just on the spur of the moment."

John Marco turned to her.

"I've told Mr. Kent that we shall wait," he said in the same calm voice of authority that had impressed Mr. Kent. "We shall wait until I can give Mary everything she's been used to. I was telling her just now that no matter how much we want it for all our sakes it can't be at once."

Mrs. Kent opened her eyes a little wider. He seemed to be such a reliable, level-headed young man; and the fears that she had been suffering, subsided a little. When he came to say good-bye Mrs. Kent did the most astonishing thing: she kissed him. He kissed her obediently in return.

Then Mr. Kent took Mrs. Kent by the hand because she had suddenly started crying again, and they thoughtfully allowed Mary to see him off alone. The two lovers stood out in the dim, narrow landing together.

"May I see you to-morrow night?" he asked.

"We'll see," she said.

They kissed again, and he held her there so that the gas-light fell on her face; her hair shone.

"We'll go together and buy a ring," he said. "We'll buy it on Thursday."

"I shall be so proud," she told him.

"I'll give you this now," he said suddenly.

He felt in his pocket and produced a thin gold ring which had once been Mrs. Marco's.

"We'll break it and each keep half," he added.

"You won't be able to break it," she said.

He smiled and, pressing the tiny circle of metal between his thumb and forefinger, he destroyed it.

"There," he said proudly.

"I'll keep it always," she said.

She came right down to the bottom of the stairs and they

kissed again, foolishly in the manner of lovers afraid of separation. Then he opened the front door and stepped into the windy emptiness of the street.

But the street was not empty. Standing opposite, under the solitary street-lamp was a woman. She was motionless, gazing up at the window of the room in which he and Mary had been sitting. He did not need the light of the lamp to show him who it was. She was dressed all in black and he had seen her face. At the sight of her a wave of coldness ran over him.

Then, noticing that the front door had opened and that there were people on the doorstep, the figure under the lamp turned and began to walk rapidly away.

Chapter VII

The January sale at Morgan and Roberts' was not a trifling affair; every department was affected, and old Mr. Morgan, who became agitated at such times, kept going out onto the pavement (a thing which in the ordinary way he never did) to see that in this annual Spring-time clearance, when the mistakes of the past twelve months were being remaindered at a fraction of their usual price, dignity was nevertheless still being observed. For, during that desperate week of cut-throat selling, the whole appearance of the shop was changed. Instead of two or three elegant china hands delicately displaying the latest fashions in kid and suède gloves, whole boxes full of gloves were piled into the window, marked "Very Special: 8/11 reduced to 5/11," or "Cannot be repeated 5/11 now 3/6." And in place of the unsmiling wax ladies who for upwards of a generation had worn the new models in millinery on their heads, the hats were simply crammed into the available space, stuck onto pegs or even left dangling on clips from a cord suspended from the ceiling.

Not that the wax ladies were altogether a loss; they were due for interment anyhow. They had aged. Their glassy eyes lacked their original lustre and somehow their very features seemed unnatural and out-of-date. Their hair, too, was thinner than it had been. With every change of hairdressing fashion, Mr. Hackbridge, who supervised the window-dressing, had been forced to let down those false chignons and comb them carefully into the mode of the day. In the result the two ladies now had bare, elderly-looking patches on their crowns that contrasted strangely with the vivid gold of their hair itself, and one of them had gone completely bald at the temples and could be exhibited only when heavily veiled like a Dowager.

But the windows were, after all, only an indication of the disturbance that was going on within. There were three temporary assistants; two extra tables heaped with oddments; and four fewer chairs—Mr. Morgan did not encourage sitting down at sale-time. The principal cash-desk, a gilded, imposing cage that held the unlovely prisoner, Miss Rawkins, was moved right up into the centre of the shop, and additional cash-desks were erected in the various departments. During the seven days of the sale the customary decorum of the house went all to pieces; assistants called out to each other instead of going across and speaking softly; wrong change was given and not detected; thirty-eight inches went as a yard; cups of tea, hastily snatched, were drunk almost within sight of the customers; and the will to sell supplanted the will to please.

It was the opening day of the sale that John Marco now faced. He was early as befitted a man with four female assistants, one a stranger, under his control, and the church clock at the corner was striking eight-fifteen as he went in through the front entrance. Mr. Morgan was there already. He lived over the shop in a suite of rooms as large and lofty as those of an Embassy, and could afford to be early. He was now pottering about, re-arranging the

90

price tickets; taking away more chairs; pushing the dud lines to the back where they would be discovered later by some desperate bargain hunter delighted by the chance of being able to buy *anything;* seeing that all the assistants had a pencil ready in their books; enjoying himself. He gave Mr. Marco a friendly good-morning: he had grown to rely on the punctuality of this young man who never varied.

By five minutes past nine the day's business had begun; they had sold a pair of outsize gloves. Between then and ten-thirty, there were forty people in the shop, and at ten-thirty the real morning rush began. Paddington suddenly descended upon them. Women with shopping-baskets, women with children, women from the wrong side of the Harrow Road—they poured in. In the depths of winter they bought sprays of false flowers for summer hats and light weight cotton combinations. Anything that was for sale was snatched up and examined and hungered for. Even the corset department in the cream and gold room up the stairs was crowded; it was as though the whole of Bayswater had been going about unsupported for weeks waiting for this moment of relief to arrive. And this was only a foretaste of the afternoon. At half-past-three the shop was so crowded that Mr. Hackbridge, the shop-manager was swept entirely to one side: he could only stand on the bottom step of the staircase help-lessly looking on while a sea of women swirled at his feet, eddying now into the Blouses and Shirt-waists, now in the Millinery, and now into the Underwear. And every few moments one or other of the assistants was crying out "Cash, please, Mr. Hackbridge," which meant that he had to wade in up to his neck (he was a tall man) and make a magical symbol of his initials to denote that the sum presented to him was right down even to the farthings. At sale time, Morgan and Roberts' had to send over specially to the bank for a whole bagful of farthings.

There was a lull round about tea-time; and during this lull Hesther Croome came in.

John Marco saw her as she entered; she was different at a glance from the other shoppers—intent on something more serious and more important. She paused for a moment, studying the scene before her; then, having located what she wanted, she came straight towards him.

John Marco felt a wave of coldness again. But he remained the perfect shop-assistant. He placed his two hands on the counter and leant forward, ready to serve her with whatever it was she wanted.

"Can I speak to you, Mr. Marco?" she said.

Her eyes met his and remained there, boldly; John Marco returned her gaze just as steadily.

"What is it you want?" he asked.

"I have something private to discuss with you," she replied.

John Marco's heart missed its beat; the words frightened him. But his manner did not reveal it. He stood there, fixed and impersonal, like any other shop-assistant. Even Mr. Morgan, who was regarding them from the other end of the shop, did not notice anything untoward in the situation.

"Will you tell me what it is?" he said.

Miss Croome glanced round her.

"I can't speak here," she said.

"There's no where else," John Marco answered abruptly.

"Then you must come to my house. You can come this evening."

John Marco's eyes contracted; he thrust out his lower lip, as he always did when he was angry, and shook his head.

"I'm sorry, Miss Croome, but that isn't possible."

"You mean not this evening?"

He bent forward over the counter till his face was close to hers.

"I mean," he said, "that my evenings are engaged."

Miss Croome might have been expecting the words; she did not waver.

"It would be better for you if you came," she said quietly.

It was Mr. Morgan who interrupted them. He had been watching them all the time and he now came importantly in their direction. As the lady had made no attempt to buy anything, and as his star assistant was frowning, he could only assume that she had come in to complain about something; and Mr. Morgan did not encourage complaints at sale time.

He gave a stiff little bow.

"Can I assist you, madam?" he asked.

Miss Croome turned towards him.

"I *am* being attended to thank you," she said. "It was only that I couldn't get what I wanted." She paused and looked at John Marco as she said it. Then, as calmly as before, she went over to the glove counter and picked up a pair of light grey ones that looked out of place beside the funereal black of her dress.

"I think a pair of these would do," she said, still looking at him. "I don't intend to go on wearing black for ever."

"You see," she went on after Mr. Morgan had moved away again, "it isn't possible to talk here—not privately. You had better come as I asked you."

John Marco's face flushed.

"I'm not coming," he said.

He turned his back towards her and walked over to the other counter. The temporary assistant, a pale, timid-looking girl, was standing there: she could not help noticing that there was some kind of trouble between her department manager and this lady in black.

"Miss Carter," John Marco said harshly, "don't just stand there like that, go and serve that lady at once."

He did not even look back to where Miss Croome was standing: he went instead straight through into the small back wash-house where the male members of the staff spruced themselves up. At this hour, of course, it was empty. John Marco did not light the gas: he stood there staring in front of him into the darkness. Then realising that his absence might be noticed, he filled the enamel wash-basin and plunged his face into it. The shock of the icy water revived him. Five minutes after he had left the counter, he was back there. His hands still trembled, but nevertheless he was the polite, the perfect counter-jumper again. "Good-afternoon, and what can I show you, madam?" he said fifty times, always with a little nod of the head and a smile, between Miss Croome's departure and closing time.

There was, indeed, something in the mechanical regularity of the thing that soothed him; each new customer meant another moment's respite from the thoughts that he did not enjoy. He was no longer the wretched John Marco tortured by a conscience and a fear; he was merely someone who measured off yards of stuff and rolled it up in flimsy paper; and wrote out flourishing cryptic bills; and helped fat ladies to try on tight gloves; and smiled and was obsequious and pleasant. John Marco, had indeed, almost forgotten about Miss Croome by the time seven o'clock came along and Mr. Morgan, taking out his gold half-hunter, gave the signal for them to close the shop and clear up after the shambles of the day.

"The front door, Mr. Marco, please," he said.

John Marco put down the roll of ribbon which he was

re-winding and went down the strip of drugget that ran between the counters. In the ordinary way it gave him a sense of position and authority to close the front-door; on the first occasion when Mr. Morgan had asked him instead of Mr. Hackbridge to close it, the staff had realised that times were changing and that it would be Mr. Marco to whom they would have to look up one day.

He pulled down the blue roller blind and clipped it into place behind the panel of plate glass before attempting to close the door. The reason for this was simply courtesy; Mr. Morgan had long ago decided that it was permissible to close an opaque door in the face of a late customer whereas it would be unthinkable to close a transparent one. But to-night, just as John Marco was swinging the heavy door shut, a woman stepped in from the pavement and came forward as though determined to get in.

From the crack of the door, John Marco gave her his usual correct little smile.

"I'm sorry, madam," he said, "but we're just shutting."

It was then, however, that he saw who the woman was; he recognised the shabby overcoat that had once been black and was now almost green with age. He recalled where it was that he had last seen that garland of moulted feathers that was a feather boa, and those wisps of grey hair that straggled over it at the back. It was Mr. Trackett's—now Miss Croome's—general servant who had come to summon Mr. Tuke on the night of the Immersionist Revival Meeting. Even the umbrella, gripped like a weapon, was the same. In her hand she was carrying a black-edged envelope.

"The young lady told me to give you this," she said. She's waiting for an answer.

For a moment John Marco thought of slamming the door in

her face and leaving her there with the envelope still in her hand. But he dismissed the thought as it came to him: he had almost betrayed himself in his manner to Miss Croome. He realised that now, more than ever, he must proceed clearly, and without emotion. He put out his hand and took the note.

The handwriting on the envelope was sharp and angular; the capital J of his Christian name was like a dagger. He tore the letter open and began to read. It repeated, almost word for word, the mysterious message that Miss Croome had delivered in person.

"*Dear Mr. Marco,*" it ran, the words set out on the paper as neatly and blackly as if a printer had disposed them there, "*I have something important to discuss with you—something that affects us both. I ask you again to come to my house this evening. The maid will be there all the time so that we shall not be alone. I can only feel that we shall both regret it if you do not come. Yours earnestly, Hesther Croome.*"

John Marco stood staring at the words. They said quietly and by innuendo, everything that he dreaded. Yet, as he looked at them, he told himself that he had nothing really to fear; Hesther Croome knew nothing that could harm him—it was only the half-demented old man who had hoarded all that money who could have betrayed him—and he was safely laid away under six feet of clay in Kensal Green. No: this was something new and unforeseen, this sinister delusion, this infatuation perhaps, of Miss Croome's. In the face of it, he would have to behave firmly and with decision.

It was only when he realised that the creature was edging round beside him trying to read what it was that her mistress had written, that he spoke. He re-folded the paper and thrust the note back into its envelope.

"There is no answer," he said quietly.

"But . . ." the woman began.

"I told you," John Marco repeated, his lower lip jutting out threateningly again, "that there is no answer."

He did not wait to hear whether she would make any further protest or not, but shut the door abruptly in her face. Through the millinery window he could still see her. She stood there, undetermined for a moment, almost as though she were afraid to go back without the reply that she had been sent for; then, shrugging her shoulders, she drew the straggling boa closer round her neck, and went off up the street.

John Marco glanced over his shoulder to establish that he was not observed in particular by anyone and then walked boldly up to the big iron stove that served to heat the ground floor of Morgan and Roberts'. Opening the top, he threw the note, just as it had come in its envelope, onto the glowing coals as though it were something trivial and unimportant, like a crumpled bill dropped by some careless shopper.

The next three hours were probably the busiest, certainly the most tiring, of the day; everything had to be straightened out in readiness for the turmoil of to-morrow. The windows, from which hats and handbags had been snatched by special request had to be re-filled and re-designed. Basket-loads of stuff had to be carried through from the stockroom and set out on the counters. The carbon-counterfoils of the orders had to be checked against the cash in the till. The "lines" that remained unsold had to be gone over so that Mr. Morgan could decide whether or not to reduce the prices still further.

John Marco worked with a rapid, fixed intensity that frightened his assistants and gratified Mr. Morgan. In his shirt sleeves now—they could afford to be informal once the front door was shut—he was taking down rows of boxes from behind him and

97

going through them one by one measuring up the remnants; discarding empty reels; correcting other people's errors—there was, for instance, a whole three yards of pure silk in among the mixtures; re-grading the colours; pairing up the gloves; smoothing out creases in odd blouse lengths; folding the stockings neatly toe to toe; and endlessly, tirelessly, sticking in the little price labels; "Special Line," "Special Offer," "Special Opportunity," "Unique Reduction."

At nine o'clock the young ladies were sent home. It was a pleasant and gentlemanly convention that, having kept the girls on their feet for twelve hours with only an hour's interval for lunch and ten minutes for tea, they should then be sent home before the men, like the weaker vessels that they were.

And it was understood that, once nine o'clock had passed, the men could go too when they were finished. John Marco had calculated, carefully and exactly, that by not breaking off even for a single minute he could get through his work by nine-fifteen. Then, by running if necessary, he could arrive at Abernethy Terrace where the Kents lived by nine-twenty-five: Mrs. Kent had told him that if he arrived no later than nine-thirty—after that it would have seemed somehow improper—he could have ten minutes of her daughter's company before the family went to bed.

But as nine-twenty was approaching—he was late already—Mr. Morgan came up to him. He seemed to take it for granted that John Marco would be ready before the others; he did not comment on it.

All that he said was: "Do you mind stepping this way, Mr. Marco. I want to re-organise the corsets."

And John Marco answered, "Very good, sir."

It was ten minutes past ten when Mr. Morgan released him;

John Marco, his arms round a pink silken bosom like a *prima donna's,* deposited the dummy on the small table over by the window and Mr. Morgan announced that they were through. He said good-night and, walking through the empty shop, left him there. John Marco followed, turning out the gas-lights as he came.

But this time John Marco did not run: there was no point in it. He walked slowly, like any other man who has worked too long; too long and too hard. Even so, he went in the direction of Abernethy Street instead of Chapel Villas.

When he got there, the shop and the rooms above it were in darkness: he stood on the pavement and gazed up at the house front. He was late. But somehow he did not regard this weary détour as wasted: she was there even if he could not see her. And he knew that every night until they were married he would be here like this; whether she were awake or sleeping, sometime during the evening he would be standing there.

Then he turned and still wearily went back to Chapel Villas and the nightly catechism of old Mrs. Marco.

He knew before he reached the house that there was something wrong, something alarmingly wrong. His mother was standing out there in the cold on the pavement waiting for him. He saw her from the end of the street, a stooping, muffled figure, swathed in all the wraps and capes she could lay her hands on. From a distance, in the lamp-light, she looked entirely spherical; it was only as he got nearer that he could see that she had wrapped a rug round herself and was clasping the two ends across her.

"What are you doing out here?" he asked. "It'll be the death of you."

"Where have you been?" she began.

"I've been at the shop," he said. "We're always late at sale-time."

But the answer did not satisfy her.

"You're not telling me the truth," she said. "You're in some kind of trouble and you won't tell me."

He took her by the arm and began to lead her up the tiled front-path.

"Come inside," he said. "You're not yourself to-night."

He was used to these moods of hers and knew how to handle her. At that moment his one thought was to get her inside so that their neighbours should not hear her; he wondered how long she had been standing there making an exhibition of herself.

But once in the tiny porch Mrs. Marco would not budge.

"She's come," she said. "She's waiting for you."

"Who's come?"

"The young lady."

John Marco felt a sudden icy wind blow across him; but he controlled himself.

"What young lady?" he asked steadily.

But Mrs. Marco was past replying; it was doubtful indeed, whether she had even heard him.

"She's there," she said. "Sitting waiting for you. She wouldn't tell me what she wanted. She only said that she'd got to see you to-night. . . ." Mrs. Marco paused. The night air had got into her lungs and she gave herself up to a fit of coughing. When she could speak again, she clung to him. "Oh, John, John," she said, "what have you done to yourself? What is it she wants with you?"

He pushed her away from him; he was rough with her by now.

"Who is she?" he asked. "Who are you talking about?"

It was only as he put the question that he realised that it might

100

be Mary, who was sitting there. Something—anything—might have happened, and she had come to him. He pushed open the sitting-room door and stood there, staring into the white face and deep eyes of Hesther Croome.

For a moment neither of them spoke. Then John Marco recovered himself.

"Why have you come here?" he asked.

"I told you I wanted to see you," she replied quietly.

"You had no right to come here," he said.

"I did it for your own good," Hesther Croome answered just as quietly. "I am giving you one more chance."

"One more chance?"

"To save yourself."

Before John Marco could answer—and he was trembling now so that he could scarcely stand—Mrs. Marco had pushed her way in front of him.

"What is it you're talking about?" she kept asking. "Why can't I be told? What is it?"

Hesther Croome looked at the old woman contemptuously, running her eyes up and down her.

"Do you want me to tell her?" she asked.

John Marco remained where he was; his face was greenish-white under the gas-light.

"We'll talk alone," he said.

Miss Croome removed a small, silver smelling-bottle and applied it first to one nostril and then to the other.

"Send her away," she said.

But it was not easy. Mrs. Marco became strident. She began abusing Miss Croome. "She's blackmailing you," she said. "She's come for money. That's what it is. I can see it in her face; she's come for money."

John Marco took her by the shoulders and pushed her towards the door.

"You don't understand," he said. "Go to bed and leave us alone."

"I won't go," Mrs. Marco replied vehemently. "I shall stay here. I'm needed."

She was still protesting, as John Marco thrust her out into the passage and turned the key on her. Then the two people inside the room heard the sound of her voice subside, and the noise of crying begin. A moment later, they heard her footsteps shuffle brokenly away in the direction of the kitchen; she was beaten. She was still crying, crying like a child.

Miss Croome was the first to speak.

"You may as well confess it," she said.

John Marco turned on her. "I don't know what you mean," he said.

"Oh yes you do," she answered. "You've got it on your conscience."

"I've got nothing on my conscience."

"Then you're worse than I thought you were. You're not worth saving."

She removed the top of the smelling bottle again and started playing with it. He noticed as she did so that her hands were calm and steady. And for the first time he began to doubt his strength against hers. But he controlled himself and spoke coolly and deliberately.

"What is all this that you're imagining?" he asked.

"You robbed the dead," she answered.

There was a silence which ran on until John Marco did not dare let it last any longer.

"You're mad," he answered. "I don't know what you're

talking about."

"I can tell you how much it was you stole," she went on. "It was a hundred and fifty pounds." She let the words linger on her tongue as she said it.

John Marco had left his place by the chair and began walking up and down the room. His mind had suddenly grown clear and resourceful again.

"Is that sum missing?" he asked.

"You know it is."

"And what makes you think I took it?"

"There was no one else."

He laughed at her.

"No one else," he said. "It might have been anyone. It might have been the servant. She was in and out of the room the whole time. It might have been the lawyer: he wouldn't be the first lawyer to steal his client's money. It might have been the doctor—people trust doctors. It might have been Mr. Tuke— we've only got his word for it. I gave the box to him in the bedroom."

Miss Croome was regarding him again: she was smiling now.

"How do you know it was that night it was stolen?" she asked.

"I know nothing about it at all," he answered.

"Yet you accuse all those people," she said. "*Good* men like Mr. Tuke and Dr. Preece."

"I accuse no one," he retorted. "You're forgetting that I— don't even know that any money *has* been stolen. Women," he looked hard at her—"especially unmarried women, have delusions sometimes. They get put away because of them."

"But I have certain proof," Hesther Croome answered.

At the sound of the word, John Marco stopped himself, he knew that he must be doubly calm now.

"What is it?" he asked.

"My uncle left me a letter saying how much was in the box," she said.

John Marco did not answer immediately. But he realised then that he had nothing more to fear. She had thrown her proof before him and it was useless. He began to laugh.

"He left you a letter," he said jeeringly. "A crazy old man whose mind was wandering. I don't care if he left you a hundred letters. It proves nothing. You could arrest the whole of London on that kind of evidence." Now that he felt safe he could afford to speak angrily. "And you come here at this time of night and accuse me!"

"That wasn't the only reason I accused you," she said.

John Marco paused.

"I have other proof," she continued.

"What is it?" he asked. "More letters? More imaginings?"

"I followed you," she said. "I followed you at lunch-time when you left the shop."

He felt fear strike at him again as she said it. But he continued to face her, continued to look her full in the eyes.

"What's that to me?" he asked. "What do I care if I'm followed?"

"Don't you want to know where you were followed?"

John Marco swung round on her.

"Must I be expected to endure more of this madness?" he asked.

"It isn't madness," she answered. "I followed you to your bank."

He was silent for a moment: he felt now that the net was closing round him, closing tighter than he could ever have foreseen it. But he was still calm.

"Haven't I the right to go to my bank?" he asked.

"It was a lot of money you paid in," she said.

He saw a loop hole there, one dwindling gap which the mesh-work had not yet covered.

"That had nothing to do with your money," he said.

"That was something of my own. Do you want to know how much it was? It was fifty pounds."

"I know already," she answered. "I heard you tell the cashier."

The thought that she had been so close to him, that she had been in his shadow at that moment alarmed him still further. But he kept his voice level.

"What did I do with the rest of it then?" he asked. "Waste my substance in riotous living?"

"You aren't that sort of man," she answered. "You paid it into other banks. You went to Parr's Bank, in Bayswater, on the Wednesday and to Fowler's Bank, in Edgeware Road, on the Friday. You haven't been into a bank since."

When she had finished speaking, he sank down. He was cold, desperately cold, and his stomach was sick inside him. It was not merely that he was trembling now, he was shivering.

"Is that the whole of your proof?" he asked; he managed to jerk the words out of him.

"It is," she answered.

"Then go to the police with it," he said. "Go to the police and make yourself a laughing stock. Go to the police and see if you ever dare to show your face inside the Chapel again."

She got up slowly and drew on her gloves again.

"Very well, then," she said. "I *will* go. I shall go to the police."

He stood up and let her pass and she went out into the inky hall. Then he followed her to the front door and opened it for her. He was breathing heavily and his heart was pounding.

"Is that your last word?" she said from the porch.

"It is," he said, without looking at her.

But when she got to the gate he called her back.

The room was in silence. The only sound—so slight that it only made the silence seem deeper—was the everlasting *ting-ting* of the ornamental marble clock on the mantelpiece with the bronze figure of Father Time swinging in an endless and silly see-saw beneath. They had been sitting there in that chilly front parlour for nearly an hour, the two of them, but for the last five minutes John Marco had not spoken. His eyes were fixed on that maddening pendulum, aimlessly crossing and recrossing its path in space.

"I'm still waiting for your answer," Miss Croome said quietly.

John Marco started.

"I've told you I'll give you the money back," he said.

"I don't want you to give it to me back," she answered. "It isn't that I came for."

"But I can't do it," he said. "It's not in reason to ask it."

"There's no other way," she reminded him.

"Yes, there is," he said. "I'd go to prison sooner."

"You're not the sort of man who lets himself be put in prison," she answered. "You're too fond of the future. Think of the shame of it if they arrested you. Think of what they'd say about you in the Chapel. Think of what would happen to your mother if they *took you* away. You'd never get another place in a shop, remember. You have to handle money. They wouldn't trust you again. This has got to be a secret between the two of us."

"I won't do it," he said again.

"Is it because you're in love with Mary Kent?" she asked.

It was the first trace of emotion that had crept into her voice at all.

He got quickly to his feet at the mention of Mary's name and came over to where Hesther Croome was sitting. The movement was so sudden that she drew back involuntarily at his approach.

"Yes," he said recklessly as if he did not care who heard him. "I'm in love with Mary Kent. Put me in prison, and she'll wait for me until I come out. Try to ruin me, and she'll stand by me. Do what you like but you can't come between us."

"You think that?"

"I know it."

Miss Croome paused. Her eyes were fixed very steadily on his as she spoke.

"Then I shall go to her," she said. "Perhaps she can save you."

"You'll not go near her," he shouted. "You'll not say a thing to her."

"I shall go to-morrow morning," she answered. "I shall tell her everything."

"She'll not listen to you."

"If she loves you she'll want to save you. She won't let you be sent to prison."

"How can she stop it?"

"She'll give you up. She'll refuse to marry you."

He turned away from her and leant against the mantelpiece, passing his hand across his face as though to wipe something away.

He looked very different now from the John Marco who had entered the room and found her sitting there. The spruce counter-jumper had been obliterated: this was someone else. This man's hair was tousled where he had run his fingers through it, and his collar had sprung open. His nerves, too, were on fire: his fingers were twitching. Without moving he snatched the pendulum from the clock and threw it into the empty grate. Without its pendulum the clock subsided. The silence of the room was now complete.

"Hadn't you better give me your answer?" she asked him.

"I've promised nothing," he told her.

"I shall give you until the morning," she said. "You're tired. You can decide after I've gone."

"No: give me longer," he said desperately. "Give me time to think."

"Only till the morning," she answered. "I shall do nothing until then if I can trust you."

"But I've got to think, I tell you. I've got to think."

It still seemed at that moment that there must be a hole in the net somewhere, a tear in the mesh-work through which he could still escape.

In her high bedroom in Abernethy Terrace Mary Kent suddenly cried out. It was a cry of pain followed by what sounded like a sob. Her mother heard her and went in. But Mary was sleeping. She was lying there with her cheek resting on her hand and with her fair hair like a cloud trailing across the pillow behind her. She looked very young. Mrs. Kent drew the covers closer over her and went out again. She never failed to remark that, in her sleep, Mary still looked as she remembered her as a child; she had cried out then sometimes, even though she was happy really.

Chapter VIII

The Second Day of the sale was the most sensational in the whole history of Morgan and Roberts. Mr. Jamieson, the manager in the Fancy Goods Department, was away (which was bad enough in itself at Sale time), and there were police in the shop. The latter came in through the stock door at the back and, with a somewhat ostentatious display of secrecy, went up heavy-footed to Mr. Morgan's private office. The whole place buzzed with the news; it was the first time that the force had ever been on the premises.

Up to the moment of the police's arrival, John Marco had seemed at first glance to be entirely normal; he was courteous and helpful and efficient. It was only on more intimate inspection that the strain, the cracks even, began to show: he looked older somehow. He was paler, too, much paler than usual; and his face was drawn as though invisible cords inside it had been knotted and pulled tight. He was, moreover, shut off from everything that was around him; he was isolated in a frigid, silent world of his own. So complete was the isolation, that before long the girls who worked beside him began to notice that he seemed vaguely queer. For all the contact there was between them he might have been someone serving in another shop.

And when Mr. Hackbridge, with a look of immense gratification upon his face, came strolling down the aisle and whispered something in John Marco's ear, it was the moment of climax. John Marco gripped the edge of the counter.

"Will you say that again, Mr. Hackbridge?" he asked. And as he spoke a sudden wave of terror broke over him.

Mr. Hackbridge tweaked the waxed ends of his moustache and gave the conceited smile of a man who is the bearer of important tidings.

"I said," he repeated, "that the Old Gentleman has a couple of police officers with him, and they're come to make enquiries."

The shop and Mr. Hackbridge's wide waistcoat and the young lady assistants all went black for a moment and disappeared, and John Marco thought that he was going to faint. But the darkness cleared away again and left him standing there.

Mr. Hackbridge was clicking his teeth at him.

"You look," he said disapprovingly, "as though you'd had a night on the tiles, young man."

The words brought John Marco up sharply. He passed his hand across his forehead.

"It's nothing," he said. "It's just that I don't feel very well this morning."

Mr. Hackbridge, however, was not listening; he had passed on down the shop and was rubbing his hands over a customer.

"Germornin' madam," he was saying in a voice of treacle, "and what may we have the pleasure of showing you this morning?"

But John Marco was oblivious to it all. He was still standing at his counter staring blankly in front of him at the patch of air where Mr. Hackbridge had just been.

Then little Mr. Lyman, who looked after the accounts, came down, and said that the Old Gentleman wished to see John Marco in his office for a moment. As he heard the words, John Marco became aware of a strange fatalistic sense of pre-knowledge; he had waited for this summons so helplessly that it came almost as a relief. Ever since that one fatal act of folly that had jeopardised everything, he had been expecting this. Now that it had come, he only prayed that he would know how to meet it. Mr. Lyman had dropped his voice discreetly as he delivered the message—he was a bit self-conscious about it himself. But even so he was audible; the girls momentarily stopped serving and listened. John Marco was perfectly aware of their behaviour. That was why he merely gave a polite little nod and followed the diminutive Mr. Lyman with squared shoulders and his head carried high; at first glance it might even have been thought that it was Mr. Lyman whom the police wished to interview and John Marco who was his escort.

They were all sitting there when John Marco reached Mr. Morgan's room. Mr. Morgan was seated at his desk with a plain-clothes man on either side of him. In front of the desk was one empty chair; John Marco looked at it and knew that it was for him. He caught a glimpse of Mr. Morgan's face and saw how white and anxious it looked.

"Come in, Mr. Marco," Mr. Morgan said with rather more formality than was necessary. "Come in and sit down. These gentlemen are police officers. They want to see if you can help them. Don't be afraid to answer quite frankly."

John Marco seated himself under three pairs of eyes and waited. He could hear his blood battering against his ear-drums as he sat there.

And then he became aware that Mr. Morgan was speaking again.

"It's about Mr. Jamieson," he was saying; "you will have noticed that he is not here this morning. I have to tell you that he met his death last night on the railway."

"Do you want to speak to me about Mr. Jamieson?" John Marco asked.

And as he said it he laughed at the relief. With those three men staring at him he sat there and heard himself laughing.

Mr. Morgan looked shocked and startled.

But the Inspector was master of the situation.

"Take it easy," he said. "I want you to tell me anything you know. Did he drink or bet, for instance?"

John Marco paused.

"I have seen him reading the racing editions, if that's what you mean," he said; and out of loyalty to the departed spirit of his ex-colleague, he added, "—out of business hours, of course."

As he said the words, the picture of Mr. Jamieson flashed across his mind; it was the picture of a small man in a seedy frock coat, crouched down behind a cupboard in the stockroom, assiduously working out with the stump of pencil on a piece of paper the chances of one dark horse against another over the five furlongs of unseen, distant turf somewhere near Newmarket.

Mr. Morgan shook his head over the reply.

"Horse-racing's the devil's pastime," he said. "It's the high road to ruin."

"And drink?" the Inspector went on. "What about drink?"

"I have never personally seen Mr. Jamieson the worse for liquor," John Marco answered. "He always seemed the most sober of men."

Mr. Morgan shook his head.

"I can't understand it," he said. "The two things usually go together."

John Marco looked at him with contempt: the whole shop knew that Mr. Jamieson drank like a sink. Every day after lunch he used to stand on the pavement outside chewing a clove ball before he came in. But if Mr. Morgan hadn't discovered it during all these years, John Marco did not feel inclined to tell him now.

"Did he ever discuss any money worries with you?" the Inspector asked.

"No," said John Marco. "Never."

"And you hadn't any reason to think that he might take his life?"

John Marco raised his eyebrows a little. So that was it: they had simply been polite to the dead man when they said he had met his death. It was evident that they all thought that he had arranged the meeting. But John Marco merely shrugged his shoulders.

"Really," he said, "I hardly knew the man."

The answer did not seem to satisfy Mr. Morgan. He leant forward and addressed himself to John Marco.

"Mr. Marco," he said, "I will be frank with you. Mr. Jamieson was under suspicion: he was fourteen-and-seven-pence short on his day's takings: I had to speak to him about it. And it wasn't the first time it had happened." He dropped his voice almost to a whisper. *"He was nearly three pounds short altogether last month,"* he said. "I told him that if he couldn't explain it, I should have to send for the police. And the same night he fell under a train."

"Threw himself under a tank-engine, you mean, sir," said the Inspector cheerfully.

Then the other policeman came into life.

"Had you actually dismissed him, sir?" he asked.

Mr. Morgan shook his head.

"Of course if I'd been able to find out anything *definite* he'd have had to go," he answered. "You can't afford to employ a thief in retail business."

John Marco could feel a cold sweat breaking out upon his forehead: it seemed that in some inscrutable way the unlamented Mr. Jamieson had been sacrificed as an example: what twenty-four hours before had been a man was now merely a bloody and terrifying warning to sinners and the undetected.

"Did you see the widow?" Mr. Morgan was asking, turning towards the Inspector. "How was she taking it?"

"Sort of dazed, sir," he answered. "They usually are a bit at first. She's an invalid, you know. Been bed-ridden for years."

John Marco half-rose.

"Will you be wanting me any more, sir?" he asked.

He felt that he could sit there no longer. This little comedy at which he was both spectator and actor was too grim for him. And he did not know how much longer his self-control, his beautiful self-control, would last.

He wanted to jump up and shout out: "Don't go on chattering about poor old Jamieson. He's dead anyhow, you fools; he got clear. Take a look at me. I'm a real thief. I didn't just pinch a few shillings here and there. I stole bank-notes, handfuls of them."

But all that happened was that Mr. Morgan beamed on him.

"Quite right," he said. "We mustn't forget the Sale. We mustn't let this other affair interfere with business." And when John Marco had got to the door he went after him. "I shall have to put you in charge of the fancy goods as well," he said. "They're very important at Sale time remember; they're quick turnover." He paused. "And if I find you can manage it," he added, jingling his small change in his pockets as he spoke, "I may give you both departments for good. Then we'll have to see about your salary: it may mean an increase, you know."

"Thank you, sir," John Marco said and left him.

As soon as he was in the corridor he took out his handkerchief and wiped the inside of his collar with it: the handkerchief came away quite moist.

By eleven o'clock when Miss Croome had not arrived, John Marco began almost to doubt that she would come at all. The theft, *his* theft and the threat of exposure that she was hanging over him, did not seem any longer to belong to this world at all. And this one was the real world, this retail world of inches and farthings. The other was simply the finale to a nightmare that somehow or other had not vanished at morning. And then he remembered that Mr. Jamieson must often have felt like that while an unseen race-horse with five stolen shillings of Mr. Morgan's money on it was winning or losing on one of the thumping tracks of England. But Mr. Jamieson had been wrong: only yesterday he had discovered that reality and the nightmare can become one.

And at twelve o'clock, just as Mr. Morgan and the two policemen came down the stairs and began to tour the shop, Miss Croome came in; John Marco's eye was on the door as she entered; it had been there all the time in fact. But she looked different now; he noticed that at once. Even the mourning which she was wearing was not the same. She had brought a black, handsome fur and wore it slung across her like a prize. Somehow in the midst of death she had become fashionable.

She walked up to John Marco, and this time stood there without even making the pretence of buying anything.

"Have you decided?" she asked quietly.

John Marco's throat was dry. At the end of the counter Mr. Morgan and the two police officers were standing.

"I have," he said.

"Then you will?"

"Yes," said John Marco.

He said it so faintly that only Miss Croome knew what it was that he had said.

Chapter IX

Mr.Tuke was standing in front of his drawing-room fire-place, his long coat tails tucked under his arm, so that the fire could get on with its business of warming, unimpeded. All Amosite Ministers affected the frock coat; it was their reply to the cope, chasuble and stole of the older Christian Orders. Only on the Immersion Nights was the frock coat, for obvious reasons, changed for something lighter and less shrinkable. And he made a fine figure as he now stood there—bland, enormous, uncontradictable. He seemed, too, to be in an unnaturally good humour about something. Spread over his wide face was a smile like a sunset.

Mrs. Tuke, her eyes cast down to the hearth-rug, was sitting at his feet, wearing that expression of negative receptivity which Mr. Tuke liked to see when he was talking to her.

"And to think," Mr. Tuke was saying, passing his tongue over his lips as he said it, "that it was I who engineered it."

"I'm sure they ought to be very much obliged to you," Mrs. Tuke remarked.

"They're so exactly cut out for each other," Mr. Tuke went on. "Two such sensible people. Steady and unspoiled."

"She's a good bit older than he is, isn't she?" Mrs. Tuke put in suddenly.

Mr. Tuke paused: he looked at Mrs. Tuke in astonishment.

"A year or so, perhaps," he said. "I attach no importance to it. They're neither of them children."

"They fell in love like children," Mrs. Tuke observed.

There was a note of bitterness, of envy even, in her voice as she said it. She had not forgotten her own engagement to Mr. Tuke. It had lasted through three winters and four summers; during that time she had seen other girls fall in love, marry and produce children—while all she could look forward to was a chaste embrace on Sundays over the hard edge of a clerical collar. By the time she had married Mr. Tuke it had been almost like marrying a bachelor uncle. She had been pretty Miss Westrope then; and in the face of this five minute romance which had abruptly blossomed under their noses she was surprised to find how much of the original Miss Westrope still remained.

But her spouse was speaking again.

"We mustn't misjudge them," he declared. "She was lonely and he took pity on her. You must remember they met in very exceptional circumstances."

"The old man hasn't been buried a week," Mrs. Tuke said almost to herself.

"But they aren't thinking of getting married immediately," Mr. Tuke replied. "There'll be nothing unseemly. She told me so herself."

"I'm not so sure," said Mrs. Tuke rather sharply. "She didn't seem so patient to me. She looked as though she was simply asking for it."

Mr. Tuke let his coat tails drop.

"Really," he said. "Really."

He turned with dignity, rather like a large cart-horse being manoeuvred in a small space, and went out of the room. He had never ceased to marvel that anyone without meaning it could be quite so quietly maddening as Mrs. Tuke.

He remembered, however, that he had work to do: his visiting. In the course of a year he must, he had often reflected, have walked as many miles as a postman. And for the next hour and a half, he was the good shepherd working, unfortunately, without the assistance of any kind of dog to get the flock together. He knocked at doors, rang bells, climbed up to attics, descended into basements, and was shown into drawing-rooms, criss-crossing the whole of Paddington and half Bayswater on his mission. He sat —only for a minute or so of course—at three bedsides; he comforted a widow; he patted a family of young children on the head, some twice; he discussed with an anxious parent the incipient atheism of a backward boy of fifteen; and he visited a household where the mother of the family was lying coldly on a beautiful bed of lilies behind the drawn blinds of her own bedroom. In the course of it all he ranged the whole social scale from Westbourne Terrace to Chaffinch Row; and within each home he was a different human-being, tender, stern, paternal and philosophic by turn. Only one characteristic remained constant and unchanged: wherever he went he was still the messenger of grace abounding; the odour of sanctity surrounded him like an envelope. Even after he had gone, a little bit of it seemed to linger on in the corners like the aroma of a good cigar.

By the time four-thirty came round, he was an exhausted man. He had been disappointed in a chance visit to Southwick Crescent where one of the very best of his followers lived. Tea was served there from silver into egg-shell china, and the conversation was of the highest. But he was thwarted. The good lady was out, and he could do no more than leave a tract with the maid. He walked disconsolately back towards the Harrow Road, tired and thirsty, casting round in his mind for other duties that he ought to perform. Then he remembered the Kents, and doubling on his tracks, he went off in the direction of Abernethy Terrace.

The Kents were more than pleased to see him; they were gratified. He spent a few moments talking to Mr. Kent down in the shop amid the pendants and hair brooches and the innumerable watches, and then went upstairs where tea was on the table. Mrs. Kent had been busy while Mr. Tuke had been talking. She had cut bread and butter, laid a table and cleared away her mending. Mr. Tuke drew a chair up to the table and was well satisfied; this always seemed to him a singularly restful roof to come under. God was so very obviously in the house.

Mrs. Kent entertained him while Mary infused the tea. He sat back, not listening, watching Mary go first over to the tea-caddy and then outside to the scullery and finally come back into the room again carrying the big brown tea-pot, and reflected on what a beautiful child she had grown into; delicate, but beautiful. He was still thinking how charming—how "nymph-like" was the word for which he was actually searching—when he bowed his head and invoked a blessing.

During the meal the conversation turned to lighter topics.

"We have—another romance—inside the Chapel," he remarked pleasantly, blowing across the scalding surface of the tea as he did so. "Another nuptial."

"Indeed," said Mrs. Kent with reviving interest, "and who is the lady?"

(It was always the lady on these occasions who was enquired after first.)

120

"I am pleased to say it is our poor Miss Croome," he said suavely. "The young lady who was so recently bereaved, you know."

"That one," said Mrs. Kent turning down the corners of her mouth as she spoke. "And who's she marrying?"

"Such a splendid young man," Mr. Tuke replied. "A pillar. It's young Mr. Marco."

He reached out his hand and drew the glass dish of bramble jelly towards him. Of all preserves, it was bramble jelly to which he was most partial, and he spooned himself a large translucent blob of it like a quivering amethyst. Then, just as he was about to smear it over the rich, golden butter, he became aware that his two companions were staring at him. Quite motionless, they were sitting there staring. They had stopped eating, and from their appearance they might even have stopped breathing as well.

He turned from one to the other in some surprise and saw now that Mary was blushing. She looked charming, quite charming, he thought. But it was more than an ordinary girlish blush that he was regarding; her whole face was suffused. And as she sat there he saw that her eyes were filled with tears.

It was only because he was a man of the world as well as a minister of the gospel, that he knew how to meet this situation. His quick mind jumped to it and he smiled as he realised that he must, all unknown, have stumbled on some shy infatuation. He leant over and patted Mary Kent on the hand with his forefinger.

"Your turn will come, my dear," he said. "There's a lucky man waiting somewhere."

But his piece of tact was ignored; simply ignored. It was as though he had not even spoken. And he observed to his further surprise that Mrs. Kent was looking at him as though she hated him. He might just have insulted her daughter instead of having tried to pacify her.

"Did you say Mr. Marco?" Mrs. Kent asked.

"Why yes," Mr. Tuke replied. "Mr. *John* Marco. Our Sunday School teacher."

There was another extraordinary silence. The two women seemed ready to leap on him.

"I only heard a few hours ago," Mr. Tuke went on, searching desperately for anything to say that would break this awful silence. "It's all very delightful and unexpected."

"Very!" said Mrs. Kent shortly.

She went over and put her arm round Mary's shoulders. And Mary, quite suddenly after all the reserve that she displayed, broke down. She slumped forward, scattering the plates and tea-cups and buried her head in her arms. At the same moment she began to cry. She cried noisily and shamelessly, her shoulders shaking.

Mrs. Kent looked across at Mr. Tuke. There was no trace of civility left in her.

"You'd better go," she said. "I've got her on my hands."

Mr. Tuke found his own hat and coat and let himself out. He paused for a moment at the foot of the stairs. The sound of crying was still painfully plain. And there was another sound as well: it was Mrs. Kent hammering on the floor with her heel as a signal to Mr. Kent that she wanted him upstairs at once.

Mr. Tuke shut the door and walked hurriedly up the street before he was any deeper involved. In all his twenty years in the Ministry he had never known such another case. And his tea! In the excitement that had been entirely forgotten. They had simply overlooked it. It was too late now to expect Mrs. Tuke to give him anything: it would get in the way of supper. The strange behaviour of the Kents would mean that he would have to go hungry right on until eight o'clock. He was a big man and he felt it when he missed a meal.

ii

Tuesday, the second day of the Sale, had been one of the busiest that Mr. Morgan could ever remember. Despite the unpleasant affair of the police officers the day had been a success; and they hadn't been able to get up fresh supplies from the stockrooms quickly enough. It had made Mr. Morgan feel quite queer to see the crowds thronging into the Fancy Goods Department and no Mr. Jamieson there to attend them. And Mr. Marco with two departments on his hands was going about like a man in a daze. Mr. Morgan only hoped that he wasn't making mistakes.

If he had known the real state of John Marco's mind he would have been more anxious still. He did not see him cut savagely right across a length of good silk ribbon rather than rewind it, and then toss the remnant casually into the oddment tray. He did not see him replace one of the cases so violently that the cardboard end flew open. He did not see him hand customers the change as though the pennies were red hot. He did not see . . . but the other assistants saw. They knew that for some reason, obscurely connected with the visit of the smart young lady in black, Mr. Marco was a man to be avoided.

At nine-forty-five he took his coat down from the peg, jammed his hat on his head and went out saying goodnight to no one. The air in the street was cold and he stood there gulping at it. The hardest part of the day was still to come: he had got to see Mary and confess to her. Simply at the thought of Mary his mind

123

cleared for a moment. She was so pure herself that she could afford to take his evil onto her; and in that instant it seemed less dreadful that he should lose her than that she should misjudge him for ever.

He turned and walked rapidly in the direction of Abernethy Terrace, praying for strength as he walked.

"Oh God," he said, speaking the words half aloud to himself, "give me the power to be strong."

But as he drew nearer his courage failed him. Was he brave enough, he wondered, to thrust her away as she came towards him, to pull his lips back from her eager ones, and tell her that never, after what had happened, would she be in his arms again? He feared that once she was beside him again he would never be able to let her go—and then this never-ending corridor of horrors would re-open up before him. No! He must tell her when he saw her: the very second, before he had time to feel her touch. But to hurt her: that was the torment of it. He would have to stand in front of her, robbing her of everything that they had planned together, destroying in the moment of meeting a life that had not yet had time to live. He closed his mind to the thought, but told himself nevertheless, that he could not turn back. Had he loved her less, it would have been simple: he could have written her a letter, could have filled it with phrases that healed the wound as they opened it, could have avoided looking into her eyes while he told her. But their love had been too great for that. And he was not a coward, not that sort of coward at least. Because he loved her he would have to hurt her, to hurt them both; he would have to confess and humiliate himself and then go away again—alone.

When he reached the house he stood for a moment looking up at it. He saw that it was all in darkness and, for the first time it occurred to him that perhaps it was too late, perhaps time alone had defeated his resolve. It added a new terror to his purpose to have to wake her from her sleep to tell her this thing. He paused undecided. But, as he looked, he saw the corner of one of the blinds move slightly, though the window itself was fast closed. And he knew that someone inside was awake and watching him; knew that Mary herself by waiting for him had made it almost easy. He could tell her alone. His lips were quivering and his face was white and drawn as he crossed the road and raised the knocker.

The door was swung open before the knocker had descended, and the black cave of the hall appeared before him. But it was not Mary who stood there: it was Mr. Kent. He presented a distraught, desperate figure. His hair was dishevelled—it stood up all over his head in little white wisps like feathers—and in his hand he held a thin malacca cane that he sometimes carried on Sundays. In his shirt sleeves and wearing a pair of gaudy carpet slippers, he was like a man possessed. Before John Marco could speak, he had raised the walking stick and brought it down full across John Marco's face.

"You blackguard," he screamed in a voice like no voice that John Marco had ever heard before. "You seducer."

John Marco raised his hand to his mouth. It came away wet and sticky. Mr. Kent's blow had cut his lip and the blood was running down onto his chin. And as he stood there he saw that the little man was preparing to attack him again. He did not attempt to defend himself.

"Let me explain," he said. "I've come to explain everything."

The second blow fell across his shoulders: it was harmless. But Mr. Kent had lost all control of himself by now.

"Don't you dare to speak to me," he was shouting, still in the same terrible voice. "Don't come near this house again."

As he said it, he raised his stick above his head for the third time and made a fresh run at John Marco. But John Marco was ready for him. He caught the stick as it fell, and snatched it away. Then he broke it across his knee. It snapped like firewood. The silver band made a silly tinkle as he threw the broken stick into the gutter.

"You fool," he said. "You fool. Why wouldn't you listen?"

Mr. Kent stood for a moment looking at his stick, his beautiful stick, being broken in front of his eyes and then tried to throw himself on John Marco. It was a pathetic attempt. Mr. Kent was sixty and an invalid. When John Marco caught him by the arms he could do nothing: he struggled vainly like a pickpocket in the grip of a policeman. But he made one last helpless heroic effort; he spat in John Marco's face. And when John Marco thrust him angrily from him in disgust he simply collapsed against the railings and remained there supported by the ornamental scroll work of the balustrades.

John Marco turned and walked away. He felt sick and faint. He did not even pause when he heard a voice-it was Mrs. Kent's by this time—shout something after him. The words themselves were lost, but their meaning was clear enough; they came through the air like so many wasps. John Marco walked straight on in a kind of icy trance. He was trembling, trembling so violently that his foot-steps were jerky and unsure. A sweet, sickly taste filled his mouth and he found that he was still bleeding. Mr. Kent's malacca cane had cut his lip clean open.

He pushed open the squeaking gate and turned up the sedate tiled pathway of his house. It was quiet, very quiet there; it was somewhere where he could lie down and forget. He was still

126

trembling and had to steady his hand before he could insert the key; but, as the door swung open and he stepped into the hall, he felt suddenly at rest again. There was a single high-chair beside the hat-stand and he sat down upon it exhausted, utterly exhausted.

As he did so, the door of the sitting-room opened and a woman came out. But it was a younger woman than his mother, dark-eyed, and bathed in a deep, musky scent.

"You're hurt," she said. "You're bleeding."

She took out her handkerchief, a small lacy one, and, gently, lovingly, it seemed, applied it to the wound.

Chapter X

John Marco and Hesther Croome were married three months later in the Tabernacle.

But it was not like a real wedding at all; and the half-crown which Mr. Morgan gave to the verger seemed more in the nature of hush-money than a tip. Mr. Morgan in fact was the only guest. He turned up wearing a wide butterfly collar, and a large white buttonhole. His pink face behind the bright pebble spectacles glowed until he saw the rows of empty pews stretching all round him like the streets of a deserted city; then the geniality vanished and he consoled himself with memories of the happy day nearly half-a-century ago when half Merthyr had turned out to see him and Mrs. Morgan get married. He would have liked something of that same atmosphere of jostling and excitement here. A trace of paganism did not seem out of place at a wedding, and he relished a bride who blushed whenever anyone caught her eye. Miss Croome whom he had only met once before struck him as a singularly cold young woman.

Old Mrs. Marco's presence did nothing to enliven the occasion. Her rheumatism had knotted her up fearfully and she had to be carried into the Tabernacle. They dumped her down in the front pew and left her there, an isolated figure in a complicated assortment of black.

She had ransacked her cupboards for finery; and, when the lights above her head were put on, the jet on the garments glittered, like a scuttleful of coals. She cared nothing for her appearance, however. She was still too much dazed and bewildered by everything that had happened: her son, her dutiful son, had suddenly been snatched away from her and she was expected to be radiant about it. Less than two months before she had never even seen this adventuress and now she was going back to share her home with her. She felt in no mood for celebration: she was simply a poor widow woman who had been robbed. Burying her face in her gloved hands she wept.

Three rows behind her, sat the woman who had been Mr. Trackett's maid. She was still in mourning but she was decked out in tribute to her new mistress. She had run a white piping round her black dress and had stuck a band of blue flowers into the side of her dark velvet hat. Apart from them, the Chapel was entirely uninhabited; and those three figures seated there had about them the air of survivors of a lost world—they seemed so small and desolate amid those polished expanses of cheap polished pine.

There was, of course, no one to give the bride away and no best man; Amosites do not hold with such primitive survivals. Instead the bride and bridegroom-to-be, assemble privately in the vestry with their minister, and there is an interval for silent prayer until, under guidance from above, the spirit moves the two parties. (For it to move only one of them is not enough.) The minister takes no action at all in the matter; he is, after all, merely Jehovah's witness. And Mr. Tuke had known this period of silent prayer, especially when it was mature serious people whom he was marrying, last for as long as twenty minutes. But in the ordinary way he gave the young couple about five minutes by the clock and then coughed. The cough nearly always worked; and the spirit, realising that it was holding up the proceedings, came promptly through.

To-day Mr. Tuke glanced at the two of them and closed his eyes. He was displeased. Miss Croome was not suitably dressed. She had almost discarded her mourning and was wearing a dark tailor-made costume trimmed with fur, and a smart toque with a blue feather. The effect on his mind was almost that of wantonness; a veil and orange blossom would have been easier to condone. Perhaps Mrs. Tuke had been right; perhaps Miss Croome *was* sinful in her desires. But it seemed surprising: he had never known Mrs. Tuke to be right about anything before.

John Marco was on his knees, his eyes closed. But it was as though by closing his eyes he had opened a window in his mind, and the images that he had wanted to exclude came flooding in. He saw Mary again, saw her in a hundred different ways—clad all in white descending into the Jordan Tank on the evening of her baptism; smiling up at him in the dim light of the staircase as she had kissed him; stroking his hair on that evening when he had told her that she must never leave him.

She was far away at this moment; Mrs. Kent had given it out that she had suffered some kind of breakdown and had sent her away into the country to recover. He did not even know where she was, and the letters that he had written to her had remained unanswered. He doubted, indeed, whether they had ever reached her; and he had posted the last one, the final desperate attempt to explain, with the pre-knowledge that it would probably be the fiery eyes of her parents who perused it.

Mr. Tuke coughed and John Marco started. He was ready, he

supposed; as ready as he ever would be. He sat back and caught Mr. Tuke's eye. But there was still no sign of movement from Hesther Croome: she was praying. Mr. Tuke looked hard at her. If there was one thing he was really expert in it was prayer: he knew the difference between mere muttering and the real stuff. And this was real: Hesther Croome was praying in deadly earnest. She was cut off from everything around her and was engaged in some struggle of her own. The knuckles of her clapsed hands showed white and sharp. She was praying half aloud.

"God grant that it may come right," she was saying. "God grant that he may grow to love me and that I may be a good wife. God grant that this isn't a sin that I'm committing, I need him so." Mr. Tuke coughed again, but the praying went on. "Forgive me my evil desires. Let my life show the face of innocence and humility. Let the evil I have done be washed away and let me bear his sin on my shoulders. Be with me, Christ Jesus, now and forever more."

She sat back and took John Marco by the hand. In front of Mr. Tuke she kissed it.

"Come, John," she said.

Mr. Tuke opened his Bible at the page where the purple velvet marker hung downwards and led the way.

He had caught only some of the words which Miss Croome had uttered; but he had caught quite enough.

ii

They all went back to what had been Mr. Trackett's stucco mansion in Clarence Gardens.

John Marco handed Hesther into the bridal carriage—the verger encouraged by Mr. Morgan's generosity had put a bunch of white flowers into it—and had climbed in after her in silence. Now that it was over he was calm, quite calm, again: the future held no new terror because there was nothing at all that was worth living in it. They reached the end of Chapel Villas without speaking. Then Hesther drew off her glove and thrust her hand into John Marco's; but it lay there without his fingers closing over it and after a few moments she withdrew it and put on her glove again. They still had not spoken.

The party on the steps of the Tabernacle watched the cab recede into the distance, and Mr. Tuke announced that he would look after old Mrs. Marco. She was still sitting there in her pew, weeping, and the sight of her vaguely annoyed him. She was another proof of the fact that Mrs. Tuke's reading of the whole situation had been the right one. He comforted himself, however, with the thought that most mothers weep at weddings; and putting his arm under hers, he started to lift her to her feet. As he did so, he was reminded irresistibly of an occasion years ago when he had assisted in carrying a drunk out of what the landlord had called a respectable licensed house and what Mr. Tuke had called a common gin-palace. The verger, too, had put out the lights and the large chapel was in semi-darkness; a pale, greenish glow was all that filtered in through the tinted windows. As Mr. Tuke stood wrestling with Mrs. Marco he felt suddenly like a diver struggling with something heavy at the bottom of an aquarium.

He got her finally into the last of the carriages, but even inside the carriage old Mrs. Marco went on crying; huddled up in the corner she put a handkerchief across her face and moaned into it. Nor was it better after they had called and picked up Mrs. Tuke. The women, moreover, immediately sided together; they formed a feminine alliance against him. He was forced to give his seat up to his wife and was now sitting on the hard, inadequate tip-up seat opposite. It was not made for a man of his weight and figure. Every time the driver whipped up his horse Mr. Tuke suffered.

But Mrs. Tuke seemed oblivious of her husband's discomfort. She had her arm round old Mrs. Marco's shoulders and was consoling her.

"You poor dear," she was saying. "I know how you feel. There's one of us who understands."

The house was empty when John and Hesther got back to it, quite empty. It loomed up like an iceberg, the front broken only by the dark, blind-looking windows. And inside it was silent—an ominous absorbing silence; it was as though the spirit of the departed Mr. Trackett had just recently passed through subduing things. Coming in from the populated streets of Bayswater, it was like entering a pocket in creation.

They closed the door behind them and stood there, man and wife, in what was to be their future home.

"Kiss me," Hesther said. "Kiss me and say now that you forgive me."

But he turned away from her still without answering and, as she threw her arms round him and he felt her body draw close to his, he drew back. There was something in the eagerness, the urgency of it, however, that made him pity her. She was asking for something that he could not give, would never be able to give. She had told him frequently in those last few days before the wedding that she knew he would grow to love her; she was recklessly building her whole life upon that pale hope. And instead of drawing back and saving herself, she had gone blindly on. She had bared herself for all the pain the years could inflict on her.

That she loved him already, had loved him from the moment she saw him in that awful bedroom—he had grown to accept. Every time they had met she had tried vainly and pathetically to disguise from both of them that this was not like other betrothals: she had talked cheerfully, like a child, of the things they would do together when they were married. Throughout it all ran the same hopeless thread of illusion that they were lovers. Sitting back in her chair, her dark eyes fixed on him, she had resolutely imagined for the two of them.

Disengaging his arms, he drew off his gloves and began to undo the buttons of his overcoat.

But she did not remain standing silently before him for long. She was still desperately seeking to make the illusion a reality; her mind was fixed on an image of life that did not yet exist.

Opening the door of the dining-room, she beckoned to John Marco to come forward.

"I've got it all ready," she said. "It's our wedding-breakfast."

The room had been arranged for a party, a party three times the size of the one that was coming. As he saw the row of chairs against the wall, John Marco recognised that she had calculated and been wrong. Up to the last moment, up to the very instant when they had left the vestry, she must have thought that some of his friends would be there to see them married. She had never guessed that any wedding could be quite so empty.

On the long table under its white damask there was food for a company. John Marco looked at the dishes and cakes and dainties and his feeling of pity for her returned; she had prepared all these herself so that the outward appearance of festivity should be there; she had tried hard to make this a happy wedding. And the cake was magnificent. It rose in three sugary tiers to an icing

134

temple on the top. There were bells and horseshoes and lucky shamrocks all cut out of silver paper decked round the sides of it.

"Do you like it?" she asked.

But John Marco's answer was cut short. Mr. Morgan had arrived. He came sidling into the room a little astonished by the size of the place. It was a gentleman's house this, a pretty substantial property. It wasn't like an assistant's house at all, and he envied John Marco his good fortune. But he gave him his due. Marrying for money could be just as hard work as earning it in any other way; and glancing across at Hesther as she stood at the top of the table he reflected that he had seen younger and fuller-blooded brides. But he did what was expected of him. Going up to her, he kissed her ceremonially on both cheeks.

"An old man's privilege," he said.

Then he came over and patted John Marco on the back.

"Have to go straight home in the evenings now," he said. "Have your wife after you if you don't."

He continued in the same vein until the others arrived. He was a different Mr. Morgan from the Old Gentleman in the shop; there was something vaguely and rather innocently salacious about him. Between some of his remarks he even winked. Evidently in a life that had long been devoid of it, the thought of sex had revived old, boisterous memories. For those few private minutes while he was alone with the young couple this white-haired Amosite Elder became a kind of plaintive Pan in a frock-coat; over his bright spectacles he leered. Then Mr. Tuke arrived too, and all was respectable again.

It had been Mr. Tuke's intention not to stay very long. But at the sight of so much good food his intention wavered. He began passing things; and in between passing them, he ate. For every dainty that Mrs. Tuke got, he had two. And when tea was brought in he became quite reconciled to staying. The quantity of tea that he could drink—the quantity of tea, indeed, that he seemed to *need* to drink—was quite surprising. He drank three cups straight off, passing up his cup each time as though it were someone else's.

Mrs. Tuke was still engaged in comforting old Mrs. Marco. She was trying to get her to eat something and kept patting the back of her hand as though she were just emerging from a faint.

"You'll like it here when you get used to it," she was saying. "It's very nice of your daughter-in-law to want to have you to live with her."

"I was happy where I was," Mrs. Marco protested. "I'd lived there ever since Mr. Marco died."

"But think how lonely you'd have been," Mrs. Tuke reminded her. "Think of what it would have been like without your son."

Mrs. Marco pondered over the point for a moment, without replying. She was sitting huddled up in her chair with her shoulders hunched up like a monkey's. It was obvious that in spirit she was not of the party at all. And when Mrs. Tuke passed her anything she waved it away as if it had been poisoned.

"I'd rather have seen him dead," she said suddenly, "than married to her."

Mrs. Tuke patted her aged hand more vigorously. "You're over-tired," she said.

"I may be over-tired," Mrs. Marco answered. "But that doesn't alter that she stole him. He was all I had."

"You'll feel better in the morning," Mrs. Tuke told her. "See what a good night's rest does for you."

"Good night's rest," Mrs. Marco spat the words out. "I shan't sleep a wink under the same roof with her."

She shifted herself round in her chair until she was facing

Hesther as she said it.

Mr. Tuke detected at once that something was amiss and he recognised this as one of the occasions when tact, exemplary tact, would be needed to gloss it over. So, turning towards Hesther, he allowed his voice to swell until Mrs. Marco's remarks were drowned and inaudible.

"And has to-day been everything you could have wished?" he asked.

"Everything," Hesther replied briefly.

"If only your dear uncle could have been here," Mr. Tuke went on. "Such a loss. Such a sad loss."

"If my uncle hadn't died we might never have got to know each other," Hesther answered.

She looked sideways at John Marco as she spoke; but though he was standing by her he gave no sign of having heard.

"Perhaps not," Mr. Tuke agreed. "Who shall say? How little we any of us know what is in store for us."

While he was speaking his eye had been roving up and down the snowy terraces of the cake; it was still whole and unbroken as it had been when it was delivered from the shop.

"Isn't it time for the bride to cut the cake?" he suggested. "Isn't it time she plied the knife?"

As Hesther moved up to the middle of the table, Mr. Tuke followed her. He waited until she had the large silver-handled knife in her hand and then reached down and taking John Marco firmly by the wrist placed his hand over hers.

"Like that," he said. "Together."

He stepped back, smiling, and caught Mr. Morgan's eye.

"So much to learn," he said. "So far to go."

John Marco's hand, however, dropped to his side again.

Mr. Tuke could not help remarking the gesture: it was almost as though the young man were *reluctant* to have his hand on hers, as though he did not *want* to touch her. And what was more extraordinary was that the bride herself did not seem to expect it. To cover up the incident, Mr. Tuke took hold of the knife himself.

"With your permission," he said. "Allow me . . ."

It was at that moment that Mrs. Marco suddenly reasserted herself. She had been watching everything going on around her with a kind of hostile intentness. And she leant forward intently, her old finger pointing.

"That's my tea-kettle," she said.

"But you're forgetting," Mrs. Tuke reminded her. "All your things have been brought round here. This is where you're going to live."

"I'm not going to have that woman using my tea-kettle," Mrs. Marco asserted loudly.

John Marco left Mr. Morgan to whom he had been talking and came over to her.

"You'd better go to bed," he said. "You've done too much."

Mrs. Marco stared at him for a moment before she answered.

"You want to get rid of me," she said. "You want to be alone with her."

"Go to bed," he repeated; and leaning over her he began to lift her from her chair.

"Don't you dare to lay hands on me," she said. "I can walk."

It might, even then, still have been all right if Mrs. Tuke had not again intervened.

"This isn't a very good start," she said reprovingly. "This isn't being kind."

"Was it kind of her to break my home up for me?" Mrs. Marco demanded. "Did I ask her to do that?"

But John Marco did not wait any longer. He gathered old

Mrs. Marco up in his arms and, holding her almost like a baby, was proceeding to carry her out of the room.

"Put me down," she screamed. "Put me down."

At the door he paused and turned to Hesther; it was the first time that they had heard him speak to her.

"Which room have you given her?" he asked.

Hesther's eyes met his: her dark ones were steady and unwavering.

"My uncle's room," she said. "I'll come up with you."

By the time they had got downstairs again, the company was just leaving. They had been sitting there in silence, ever since the others had left them. Even Mr. Tuke's usually boundless tact suddenly failed him; he just stood there gloomily eating. And when John Marco entered, Mr. Tuke made no pretext of wanting to remain. He went straight up to Hesther and shook her earnestly by the hand.

"We leave you," he said simply, "in one another's arms."

Then the others said good-bye as well, and Mr. Morgan went back to the shop. He was at heart a little vexed; vexed and disappointed. All the week he had hoped that this was going to be a jolly occasion: he had looked forward to enjoying himself. And he hadn't enjoyed himself a bit. And what was more he knew the reason for it: the two young people had tempted Fate and got married before the shadow of death was properly off the house. He was at heart considerably shocked that his star-assistant should have been so impetuous.

On the way back Mrs. Tuke, too, was silent and preoccupied; she did not even always answer when Mr. Tuke addressed her, and she abruptly interrupted his remarks with an observation of her own.

139

"I don't like it," she said. "There'll be a tragedy in that house as sure as I'm alive. He didn't even know where his own mother was sleeping. And you can see that he isn't in love."

"Indeed," said Mr. Tuke. "Then if he isn't in love why did he have to apply for a special licence?"

"I can think of one good reason," said Mrs. Tuke grimly.

Inside the house Hesther and John Marco were alone together. They were not talking. They simply stood there, eyeing each other across the loaded table on which stood the enormous wedding-cake, still uncut.

iii

It was ten o'clock the same evening.

There was to be no honeymoon—John Marco had insisted that he should be back at his counter by nine o'clock on the Monday morning—and they were seated at either side of the veined marble fire-place in their front drawing-room. Hesther was embroidering the collar of a dress. There were long pauses between the stitches; and sometimes for minutes on end she sat gazing into the fire. John Marco was staring into the same fire. But he was seeing different things.

Then Hesther broke the silence.

"You did better than you realised when you married me," she said.

John Marco turned to her.

"What do you mean?" he asked.

"You're not a poor man any longer," she said.

His mind kindled as he heard her. From nowhere Mr. Tuke's voice intoning the twenty-third psalm came back to him. "The

140

Lord is my Shepherd: I shall not want. . . ." But somehow the words frightened him. It was punishment that he had been expecting; and this was reward. "I shall not want," he repeated to himself; "I shall not want." And then as he said them the image of Mary rose up before him, pale and slender, and he began to understand.

But Hesther was addressing him again.

"He left me all his money," she was saying. "Except what the Chapel got."

Her eyes were on him as she spoke: she was watching him.

"What are you going to do with it?" he asked.

"It can be yours if you want it to be," she said.

He made no movement and she held out her hand to him.

"Come over to me," she said. "Bring your chair beside mine."

He shook his head.

"No," he said. "Go on talking to me as you are."

She drew in her lips at the answer; but she resumed.

"Aren't you interested in knowing how much it is?" she asked.

He was looking hard at her, his eyes fixed on hers.

"Tell me," he said.

"It's twelve thousand pounds," she answered. "Twelve thousand pounds and this house."

John Marco got up and began to walk about the room.

Twelve thousand pounds! So the Chapel had been right in what they had whispered about Mr. Trackett: he had died a rich man. And his fortune was the kind of fortune out of which larger fortunes could be made. With that amount behind him, John Marco could go forward to anything. He could ride the world.

"It's a lot of money," he said slowly. "You must be careful of it."

He was passing her chair as he said it and she caught him by the hand. She clung to him.

"I told you," she said. "It can be yours if you want it to be. I shall trust you with it."

"You trust me?" he replied.

"Yes," she said. "I trust you with everything now. You're my husband aren't you?"

Her other hand was on his fore-arm by now, she was trying to pull him down to her.

"Kiss me," she was saying. "Take me in your arms and kiss me."

But he forced her hand away from him and stepped back.

"Don't you see that it can't be like that?" he said.

"But you've got to love me," she said. "You've got to."

She slid out of her chair as she said it and went down on her knees with her two arms round him so that he could not free himself.

"You can't think that I married you so that you could go on hating me," she said. "I want to be loved. I want *you* to love me."

Then, because he did not answer, because she realised at last that he intended never to give her the answer that she wanted, she went on in a lower voice almost as though speaking to herself this time.

"I want a child," she said almost under her breath. "I want your child."

Her arms were still round him and he was looking down on her. Her dark head was pressed against him; it seemed that in some hopeless fashion she was seeking refuge from what she had done.

John Marco paused.

"There can't be children," he said. "Not in a marriage like this."

"You mean never?" she asked.

"Never!" he repeated.

Her arms dropped to her side and she released him. He went over and stood by the mantelpiece with his back towards her. But Hesther did not move. She remained half-sitting, half-kneeling on the mat in front of the fire.

"If you give me a child," she said, "you can have all the money." She paused. "That's what I had always wanted to do with it—give it to my husband."

She rose to her feet as she said it and began going round the room in the manner of a woman preparing for the night. She went over to the windows to see that they were latched and then crossed over to the door.

"I shall leave you now," she said, still in the same quiet voice. "You can come up when you're ready."

The room seemed very quiet after she had left him. The whole house was quiet; it hadn't warmed yet to the new life being lived within it. Instead, it was trying to absorb him into it, to enfold him in the kind of existence that it had always known; he could feel the four walls closing in on him. But the mood passed, and he saw the room in its old light again. It was a prosperous, solidly-comfortable sort of room. The rich ox-blood red of the paper set off the dark glow of mahogany. And over on the side table was a fine gleam of silver. It was all his. Already he had got so much. But how much more was he prepared to take?

The thought set him trembling. His heart began to hammer. He paused uncertain for a moment. Then turning out all the lights he began to mount the stairs.

Outside her door, he paused again. Then he passed his hand across his forehead and went in to her.

143

She was seated in front of the mirror brushing out her hair. It fell about her shoulders in dark heavy waves. The pink wrap she had on was new. He could tell that it had been bought specially to please him; there was a luxury, a wantonness, about it. It was gathered in under the bosom with a thick silk cord and spread out over the hips in long shining folds. He had never seen a woman in such clothes before. And the room was full of scent; his nostrils were filled with it as he stood there. Her hair, too, was fuller than he would have imagined. By day she wore it screwed up to nothing in a hard unshapely roll; he had hardly noticed it. But now it covered her. And in the light of the two candles in front of the mirror it glistened. He stood where he was, looking at her. In that gown and with her hair all about her she was almost beautiful.

When she heard the door close she got up and came over to him. She put her arms round him again.

"Hold me," she said.

She could feel his breath on her face, as his arms came round her. This was the happiness for which she had been waiting. She wished for his sake that she had been younger, fairer. He seemed so firm and powerful himself. The child that would be born to them would be strong and upright like its father.

She let her whole body go limp so that he had to support her. She closed her eyes.

"Say that you love me," she said. "Say that you love me. Tell me that you don't regret Mary now. I'll give you . . ."

But at the sound of Mary's name his mind cleared. He no longer smelt the scent in the room and felt the softness of her hair brushing across his hand. He pushed her away from him.

"You fool," he said. "Why do you have to remind me of her?"

He stood for a moment longer, then turning his back on her

144

he crossed the room and swung the door to behind him. As he went down the stairs he saw only a face with grey, wide eyes and a coil of gold above a white neck, in the darkness ahead of him.

The sound of crying, bitter humiliated crying, came through the darkness after him.

He was asleep in the big armchair before the burnt-out embers of the grate in the drawing-room when Emmy found him next morning. He was sleeping so soundly that she had pulled back the velvet curtains on their runners before he stirred. Then he roused himself suddenly as though not knowing where he was and stood staring into the yellow March dawn of Bayswater.

Emmy did not move. She just stood there, nodding her head knowingly as she looked at him.

Book II

John Marco, Elder

Chapter XI

The election of the Synod was a triennial affair; it had occurred in the year when John Marco had got married and now it had come round again. Six new pillars of the Chapel had to be elected—or the old ones chosen anew: there was no limitation to the length of service. Only this year there had to be at least one fresh one: Mr. Chilp, who had been an Elder for upwards of eleven years—he had been sixty-three when he was first called upon—had gone the way of Mr. Trackett and had been trundled off to Kensal Rise in a handsome oak coffin lined with crinkly satin.

They met in the vestry for the task of election. It was a high bare room, painted in moderate pea-soup tones and with a large coloured photograph of the Rev. Mr. Sturger hanging over the chairman's table. There was something in the photograph that gripped the beholder. Perhaps it was the eyes, small and deep-set, like twin jewels. They had been famous eyes in their time. But they were undeniably uneven. The left one pierced straight to the heart of the onlooker while the right gazed mildly past his ear into space. In some miraculous fashion they contrived in that divided look to combine knowledge of the world with meditation. And the eyebrows were bafflingly individual, too. The one over the intense eye was high and arched like a comedian's; the other was beetling and set in a perpetual frown: it threatened. It was, of course, impossible to say what expression the mouth was wearing: it was obscured somewhere in the dense jungle of his beard. And now all that was left of him, of his thunderings and his comminations, his gentleness with little children and his tears over repentant sinners, his fearlessness in the pulpit and his adroit handling of finance, was this enigmatic Mona Lisa-like portrait which hung in the Chapel of the Sect that he had founded.

John Marco took his seat under the portrait and waited for the room to fill up. He looked a trifle older, perhaps; his face was leaner and the hard lines on either side of his mouth had grown deeper and more sharply cut. But this served only to accentuate the look of strength, of authority even, that he possessed. He was better dressed than he had been. Very obviously, he was the one tailored man in the whole vestry. But it was not his clothes that distinguished him in that baggy, unfashionable company of Paddington tradesmen. It was the way he sat. With arms crossed and his chin tilted upwards over the hard points of his collar he seemed to command the rows of chairs in front of him.

Beside him sat Hesther. She was dressed expensively in black and heavily veiled. She sat with bent shoulders and her hands folded in her lap.

There were usually fifty or sixty present at these elections; the real, solid bed-rock of Amosism was there. By the time seven-thirty came round, it would have been impossible anywhere in London to find more four-square fundamentalists gathered together in less space.

And punctually to the minute, Mr. Tuke came in, put down

his gloves and his tall hat and declared the meeting open. The five existing Elders sidled into the room after him. Their average age was sixty-eight; they were dignified respectable persons, not exactly exciting perhaps, and with a faint air of the moth-bag about them; but staid, incorruptible, reliable.

The vestry was almost full by now; those who arrived late would have to stand. Mr. Tuke liked to see it like that, liked to see visible and manifest proof of the democracy of the Order. It was a Brotherhood, a sodality, meeting to choose its own spokesmen, and their first duty after election would be to confirm Mr. Tuke's own appointment. He was in no doubt as to the outcome, of course; but there was something so reassuringly simple, so Galilean, about it all—so different from the Church of England in which an agnostic Prime Minister could choose the Bishops and rich, ungodly men gave away the livings.

Mr. Tuke's address was manly and to the point. He reminded them that this was a solemn and important occasion and urged any who were unserious or frivolous at heart to leave now before the proceedings commenced. As no one left, Mr. Tuke accepted his audience at their face value and went on to outline the character of the ideal Elder. He must be experienced in life's lessons, he said; inflexible in the face of opposition but humble in his own soul. He must be a lion and he must be a lamb. Mr. Tuke glanced round last season's Synod as he said it and prayed hard that the Lord might release him from this gaggle of grandfathers. And before he closed he made a brilliant rhetorical appeal for youth.

"We cannot," he said, his voice rising like a singer's, "ever be blessed with too much young blood. We need a great bowl of it into which we can dip." He paused in one of those sudden silences that are as eloquent as words. "How beautiful," he went on, "are the lines of the hymnist: 'There is a fountain filled with

151

blood drawn from Emmanuel's veins'. It is a gushing youthful fountain shooting up to the ceiling and lapping over the edges in its fulness." The image had become too sanguinary, however, and he discarded it. He allowed his voice to drop to a lower register, almost a conversational one, and said pleadingly: "After all, our Lord wasn't an elderly man, remember. He had no grey hairs, no aching bones. He was young, he was vigorous, he was athletic. We need all kinds of soldiers in our fight against the Devil—strong arms as well as white heads. So let us see if there isn't anyone young amongst us—young but nevertheless married and with the experience which springs from marriage—who has shown by his bearing, and by his record of attendance both in Chapel and in that blessed nursery, our Sunday School, who could be raised to sit in the conclaves of the Synod."

With that Mr. Tuke sat himself down. Without actually mentioning John Marco's name, he could scarcely have been more explicit. The incongruous impetuosity of the wedding arrangements had now been forgotten, obliterated by three years of exemplary, unexceptional conduct; whenever the young man was not working he seemed to be worshipping. He now taught for two full periods every Sunday, and as often as not he attended the evening service as well as the morning. Moreover, with his address in Clarence Gardens he was a man of some position and standing in the neighbourhood. And Hesther Croome had proved herself a model as Mrs. John Marco; she would be so suitable as an Elder's wife. As yet unfruitful, they were nevertheless of the obvious stuff of parents.

After waiting long enough for the last of the late-comers to arrange themselves, Mr. Tuke pushed back his chair and slid forward onto his knees onto the hassock that the verger had left for him.

152

"Let us open the proceedings with a silent prayer," he said. "Let us ask God's guidance in our selection."

The sixty men and women in front of him all got down onto the hard floor of the vestry—there were no hassocks for them—and an intense, charged stillness filled the room; it was as though a dynamo were running. Mr. Tuke kept them there on their knees for two minutes by his watch and then, getting up onto his feet, addressed them in a bright, refreshed kind of way.

"We're ready for nominations, now," he said. "Suggestions, please."

The name of Mr. Hartshorn was put forward first. Mr. Tuke looked towards him with disappreciation. He was seventy if he was a day, and wore a false, celluloid-looking dicky. But it was all right; he was not supported. Only a thin flutter of hands was raised on his behalf. Then Mr. Tottel and Mr. Cheeble, both well into their sixties, were proposed—and rejected. No candidate, it seemed, met with anything like general approval. In the fifth row, John Marco was sitting with his arms still crossed. His mouth was tightly closed and he seemed aloof from the whole proceedings. He had apparently no nomination to make, and had taken no part in the voting so far.

Mr. Tuke could stand it no longer: he expanded his chest like a swimmer.

"Come, come," he said. "Are there no young men in this parish whom we can trust? Will no one propose a brother who is in his prime?"

"I propose Brother Marco."

It was Mr. Morgan who spoke. An Elder himself, until his health had forced him to relinquish his position, his voice was listened to. And he liked the idea of having his best assistant in the Synod: in a sense it was more distinguished to employ an

Elder than merely to be one.

"Bravo," said Mr. Tuke loudly. "Those in favour."

There was a general stir in the vestry this time as the hands came up. Soon the air was filled with them. So far as Mr. Tuke could see John Marco's and Hesther's were the only ones not raised. He smiled; this was not the first time he had swayed a congregation. But he proceeded to do his duty according to Mr. Sturger's Book of Rules.

"Is anyone opposed to our Brother's election?" he asked. "Does anyone wish to raise his voice against?"

"I do."

The words uttered in a shrill, strained voice came from the back of the vestry. For a moment, Mr. Tuke could not believe them. In all his experience of these elections he had never before encountered such a thing. He felt personally insulted. And the effect of the interjection was deplorable. Every head in the room was twisted round in an effort to see who it was who had spoken, and some people were actually kneeling on their chairs to see. As for the interrupter himself, he was invisible, obscured somewhere behind all those rows of Brethren. Out of the whole company, indeed, only two people preserved their dignity—Hesther and John Marco. They had not moved. With faces rigidly fixed in front of them, they sat there as though nothing had happened. But John Marco had gone pale.

Mr. Tuke looked at the curious inquisitive ones, and clapped his hands together loudly, like an irritated schoolmaster.

"Please, please," he said. "Remember you are in God's house."

He came forward to the front of the table and held up his hand baton-wise.

"Will you all kindly sit down?" he said.

There was a scraping of chairs and the congregation, rather shame-facedly, one by one re-seated themselves. Mr. Tuke towered above them.

"And now will the Brother who spoke be so good as to stand up," he asked.

There was a moment's pause and someone by the door got to his feet: it was Mr. Alexander Kent.

Mr. Tuke stared at him in amazement.

"Do I understand," he asked, "that *you* oppose Brother Marco's election?"

"I do."

Mr. Kent's eyes behind his small, steel-rimmed spectacles had fixed on Mr. Tuke as he spoke. He was quivering with emotion, and the corners of his mouth were twitching. As he stood there he kept twisting his bowler hat in his hands as though he were trying to break it.

"May we be told the reason?"

"Because I don't regard him as a fit person to hold office."

The words were jerked out. They came in a vicious rush, and Mr. Tuke was astonished at the amount of bitterness behind them. Someone beside Mr. Kent—a woman, Mr. Tuke noticed, pulled at his sleeve to make him sit down, but he shook the hand angrily away, and remained there defiantly facing Mr. Tuke. He looked like a fierce, cornered little animal.

His reply, of course, had caused a second sensation. The Brethren began to turn round again, but Mr. Tuke checked them.

"Perhaps Brother Kent would like to come out to the front," he said, "where everyone could see him."

"I'm all right where I am," Mr. Kent answered back. "I've said all I have to say."

With that he sat down again. At once, everyone, who until that moment had been trying to see him turned towards Hesther and John Marco instead; they wanted to see how *they* were taking it. This and the time when the woman had broken into the Immersionist Service, looked like being the two most sensational nights in the history of the Tabernacle: and the remarkable thing was that John Marco had been the central figure of both.

Mr. Tuke returned to his table. He recognised this as a moment for supreme control and authority. His manner became Mosaic as he sat there.

"You have all heard what our Brother has said," he declared. "I will ask our Brother once again if he will explain himself."

Mr. Kent anticipated him, however. He was on his feet before Mr. Tuke had time to finish speaking. And when he was standing he looked such a little man, such a shoddy, insignificant little man. But he was showing his teeth.

"Mr. Marco knows," he said, his voice trembling. "He knows what I'm talking about."

With that he sat down again; he was so small that he simply disappeared into the back row. Mr. Tuke found himself staring into space.

There was a strained nervous silence. Then Mr. Tuke spoke.

"Does Brother Marco wish to say anything?" he asked.

But John Marco made no attempt to speak. He did not seem to have heard, and he did not even uncross his arms. When Hesther bent over and whispered something in his ear he took no notice.

"Then we will put the matter to the vote," Mr. Tuke said in a dangerously sweet voice. "You must all do as your conscience dictates. Only remember, God is watching. He is here with us in this room. Those in favour?"

156

The hands were a little slower in coming up this time; they hesitated. There was always the possibility that they might be voting for a wife-beater or atheist. But soon there were thirty-five raised hands. Mr. Tuke counted them gloatingly.

"Those against," he said.

Only Mr. Kent's hand went up. It rose—bony and withered inside its stiff shirt cuff—a solitary symbol of dissension. The rest of the Brethren who had not voted all sat there with their eyes lowered.

"Then the Ayes have it," said Mr. Tuke. "Brother Marco, you have been elected to the Synod."

The words seemed to come to John Marco from a long way off. He started. Then he rose and went slowly towards the empty chair beside Mr. Tuke's.

As for Mr. Kent, he took John Marco's election as the signal to leave the building. He squeezed his way out of his seat and began to make off through the doorway at the back. John Marco watched him go, contemptuously. He stood there in front of them a half-smile on his face, looking at the narrow back of his defeated enemy.

It was then that he noticed that Mr. Kent had not gone out unaccompanied. There was a young man beside him, a stranger, in a bright, new-looking mackintosh, who went out beside him. John Marco wondered who he was: he had not seen him before. And there was a girl with him: she had her hand on his arm. It was when she got to the door and turned round that he saw that it was Mary. For a moment she stood there, her face towards him. Then the young man in the new mackintosh said some-thing to her and she turned away again.

Mr. Tuke was speaking again. But the words did not reach John Marco. At that one glimpse, the whole strategy of his life,

157

the plans for his immense future, his riches, the lesser people that he would some day govern, the magnitude of his eventual operations—were all destroyed. He had seen Mary again; and the world was worthless. He sat there, oblivious to everything around him, staring blankly at the door through which she had just passed.

Hesther was watching him intently. He looked very pale. She wondered if Mr. Kent's interruption had upset him more than he had shown.

Chapter XII

The pain under the side pocket of Mr. Morgan's waistcoat had grown worse. It had started as no more than an occasional twinge, a tiny pin-point of sensation. But the pin-point had enlarged; it had developed. It had grown into something about the size of a threepenny piece that seemed to be red-hot for half the time. And when it was not burning, it ached. Mr. Morgan had deliberately ignored it at first, had told himself that most men of his age get little pains that they cannot account for. But when it began to wake him up at night, this piece of fiery anger inside him, he knew that he must see a doctor. The doctor had been consoling: he had prescribed bismuth. Mr. Morgan had taken the stuff: his mouth had seemed never free from the taste of it. But the pain had gone on just the same: it had been going on for two or three years now. Mr. Morgan had forgotten exactly how long, it had grown to be so much a part of him. And now it was no longer in that spot alone: he could close his eyes and feel it stabbing at him from half-a-dozen points at once.

After the doctor and his bismuth had admitted themselves to be defeated, Mr. Morgan had tried other remedies, desperate ones advertised in the back pages of magazines. He had eaten strange herbs. He had drunk magic potions. He had worn an electric locket. But still the pain had advanced. And when it had become so bad that his whole body seemed to be contributing to it, he had called in his own family doctor again. The doctor was startled this time; startled and resentful. He had invited another opinion and sent Mr. Morgan off in a hansom cab to Harley Street to get it. And the verdict (it had been more than an opinion) had been that Mr. Morgan—white-haired benevolent Mr. Morgan—the employer of twenty-three assistants, was in the grip of something too powerful to be resisted. The specialist said that it was . . . but he wrote the word in a private and confidential letter to Mr. Morgan's doctor; at the time of the consultation itself he had merely pocketed the three guineas and agreed politely that Spring seemed to be later than usual this year. It was the doctor who had broken it to Mr. Morgan—he was relieved that there was no Mrs. Morgan who had to hear the news as well. And Mr. Morgan after a few seconds' incredulity that his Maker should have chosen him for such an end had been very calm and dignified about it. He had shaken the doctor sadly by the hand, rather as one might shake the hand of an unwilling executioner, and had sent for Mr. Hackbridge; Mr. Hackbridge, large toothy and self-important, was standing in front of his desk at this moment.

It was significant that Mr. Morgan had not sent for John Marco. A week ago he would have done so, he had grown to rely on the young man. He was so obviously of the stuff that managers are made of. But the episode in the vestry on the night of the election had shaken Mr. Morgan. He knew Mr. Kent, had known him for years in the way in which a large and important shopkeeper knows a small and unimportant one who happens to worship in the same Chapel. And he was convinced that Mr. Kent would not have spoken without conviction, without evidence. There must certainly have been something behind that outburst. But what? It was that which was troubling Mr. Morgan. In a sense, the uncertainty was worse than actual knowledge: Mr. Marco might have been guilty of *anything*. And so it was, with the pain remorselessly advancing all the time and with so little time to lose, Mr. Morgan had sent for Mr. Hackbridge instead. He felt that in an emergency like the present he could not afford to place his business in the hands of someone over whom even the faintest cloud of dubiety had ever rested.

"It may be six months, it may be a year," Mr. Morgan was saying. "They can't tell."

"You have my deepest sympathy, sir," Mr. Hackbridge replied. "It has come as a great shock to me."

Mr. Morgan paused: in a strange way he was rather enjoying shocking Mr. Hackbridge.

"And after I'm gone," he continued, "there'll have to be someone to carry on."

"Quite so, sir," said Mr. Hackbridge, in the same deliberately melancholy voice. "I see your point."

"I shall probably sell the business eventually," Mr. Morgan went on. "I shall go back to Swansea and get ready for the end. Until then I shall need a manager—someone I can trust."

"Quite so, sir," Mr. Hackbridge agreed again. He twirled the fine points of his moustache as he spoke and shifted his feet a little more widely apart.

"And I've decided to ask you to keep your eye on things in my absence," Mr. Morgan said. "If you show that you can do it—I mean the buying and the accounts and everything—the new people will probably want to keep you in the same position. It's your big chance, Mr. Hackbridge. It's your opportunity."

161

He came over and put his hand on Mr. Hackbridge's shoulder.

"And we shall have to consider the financial aspect," he wound up. "You get three pounds ten a week—don't you?—at the moment. Well, we'll bring it up to four. It's a big jump, Mr. Hackbridge. A big jump."

ii

Mr. Morgan's consternation over Mr. Kent's attack was, after all, only symptomatic of the wave of unrest that had run through the whole Tabernacle. People talked of nothing else. Wherever Mr. Tuke went on his visiting, he heard sly references to the occurrence. In the end things had become so bad by the Saturday night that he re-wrote his Sunday Sermon to counteract it: he preached on slander.

Not by any means that he was convinced of the baselessness of the whisperings. Like Mr. Morgan he had the agonised conviction that behind so much smoke there must be at least a tiny central core of fire. And the fact that John Marco was now an Elder, that he himself had been responsible for making him one, only alarmed him still further.

At last in an effort to clear up the whole mystery he had done the straight and manly thing: he had gone round to Mr. Kent and had asked him point blank for an explanation. But Mr. Kent had refused to say a word. He had been more than reticent: he had been secretive. And he had stood on his rights under the Amosite Charter.

"I don't have to give any reason," he had said. "The book says that anyone who opposes the Election of an Elder shall say so in open convocation, and that's what I did. I said everything that

I'm going to say."

"But think of the effect within the Chapel," Mr. Tuke had reasoned with him. "Think of the effect on our Brother."

"That's his affair," Mr. Kent had replied bluntly. "His and his Maker's."

And though Mr. Tuke had stayed on, by turns wheedling and magisterial, the result had been the same. Mr. Kent had been adamant and Mrs. Kent had supported him. When Mr. Tuke had finally left them he was more aggravated and mystified than ever. That was why he had decided that he would pay an informal evening visit on John Marco to see if he could glean even the least hint of what had gone before.

He delayed his visit until nearly nine o'clock: he wanted to be quite sure that John Marco would be in when he got there. It was an unpleasant sort of night, wet without being cold; and inside his mackintosh Mr. Tuke steamed. By the time he had reached Clarence Gardens he was hot and sticky, and he could not help asking himself how many ministers of his standing would have turned out on such a night merely to lay a rumour. As he stood on the porch shaking his umbrella out into the darkness he envied other men whose day's work was done once they had crossed their thresholds in the evening.

But as he tugged at the massive handle in the socket beside the front door and heard the tinny rattle of the bell in the basement depths below, he was aware of a new and indefinable sensation; it occurred to him with the suddenness of a revelation that this was not a *happy* house. He could not say exactly what it was that put the notion into his head. It might have been merely the melancholy bell-notes below stairs; it might have been the blind, curiously deserted appearance of the front; it might have been its size, so out of proportion to the number of people who lived in

163

it; or it might even have been simply the wetness of the night and his own soaking legs. But Mr. Tuke felt sure it was none of these. It was something intrinsic. Something in the bricks and mortar of the place. It seemed to Mr. Tuke in that inexplicable moment of clairvoyance to be the sort of house in which flowers would wither, fires prove heatless and laughter die away inaudibly on the lips.

Then Emmy opened the front door and Mr. Tuke pulled himself together with a jerk. He was not given to day-dreaming of this kind and wondered if he had caught a chill and were feverish.

"And is Mr. Marco at home?" he asked in his full, rich voice. Emmy shook her head.

"He's gone out for a walk," she said.

"In this weather?"

"That's what he said."

Mr. Tuke paused.

"Is *Mrs.* Marco in?"

"The old one is," Emmy answered. "She's in there."

She jerked her head towards the drawing-room as she spoke.

"Then perhaps I may be allowed to pay my respects," Mr. Tuke replied.

He stepped into the high, dark hall as he said it. He did not like being kept hanging about on doorsteps like a tradesman, and he had never been able to get this draggled maid-of-all-work to treat him with the kind of respect to which he was entitled. He handed her his dripping umbrella and stooped down to remove his goloshes.

"Perhaps you could get rid of these somewhere and then announce me," he said curtly.

But Emmy did not get rid of them. She held them in her arms

with his saturated mackintosh on top and the valuable silk hat somewhere underneath it, and opened the drawing-room door with her free hand.

"The Minister," she said.

Mr. Tuke pushed past her—he had to push: the creature did not even have the good manners to step back for him—and entered the room. As he did so, there was a chuckle of delight from the far side of the fire and old Mrs. Marco half rose to receive him.

She had changed a good deal in those last three years. With someone to look after her and bring her regular meals, and nothing to do all day but read her Bible when she felt like it and ring for cups of tea, she had become strikingly different from the rheumatic old witch who had hobbled about the cold passages in Chapel Villas. She wore her best all day now. And she was cantankerous in the way that old women with an assured livelihood can afford to be.

"Shut the door, Emmy," she screamed over Mr. Tuke's shoulder as she rose to meet him. "You're leaving me in a draught."

Then she held out her hand in its ribbed, black mitten.

"I wanted to see you," she said. "I wanted to hear all about it."

"About what?" Mr. Tuke asked.

"Oh, don't try to pull the wool over my eyes," she answered with a hard, vindictive little laugh. "I heard, what happened. And I want to know exactly what he meant."

Mr. Tuke pulled a chair to the fire and sat down. As he did so he saw how very false his imagination out there on the doorstep had played him. The fire was toasting his legs already and on a table by the window a bowl of hyacinths was blooming. He was somewhat taken aback, however, by the directness of Mrs. Marco's onslaught. The only thing to do was to play for time.

"Whose meaning is it that you want to understand?" he asked suavely.

"Mr. Kent's," Mrs. Marco told him.

"So someone has told you all about that little affair," Mr. Tuke replied.

"It isn't a little affair," Mrs. Marco contradicted him. "He's my son and I want to know what Mr. Kent meant by it."

Mr. Tuke put the tips of his fingers together.

"Really," he said, "I haven't the least idea what he meant. He didn't tell me."

"Then why don't you ask him?"

"I did."

The words slipped out unintentionally. He was about to cover them up with something else, but Mrs. Marco had already pounced on them.

"And what did he say?" she asked. "Now I shall hear something."

"He declined to say anything," Mr. Tuke answered. "He merely said that he opposed your son's election."

"Pah!" Mrs. Marco blew out her lips with anger. "Everyone's trying to keep things back from me these days."

"Then why not ask your son yourself?" Mr. Tuke suggested cunningly.

"He wouldn't talk about it either," Mrs. Marco admitted.

There was a pause, and Mrs. Marco drew one of her shawls closer about herself. Then in the manner of old people Mrs. Marco's whole nature changed suddenly. She became pitiful and appealing.

"You've got to help me," she said. "I can't stand not knowing."

"I shall do all I can to clear the matter up," Mr. Tuke answered her. "I've prayed about it."

But Mrs. Marco ignored his prayers.

"He hasn't been the same since it happened," she went on. "He hasn't spoken to anyone. He's just spent his evenings walking up and down in his room. Emmy's seen him. And sometimes he goes out in the evenings. He's out now."

"I can understand that it upset him," Mr. Tuke said consolingly.

"He isn't upset," Mrs. Marco answered, her old contempt returning for a moment. "It would take someone better than Mr. Kent to upset him. It's his conscience that's troubling him. That's what it is: he's got something on his conscience."

Mr. Tuke's reply was interrupted by Hesther. She opened the door and stood there in the doorway as though listening.

"What were you talking about?" she asked.

"Oh nothing, nothing," Mr. Tuke said hurriedly as he rose to say good-evening. "We were speaking of Mrs. Marco's health."

"No, we weren't," said Mrs. Marco promptly. "We were talking about what Mr. Kent said about your husband."

"Need you worry her with it?" Hesther asked in that flat, quiet voice of hers.

"Mrs. Marco began it," Mr. Tuke replied. Then he realised that the answer was somehow below his dignity; it was school-boyish. "I'm afraid," he continued, "that tongues have been wagging. Idle gossip has been abroad again."

"Well we don't want it here," Hesther said. "We shut our ears to it."

"That's right," Mrs. Marco agreed in her high cracked voice. "We shut our ears to it."

Mr. Tuke shifted in his chair. He felt uncomfortable in the presence of these two women. They were somehow hostile to him; they misunderstood. He was an intruder from the outside world that was saying things about John Marco; and they resented him. The whole household—or at least the women in it—was on the defensive.

"And *I* do more than shut my ears to it," he replied. "I have threatened that if I find out the offenders I shall expose them."

Hesther made no reply. She went over to the window and parted the slats in the long Venetian blind. Then she stood there looking out into the street.

Mr. Tuke coughed.

"Is your husband likely to be long?" he asked.

Hesther shrugged her shoulders; there was an air of complete helplessness about the gesture. It seemed to convey that she didn't know where he had gone, why he had even gone at all. And in front of Mr. Tuke, his absence was a humiliation.

"It's most uncharitable weather to be out in," Mr. Tuke observed. "Most uncharitable."

As he spoke a fresh cascade of water hit the window; it was as though someone outside were sluicing it with a bucket. Hesther shivered.

"I can't believe that he'll remain out very long," he went on. "Not on a night like this."

"He'll be back in his own time," Hesther replied.

She left the window and came over to the fire. Then she stood there looking down on Mrs. Marco.

"It's time you were in bed," she said. "You'll be tired in the morning."

"But I wanted to see if John was all right . . ." she began.

"I shall be waiting up for him," Hesther answered. "There's no reason to have the whole house disturbed."

Mrs. Marco got reluctantly to her feet and began gathering her things together. She proceeded with the unhurried thoroughness of the aged.

"I don't like it," she said. "He was never like this when he was at home."

"This *is* his home," Hesther answered sharply.

"I know," said Mrs. Marco. "It's not your fault. It's just that he's not at rest here." She turned to Mr. Tuke. "Please say something to him," she said. "You can: you're a minister. Tell him it isn't right for any husband . . ."

But Hesther cut her short.

"You're over-tired," she said. "You've been doing too much."

"I only wanted to ask Mr. Tuke to make it all right," Mrs. Marco explained. "I only wanted him to . . ."

"You can tell him some other time," Hesther replied. "You'll only be having another of your fainting attacks if you go on now."

The suggestion of one of these attacks seemed to frighten Mrs. Marco: she put her hand on her bosom over her heart.

"Perhaps you're right," she said feebly. "It's always hammering. Perhaps I ought to lie down."

She gathered her skirts together. Then she picked up her reticule and her spectacle cases, her extra shawls and her bottle of tablets. There was something practised and precise about the way she loaded herself with her belongings; it was evidently a part of some invariable bed-time ritual in which she would let no one help her. Then, when she was ready, she beckoned for Hesther to come over. And leaning heavily on her arm she prepared for the ordeal of the stairs.

Left alone in the room, Mr. Tuke felt drowsy. The air was close and oppressive, and after a few minutes when Hesther had not returned, he sat back and shut his eyes. He did not actually drop off: of that he was certain. He was not the sort of man to indulge in cat-naps. But when he sat up again and opened his eyes, he saw John Marco standing there. It was as though, invisible when he had entered, John Marco had suddenly and silently materialised in front of Mr. Tuke's chair.

And he presented a strange figure. His clothes were drenched and his trousers, too, were clinging to his legs; they seemed to have been splashed by every passing vehicle. Even his face was spattered by the rain.

Mr. Tuke started forward.

"Ah!" he began. "So the wanderer has returned."

"You wanted to see me?"

"That's what I came for," Mr. Tuke told him.

"On Chapel business?"

"On private business."

"It's very late for private business," John Marco answered.

"But this is important," Mr. Tuke replied. "Very important."

John Marco did not move; in the warmth of the room his clothes were steaming, but he did not seem to notice their wetness.

"Go on," he said.

"It's about that little affair at the vestry meeting the other night," he began.

"Is that all you wanted to see me about?" he asked.

"Isn't it enough?" Mr. Tuke asked in astonishment. "Isn't your good name at stake?"

"It's over and done with," John Marco answered slowly. "It's better forgotten."

"But you're an Elder remember," Mr. Tuke told him. "People are bound to talk."

"Then they must talk."

Mr. Tuke came over and put *his* hand on Mr. Marco's arm.

170

"Why not tell me everything?" he asked. "Why not let the sunlight in?"

"There's nothing to tell," John Marco answered.

The tone of his voice startled Mr. Tuke; it sounded so hard and bitter. He dropped his hand.

"It's very sad," he said, "when people harden their hearts." He paused and gave what might have been a little sigh as though to show that the formal object of the visit was over. "I saw Mr. Kent to-day," he added by way of conversation. "His daughter's back, you know."

For the first time John Marco's air of reserve slipped from him.

"Was she there?" he asked. "Have you seen her?" Mr. Tuke nodded.

"Yes, she was there," he answered. "And she's grown into a very fine young woman. I remember her as scarcely more than a child."

John Marco was walking up and down the room by now; crossing and re-crossing between the door and the window. Mr. Tuke was watching him out of the corner of his eye; he thought that he had never seen anyone so restless.

"Did you find out why she's come back?" John Marco asked suddenly.

"I did," Mr. Tuke replied. "Her parents told me. She's come back to get married."

John Marco stopped. He stood motionless, facing Mr. Tuke.

"Are . . . are you sure of this?" he asked.

"Perfectly sure," Mr. Tuke assured him, a trifle coldly. "I've been introduced to her intended. A most estimable young man."

"But what's he like?" John Marco came up close to Mr. Tuke as he spoke. He was peering into his face.

171

Mr. Tuke raised his eyebrows in surprise.

"Really," he said. "I couldn't tell you. I only saw him for a moment. I believe him to be a chemist's assistant."

"Does she seem happy?" John Marco asked. "Could you tell that?"

"People in love always seem happy," Mr. Tuke replied.

John Marco made no answer. He began walking up and down the room again.

"When are they marrying?" he asked at length.

"Sometime after Easter," Mr. Tuke answered. "I'm putting up the banns straightaway."

But John Marco did not seem to have heard him. He had paused by the window with his back to Mr. Tuke and was staring out into the street through the slats of the blind that Hesther had left parted when she had grown tired of watching for him. His handkerchief was in his hand and he was screwing and rescrewing it between his fingers as if he were trying to tear the fabric into fragments.

Mr. Tuke regarded him. Then he did one of the few brave things of his life. He went over to John Marco and stood by him.

"It's not too late for me to help you," he replied. "You have a load of sin on your mind. Tell me why Mary Kent's return has affected you this way?"

But John Marco merely held out his hand.

"It's very late," he said. "Good-night."

When Mr. Tuke had gone (and he left so hurriedly after his dismissal that he had to stand in the darkness of the porch fumbling with the buttons of his coat, for it was still raining), John Marco went upstairs.

The house was very quiet by now, he had that strange isolated

172

feeling of being the one waking person in a sleeping household. He went straight to his room. But it was not Hesther's room. Ever since that first night which he had spent in the chair where Emmy had found him, he had slept alone. It was a small room that had once been Mr. Trackett's dressing-room which he now occupied. There was space in it only for a narrow bed, a chest of drawers and a pile of round cardboard hat-boxes that had once been Mr. Trackett's. They had been there when John Marco moved into the room and he had left them where they stood. It was in a way significant of the fact that he had never felt this house to be his own.

Opening one of the drawers in the chest, he removed a small box from it. His personal possessions were in that box. He unlocked it and from an envelope at the bottom took out the remaining half of the ring that he had broken for Mary. Then he pushed up the window. Beneath him lay the dark shrubbery: the tangle of bushes was thick there. The half ring could lie for years among the roots, undiscovered. It was worth nothing now; after what Mr. Tuke had told him it had become simply a silly piece of broken jewellery. So, parting the curtains, he stood there ready to throw. But at the last moment his resolve failed him. The ghost of its old meaning still seemed to cling to it, and even now he did not doubt that the two halves would somehow join again.

And as he stood there he heard a movement behind him. He turned guiltily as though he had been surprised in something disgraceful, and he saw Hesther standing in the doorway.

She was wearing the pink wrap that he had seen for the first time on their wedding-night. But it was faded now; it clung to her in folds. But it was the fact that she was there at all that surprised him—she had never been to his room like this; they

173

were careful to respect each other's privacy. And already Hesther was closing the door behind her. Once it was shut, she stood with her back against it.

"I want to talk to you," she said.

John Marco turned to her, the half ring still held in the hollow of his hand. He could see now how drawn her face was; she no longer looked even a young woman. Her hair, dragged tightly back from her head, fell between her shoulders in a tight, leaden looking plait.

"What is it you want?" he asked.

She paused. "It can't go on like this any longer," she said at last. "It's more than any woman could bear."

"So you regret it, do you?" he asked.

She bowed her head.

"It was sin," she answered. "Sin, and I've been punished for it."

"We've both been punished for it," he replied. "And we've both paid."

"We're both sinners," she reminded him. "That's what still gives me hope."

He looked at her incredulously.

"Hope?" he said. "For us?"

"Yes," she answered. "Every sinner needs someone to bring him back to God. It is for us to be each other's salvation."

She made a little involuntary movement with her arms as she spoke as though she were about to hold them out to him. The movement was no more than a flicker, however; it died away before it was born. And she was left there, her arms to her sides, a rigid, expressionless figure in that drab, pink silk dressing-gown.

"So you've been talking to Mr. Tuke, have you?" John Marco

asked. "Those aren't your words. They're his."

"I said nothing to Mr. Tuke," Hesther answered. "He knows enough without my telling him."

"Knows what?" John Marco demanded.

"That we're not truly husband and wife," Hesther answered. "That this isn't a real marriage."

"So he knows *that*, does he?"

"Everyone knows it."

John Marco did not reply immediately. His lower lip was thrust out a little.

"How do they know?" he asked. "How can other people know what goes on here?"

"Do you expect Emmy to notice nothing?" Hesther replied. "Doesn't this room speak for itself?"

"If *she's* been talking," he said, "dismiss her. I don't like having my affairs discussed by servants."

"You needn't dismiss Emmy," Hesther answered, quietly. "I shall take her with me."

"Take her with you?" he repeated.

"That's what I came to tell you," she said. "I'm going away."

There was silence, complete silence between them. They stood there, looking at each other like strangers. Only they weren't strangers any longer. They had come face to face with each other at last, and Hesther had uttered what for three years she had refused even to admit.

"You mean you're leaving me?"

"I do," she said.

He paused. "When are you going?" he asked slowly.

"I may be gone by to-morrow night," she replied. "It may take longer; I can't tell."

"Is your mind made up?" he asked.

"Yes," she answered in that same quiet voice. "That is unless you're willing."

"Willing?"

"Unless you'll give me a child."

He stood staring at her. A child: so she was tempting him again. And he would refuse; of course he would refuse. But was this house nothing after all? Didn't it count for something to be an Elder and live respected within the Chapel? As a man who was separated from his wife he would even have to resign from the Synod of the Tabernacle. And old Mrs. Marco? It would be like drawing a knife across her remaining years to expect her to scrub her own kitchen again—she had been living the life of a gorgeous and pampered invalid for three years now. Hesther was still dangling Mr. Trackett's hoard before him. It could be his, all his, if he stretched out his hand for it; and the future could then lead on, magnificently as he had so often imagined it. His throat went dry and his heart began to hammer. But suddenly he stopped. In the palm of his left hand there was a single violent stab of pain. He opened his hand and, from the tiny wound where the broken ring had punctured the skin, a little trickle of blood was oozing.

As he moved his hand, the blood gathered itself into a ball and ran down to his wrist, leaving a bright trail behind it. In the centre of his palm the mark of the half-ring where he had gripped it, still showed clearly imprinted in the flesh.

Then he turned to Hesther.

"Go away if you must," he said. "We've never belonged to each other."

Chapter XIII

It was eventually to be Mr. Hackbridge's downfall that he was not an Amosite. Had he been even a Rechabite, the larger lapse could have been overlooked. But he was none of these. He worshipped in slack, desultory, Anglican fashion in St. George's Parish Church, Hammersmith; and it was typical of the laxity of his religion that he regarded alcohol as no sin. That is not to say that he drank to excess; the temperance advocate's picture of the drunkard was simply not in him. It was merely that he liked a little whisky before going home; and from time to time he would slip into the William the Fourth (which was far enough away from the shop for his entry not to be observed) to drink a solitary glass. Nothing could have been more moderate or more seemly than his behaviour on these occasions. But it was to be his undoing just the same.

Ever since Mr. Morgan's private talk he had been a little above himself. He no longer came immediately the assistants uttered their shrill "Sign please"; he came instead in his own time, keeping both the assistant and the customer waiting long enough to show that he was a person of some importance. And his signature had changed. Always sprawling, it was now flamboyant. As often as not the point of his pencil went right through the sheet and ripped up the carbon paper underneath as well. His manner, moreover, towards the other assistants had altered appreciably; it had deteriorated. He now bullied unmercifully. And the young ladies, always faintly apprehensive, now went in fear of him. He would wait until the department was empty and then pounce on an error in addition, or point to a box lid that had not been shut down properly, and shout at them about it.

It was only John Marco that he left unmolested. He was not sure enough of him; there was something about John Marco that warned Mr. Hackbridge not to interfere. Not that there was anything that *could* be found fault with. John Marco's departments, even the subsidiary Fancy Goods one that was difficult to keep tidy, were models of what retail departments should be. Mr. Hackbridge, indeed, was gratified to think that he would have such a key assistant under him. He was also gratified to think that it would soon be in his power to humble the younger man. For nearly four years now it had been of the gall and wormwood of his life to think that while he lived in one of a row of inferior dwellings John Marco should reside in a mansion. He looked forward with delicious anticipation to getting his social superior to run messages for him.

It was one evening just as he was about to slip in for his drink that he saw John Marco. He looked again and saw how drawn his face was; as he walked he was staring down at the pavement in front of him. He's got something on his mind, something that's eating him up inside, Mr. Hackbridge said to himself; perhaps he's quarrelled with that rich wife of his. And he saw in this the opportunity that he had been waiting for. It would be something else on John Marco's mind to learn that soon he would be serving under Mr. Hackbridge.

He crossed the road and tapped John Marco on the shoulder.

"Just a moment, young man," he said.

He was quite surprised, however, at the way John Marco turned round on him. He looked so angry, so positively angry. Mr. Hackbridge drew away a little.

"What is it you want?" John Marco asked.

"I've got something to tell you," Mr. Hackbridge said. "Something that may make you sit up a bit."

John Marco stood where he was.

"Very well, then," he replied. "Tell me."

Mr. Hackbridge was taken aback.

"Not here, I can't," he said. "Let's go in somewhere."

He took John Marco by the arm and began to lead him towards the glass frosted doors of the public house.

"In here," he said. "I'll tell you over a drink."

But on the threshold John Marco stopped.

"You forget I'm an Amosite," he said.

Mr. Hackbridge looked surprised.

"What's that got to do with it?" he asked.

"We don't drink," John Marco replied.

At that Mr. Hackbridge pursed up his lips.

"I see," he said. "It's all right for me to go into a public house, but it's not good enough for you, is that it?"

John Marco nodded: he did not seem in the least concerned to hear Mr. Hackbridge's secret.

But Mr. Hackbridge was disappointed.

"Not so hasty," he said. "It's very important what I've got to tell you."

"Then why don't you say it?" John Marco asked.

Mr. Hackbridge put his hand on John Marco's shoulder.

"Come inside like I asked you to," he said. "You don't have to drink just because you're in a public house."

They went in together and Mr. Hackbridge ordered whisky. John Marco himself drank something non-intoxicating; it was a sparkling glass full of juvenile rubbish that the barman had put before him.

"I expect you've noticed that there's been something on," Mr. Hackbridge began.

John Marco nodded: he had no notion of what Mr. Hackbridge was talking about.

"Well, Mr. Morgan's retiring: that's what's on," Mr. Hackbridge told him.

John Marco's face did not express any surprise. Mr. Hackbridge looked hard at him to see him lift his eyebrows when he heard the news, but he was cheated.

"Is that what you wanted to tell me?" was all John Marco said.

Mr. Hackbridge took a deep drink and sat on in silence for a moment.

"You're the only other person who knows," he remarked.

There was another pause.

"What's going to happen to the shop?" John Marco asked.

Mr. Hackbridge smiled a slow superior smile.

"Wouldn't you like to know?" he said.

"I thought you were going to tell me," John Marco answered.

Mr. Hackbridge raised his glass and drained it.

"I've been pledged to secrecy," he said.

"I see," replied John Marco quietly.

Then he looked towards Mr. Hackbridge's glass.

"Will you have another drink?" he asked.

"If you do," Mr. Hackbridge replied.

"Very well," John Marco answered. "Another whisky and a ginger ale. . . ."

"I said a drink," Mr. Hackbridge interrupted. "A real one. Not that stuff."

John Marco hesitated. He knew perfectly well what the challenge meant: if he accepted it he would be the first Amosite ever to touch liquor in public, perhaps the first Elder ever to touch liquor anywhere. It would be the betrayal of a vow; the committing of the eighth deadly sin. He had seen men turned out of the Chapel for less. But he had to know Mr. Hackbridge's secret. And he did not doubt for a moment that Mr. Hackbridge had brought him in simply to break it to him.

"Very well," he replied. "Two whiskies."

"Now you're talking," Mr. Hackbridge said admiringly.

He sipped the drink that John Marco had brought for him and gazed dreamily into space. "Would it surprise you," he said at length, "if I told you that Mr. Morgan had appointed me as manager?"

This time Mr. Hackbridge was not disappointed. John Marco drew in the corners of his mouth sharply.

"Is that so?" he said.

Mr. Hackbridge smiled unpleasantly.

"Why do you think I should be telling you if it wasn't?" he asked.

John Marco did not answer. He sat back and stared at the rows of casks and bottles opposite. So that was it! Mr. Morgan, the elderly Mr. Morgan, who couldn't even check over his own stock-room accounts without getting him in to help, had passed him over, had passed him right over and given the prize to this fool in a frock-coat, this whisky-drinker. His anger mounted inside him so that he could not trust himself to speak; there was nothing now that remained of his prodigious future.

Mr. Hackbridge, however, did the speaking for him.

"If you mind your p's and q's," he was saying, "I may be able to do something for you."

"For me?"

"Yes, I may be able to put you in the way of a bit of promotion. How would you like my job? How would you like to be shop-walker instead of me?"

"I'll think about it,' John Marco answered.

The answer annoyed Mr. Hackbridge.

"Oh no you won't," he said. "You won't do anything of the kind. If I want you to be a shop-walker you will be. And if I don't you won't."

He finished up his drink and tapped loudly on the counter with a florin.

"Same again," he said. "And hurry up with it."

Then he turned to John Marco.

"You don't seem to realise who you're talking to. I tell you I'm going to be manager. I'm going to have things done my way in future."

He sat back as he said it and thrust his thumbs through the arms of his waistcoat. His top hat was tilted a little over one eye and his face was flushed.

"When is this change going to take place?" John Marco asked.

"Whenever I bloody well want it to," Mr. Hackbridge replied. "Whenever I choose to go to Mr. Morgan and raise my little finger."

John Marco left him. It was still evening outside. A pale yellow light filled the sky and the chimney-pots were like gold. He walked away rapidly; walked at random without any destination.

182

Even the streets were better than going back to Hesther. And no doubt she had already told Mrs. Marco of her decision—there would be two women now, not one, to face when he got back.

The street which he had taken led him in the direction of the park. It was quiet there, dark and silent under the trees. The lights of London showed simply as so many fairy lamps set round the boundaries of this open wilderness. In front, away from those lights, a man might lose himself; it was somewhere that did not belong to this world at all. He set his feet towards this mysterious inner darkness and walked on. He was not alone, however. Women spoke to him. He saw their shadowy faces, smelt the cheap reek of their scent. The whole air seemed full of powder and patchouli. He brushed past them and went on. He did not stop until he came to the great sheet of water that lay in front of him. In the gloom it stretched out like a great inland sea, and came lapping lazily at the pavement beneath his feet. It pacified him. He stood there, and his thoughts started to unravel: he began to see the future again. An hour later when he came away, his mind was made up.

The house was quite dark when he got there; the curtains were still drawn and the windows bolted. It was like entering a cold handsome tomb. But he did not pause. He lit the light with fingers that were shaking. And then in the cold bleak hall he stood staring.

There were trunks and boxes all round him. They were labelled and corded, ready.

His heart still hammering, he began to mount the stairs.

And at the top he turned, not towards his room, but towards Hesther's. It was not, however, until he actually heard her voice in the darkness that he knew whether she was still in the house or not. Then, he closed the door behind him. He was alone with her.

"I've come to you," he said.

There was a sound from the bed that was almost like a sob.

"I've been waiting," she answered. "Waiting so long."

Chapter XIV

Hesther woke before him in the morning. She lay there filled with a rich happiness. This other body, with a warmth of its own, seemed still to be giving her a share of the life within it. It was strong and satisfying. Even the regular sound of the breathing was reassuring. With him beside her she felt that she could never be lonely again.

The light was already shining through the slats of the Venetian blind when she stirred; it fell across the counterpane in a crumpled design of black and yellow. Very gently so as not to disturb him, she raised herself on one elbow. She had never watched him sleeping before and she bent over him, fascinated. In repose his face seemed strangely different; it was younger. The hard lines beside the mouth had disappeared arid his frown had gone. And as she sat there her face became gentler, too. She watched him for some minutes and her lips began to move. "Oh God," she was saying, "make him love me. Make him need me more and more."

Then she drew back. She felt proud as well as happy. It had happened, and the years of her humiliation were over. She was a woman. And because it was her victory, because of all the days of her life this was the greatest, she wanted to share the moment: it was a secret too important to be kept alone.

So slipping from the bed with the same silent, stealthy movement she went over to the dressing-table and stood gazing into the mirror. The face that looked back at her was paler than she liked, paler and more drawn. "I'm getting old," she thought. "Old"; and she loosened her hair at the temples and drew it forward. Then she searched for something to put round her; the plain linen nightgown that buttoned in at the wrists like a surplice and the faded dressing-gown were not what she wanted this morning. Finally she opened the scent bottle (she had given up using scent again; the bottle had stood there half-full on the dressing-table for years) and sprinkled some on her wrap.

She was ready now. Going over to the fireplace she rang the bell. The sound surprised Emmy. But obediently she put down her dust-pan and brush—she had been about the house cleaning ever since half past six—and began to climb the vast Niagara of stairs that descended in a twisting cascade of woodwork from the roof to the basement: she had toiled up them so many times that she had grown to think of them as being built that way.

She was inside the bedroom before she noticed John Marco's head on the pillow. Then he stirred and she saw him.

Hesther was saying something about bringing the master's tea up to this room instead. But Emmy was not listening: she knew perfectly well why she had been sent for. She turned and caught Hesther's eye. The two women understood each other.

ii

When John Marco returned home that night he found it converted. Hesther and Emmy had brought all his things through

186

into Hesther's bedroom; his suits were now hanging in the big mahogany wardrobe alongside her dresses. And she had even set out his brushes with hers on the dressing-table. His own bedroom was now simply a box-room again.

The rest of the house, too, had undergone a change. There were flowers in the hall and a rug that he had not seen before covered the cold tiling. Even the Venetian blinds were drawn up higher so that the evening light could get in. And Hesther herself was wearing a brown velvet evening dress with a brooch on it. It was very different from the black satin in which he was used to seeing her. She looked a woman; and when she came to the door to meet him—she had been standing there apparently waiting— he smelt perfume again. Before he had time to remove his coat she had kissed him.

"John," she said.

And she paused as though hoping that he would utter her name. But he only smiled, smiled pityingly it seemed, and turned away. And then, still as if he were sorry for her, he came back and putting his arms upon her shoulders he kissed her on the forehead.

He felt a kind of relief as he did so. Now that the struggle was resolved, now that at last he had decided to take everything that Hesther had to offer, he was freer. He had waited long enough; no one could deny that. He had tried to remain faithful. But somehow the miracle had not happened. He had lost Mary for ever: he realised that now. And in her place he had got a mansion and a future; the Lord, he supposed, had been a good shepherd to him after all.

And Hesther was another woman to him: she bloomed, like a wife who is cherished. At dinner she kept smiling, caressing him with her eyes from the far end of the table. When he told her that he was going to the lecture at the Tabernacle she only nodded her head and smiled again. She would not come too, she said; she was happy to remain at home now, waiting confidently for his return.

The subject of to-night's lecture was the transgressions of Moab; the lecturer, the Reverend Samuel Carver, had come all the way over from the Putney Tabernacle to discuss them. He was a poor speaker and of no presence—beside Mr. Tuke he looked no more than an impostor. But his reputation as a wizard in theology had spread before him, and in consequence the pews were crowded to hear his exposition of what the Lord had really meant when He said that because of the three transgressions of Israel and because of four, He was not going to turn away the punishment thereof. But when Mr. Carver came to the Lord's threat: "I will kindle a fire in the wall of Rabbah, and it shall devour the palaces thereof, with shouting in the day of battle, with a tempest in the day of the whirlwind," Mr. Tuke turned in his toes: he wished that *his* voice instead of Mr. Carver's thin, piping one could have been given a chance of showing them what the Lord really sounded like when He was angry.

John Marco had been sitting listening for some time before he became aware that there was another power than the lecturer's in the room. It was a stronger power and it lay somewhere behind him. He began to stir uncomfortably in his seat and, when the speaker was reading verbatim from an apparently endless tract of Mr. Sturger's on Sin, he turned round. It was not immediately, however, that he could find what he was looking for; at first he saw merely a blank bank of faces. Nevertheless, he was aware at once that the power had increased, that he was now in the full play of it. Then on the far side of the Chapel against the wall he saw one face different from all the others: he saw Mary. She was alone. And she was looking towards him.

When John Marco turned towards the lecturer again he was trembling, and his knees were weak. Mr. Carver was ingeniously proving that when the Lord had said Damascus, Tyre and Edom He had really meant Bayswater, Paddington and Marylebone and the people thereof. But John Marco was not listening to him. He had seen Mary again, and already the whole of this new life of his was crumbling.

He folded his arms and sank deeper into his seat. This was the very thing that he had told himself he must never do, to let the past come creeping up into the present. But as he sat there, he could still feel this power beating on his back, forcing its message through to him, and he knew that Mary's eyes were still fixed on him.

But when the lecture was over and he was able to turn round again she was gone. Her place was empty and the whole Chapel seemed suddenly to have gone cold. For a moment he wondered if he had been deceived and if it were someone else with gold hair and slender shoulders whom he had seen sitting there. But he knew in his heart that there had been no mistake.

The warmth had gone from the air by the time he got outside. The last vestiges of daylight had gone with it and the streets were desolate, lamp-lit chasms again. John Marco did not linger. He picked his way through the dispersing crowd on the Chapel steps and walked off rapidly like a man who is not anxious for company. Soon he was alone, except for a few late stragglers returning to their homes, and he slackened his pace a little. His path lay down Chapel Walk where it was dark, very dark, under the plane trees. The walk was short—a mere hundred yards or so—and he was halfway down it before he was aware that there was someone, a woman, standing in the shadows beside him. And this time he knew at once who it was. His heart seemed momentarily to stop altogether and then begin racing furiously as he came up to her.

"Mary," he said. "It's you."

She came towards him and laid her hand upon his arm.

"I had to see you again," she said. "I've been trying to see you ever since I got back."

"Trying to see me?" he repeated. "Why should you ever want to see me again?"

"I wanted to know if you were happy," she answered.

She had turned her head a little and the light of the lamp now fell upon her face. For a moment he dared not look at her. Then he raised his eyes and, as he did so, the three years since he had last seen her disappeared. He was back again at the night of the Immersion; his eyes had been fixed on her then. Everything that had happened since that night was a phantasy which only this moment could dissolve.

"I was asking if you were happy," she reminded him.

He started.

"Why do you want to know?"

"Because I'm getting married too," she told him. "I shouldn't feel free to be happy if I knew that you weren't."

There was a pause, and he ran his tongue over his lips to moisten them.

"Yes," he said deliberately. "You can think of me as happy."

They did not speak again for a moment and they began to walk along slowly, side by side.

"Did . . . did you get those letters I wrote you?" he asked.

She shook her head.

"No. But I knew that you must have written. I was sure of it."

"I told you everything in them," he said.

She was frowning, puzzled.

"What was it you told me?" she asked.

But his face darkened and he did not answer.

"It's too late now," he said. "It's all over. It doesn't matter." He paused: "Are you in love with this man you are marrying?" he asked abruptly.

"Yes," she answered. "You can think of me as happy, too."

He turned on her.

"That isn't the same thing," he said. "I asked if you loved him?"

"Do you love Hesther?" she asked quietly.

They were nearing the end of Chapel Walk by now. Its darkness and its trees came suddenly to an end in a thoroughfare along which lighted buses trundled. All privacy stopped there. He laid his hand on her arm.

"Stop here a moment," he said.

He put his arm round her.

"I love *you*," he said. "You know that. I shall go on loving you for ever."

"I love you too," she answered. "I can't tell you how much."

He looked into her face and saw that she was crying. His heart which had become normal again now began to hammer uncontrollably once more. He could feel little frantic pulses all over him.

"Come away with me," he said suddenly. "Come away before it's too late. We'll manage somehow. I'm strong. I can support you. Come away to-night . . ."

But she put her hand over his mouth to stop him.

"Don't ask me," she said. "Can't you see that it's wicked?"

"It's not wicked to love you," he answered.

She took hold of his hands and drew them away from her.

"It *is* wicked," she said. "Hesther's your wife now. We mustn't see each other again."

Her voice was calm as she spoke; so calm that he felt his desire passing out of him. Only the misery of separation remained.

"Then kiss me," he said. "Kiss me this last time."

"I hoped you'd ask that," she said.

They were still embracing, his lips on hers, when Mr. Tuke, the total of the collection in his bag, passed hurriedly down Chapel Walk on his way back to the Presbytery. He was frowning as he walked; he knew that lovers used these shadows and, in his mind, the street reeked of Babylon and its devices.

But he was utterly unprepared for what he saw to-night. A chink of light penetrating between two of the trunks illuminated the figures and there was no mistaking them. For a moment this man of God thought of striding up and tearing them apart as Joshua or Isaiah would have done. But he checked himself: he was actually so dumb-founded that he could think of nothing to say. So, instead, he went on hurriedly—almost running in fact to avoid their seeing him—as though it were he who were guilty, and they who were standing in innocence beneath the trees.

Chapter XV

Old Mr. Morgan did not ever get so far as Swansea as he had once intended. The rooms were booked, the nurse, a grizzled-haired old veteran, was installed, and then the doctor said that things had gone too far and Mr. Morgan was not to be moved.

In his heart Mr. Morgan knew that the doctor was right. The last three months during which he had been carefully tying up the business and putting all the ends into Mr. Hackbridge's damp, fumbling hands, had been painful and terrifying. He was now a groaning lump of misery with a kind of octopus inside him that stretched out one of its eight legs and caught him whichever way he turned. Had he attempted the journey, indeed, he doubted whether he would ever have reached his destination; and there seemed something downright improper in a man's meeting his Maker in a private compartment on the Great Western Railway.

So it was arranged that the flat over the shop should be opened up again and that Mr. Morgan should stop there. The result, of course, was chaos. It was agony to the Old Gentleman to lie there in the big, brass bedstead in front of the window and know that two floors underneath him, Mr. Hackbridge was making a mess of things. The nurse, moreover, had deserted him. When she learned that he was not going to Swansea after all, she threw up the case altogether. She felt that, at her time of life, she was entitled to a little consideration, too; and she definitely preferred death at the sea-side to death anywhere else.

The new nurse was a very different kind of citizen. She was a charmer. She was small and well-preserved and chestnut-haired. Out of an unvaryingly complexioned face, there gazed a pair of bright, china blue eyes that were as blandly innocent as a child's. Nothing disturbed her; nothing interfered with her sleep. She was smooth and efficient and silent. The Association that had sent her, spoke of her in the highest possible terms, and she carried the references of an angel. Altogether she was a formidably presentable companion. Mr. Morgan, elderly widower as he was, used to lie on his back and wonder which side of forty she belonged to. One day he asked her, and she told him that she was thirty-five.

And under her care, as expert and proficient as a vet's, Mr. Morgan lingered on. Nothing fearful happened, nothing alarming. May turned to June, and June gave place to July and Mr. Morgan and Nurse Foxell were both of them still there. The Old Gentleman of course was in a daze for most of the time. The doctor had given her a bottle of Liquor Morphia to exhibit to the patient whenever the pain became too unbearable, and she administered it constantly, compassionately. The doctor was satisfied that it should be so; and so, in his wakeful moments, was Mr. Morgan.

It was these wakeful moments which were the trouble. His anxiety about the shop returned then and he would wonder whether the windows were being looked after properly and if the corsets were being really carefully rolled up before they were put away again. Sometimes he could stand the uncertainty no longer. And there would follow the strange spectacle of a nurse in uniform, gleaming all over with chaste starch, walking through the departments on a tour of investigation. Needless to say, Mr. Hackbridge resented these tours, and tried to show his resentment by following her round on his big, spongy feet until she returned to the sick-room where she belonged.

But Mr. Morgan already resented Mr. Hackbridge and was so sharp in his dealings with him that Mr. Hackbridge had no opportunity to complain. Every time, in fact, when Mr. Morgan saw his manager on one of the periodic visits that he insisted on he wondered if he had not blundered in his choice and should not have picked on John Marco instead. Mr. Hackbridge was such a sloppy sack of a man, and John Marco was always so ready and alert. Mr. Morgan actually spoke once or twice to Nurse Foxell about sending for John Marco and making some new arrangement: but each time Nurse Foxell dissuaded him. She said that he must forget all about the shop and simply take care of himself.

And, what was odd, Mr. Morgan obeyed her. During the ten weeks in which she had looked after him he had come to rely on her so completely for everything that it did not occur to him to question her authority. Whenever he became in the least obstreperous she would purse up those red lips of hers and begin fumbling with the small blue bottle of Liquor Morphia. There was never any disputing *that;* and after he had greedily drunk from the spoon which she had held for him in cool, steady hands, he would drift gratefully off again into oblivion. Best of all, he liked those afternoons when he was no more than sensuously drowsy and could lie, propped up with pillows while Nurse Foxell sat beside him stitching, endlessly stitching, at some piece of everlasting needlework.

It was on one of these occasions when he had been left alone with Mr. Tuke after tea—Mr. Tuke's visits seemed always to synchronise with the tea-tray—that he was able to voice his feelings.

"I'm worried," he said faintly. "Very worried."

"God will take care," Mr. Tuke assured him.

"God doesn't take care of retail drapery," Mr. Morgan said peevishly.

Mr. Tuke raised his eyebrows but did not dispute the point, and there was a brief silence.

Then Mr. Morgan spoke again.

"I've made some bad mistakes," he said. "Some very bad ones."

"We all have," Mr. Tuke replied. "We all have a load of errors with which to reproach ourselves."

"I don't mean that kind of error," Mr. Morgan replied. "I mean about Mr. Hackbridge."

Mr. Tuke, however, did not seem to be interested in Mr. Hackbridge: he treated the whole affair as though it were trivial. And it was not until Mr. Morgan mentioned John Marco that he showed any interest at all. Then the effect was remarkable. He bared his teeth.

"Don't speak of that young man," he said. "An Elder, too."

From the bedclothes Mr. Morgan stared up in dismay.

"Oh dear," he said. "Oh dear. What *is* it that's wrong with Mr. Marco?"

"Everything's wrong with him," Mr. Tuke answered. "He is walking in sin."

"But what kind of sin?" Mr. Morgan persisted. "Not thievery?"

"Carnal," said Mr. Tuke briefly. And having said as much he would say no more.

But it was enough. Mr. Morgan was now thoroughly unsettled, and when Nurse Foxell came back she treated Mr. Tuke as if he had been trying to murder the Old Gentleman. She went first over to the bed, and then crossed to the table by the fireplace and came back with Mr. Tuke's hat and gloves. The crudity of the thing appalled him. During all his years in the Ministry he did not ever remember having been treated so abruptly by a woman before. But while he was sulking on his way downstairs Nurse Foxell had quite forgotten all about him. She was already immersed in her sacred duty of healing again; with one cool hand she was smoothing the poor, tortured forehead while with the other she was loosening the stopper in the magical bottle of Liquor Morphia. In the sick room she was queen; and she knew it.

Nor were Mr. Tuke and Mr. Hackbridge the only ones to feel aggrieved about the state of siege in which Mr. Morgan existed. The bedroom was practically barred against all visitors. And, when a sister and two cousins came up by excursion train all the way from Llanelly to catch one last glimpse of the sufferer, they were actually reduced to the humiliation of having to sit about in the drawing-room like strangers for nearly forty minutes while this auburn-haired houri flounced in and out of the sickroom in front of them.

Even Mr. Hackbridge now gave his daily report into her hands instead of direct into Mr. Morgan's and for all he knew Mr. Morgan might have been dead for weeks and Nurse Foxell carrying on a sinister pantomime of showing him things. Mr. Tuke was therefore not entirely unprepared (for, without listening to scandal, he picked up all that was going on in the parish) when Mr. Morgan sent for him one day because he wanted to talk privately: he arrived expectant and disapproving.

Nurse Foxell met him at the top of the stairs and told him to mount quietly because the invalid was sleeping. Mr. Tuke said nothing to this piece of impudence; he behaved simply and with dignity, and followed her up with robust, manly footsteps that made the wood-work creak. When they reached the drawing-room Nurse Foxell allowed him to get seated properly—Mr. Tuke was always rather ponderous about sitting, it took him several minutes to get settled—and then drew up a chair opposite.

"Mr. Morgan wanted to see you privately," she said, not raising her eyes from the piece of needlework which she produced from behind her.

"So I understand," Mr. Tuke replied. "That is why I came."

"But he finds now that he doesn't feel strong enough to tell you himself," Nurse Foxell went on. "So he asked me to tell you instead."

"He asked you?" Mr. Tuke repeated incredulously.

"Why not?" Nurse Foxell answered. "Why shouldn't he?"

Mr. Tuke was not prepared to argue.

"Go on," he said coldly.

Nurse Foxell stitched the tendril of a spray of honeysuckle into the pattern of her embroidery, and gave a little sigh.

"The fact is," she said, "he wants to marry me."

Mr. Tuke kept himself rigid. He was careful to show neither resentment nor astonishment. Instead he presumed on his high position and on her lowly one.

"You are either a very simple woman," he said, "or else a

198

very scheming one."

Nurse Foxell was naturally a little offended; but she was not abashed.

"I don't see why you should say that," she replied.

"Because Mr. Morgan is a man of nearly eighty whereas you are only on the threshold of middle-age," Mr. Tuke answered back. "It's not seemly."

"You mean you don't approve?"

Mr. Tuke nodded.

"Then perhaps I'm really wasting your time," Nurse Foxell replied. "Mr. Morgan said if you were difficult we should simply have to find someone else."

But Mr. Tuke was hearing no more of it. He rose to his feet and confronted her.

"Mr. Morgan said no such thing," he thundered. "Mr. Morgan is one of my oldest parishioners."

Even this, however, did not seem to dash Nurse Foxell. She went on in a different colour with the petal of a honeysuckle, and merely raised her eyebrows a little.

"I can only suggest that you ask him yourself," she said. "He's probably awake by now."

She crossed over to the door of the bedroom as she said it, but Mr. Tuke crossed faster. His hand was on the doorknob before Nurse Foxell had got there.

"I will see for myself," he said.

Mr. Morgan was awake all right. He was lying on his back staring helplessly in the direction of the little bottle which Nurse Foxell had left foolishly in full view on the mantel-shelf.

The sight of Mr. Morgan shocked Mr. Tuke. He had seen him a week or so ago but even in that brief interval, there had been a change. He was no longer the plump Old Gentleman whom they had all known. In fact he wasn't plump at all now: he was rapidly disappearing before their eyes. The genial curve of his cheeks had vanished already and all that was left was the grim ominous bone work of the face covered by tight, transparent-looking skin. Only the eyes remained. They were larger and more bright than ever. And as Mr. Tuke stood there they turned towards him and he could see that they were frightened eyes.

It was Nurse Foxell's voice that roused him. She was standing just behind Mr. Tuke and she spoke over his right shoulder.

"It's Mr. Tuke," she said. "I've told him our news."

Mr. Morgan did not move at first. Then very arduously as though it were an effort too great to be attempted he removed a very pale hand from the bedclothes and beckoned Mr. Tuke to come nearer.

"That's right," Nurse Foxell said from the doorway. "You two talk it over together."

When Nurse Foxell had left them it was Mr. Tuke who opened the conversation.

"I don't like what I've just heard," he said. "It's wanton."

"But she's very devoted," Mr. Morgan protested. "I've never been looked after like this before."

"That's no reason for marrying," Mr. Tuke replied sternly.

"She won't stop unless I marry her," Mr. Morgan went on. "She told me so."

"Then she isn't worthy to be a Nurse," answered Mr. Tuke. "She should be exposed. The Association should be told of it."

"That wouldn't help me," said Mr. Morgan sadly. "I can't get along without her."

Mr. Tuke pursed up his lips disapprovingly.

"Then you ought to be able to," he said. "Your mind should

200

be on other matters. You ought to be preparing yourself."

"I'm ready whenever He calls," Mr. Morgan replied. "I'm the one who's waiting."

There was a pause, a long heavily charged silence that was broken only by the sound of the difficult breathing from the bed. Then Mr. Tuke spoke again.

"At your time of life, too," he said abruptly. "You must be twice her age."

"She's thirty-five and I'm seventy-two," Mr. Morgan replied. "That's why it can't last very long."

"Why it shouldn't ever take place you mean," Mr. Tuke retorted.

There was another long awkward pause after that. Mr. Tuke's intransigence was proving too much for Mr. Morgan. In his present feeble state he did not feel equal to arguing with anyone. His eyes suddenly overflowed and large, pear-shaped tears ran down his cheeks.

"Don't . . . don't you want to marry us?" he asked.

"I do not," Mr. Tuke replied.

Poor Mr. Morgan gave a fresh sob at the answer.

"Oh dear," he said. "It's very difficult. Perhaps you're right. Perhaps I'm making a big mistake. I can't think very clearly these days."

At that moment the door opened again and Nurse Foxell entered. Without giving a look at the invalid she went straight up to Mr. Tuke.

"You ought to be ashamed of yourself, you ought," she said. "Coming in here and upsetting the patient like this with all your silly talk."

Mr. Tuke trembled with rage.

"My talk was not silly," he replied allowing his voice to swell suddenly to its true proportions. "It is you who should be ashamed. . . ."

But his anger apparently had no effect on Nurse Foxell: she all but ignored him.

"Oh get along with you," she said contemptuously. "I've got my work to do."

Mr. Tuke then left them—he left silently and in dudgeon—and Nurse Foxell came over to the bed and stood looking down at the invalid.

"How are you feeling?" she asked. "How's the pain?"

Mr. Morgan bit his lips.

"It's terrible," he said. "Terrible. Give me another dose of the medicine."

But Nurse Foxell did not budge.

"Not just yet," she said. "Your mind's clouding. I heard what you said to the Minister as I came in. I don't want you going back on your word."

The Old Gentleman's end was very near by now. By some sort of tribal magic everyone seemed to know of it, and the trains from Cardiff and Newport and Swansea swarmed with hopeful and expectant relations all making their way to London to be in time for the final parting.

It was one thing, however, to get as far as Paddington Station and quite another to penetrate into the sick-room itself: the relatives agreed afterwards that it was the last six yards of the two-hundred-mile journey which were the most difficult. For Nurse Foxell kept them at bay. Polite and pink-and-white and smiling, she admitted them one at a time for a space of a few minutes or turned them away altogether on the pretext that the patient was sleeping. Even those who got inside did not profit very much. They found the Old Gentleman wrapped in a sort of morphine cocoon. They spoke to him and he didn't answer. They fondled his hand and it slid limply back onto the bedclothes. They said good-bye, and he did not seem to notice that they had left him.

Nurse Foxell herself appeared quite unperturbed by such behaviour on Mr. Morgan's part. She told them frankly that she was giving him as much of the drug as the doctor would allow, and added that you couldn't want to make a man suffer just so that you could talk to him. There was a note of rebuke as she said it; she spoke as one who does not encourage idle sight-seers in a death chamber.

After the relatives had gone, Nurse Foxell allowed Mr. Morgan to see his lawyer. He had been asking for him before, but she had said that it would only lead to bickerings if he came while the house was full of people. She said that he could see the lawyer first and then if it didn't tire him too much he could see the Minister again to-morrow.

The lawyer was with Mr. Morgan for nearly an hour and Nurse Foxell was there all the time—she had to be for Mr. Morgan was in great pain. There was a whole new will drawn up by the time he left and Mr. Morgan in a voice broken with pain and anxiety, pleaded that it should be signed on the spot. In the end Mr. Hackbridge and Mr. Lyman, from the counting-house, were sent for to witness the signature: Nurse Foxell herself could not sign as she was now a beneficiary.

Then, when the lawyer had gone away again, Nurse Foxell gave the Old Gentleman the sort of dose of morphia he craved for. He floated off on a blissful and anaesthetic cloud into a world in which there were no lawyers and no pain and no Nurse Foxells.

It was, however, the last piece of floating that he was to do for nearly forty-eight hours. For Nurse Foxell suddenly cut the morphia right out and gave him aspirin instead. The aspirin was no better than useless; the bayonets of pain went through its thin armour without stopping. Mr. Morgan writhed under it. He begged for morphia. He wept. But Nurse Foxell was adamant.

She said that if she went on giving him the stuff, people would think that she was simply trying to murder him for his money.

ii

The end when it came was sudden and dramatic. It was a Sunday evening and the relatives were gathered round again in the front sitting-room. There were seven of them, five anxious Welshmen and two of their womenfolk: they had come as a deputation determined to see the Old Gentleman and put their point of view. They were ready to use persuasion—or force, if necessary; and nothing that Nurse Foxell could do was going to prevent them.

But to their surprise Nurse Foxell was sweet and very pleasant; she invited them in and even found chairs for them all. When they said that they wanted to see Mr. Morgan she placed no obstacle in the way. She merely went into the room first to tidy up—they could hear the poor Old Gentleman's groans as soon as the door was opened—and, as she came out again, she placed the morphia bottle, which he had not seen for the last two days, on the table beside him.

It was the relative from Llantyglos who was the first to go in. And it was therefore he who was the first to see the tragedy. Nurse Foxell herself did not see it at all. She had stayed behind and was quietly embroidering by the fire in the other room. It was the terrible cry of "Nurse, he's got the poison bottle," that roused her. Throwing down her needlework in a heap on the floor she ran in to try and save the Old Gentleman. But it was too late. The bottle clutched in his stiff, white hand was pressed tight to his lips: it was empty. Two fluid ounces were inside him and his eyes stared at the ceiling with the look of innocent astonishment of a child who at last has got what it has wanted. Nurse Foxell snatched the bottle away of course, and telephoned at once for a doctor. But she warned them that there was very little hope: in the ecstasy of his relief, the Old Gentleman had drunk enough to put a regiment to sleep.

Nurse Foxell was right. The doctor could do simply nothing. By the time he arrived, Mr. Morgan was already halfway over the precipice into space; he was slipping visibly while they stood there. And it was evidently not to be the kind of end in which the patient rallies for a moment and says a few clear words before he departs. With every minute that passed the Old Gentleman was sinking deeper and still deeper. His breathing had become spasmodic and absent-minded; so spasmodic, indeed, that they never quite knew when the finish really came. It was simply that they all stood waiting for the next of those hoarse, creaking breaths— and it did not come. And by then, of course, Mr. Morgan had already taken the final plunge and was at last careering headlong through the oceans of space.

The effect on the relatives as soon as the truth was known was tremendous. They were Welsh. And they were not unnaturally keyed up. Burying their heads in their hands and pulling out brilliantly coloured handkerchiefs, they sobbed and moaned over the departed. One of the relatives, the sour, crabbed little man from Llantyglos, was the most strangely overcome of all: he unbuttoned his waistcoat and loosened his front collar stud and howled. All other grief in the room was inaudible by comparison.

Nurse Foxell and the doctor were indeed the only two who showed any command over their emotions, and even the doctor was moved. It was really Nurse Foxell alone who came through the ordeal with flying colours; the relatives admitted that much. In the midst of the turmoil she did not give a thought to her own good name and how it would be affected by her carelessness in having left the bottle somewhere the sufferer could get it. All that she thought about was the Old Gentleman's reputation. With tears in her eyes—the tears made her china-blue eyes brighter and more appealing than ever—she besought the doctor not to let it be known that Mr. Morgan had died by his own hand.

She could bear anything but that, she said.

iii

The relatives, of course, had all been home again for months by the time the Will was proved. And perhaps it was just as well. There had been considerable revision in that last version the lawyer had drawn up. Two codicils now changed the whole complexion of it. Under the first, the sum of five hundred pounds had been left to the Old People's Homes, Rhondda, where Mr. Morgan had been brought up as a boy. That in itself was nothing; the legend of Mr. Morgan's wealth was able to take the sum of five hundred pounds in its stride. It was the second codicil that counted. Under this, the residue of all of which Mr. Morgan died possessed passed into the stainless hands of Susan Augusta Foxell, spinster.

The residue included, of course, the business. And Nurse Foxell, without wasting a moment, packed up her bag and put the house of Morgan and Roberts onto the market.

Chapter XVI

The effect in the shop of Mr. Morgan's death (and the news leaked out at once that it was suicide) was deplorable. It left everyone temperamental and unsettled. As much as a fortnight after the memorable and awful day when the handsome oak coffin had been carried down those winding flights of stairs, and black upright boards had been nailed over the windows, mistakes in simple addition were still being made by the cashiers and wrong lengths of expensive materials were unaccountably measured and cut off.

The sale of the shop, however, did not promise to be easy. The auditors judged the price at six thousand pounds, and wanted to put the property on the market at that figure. But Miss Foxell (she had dropped the "Nurse" altogether now and was offended and rather surprised when anyone called her by it) insisted on seven thousand pounds. She said that seven thousand pounds was the sum the Old Gentleman had mentioned to her and it would make him turn over in his grave to think of his beautiful shop going for a mere six thousand. For her part, she made it clear, she merely wanted the whole thing settled as soon as possible so that she could go away somewhere and forget all the pain and heartbreak that was attached to it.

During the time the negotiations were proceeding Miss Foxell—sedately, but nevertheless elegantly dressed in black—lodged in a small private hotel in Lancaster Gate. She had the good taste not to hang around the shop; but, as days passed into weeks and weeks became a month, she developed a habit of sending over to ask Mr. Hack-bridge to drop into the hotel on his way home. She wanted to know how many customers they had served that day, whether the trade had shown any sign of falling off since Mr. Morgan's passing, and whether any new buyers had come to look over the premises.

In point of fact, Mr. Hackbridge was not anxious to see the shop sold. So long as things dragged on as they were, he was secure enough in his private room with the frost-glass door and his two hundred a year. Once a new proprietor came along he did not know what the future might hold.

And in the shop, business by now was going on pretty much as usual. In a way, indeed, there was something rather uncanny about it. Mr. Morgan was gone: the central pivot of the place had been removed, but the wheel continued to revolve just the same. Even the disturbance of Mr. Morgan's mysterious death at last subsided. The girls no longer got into little groups and whispered about it in the corners. Instead, they stood meekly behind the counter like black silk statuary and served out their ribbons and bits of stuff and fancy handkerchiefs as naturally as if at any moment the Old Gentleman himself, pink and white and smiling, might have been standing half way up the broad, curving staircase, looking down on them.

But it was John Marco who liked to stand there nowadays; stand there so that he could see the whole shop spread out at his feet like a city. Mr. Morgan had often chosen that spot for his meditations: he had stood there on and off for nearly thirty years, a small complacent God brooding over profitable retail tradings that were going on beneath him. But there was one important point of difference; one sharp dividing line in their two natures. Mr. Morgan had seen the shop as it was and been satisfied; John Marco's eyes were fixed on something that had not yet been born. When he looked, the plain wooden chairs which stood in twos beside the counter had disappeared and in their place were delicate gilt affairs with legs like spiders' and dainty wicker seats. The counters themselves were longer—nearly twice as long in fact. They stretched in an imposing line, broken only by the passage-ways to the other departments, right down to the handsome swivel doors which, every time anyone passed through them, glittered ferociously with shining plate-glass and polished brass-work. Even the space above the counters was different. It was now crossed and recrossed by a system of aerial wires along which little funicular carriages went racing with their loads of silver and small change. In fact, at those moments when John Marco stood there, he did not belong to the present at all; he had miraculously turned his back on nineteen-hundred and was peering into the heart of the impossible future of nineteen-ten.

And as a shopwalker with no counter now between him and the world he was able to indulge in his vision. In a new frock coat and glossier shoes he could afford himself this wider view. There were moments, indeed, when it seemed as though he owned the shop already; as though the counters had grown longer and the goods displayed on them more splendid. It was only the shambling, puffy figure of Mr. Hackbridge who destroyed the picture: he would go marching through the shop exacting from everyone the last morsel of respect which belongs to the chief man, and to the chief man alone, and the illusion would be shattered.

Not that Mr. Hackbridge had it all his own way: there were his worries. Miss Foxell had grown almost hysterical when she found that offers to buy her property were not forthcoming. In the dim lounge of the hotel in Lancaster Gate she would grip Mr. Hackbridge's hand which was damper than ever nowadays and beg him to find her a buyer. She said that she was simply living for the day when she could slip quietly away and go back to Cromer where she belonged. In the meantime she felt compelled to remain where she was, even though she was paying out good money all the time, just to be sure that the lawyers weren't swindling her.

But the lawyers, no matter how much they might have been ready to rob her, were not able to lay their hands on a penny with which to do so. Inside the trade, the rumours of Mr. Morgan's suicide were still circulating, and an atmosphere of doubt had got around. It was said in some quarters that Mr. Morgan had taken his life because the bank was pressing him; and gradually the flourishing retail house of Morgan and Roberts came to be regarded as a dubious property, a snare for the unwary investor. At last, even the agents became concerned. They suggested cutting the price to five thousand, then to four thousand and seven-fifty and finally to forty-five hundred. With every cut to which she agreed Miss Foxell passed through a fresh nervous crisis of hysteria. She began to suspect a conspiracy of some kind and said quite openly that she was sure that the agents were in league with the buyers.

Mr. Hackbridge sweated and protested. With his knee up against hers as they sat side by side on the sofa of the hotel he assured her that he spent every minute of his life in searching for buyers; and he almost believed it. But, in fact, with every day that passed without a single enquiry he felt more secure and contented; he now foresaw an endless idyllic existence ahead of him in which he would be able to slip out of his office at all hours of the day for little refreshers without having to glance nervously over his shoulder to see if he were observed; a future in which for ever he would be able to rest his feet which had grown tired from so much standing.

ii

When John Marco had locked up—he was the last away as usual: Mr. Hackbridge had left about five-thirty and was already seated in the lounge of the William the Fourth—he walked back to Clarence Gardens with the slow steps of a man who is not anxious to reach his home.

Once inside that massive front door he would belong to Hesther again. Her arms would go round his neck and old Mrs. Marco, watchful and apprehensive as ever, would rub her hands and look at them through eyes filled with tears to think that this fragile, ominous marriage had turned out so auspiciously after all. For Hesther made no secret of her victory. Her husband was the whole of her life now; the very centre and reason of it. She dressed to please him; did her hair to please him, spending hours before her mirror sleeking the dark heavy tresses first to one side of her head and then to the other, like a debutante; she even wore jewellery to please him despite the fact that all Amosite ministers, from the original Mr. Sturger onwards, had preached against the stuff. During the last month in particular her devotion to him had been more patent than ever. If he were so much as ten minutes late in the evenings she would be at the window as anxious and impatient as a new bride, watching for him.

He turned in at the gate, trying not to think of the kiss full on the lips which she would give him as soon as he got in. The house had not changed much since Mr. Trackett's departure; his ghost could still have wandered downstairs in the dark, crimson-papered hall and have felt at home there. For every time when Hesther had suggested that they should disperse the ghosts and have the stucco painted and the walls of the rooms re-papered, he had dissuaded her; he spoke of their capital, of the fortune that Mr. Trackett had left her, as something sacred that had to be guarded and cherished—rather in fact as Mr. Trackett himself had spoken of it. And Hesther, who while her uncle was alive, had looked forward to his death as the signal for a sudden ecstasy of spending, had at last abandoned the hope and found herself still twisting the rugs in the drawing-room this way and that in an effort to cover up the bare patches in the carpet, and going down to the kitchen to make sure that Emmy was not wasting their money below stairs.

But there was no Hesther in the hall to-night; John Marco closed the heavy door behind him, and stood for a moment in the half light that drifted in through the stained glass panels. There was the sound of voices coming from the drawing-room and as he opened the door, it was Mr. Tuke's voice that he heard.

"The reward of waiting," he was saying. "What infinite richness."

Old Mrs. Marco was sitting beside him. And they were holding hands. John Marco paused: it was obvious that he had intruded on one of Mr. Tuke's professional moments. But whatever it was, Mrs. Marco wanted him to share it. She came running up to him and threw her arms round his neck.

"Oh son, son," she said. "I'm so happy."

212

"Wonderful, indeed," Mr. Tuke repeated, getting up. "You should be a happy man, Mr. Marco. God has indeed been generous."

He spoke with more than a trace of bitterness in his voice. The man was a sinner: he stank. But this perhaps was *His* inscrutable way of saving him.

John Marco stood staring at them.

"It's Hesther," old Mrs. Marco explained. "She's just told us."

But Mr. Tuke shook his head.

"No, no," he said. "This is sacred. He must hear it from his wife's lips. We must not presume because we have been privileged."

"That's right," Mrs. Marco agreed eagerly. "Go upstairs and ask her."

Mr. Tuke placed his hand on John Marco's shoulder and almost thrust him out of his own drawing-room.

"She's waiting for you," he said. "She has news."

It was dark in the bedroom. Hesther was lying there, the blinds drawn. She called to him and, when he came over to her, she put her arms round him and pulled him towards her.

"It's happened," she said. "I saw the doctor this afternoon. Your mother went with me."

"You mean that you're going to have a child?"

She thrust up her arms trying to pull him down closer.

"It's the third month," she said. "I didn't tell you before. I wanted to be certain."

He looked down at her. There were dark lines under her eyes as though she had been sleepless. Her whole face was drawn and tired looking. In a way she looked older; but she looked happy too. He could see in the shadows that she was smiling up at him.

He paused.

213

"Do you remember your promise?" he said at last.

"What promise?"

"That if you had a child you'd give me the money?"

She did not answer. Instead, she unfastened her arms and covered her face with her hands. She was crying now.

"Is that all you have to say?" she asked. "Aren't you happy, too? Don't you love me at all? Don't you even want to kiss me?"

She turned her back on him and burying her head on her arm she lay there weeping. When at last he bent over she thrust him away from her.

iii

That same evening John Marco left the house in Clarence Gardens and turned in the direction of Lancaster Gate. He was excited and strode through the streets with his head held high. His whole future seemed to be in his pocket and, as he walked, it jangled like a bunch of keys.

Miss Foxell came down immediately when she heard that there was a gentleman to see her. At the sight of John Marco, however, she paused abruptly.

"Nothing wrong, is there?" she asked. "Nothing's happened to the shop?"

Her mind was filled with sudden terrors of fire and lapsed insurances; she saw the legacy, the fortune, everything, vanishing in vast clouds of terrifying smoke. And then she remembered that Mr. Hackbridge had assured her that the fire policy was all in order: she had been tormented by that fear before. Perhaps it was Mr. Hack-bridge himself. Had something happened to her one link with everything that Mr. Morgan had left her?

"Not Mr. Hackbridge," she said, still in the same breath.

"Not poor . . .?"

In her present mood of excitement and anxiety she looked very fragile and appealing. Her eyes, bright cornflower blue under their dark lashes, were agitated and shining.

But John Marco came straight to the point of his visit. He ignored her charms.

"I understand that you want an offer for the business," he said. "I've come to make you one."

"The business. Oh yes, the business."

Miss Foxell's white hands fluttered across her bosom. She felt perplexed and confused. Here at last was the offer that she had been waiting for, praying for. But it had come to her in a way in which she had least expected it—from her own shop-walker in fact. And he was so strange in his manner: he didn't treat her as if she were a woman at all.

"Are you ready to discuss it?" he asked.

Miss Foxell smiled.

"Well, we can't talk about it down here if that's what you mean," she replied: she was recovering herself more and more every moment. "Come upstairs and tell me about yourself."

They went into the resident's lounge of the Almeira where the palms drooped sub-tropically out of their bright brass bowls— the Almeira was of the best class—and the light filtered discreetly in through the varnish-papered windows. Miss Foxell led him towards one of the little bamboo and wicker couches with which the place was furnished.

"This is a nice surprise," she said. "Sit down and tell me all about it, Mr. . . . ."

"Marco," he told her.

She caught her breath, and her handkerchief fell unnoticed to the floor.

215

"How silly of me," she replied. "I shall be forgetting my own name next. And Mr. Hackbridge was only talking about you the other night." She paused. "It wasn't Mr. Hackbridge who sent you was it?"

Was he going to notice her handkerchief? she wondered.

John Marco narrowed his eyes until Miss Foxell looked blurred and distant, not radiant and animated and on the couch beside him.

"You haven't had many offers, have you?" he began.

She was defensive immediately.

"There were some very good enquiries," she said.

"But they came to nothing," he reminded her. "They were withdrawn before you had time to accept them."

"They weren't good enough," she answered. "I wasn't sorry to see them withdrawn."

"They were more than you'll ever get for it now," he told her brutally.

Miss Foxell folded her hands in her lap. Her small chin was set into a hard, square line and her eyes had lost some of that dewy freshness which the Old Gentleman had noticed when he first saw her.

"Hurry up and tell me what's on your mind, Mr. Marco," she said. "Perhaps we're just wasting each other's time."

John Marco smiled. He picked up the handkerchief and put it on the couch beside her.

"I've come to offer you three thousand pounds for it, just as it stands," he said.

"Three thousand pounds." She showed the whites of her eyes in horror. "Seven thousand is the price."

"It's ready money," he answered.

She shook her head.

216

"I couldn't look at it," she said. "What would the agents think?"

"They'd be glad to get their commission," he replied. "It's been on the market a long time now remember."

She got up and rang the bell.

"Will you join me in a little drink?" she asked. "What about a nice glass of port?"

John Marco shook his head.

"I'm an Amosite," he said.

Miss Foxell gave her little social smile.

"I remember now," she said. "So was Mr. Morgan. I'm Church of England myself." There was a pause while they waited for a maid to come and Miss Foxell went through a brief crisis of indecision. "Some gentlemen don't like seeing a lady drink if they're not drinking themselves," she said.

But John Marco solved the problem for her. When the maid came in he addressed her himself.

"The lady wants a port," he said. "Just one."

Miss Foxell smiled.

"You certainly know your own mind, all right," she said. She moved up a little nearer to him on the couch. "Is three thousand all you've got?"

"Three thousand is all I'm offering," he corrected her.

She remained silent for a moment and then an idea came to her.

"Why not three thousand for a half share?" she asked. "Why not you and me together?"

"I offered you three thousand for the whole business," John Marco answered. "I'm not interested in half shares."

But Miss Foxell was crying. The strain of bargaining with a man stronger than herself had been too much for her and her shoulders were shaking. She found herself at a disadvantage, however, with no handkerchief. And despite the fact that she kept indicating it with the toe of her shoe John Marco seemed incapable of noticing it a second time. In the end, she bent down and recovered it herself.

"It's so difficult for me," she said in between the sobs. "I'm only an inexperienced woman and you're a man of the world."

"I'll deal through the agents if you'd rather I did," John Marco answered.

The reply served to rouse her: she began patting at her hair.

"Why did you come here at all?" she asked. "It isn't regular you know. Did you want to come and see me?"

"I came because I wanted everything fixed up to-night," he answered.

Miss Foxell disregarded the snub. There was the light of admiration in her eyes.

"If only I'd met you before," she said. "I can see I've just been wasting my time with Mr. Hackbridge."

"Are you going to accept?" he asked.

She allowed her hand to droop until it was resting against his.

"I'll let you know in the morning," she promised.

But John Marco had already risen from his seat beside her.

"I'll give you until ten o'clock," he said.

Miss Foxell smiled up at him.

"Don't go for a minute," she pleaded. "We haven't finished." Her eyes were big and abnormally alive; the tiny mouth was quivering. "You can come up to my room," she added quietly. "We shall be quite alone there."

John Marco felt a sudden weakness run through him. Now that he was standing over her she seemed surprisingly small, small and pathetically deserted. The back of her neck was white and slender like a girl's and the hair ran in soft, sweeping waves.

Miss Foxell was holding out her hand to him. "It's only just up the first flight," she was saying.

His heart now was faster: he was in the pride of his strength. He met her eyes and saw the invitation that was there. Then he noticed her hand and stopped himself abruptly: one finger—the smallest one—was separate from all the others, raised in a little tantalising arc. Mary's finger had been raised in just that way on the first day when he had gone back home with her: the raised finger and the silver tea-pot were imprinted on his memory for ever. And with the memory of the finger came the memory of Mary as well. Her features imposed themselves for a moment on the smiling face of Miss Foxell and when they dissolved again Miss Foxell's face no longer looked as girlish and enticing: it was the eager, greedy face of a middle-aged woman who is snatching at something which every minute of life is taking away from her; the face of someone who keeps dropping her handkerchief and has an empty port-glass on the table at her side.

"Aren't you coming?"

But he only shook his head.

"You can give me your answer in the morning," he said. "You can sleep on it and let me know."

With that he picked up his hat and stick from the chair beside him and went down the broad staircase without even pausing to say good-bye.

The front of the house was in darkness when he got back; it looked cold and lifeless as he approached. But in Hesther's room the light was still burning; a pale, daffodil-coloured slit shone out across the corridor from beneath the door. He groped his way upstairs towards it.

Hesther started when she saw him. She had not heard him as he came in, and she was evidently unprepared for him. There was something guilty about her. She seemed ashamed to be seen at her own dressing-table. And then he saw how the dressing-table had been arranged. The brushes and the scent-spray and the pin-cushion had been moved to one side and the two tall candles had been lighted. The top of the dressing-table was now covered with a collection of baby-clothes. They lay there, in fleecy, tidy piles; she was gloating over them.

And already she was endeavouring to hide them, to cover them up again before he should see them. She was like a school-girl who has been disturbed playing with her dolls.

She stood there awkwardly in front of him.

"Did you get what you wanted?" she asked.

"I *shall* get it," he answered. "At the price I offered."

She turned away from him as he spoke and went on gathering up the secret hoard. He could see her face in the mirror: she was crying. After a moment he went over and put his arm round her.

"Don't cry," he said. "I'll repay you a thousandfold. We'll be rich."

But she avoided his touch and sank down on her stool in front of the dressing-table.

"Doesn't the child mean anything to you?" she asked. "Doesn't it mean anything to you at all?"

Chapter XVII

Three weeks later in the lawyer's office in Marylebone the business of Morgan and Roberts became John Marco's. The final stages seemed absurdly simple. Miss Foxell—she was still wearing black like a widow and kept pressing a handkerchief to her eyes—signed in one place, John Marco signed in another, the witnesses wrote their names, a banker's draft was passed over—and four plate glass shop windows, three waxen dummies, the fruits of Mr. Morgan's lifetime, the crammed stock-rooms, the debts, and the professional lives of twenty lady assistants and three men all magically changed hands.

At the actual moment of completion the most anxious man in London was probably Mr. Hackbridge. For no reason that he could discern, Miss Foxell had suddenly dropped him. She no longer sent for him in the evenings and she ignored his very existence. It was John Marco she asked for; and John Marco himself would say nothing. Mr. Hackbridge was afraid even to go out of the shop for a moment, and sat instead poring over piles of accounts that he could not master.

And by now the whole business was more inexplicable than ever. John Marco had sent a note round to the shop—a casual note as though he owned the place—to say that he would be absent this morning; and Miss Foxell had telephoned very curtly to ask for a pair of brass vases from the Millinery Department, which she said Mr. Morgan had promised her. Mr. Hackbridge put two and two together and did not like the total. He saw himself at fifty-four thrown suddenly onto the street with no assets but his frock coat and his striped trousers and with no living being to give him a testimonial. He sweated.

As soon as John Marco got back from the lawyer's he went straight to the Old Gentleman's room—it still seemed difficult to think of it by any other name. It was eleven o'clock, but Mr. Hackbridge was not there. At the last moment he had decided that he could stand the strain no longer without something to buck him up, and at this very minute he was gnawing his nails and drinking something short. John Marco sat himself down at the desk and began going through the papers.

They were a jumbled untidy collection; apparently Mr. Hackbridge simply emptied his pockets when he got there. Among the invoices and statements to the firm was a coal bill made out to Mr. Hackbridge, a final demand for the water-rate at twenty-seven Elzevir Road, Hammersmith, and a piece of paper with a list of football results on the back. There were also two empty bottles of pick-me-up tablets, a whisky-flask drained dry and a number of dirty pipe cleaners that had obviously been straightened out and put away for future use. John Marco was still rummaging about in all this rubbish when Mr. Hackbridge came in.

He stood in the doorway staring. His face was flushed with the high, hectic colour of dyspepsia and his hair was brushed up the wrong way like the feathers of a bird that has been caught with its back to the wind.

"What's happening here?" he began. "Who gave you permission . . ."

But John Marco interrupted him.

"Mr. Hackbridge," he said without rising from the Old Gentleman's chair, "Mr. Morgan put his business into your hands before he died, didn't he?"

"Yes, he did; and not into yours," Mr. Hackbridge replied breathing heavily.

"And you've been spending your time hanging about public houses ever since."

Mr. Hackbridge took a step forward and twitched up his sleeves at the elbows: for a moment it looked as if he were going to eject John Marco from his chair by force.

"What the Hell's that got to do with you?" he shouted.

"Only this," John Marco answered, still without raising his voice, "that now I've bought the business I shan't be requiring your services."

"You won't be requiring . . ."

Mr. Hackbridge clutched suddenly at the lapels of his coat.

"That's what I said," John Marco replied.

"But you can't mean it . . . you don't understand . . . do you realise that I've been here for eighteen years?"

"I'm sorry, Mr. Hackbridge," John Marco replied, "but it's my business now and I've decided that I can get along without you."

"Give me another chance," Mr. Hackbridge pleaded. "You won't regret it."

John Marco shook his head.

"You had your chance when the Old Gentleman died," he said.

"But I'll never get another job; not at my age."

"That's no affair of mine."

"But what about Mrs. Hackbridge? I can't let her starve."

"She's your wife, not mine," John Marco answered.

There was a pause—a long pause—and then he looked towards Mr. Hackbridge. Now that the blow had fallen Mr. Hackbridge was crying. He had sat down and was weeping. Weeping, quite openly. Large, sticky tears were running down his cheeks and onto his fine moustache. The tyrant of the front shop, the monster who walked through the departments after closing time, shouting at the assistants, was there no longer. It was this shabby, half-sick shop-walker who remained.

Mr. Hackbridge began groping in his pocket and pulled out his handkerchief: he buried his face in it. John Marco turned his back on him and walked over to the window.

What he saw held him there: he forgot all about Mr. Hackbridge. It was bright sunlight on the other side of the street, and in the sunlight two people were standing. The young man, in a rain-coat and a black bowler, was pointing at something in a shop-window, and the girl beside him, who had her hand on his arm, was nodding. The shop was a furnisher's; and it was a drawing-room suite that they were looking at. The suite was very handsome, very elegant, and in the latest Bays water style. For a moment, the couple hesitated and then, still arm in arm, they went into the shop together.

John Marco stood looking after them. It was Mary Kent and her fiancé that he had seen. And his heart had stopped for a moment at the sight. But it was not jealousy that he was suffer-ing: it was loneliness. That was happiness, real happiness, that he had been watching; and he was shut out from it. The young man had seemed so proud and confident as he stood there, and Mary had leant on his arm so trustfully. It was love that he had seen down there, and it made the good-will and the book-debts and the well-filled stock-room of this business that he had schemed and prayed for, seem suddenly empty and unimportant. It no longer appeared the kind of thing that a man might spend his whole life fretting over.

He turned and started to walk back to his desk.

And then he realised that Mr. Hackbridge was still there. His face had gone blotchy from crying and the colour had drained away from it. The corners of his mouth were working as if he were preparing to say something.

But John Marco anticipated him.

"You can stay," he said wearily. "It doesn't matter. You can stay."

Mr. Hackbridge let out a little cry and coming forward tried to shake John Marco by the hand with his cold, damp one.

ii

The change of proprietorship was discernible from the start. Even the windows looked different. The oldest of the dummies, the dowager one—was removed and a new one bought. She was a simpering little cocotte, the new one, with slanting eyes and a wealth of bright, gold hair, that Mr. Hackbridge had to dress with a pocket comb when the blinds were down. From her pedestal in the centre she delicately accosted people, and John Marco would allow only the smartest hats and the latest kind of veil to be shown on her. When fully dressed, she was the sort of thing that the Old Gentleman would never have allowed anywhere near him; and in her various stages of undress when they were arranging her, she looked positively disgraceful.

There was actually *less* in the windows nowadays. The stocking display, for instance, which hitherto had consisted of great dangling masses of them like jungle vegetation, was completely done away with. And in its place was left one pair of thin silk stockings on a couple of shapely *papier mâché* legs. People who wanted ordinary wool or cashmere had to come in and ask for them.

And there were Special Weeks and Offers and Opportunities. On one Monday, Millinery Week would start and there would be hats even in the Fancy Goods. On the following Monday there would be scarcely a hat to been seen and the shop would be devoted to blouses and shirt waists. Then in remorseless succession would occur Dress Week, Glove Week and Spring Outfitting—the labels continually being pasted onto the windows and scraped off again.

Like all revolutions, of course, the new régime produced its reactionaries. The two oldest assistants got together and complained: it was, they said, the changing about that upset them. To have graduated in Gloves and then be transferred at twenty-four hours' notice to Hosiery was something that tended to unhinge the mind. But John Marco over-ruled them, brutally and callously talked them down. And, for the simple reason that they could not afford to throw up their jobs, they allowed themselves to be persuaded; they emerged from his room, these two respectable maiden-ladies, ready to steel themselves for whatever madness the following Monday morning might bring forth. And then quite suddenly the middle-aged Miss Junip who was in charge of the corsets resigned. It was undoubtedly a loss to the firm; Miss Junip had grown up in the business and knew the busts of half Bayswater by heart. But John Marco did not hesitate. It was all over in a moment. At three-thirty one Friday afternoon

226

Miss Junip, very red in the face and with a shaking voice, said that Mr. Morgan would never have allowed her to be put upon in that way—there was now an under-vest and combination exhibition in what had hitherto been exclusively the corset salon—and that she was going to keep house for a brother in Bexhill. And at nine o'clock on the following Monday morning Miss Junip was only a memory and in her place was a dark, handsome assistant, a Madame Simone, with beautiful hands and shining, brilliantined hair. It was a startling demonstration of speed and ruthlessness; and it had its effect. There were no more complaints.

As for Mr. Hackbridge, he now worked in a frenzy of nervous energy. When shop-walking he moved with the ceaseless everlasting tread of a soldier on sentry-go and there were no more of the dartings-out for refreshers. He was even in terror lest, while actually patrolling, he should not *appear* to be doing anything. In consequence whenever John Marco saw him, he was unnecessarily re-arranging a price ticket, or opening the door for an unimportant customer, or picking up a bill which someone else had dropped. Under the strain of it all and without the constant inflow of refreshment, he was beginning to lose weight; his waistcoat sagged on him. And whenever he did pause for a moment to pass a handkerchief across his forehead he would look up only to see John Marco gazing down on him from the little landing half-way up the staircase.

It was from this landing that John Marco saw Hesther upon her first official visit. Her arrival was unexpected: she had said nothing about coming when he had left the house that morning. It was simply that the door opened and she was there. For a moment as he saw her his old feeling of uneasiness, of fear almost, returned: he gripped the balustrade and stood staring at her. The last time she had visited the shop was when she had come to deliver her ultimatum; and her entry then had been just as sudden, as startling.

But she looked strangely different now. Before, she had been pale and tense. Now she was confident and at her ease. She stood there, gazing round her with a half-smile upon her face.

Mr. Hackbridge himself did not recognise her; he selected instead another customer, an old lady in a heavy fur, for his special attention and for a moment he turned his back on Hesther. Then, when he found that she was still waiting, he came forward a second time, bowing and smiling, and asked what he could do for her. As soon as he learned the truth, Mr. Hackbridge snatched up a chair, like an acrobat arranging a stage, swept it through the air and placed it at Hesther's feet. Then he clapped his hands together.

"Tell Mr. Marco that Mrs. Marco has arrived," he said.

As he spoke he kept pulling down the waxed ends of his moustache and letting them fly up again: it was an old trick of his when he was being professionally fascinating.

But Hesther would have none of him.

"Thank you," she said. "But if you would show me the way I would rather go up myself."

"Certainly, certainly," he replied; and, removing the chair with a flourish, he led her down the aisle as though she were a bride and he conducting her to the altar. At the foot of the stairs John Marco was standing ready for them. Mr. Hackbridge withdrew backwards as from Royalty.

John Marco looked at Hesther questioningly. Inside the shop, she did not belong at all; the shop was his world.

But she was smiling again, almost as though to reassure him, and she took hold of his arm. There was something open and defiant about the geslare: it was as though in front of all the shop assistants and the customers she wanted to show that she was his wife, that his arm was there to be taken when she was in need of it. And the gesture did not pass unnoticed. The young ladies stopped selling for a moment and looked, fascinated; it was not often that salesmanship was tinged even so slightly by the disturbing element of sex. John Marco turned his back on them all and began to lead Hesther up the stairs towards his room.

When they had reached it, John Marco stepped back and let her enter. He was watching her closely now. Here, more than ever, she did not belong; it was the very centre of his separate life, this room. It expressed him. The desk was as orderly as a magistrate's; and even the little pigeon holes were labelled. The rest of the room, too, had the same unremitting air of system. The sample boxes were piled neatly by the empty fireplace and the next weeks' window cards were all set out upon a table.

He closed the door behind him and came over to her.

"Well?" he asked.

But Hesther ignored him; it was as though she had not heard him speak. She was looking round her in a critical, appraising manner, rather as a new tenant might inspect a room. Then she went over and sat down in his chair; sat down in his chair at his desk.

"So this is where you work?" she said.

John Marco paused, still eyeing her.

"You wanted to see me about something?" he asked.

She smiled at him again in that quiet, re-assuring way.

"Not you alone," she said. "I wanted to see the shop."

His heart gave a great leap at the words. For the first time in his life he found himself within an ace of loving her.

"You wanted to see the shop?" he repeated.

"That's what I came for," she answered.

"Then come out here," he said. "Come out and I'll show you."

There was something eager about him now; something that she had never been able to rouse before. He led her back onto the little landing on the stairs and threw out his hand.

"There it is," he said. "My shop."

She put her arm through his again.

"I think this is the first time I've ever seen you look happy," she said.

Chapter XVIII

It was Mr. Tuke who broke the actual date of Mary Kent's marriage. And he was quite deliberate about it. He wanted to test John Marco's guilt or innocence, to establish by his manner whether it had merely been a trick of the lamp-light or, whether on the evening after the sacred lecture, he had really seen his own chosen Elder in the arms of another woman.

They were drinking tea one Sunday afternoon in the drawing-room at Clarence Gardens when Mr. Tuke referred to it. He put down his cup and observed John Marco closely out of the corner of his eye.

"Dear Mary Kent is getting married on Tuesday," he remarked quietly.

There was a pause and, because no one added anything to the remark, he spoke again.

"At twelve o'clock," he said, not removing his gaze from John Marco's face, "Mary Kent will become Mrs. Petter."

But Mr. Tuke was defeated in his strategem. It is true that John Marco got up when he began speaking. He even put down his own cup and faced Mr. Tuke, but what he said was social and non-committal.

"You're eating nothing," he complained.

And picking up the plate of soda-cakes he passed them for the fourth time to Mr. Tuke. In his disappointment, Mr. Tuke took one; and then, because he was eating again, he had to have more tea as well. Mrs. Tuke looked at him reprovingly. Of recent months his indigestion and attacks of heartburn had been such that they were interfering seriously with his efficiency as a minister: she wished that in this direction at least his appetite could have been just a little more chastened.

It was Hesther who took up the original topic.

"Where are they going to live?" she asked.

"Still close beside us," Mr. Tuke replied. "Still in our midst. Mr. Petter is opening a business in Harrow Street."

"What sort of business?" old Mrs. Marco enquired sharply. It was her habit in conversation to fix abruptly on some minor, irrelevant detail.

"Mr. Petter is a dispenser," Mr. Tuke replied. "An apothecary."

"He means a chemist," Mrs. Tuke explained. "He's opening a chemist's shop."

"That ought to be useful to her when the baby arrives," old Mrs. Marco observed. "I used to be always round at the chemist's."

"But there's no talk of a baby," Mr. Tuke said hurriedly. "Not yet."

Old Mrs. Marco gave a little titter.

"Not yet," she observed. "But you wait."

She regarded Hesther affectionately as she spoke, running her eyes up and down her. As she grew older, Mrs. Marco was becoming appreciably more interested in babies. She referred to them as a kind of dark secret that was shared only by others of her sex; at the mere mention of an engagement her mind irresistibly fled onwards towards the accouchement. And she could not bear to let the subject drop so simply. Her mouth began working again at the corners as it always did before she spoke, and she suddenly uttered the sum of her wisdom.

"Any man that's worth his salt gives his wife a baby," she observed.

There was silence for a moment and then Mrs. Tuke coughed. But Hesther had had enough of her mother-in-law for the afternoon.

"It's your rest time," she said.

"It's always my rest time," Mrs. Marco grumbled. "It's time I was dead."

She began gathering her things obediently together, however, and waited for the visitors to come over to her chair to say good-bye to her; she had at that moment the extreme dignity which invests old age. But the dignity vanished alarmingly when she reached the door. She swung round suddenly and addressed the whole room.

"Of course there'll be a baby," she said. *"That is if he loves her"*

With that, she closed the door behind her. There was silence again in the room she had left, just as she had guessed there would be. And alone in the emptiness of the hall, old Mrs. Marco chuckled. She had never liked Mr. Tuke and she enjoyed making him uncomfortable. In her day Amosite ministers had been big, hairy men like Mr. Sturger with a whole quiverfull.

ii

On the morning of Mary Kent's wedding John Marco shut himself in his room seeing no one. Time now seemed endless as it approached this moment which he had hoped would never come. He got up and began walking backwards and forwards with short uneasy steps. It was the final betrayal, this wedding: his own marriage had destroyed half the pattern of his life and now this one was shattering what remained. Henceforth John Marco and Mary Kent would merely be two tiny points of humanity, tracing a course that led them farther and farther apart. "Some day," he told himself, "the two points of the curve will come together again: I feel it inside me." But as the idea came to him he laughed at it. The plan of his own life was simple enough now: he saw it stretching away into the future, the steadily rising arc of a merchant's destiny. It pointed upwards towards heights that Mary Kent would never know. She, too, had chosen; but she had chosen more humbly.

He paused for a moment in his stride and looked at his watch: it showed fifteen minutes past eleven. For an instant his heart missed its beat. At this moment Mary Kent would be putting on her wedding dress in that high bedroom in Abernethy Terrace; she would be sleeking her pale gold hair ready for the veil. (There was a knock on the door and Mr. Hackbridge's thick voice reported that Messrs. Fawcett's traveller was there with a special line of taffetas; John Marco replied through the closed door that he could not be disturbed and went over and stood by the window looking out into the street.) She would be wearing white and there would be a sheaf of lilies in her hand; the heads of the lilies would be resting against her bosom. He picked up a letter from his desk and began to read it: it was a letter of complaint from an important customer—the sort of thing that he usually answered the same morning in his own hand—but to-day he threw it down again unfinished. And orange blossom too; she would be wearing a wreath of orange blossom across her forehead.

He could not bear to look at his watch again: the hour was too near now. But there was a clock which stood on the mantelshelf; it was impossible to work while that was accusing him. Without looking at the hands he went and turned its face to the wall. Then, in that room that was devoid of time and cut off completely from the world, he began to work. At eleven-thirty he was bent over his desk engrossed in a pile of invoices and statements, bills of delivery and credit notes, offers of settlement-discount and manufacturers' specifications, and the whole miscellaneous jumble of paper which comprises the mad world of business. At eleven-forty-five he was still working, carefully ticking through each item as he attended to it.

But at ten minutes to twelve the room was empty: John Marco was striding down Paddington Grove towards the Tabernacle.

His mind cleared as he walked. To see it happen, actually to be there when the ring was placed on her finger: that was the only way of resolving this conflict. Then, having lost everything, having watched himself lose it, he would be able to walk out of the Tabernacle again, a free man, with only the future, and not the past as well, to contend with.

At the end of Chapel Walk he held back for a moment, fearful suddenly that he might been seen. But it was twelve o'clock already and the guests had all passed inside. The road looked empty and ordinary as though nothing were happening there; even the crowd that collects to see every bride had dispersed.

Squaring his shoulders he walked boldly up to the Chapel and mounted the high flight of steps. In the porch, however, the verger met him; he seemed excited and agitated.

"Come on in, Mr. Marco," he said. "You're missing it. I was just closing the doors."

He put his arm behind John Marco as he spoke and tried to force him inside. But John Marco shook his head.

"I'm going up into the gallery," he said.

"But you'll never see the bride from there," the verger replied hoarsely. "Not right from the gallery."

"I shall see all that I want to see," John Marco answered, and he began to climb the dark flight that twisted upwards into the ceiling.

The Amosite Chapel was the tallest in Paddington and John Marco was out of breath when he reached the narrow landing and pushed open the baize door of the gallery. The gallery itself was in darkness but the body of the Chapel was lighted: it shone up at him like a stage. Groping his way down the tiers, he slid into the front pew and, gripping the rail in front of him, stared down into the arena.

But now that he was there, the scene before him no longer seemed real. It was an actor playing the part of Mr. Tuke who was standing before the plain wooden altar; and it was a toy bridegroom that he had beside him. Even Mr. Kent, smothered in an unaccustomed frock-coat, looked imaginary; and Mrs. Kent, passing a lace handkerchief across her eyes, was a figure in a play.

There was one person, however, who was still real; and for a moment John Marco could not bear to look at her. She was sitting very upright on the high stool that was reserved for the bride. But even across the width of the Tabernacle he could see that she was pale, just as she had been on the evening of her Baptism. The whiteness of her dress and the sheaf of lilies that she was carrying filled the air around her with light. She was the one bright, living thing in that looming Chapel. Across her forehead and over her golden hair was a wreath of orange blossom.

Mr. Tuke was praying now. There was a shuffling among the scattered rows of congregation and they all got down onto their knees. Instinctively, John Marco covered his face with his hands.

But it was not in Mr. Tuke's prayer that he was sharing. "Oh God, God," he was beseeching, "rid my heart of all sinful lusts and vain longings. Let me forget this woman. Make me not wanton, sensual, having not the spirit. Give me strength to crucify the flesh in Thy name. . . ." Mr. Tuke, however, had stopped. His hands were raised in benediction over Mary Kent and Thomas Petter. John Marco closed his eyes. And when he opened them again, the ring was on her finger and the little company of players were going through into the vestry to sign the register.

He waited, knowing that they would come back, that in coming back they would pass close beneath him. The aisle ran right under him, and the front of the gallery was not more than ten feet over it at that point. He would be able to catch one last glimpse of her then that would have to satisfy him for the rest of time.

It was a burst from the organ that roused him and he saw her approaching. Her hand was on Thomas Petter's arm now but he did not notice him. His eyes were fixed on Mary. She was paler even than before; she came down the aisle like a ghost. And as she drew nearer he could see that there were tears on her cheeks; her lashes glistened. The sight overcame him. He no longer sat back, huddled in the darkness of the gallery. He leant forward instead, his forehead pressed against the iron bar that ran in front of him. His hands were tightly clenched and he was breathing quickly and unevenly.

Then, just as she was about to pass beneath him, she raised her head and her eyes met his. For a second she paused and the two of them, Mary Kent and John Marco, were alone together in the Tabernacle; and through her tears, he saw that she was smiling. John Marco half rose to his feet and bringing his hand to his mouth he threw a kiss.

When he sat back he was weak and trembling. That kiss would remain his secret, his secret and Mary's, until they died. For, when the others had looked upwards, too, following Mary's gaze, they had seen nothing but the sweep of scrolled woodwork and the curving iron bar.

He sat there in the half-light until the slam of the door told him that the last of the congregation had passed out. Then, on tiptoe, he rose and followed them. But as he turned he saw something that made him stop and step back a pace.

Three rows behind him, in the corner of one of the high pews, Hesther was sitting; there was a crumpled handkerchief in her hand which she kept pressed up against her face.

iii

That night when he returned home was the first for months that Hesther was not waiting for him. Instead, she was sitting alone in the drawing-room her hands folded in her lap. She seemed indifferent, and scarcely looked up when he entered. Already, the child within her had changed her figure; she was heavy and gross. And she filled the whole room with defeat.

He stood there regarding her. Was she going to say anything? he wondered. But a sudden knocking on the ceiling interrupted him. There were three hard knocks followed by a volley of short, irritable ones. He knew the signal well: it was Mrs. Marco from the luxury of her bedroom sending down a summons for her son.

When he got upstairs, however, he did not go in to the old

lady immediately. The door in front of him was open and he was aware that the bedroom—his bedroom and Hesther's—was, somehow different; it had been re-arranged. In front of the cupboard that had been his there now stood a tall, cheval glass and his round cardboard hat-box was missing. There was an empty space on top of the wardrobe where it had always stood.

He paused for a moment and then crossed the corridor and went into the small dressing-room that he had occupied before. He saw that it was now furnished again. On the table in front of the mirror his brushes and combs were set out. The cardboard hat-box was standing in the corner.

It was old Mrs. Marco who explained things to him. She was sitting up among the pillows in a profusion of shawls and bed-jackets and she waved a hooked hand in his direction.

"Don't take any notice of what's happened," she said in a high breathless rush. "It doesn't mean anything. Women get like that when they're expecting. Everything'll be all right. She'll want you back again. Everything'll be all right."

She kept repeating it as he stood there, as though desperately striving to re-assure herself as well. In her heart she felt frightened and bewildered: no sooner had her children built up their house than it had come crashing down again.

"Go downstairs and pet her a bit," she advised. "Bring her some flowers. Why don't you buy her something special to eat? Everything'll be all right again, I tell you."

She lay back and closed her eyes. It was all so different from what it had been like when she was a girl. Husbands and wives hadn't gone about shutting themselves away from each other then; Mr. Marco had been in the big double bed beside her two hours before her son was born. Marriage had been marriage in those days.

Downstairs, John Marco faced Hesther across the wide dining-table. It was a grim, silent meal; they scarcely raised their eyes from above their plates. And when the meal was over Hesther rose from her chair without speaking and left him. He heard her go up to her room and close the door behind her. But he sat on, staring through the window at the blank faces of the houses opposite. He was still there when Emmy, impatient at being kept waiting any longer, cleared away the rest of the china and silver, leaving him seated there at the head of the table like the host at a vanished banquet.

It was already late. Very soon it would be night-time. And it was only now that he was tasting the real bitterness of having lost Mary for ever. At this very moment another pair of arms would be round her, other fingers loosening the tresses of her hair. Because he could bear it no longer he pushed his chair back from the table and went blindly upstairs to his room.

But he had still not escaped from himself. The same pictures and images came crowding in. And in the surrounding darkness, he and not Thomas Petter was the bridegroom; it was he who saw Mary's white form in the shadows, felt her breath upon his cheek.

A clock struck somewhere and he roused himself: it was midnight. He went over and stood at the open window gazing down into the street. The street was bare and deserted; it slept.

At that moment he might have been the last man in London contemplating the empty pavements of a ruined city.

Chapter XIX

To the west, the shop next door to Morgan and Roberts' was a gentleman's outfitters. It was a dignified, rather shabby kind of shop. The gilt lettering on the front had tarnished and come loose in places and the window blind was generally caught up at one corner as though it were someone slovenly and impatient who had lowered it. But the shop did a good enough business in its way, not so much in the large things of life as in oddments like braces, collars, and false cuffs. Occasionally too, someone would buy a raincoat or a Norfolk jacket; and when that happened Mr. Skewin, the proprietor, would feel that trade was showing signs of improvement and that it would only be a matter of months, perhaps even weeks, before he could afford to have the whole shop front properly done up again. He was an Amosite himself and his faith had reconciled him to adversity.

The consciousness of those faded premises next door had begun to obsess John Marco. Whenever he was not working, he was thinking about them. Even the architecture was the same; they were really one building already. On the blotting paper of his pad he had made innumerable small drawings of an enlarged Morgan and Roberts, an imposing frontage of five plate-glass windows instead of four. Sometimes, too, he allowed his pencil to run on, sketching in the shadowy outlines of other windows, other entrances. He had only to close his eyes a little to see a shop-front so long that no sign-writer could devise one set of lettering to cover the whole of it; so long that the name would have to be repeated time and time again, like a chorus.

A week ago he had made the first tentative approaches to Mr. Skewin; and Mr. Skewin, in his shiny suit with the cuffs all frayed and serrated at the edges, had turned him down. He had listened attentively to his visitor in the gloomy interior of his shop into which no important customer ever came, and had smiled a sad incredulous smile and shaken his head. It was exciting, of course, and rather flattering to be offered money for his business; but it was also deeply terrifying. It would mean starting again. And he knew that he was not the sort of man to change; not the sort to endure the anguish of launching out afresh.

Besides he was really very comfortable where he was. He was accustomed to unsuccess, and the bare patches in the oil-cloth and the broken roller blind held no shame for him. So he merely gave a little bow and went on with his work as though a little resentful that he should have been interrupted: he was industriously writing out his own price tickets on small oblongs of cardboard which he snipped off old boxes carefully kept back for the purpose.

After his dismissal, John Marco left Mr. Skewin for a time severely alone: the man was untemptable. Like a lay saint, money meant nothing to him. John Marco put all thoughts of gentlemen's outfitting out of his head and buried himself in the management of what he already possessed.

Then he saw something that set the notion raging inside his brain again. There was a "To Let" notice pasted across the shop next door to Mr. Skewin's. The shop had been a stationer's once; the windows had always been full of die-stamps and boxes of envelopes and picture postcards. Only the sudden death of the proprietor—pneumonia, it was: two days, not more—had thrown the shop into the market; and the rival stationer's opposite had bought up everything, the lease, the stock, the book debts and the prized lists of printed note-paper customers. As a shop, the stationer's was admittedly no more than second-rate; it was really on the lock-up level. But to John Marco it was everything: he saw it as his first colony.

The rest of Paddington and Bayswater, however, saw it too; the Terrace was one of the classic shopping thoroughfares of the district and any business there had its place in the sun. A dozen other acquisitive tradesmen were after the shop within twenty-four hours.

John Marco watched them with amusement as they came and stood outside the premises and then went into the agents' opposite to ask for the keys. He could afford to be amused. For at two minutes past nine on the morning when the board had been put up he had gone into the agents himself and had accepted their terms.

He had the lease in his hands at that moment. And as he read it he smiled. It was all so pathetically silly, so lamentably wide of the mark. The lawyers who had drawn it up had stipulated that in no shape or form should it re-open as a stationer's shop; and they went on, after the manner of their kind, to define what a stationer's shop was, ingeniously countering the possible evasions one by one. John Marco shook his head at their innocence; if they thought that he wanted to waste time on stationery they were wrong. He had other and more sensational plans in mind.

A month later, when the front had been decorated and the sign board re-painted in distinctive style, John Marco opened the shop as a gentleman's outfitters.

ii

On the day after the opening John Marco returned home to find the house in chaos.

At the sight of him, old Mrs. Marco uttered a shrill cry of relief.

"Come on in, son," she cried. "It's Hesther. She's just on her time."

John Marco slowly undid the buttons of his long great-coat.

"Has the doctor come?" he asked.

"I've sent for him," old Mrs. Marco went on. "He was having his supper but he'll be round at once."

"Is the nurse there?"

"She came at lunch-time," old Mrs. Marco answered. "But she's no good," she added in a whisper. "She's too young. I shall have to look after things myself."

John Marco left her and began to mount the stairs. On the landing the nurse met him. She had that startling appearance of cleanliness which is common to all nurses; under her stiff cap her hair might have been starched too. She gave John Marco a quick mechanical smile.

"She's been asking for you," she said. "You can go straight in."

The bedroom, with only Hesther in it, looked very large; and Hesther in the wide double bed, very small. She had obviously been suffering and the lines in her face had deepened. She looked older. Strands of silver showed up in the heavy coil of her hair and her hands were thin and blue-veined. She beckoned him to come over.

"I want to talk to you," she said.

He pulled up a chair and sat down at her bedside.

"Mr. Tuke was here this afternoon," she said. "We've been praying."

John Marco nodded. Ever since Hesther had expected this child, she had been growing steadily more and more religious. She spent most of her time nowadays reading her Bible. And she read it greedily, anxiously, as though searching for some crumb of comfort amid that heaped-up mass of words. As he sat there he could see a book of Mr. Sturger's sermons on the table beside her.

"Did the prayer help?" John Marco asked.

And then quite suddenly a feeling—half of shame, half of tenderness—came to him. It was *his* child that Hesther was bearing; she had the right for his love and protection at this moment. He leant forward and began stroking the pale hand on the counterpane.

"Don't worry," he added. "It'll be all right. He's a good doctor."

Hesther turned for a moment and looked full at him, her dark intense eyes staring into his. Then she drew her hands away.

"It wasn't for me or for the child that we were praying/' she said.

"You mean that you were praying for me?" he asked.

"Yes," she replied quietly. "We prayed that your heart might be opened."

"Opened for what?" he asked: he was sitting back now, looking at her.

"For love," she answered. "No one can love if his heart is divided."

"So you told him about us?"

"Not more than he knew already. He knew all the time that you didn't want this child."

John Marco paused.

"I shall be a good father to it," he said. "You need have no fear about that."

"How can you be?"

"I shall give it everything," he said.

"You mean money?" she asked.

John Marco nodded.

"Money is not the spirit," she told him. "A child can grow up poor among riches."

"But how do you know I shan't love this child?" he asked. "Most fathers love their children."

"How can you love it?" she asked. "How can you, if you don't love me?"

The nurse entered carrying a basin with a towel spread over it. She came over and placed her hand on Hesther's forehead.

"Have the pains come back?" she asked.

Hesther shook her head.

"Not yet," she said.

"Well just ring the bell when they do," she said placidly. "I shall only be in the next room."

She spoke of pain with a kind of easy familiarity, as something that came and went away again and did not matter. At the door she stopped and smiled that bright, mechanical smile over her shoulder.

"Just you have a nice comfortable gossip with your husband," she said. "It's what husbands are for."

When she had gone Hesther turned to John Marco again. Her voice was different now: it was calmer.

246

"What's this new shop you've opened," she asked. "Why didn't you tell me?"

He looked at her in surprise; she had not been out of the house since the shop was opened.

"Who told you about it?" he asked.

"Mr. Tuke," she said. "Mr. Skewin went to him."

John Marco raised his eyebrows.

"What did he say?"

"He told Mr. Tuke that you were ruining him. He said that it wasn't right for an Elder to treat one of the brethren in that way."

John Marco gave a little laugh.

"He said that, did he?" He paused and thrust his hands into his pockets. "Anyhow it shows that he understands."

"But he's an old man. He's not strong enough to fight you."

"I gave him the alternative," he said. "He wouldn't accept it."

Hesther lay back and a flicker of pain passed across her face.

"Why *can't* you be satisfied?" she asked. "Why can't you be content with what you've got?"

She did not speak again for some time and they sat there in silence. Then she drew her lips in sharply.

"You'd better send for the nurse," she said. "I think it's time."

He got up to ring the bell and then came back to the bed and stood over her. She was paler now and there were tiny beads of sweat standing out along her forehead. Bending down he rested his arms on the pillow and kissed her. For a moment she lay motionless and then she gripped his two hands and hugged them to her. But she released them again almost as suddenly.

"Oh, John, John," she said. "If only you meant it, if only this were real."

Tears began to gather in her eyes and trickle clumsily down

her cheeks. When the nurse saw them she gave a little under-standing nod.

"Soon be over now, dear," she said. "The doctor's just coming up. We're all ready for him."

She smiled across at John Marco.

"We shall have some news for you next time we see you," she said.

Downstairs old Mrs. Marco was in a state; she was offended. She was sitting huddled up in one of the big chairs in the drawing-room rocking herself backwards and forwards in vexation.

"He wouldn't let me go up to her," she complained. "He said that he could manage with the nurse." She came over and put her hand on John Marco's arm. "But don't you go getting your-self worked up about it," she said. "You come and eat something. It'll take your mind off it."

And once they were in the dining-room old Mrs. Marco began to enjoy herself. She was usually in bed before this; and she knew it. In her present freedom, with Hesther out of the way, she was like a child that has stayed up beyond its bed-time. There was a kind of guilty delight about her.

"It'll be a long time as it's her first," she said gloatingly. "She'll probably be bad with it: they may need me there before they're through." She paused and some remote trigger was released in her mind. "Your father had to be carried upstairs the night after you were born," she said. "He'd been out at a dinner of the Lodge. He was very highly thought of inside the Order."

They ate in silence for a few minutes and then Mrs. Marco rang the bell. But it was not for Emmy to clear away; old Mrs. Marco had just conceived a very special purpose for her.

248

"Go upstairs, Emmy, and see if you can hear anything," she said. "Just hang about on the landing and find out what's going on."

There was an interval of some five minutes and then Emmy returned.

"I couldn't hear anything," she said. "Just the three of them talking."

Old Mrs. Marco's look of exultation broadened.

"What did I tell you?" she said. "I knew it would be a long one."

Then, satisfied that everything was going according to plan—her plan—of things, Mrs. Marco resumed her meal. She ate quickly and noisily as though afraid that at any moment the climax might be upon them, and she not ready for it. In her excitement she could not bear even to sit properly on her chair. She was just balanced on the edge of it, ready to dash upstairs if anything important were to happen. Thus, when the nurse came down for a moment for some more hot water, Mrs. Marco was able to dart out and intercept her. But the result was purely negative. The old lady came back and put her hand on John Marco's arm again.

"It'll be some time," she said. "Dr. Preece is going to wait."

John Marco looked at her in disgust: she was so obviously enjoying every minute of it.

A mood of bitterness came over him.

"I'm going out," he said. "I shall come back when it's all over."

She smiled.

"That's right, son," she said. "You keep out of the way. You leave all this to me."

She was impatient for him to be gone. With him out of the

way and no one but the doctor or the nurse to stop her she had every hope that somehow or other she would manage to insinuate herself into the birth-chamber. It was maddening not to know what mysteries that closed bedroom door was concealing.

iii

When John Marco left the house he walked back slowly towards Tredegar Terrace. It was not the first time that he had been there late at night, not the first time that he had thrown open the big plate glass door and stepped into the shrouded silence of the empty shop. The sense of possession was at its fullest then. It was something to stand alone amid the show cases, looking along the bare perspective of the counters, with the chairs in twos piled on them in readiness for the cleaners in the morning, and know that everything within touch, within sight, and out of sight as well in the stock-room downstairs, belonged to him. It seemed, at those moments, as though the business had a brooding secret existence of its own. The ten hours a day that it was open were only a part of it. At night the handsome mahogany staircase still curved upwards, and there was still the gleam of mirror and brasswork in the darkness.

To-night, however, he went straight to his room, and shut himself in. There was work to do in plenty; there always was. There were the endless catalogues from the wholesalers—the whole of next season's profits were hidden somewhere beneath their shiny corners, and there was a fortune to be made simply by going through them. But that kind of work was impossible this evening: whenever he cleared his mind for a moment he saw the tired, suffering face of Hesther before him. If only somehow he could have loved her, if only somehow her suffering had meant anything to him, it would all have been so easy. Not that it was her fault any longer. She had tried; had tried *hard* to be a wife to him. It was only he who had not been ready to accept. That day when she had come down to the shop had been her last, pathetic effort to enter into his life. Even the child would not bring them together now: he knew that. It would simply serve to remind him more bitterly how inextricable was the net in which he was entangled.

It was very close in the room; a heavy, drowsy stillness hung over it. Except for an occasional cab, there was no sound of traffic from the road below. He looked up once or twice at the clock on the mantelpiece. First it showed nine o'clock, and then ten. The pile of catalogues on his desk had grown smaller, there was a sheet of paper beside him now covered with jottings. Finally he pushed the last of the pile away from him. It was ten-thirty now. But it was still too early to return: he would go back when it was over. It was Hesther's destiny, this; not his; he could not help her by being near.

Sliding lower into his chair he closed his eyes and waited.

The landscape around him was golden; and corn, waist-high and red with poppies, was brushing against them as they walked. In front, there was the sea, a great sweeping arc of it. Small ships dotted it and a flock of sea birds wheeled overhead like butter-flies. It was Mary who was beside him, her hair loose flowing to her waist; the wind was teasing it, blowing tresses of it across his face and into his eyes. Because they were happy they started running; hand in hand they raced down the poppy-track towards the shore. Then as soon as they had reached the dunes and it was soft beneath their feet, they threw themselves down together and he held her in his arms and poured hot handfuls of sand over her bare feet. He felt younger, and Mary beside him was younger, too; they were like children as they played together. There was a boat pulled up along the surf-line, and Mary went over to it while he lay back idly watching her. The thought came suddenly into his mind as he lay there that he should go to her, should warn her of the depths that lay beyond. And as he watched her, he saw her climb into the boat which was now bobbing lightly on the tide. He got to his feet and started to run forward. But the sand was fine and powdery; it crumbled away beneath him. And, when he had reached the surf, the boat was already drifting out of reach. He heard Mary call something to him that he could not catch and he plunged into the water and began to swim. The sun by now had retreated; it was hidden somewhere behind a cloud. The whole of nature had gone suddenly cold and there was an undercurrent that was sucking him away from her. But he was a powerful swimmer; with deep steady strokes he overcame the current and pressed on. Yet the boat out-distanced him. It was a score of yards away by now and heading straight for the open sea. He swam harder, his heart pounding against his ribs. But, when next he looked, he could see that Mary was no longer alone. There was a man in the boat and he was rowing; with every pull of the oars the boat was growing smaller and more indistinct. Only Mary was still visible. She was sitting in the stern and in the crook of her arm she held a child. With her free hand she was waving, waving. And there were rocks, sharp, ugly ones in his way. The surge threw him against them; his knees and fingers were bleeding and the salt water stung them. And, when he looked again, Mary and the boat had disappeared. The sea was empty to the horizon.

He woke sweating. His legs were doubled under him in the chair and the room was in darkness. For a moment he sat there, dazed and uncertain. Then he rubbed his limbs back into circulation and struck a match. The clock on the mantelpiece showed two o'clock.

Old Mrs. Marco was still sitting up for him; with Hesther out of the way she was stretching her freedom to its limits. As soon as she heard his key in the lock she came groping her way towards him.

"Where have you been?" she cried.

He stood there, staring at her.

"What's happened?" he asked. "Is it over?"

"It's a boy," she answered. "It's a boy. He's just like you."

"Was it bad?" he asked. "Did . . . did it hurt her?"

"She's all right now," Mrs. Marco told him. "She's been asking for you." She came up close and squeezed his arm. "You want to see your son, don't you?"

"Not now," he said, his mind still full of the memory of the dream. "Don't disturb her. I'll see him in the morning."

Chapter XX

Mr. Skewin 's decaying business survived the opposition for the brief period of six months; and then it collapsed. The end came sooner than John Marco had expected. One morning the crooked blind simply remained lowered, and the shop was closed. The battle in retail hosiery was over.

There had, of course, been indications for some time that the climax was approaching. For the last few weeks Mr. Skewin had made no pretence of selling anything. He merely stood in the shabby doorway of his shop, watching himself being ruined. Occasionally he would mooch along and remain gazing into his rival's window, a look of fixed helplessness on his face. There was nothing that he could do about it. Ever since he had been in Tredegar Terrace he had managed to pay his way like any other business man by putting threepence on this and twopence half-penny on that. But now the shop next door had taken sixpence off everything.

Its stock, too, was new; there was, for instance, an entire window filled with fashionable ties that sold themselves simply by being shown. Mr. Skewin's own stock of ties had most of them been with him for years; he had displayed them knotted high up on the narrow part when the mode in knots was small, and knotted in great loops down at the wide end when the mode had swerved towards the Byronic. He had shown them with imitation pearl pins stuck in the middle of the knot and he had shown them without. He had spread them out in rows so that the richness of the material could be seen, and had bunched them together until the patterns merged—and for all the good it had done him he might as well have left them in the boxes they had come in.

At eleven o'clock on the morning of the closure, Mr. Skewin sucked in his lips and came over to see John Marco. It was his wife who had sent him; and he was a reluctant and resentful visitor. He entered the shop very upright and diffident, like a defeated general come to surrender his sword.

And John Marco kept him waiting for nearly half-an-hour before he had him shown into the private office.

"Yes, Mr. Skewin," he said as he entered, "you want to see me?"

He spoke as though he had no notion at all of the object of Mr. Skewin's visit.

Mr. Skewin drew himself up for a moment and then subsided. It was no use trying to appear strong and dignified when the mantelpiece in the little parlour above the shop was littered with final demands—horrible things printed across in red. So he just sat down on the chair facing John Marco and threw in his hand.

"You wanted to buy my business," he said. "Well I'm ready to sell."

John Marco did not reply immediately. And he avoided looking in Mr. Skewin's direction. He could not afford to begin feeling sorry for the man: he did not want a second Mr. Hackbridge on his hands.

"I'm sorry," he said. "But it's no use to me. You see I've got my own outfitting business now."

"No use to you!" Mr. Skewin repeated the words incredulously. "You mean you don't want it?"

John Marco nodded.

"I gave you your chance," he said. "You turned it down."

"But it was all that I had," he exclaimed. "It was my living."

As Mr. Skewin spoke, the vision of those bills grew larger; his head swam. He seemed suddenly to be caught up in a mass of whirling papers from which the words "Last Notice", "Within seven days . . . ", "Attention of our solicitors" danced before his eyes like fireflies. He made one last effort.

"What about my good-will?" he asked again.

John Marco still did not raise his eyes above his desk.

"There isn't any," he said quietly. "Not now."

"And the stock. Do you mean to say that isn't worth anything."

"Not to me," John Marco answered. "It's a different class of business."

"In that case," said Mr. Skewin rising from his chair and clasping his two hands together because they were trembling, "we're just wasting each other's time. I might as well be going."

John Marco let him get as far as the door and then called him back.

"One moment, Mr. Skewin," he said. "What about the lease? I might be able to take that off your hands."

"There's seven years to run," Mr. Skewin said bitterly. "Seven years from Christmas."

"That wouldn't worry me," John Marco replied; "not if the rent was right."

"It's a hundred a year," said Mr. Skewin. "Two pounds a week for the shop and the rooms above."

John Marco tapped his fingers on the desk.

"It's too much," he said. "I only pay ninety-five for the other shop." He paused. "But if it's any help to you I'll take it over. When can I have possession?"

"Possession?"

Mr. Skewin did not seem able to comprehend the word. He just stood there with his lips moving and no sound coming from them.

"I suppose you could move in at once," he said at last, in a limp crushed voice that faded away on his lips. "We shan't be stopping."

"I shan't need the rooms above, at once," John Marco said slowly. "The shop will need doing up first."

"As you please," said Mr. Skewin wearily. "It won't be any concern of mine."

John Marco rose and held out his hand. But Mr. Skewin ignored it. His eyes had become very moist and his lower lip was quivering.

"You're a hard man," he blurted out suddenly. "A very hard one."

John Marco regarded him coldly, running his eye up and down him as he stood there.

"I don't understand you, Mr. Skewin," he replied.

"Oh yes, you do," Mr. Skewin answered. "You understand perfectly. You tried to squeeze me out of business and you succeeded."

John Marco laughed. A brief, unsmiling laugh.

"I might have been the one to fail," he said. "I took the risk. You didn't."

But Mr. Skewin did not appear to be listening. He went straight on as though John Marco had not spoken.

"A fellow Amosite, too," he was saying. "One of the Brethren."

"I don't mix religion with business," John Marco answered.

He turned his back on Mr. Skewin as he said it and walked over towards the window. But Mr. Skewin followed him until he was only a step behind.

"That's your fault," he said. "You ought to mix religion with everything." He spoke as an elderly man addressing a young one: he was the evangelist now and not the petitioner. "You're shutting God out of your life, Mr. Marco, that's what you're doing." He raised his forefinger and tapped John Marco on the shoulder. "Why don't you draw back before it's too late?" he said. "Why don't you go down on your knees and pray? If you persist you'll find yourself pierced through with many sorrows."

John Marco turned on him. His face was flushed and angry.

"Do you want to dispose of your lease or don't you?" he demanded.

But again Mr. Skewin did not seem to hear him. His mind was continuing on another and a different level, the level of Mr. Surger and the Apostle Paul, of Mr. Tuke and the blessed St. James. Sixty years of Amosism had left its mark.

"Perilous times shall come," he threatened. "Don't forget what the Bible says about men who love themselves, covetous, boastful. Start weeping and howling for your miseries that shall come upon you. You'll find that your riches are corrupted and your garments are moth eaten. . . ."

John Marco turned and walked past him.

"Go back to your shop," he ordered. "I won't listen to you."

"That's what Mr. Tuke said about you," Mr. Skewin replied. "He said that you'd closed your ears to the Voice."

John Marco was at the door now: he was holding it open for Mr. Skewin. His moment of anger had ebbed away again, leaving

258

him cold and self-controlled.

"He said that, did he?" he remarked quietly. "Then I shall tell Mr. Tuke to hold his tongue."

Mr. Skewin's exhibition of feeling had been pathetically foolish of course. To have said anything at all in the circumstances was a simply appalling blunder; a blunder that no man of the world could possibly have committed, and it was one that drove Mrs. Skewin nearly frantic when she heard of it. But Mr. Skewin was not a man of the world: that was the whole point. He was an Amosite. He had nothing in the world to gain and everything to lose by saying anything; and his words in consequence had a disembodied, impersonal ring about them. Despite the fact that they were uttered in a small, choking voice, it was as though the Bible itself, open at the Epistles, had spoken and been wise.

Throughout the afternoon John Marco kept recalling stray sentences that Mr. Skewin had spoken. "Weep and howl for your miseries that shall come upon you": he had heard that so many times; it was one of Mr. Tuke's favourite pieces. John Marco remembered suddenly with sinister vividness those rich men whose flesh was going to be devoured by the fiery rust of the tarnished gold and the cankering silver. And he realised with a sudden sickness close to his heart that he was a rich man himself now. But St. James could not have meant quite that—not industrious shop-keepers, not honest men who worked for their livings. He was thinking of the great sultans of this world whose souls are mortgaged to their treasures. St. James could never have intended his words for one of the Brethren. Then the sound of his own words, "I don't mix religion with business," came back to him. They did not sound like the words of one who had been an Amosite, and he halted. John Marco was still sufficiently a

259

son of the Tabernacle not to question that the Devil could sometimes put such a sentence into men's mouths.

But he thought of other rich men who had apparently defied
salvation and got away with it, and his mind felt easier. There
were good and bad among the rich just as there were among the
poor: there must be. It couldn't be *all* rich men who were
condemned, or Bayswater would simply collapse of its own iniquity and Paddington be saved. And it was a part of his destiny to
be rich. The commercial grave of Mr. Skewin was merely the
first milestone on the way. There would be other Mr. Skewins
who would have to be sacrificed before he finally got there; other
Miss Foxell's to be outwitted before he reached Jerusalem. And,
as he left the shop that night, he did not doubt that he could pass
all the rivers of commerce one by one as he came to them.

ii

It was a golden evening. The sun, setting somewhere amid the
houses behind Notting Hill, was lighting up the tops of the build-
ings like a line of bonfires and casting a glow of amber into the
street below. The whole air was bright; and Tredegar Terrace,
with its long line of windows, was like a hall of mirrors in Heaven.

The street that ran off it—Lexington Street—was a poorer
affair altogether; it was the trading place of the lesser kind of
shopkeepers—greengrocers, dairymen, confectioners. The last
shop of all was a photographer's; a black velvet curtain ran across
the back of the window and against this the specimens of the
craftsman's art were arranged. There were wedding groups,
freshly christened infants and the studio portraits of plump young
ladies. John Marco noticed the shop with a kind of pitying
contempt; it was so small, so undistinguished, and tucked so far

away down the wrong kind of thoroughfare. From time to time a new photograph was put in the window as a kind of token that business was still flourishing. But in the ten years in which he had passed it he had never seen anyone going in or coming out of it. And they were always the same, these photographs; the same groups, the same infants, the same young ladies.

But to-night John Marco stopped suddenly as he passed the shop. There *was* a new picture there. It was a wedding group again; but not an ordinary one. This time it was of Mary's wedding.

It was not even, as such photographs go, a particularly good one; it teased the sitters. Against the lattice background of the studio, the guests all wore the startled expressions of people astonished at finding themselves being photographed at all. The faces were simply so many caricatures in sepia; the staring eyes of the gentlemen popped up over the unaccustomed high collars, and the bridegroom's hat was upside down on the floor beside him, with the fingers of his yellow gloves protruding like the pincers of a hermit crab. Only Mary remained as he remembered her. She was sitting with her hands folded in her lap staring straight at the camera; staring straight into it and beyond, it seemed to him.

John Marco stood gazing at the photograph. All his dreams and ambitions lay broken somewhere within the confines of the frame. A strange feeling of remoteness came over him. There on that glossy oblong of paper was imprisoned one life; here on the other side of the shop window he was in the middle of another. And in a way-it was this photograph that seemed to make it final and irretrievable. What he had seen from the gallery of the Tabernacle that day was only transient; the image on paper before him was enduring. Future generations could look on it and see how Mary Kent and Thomas Petter had become man and wife. It was an unfading statement of a world to which he did not any more belong.

He glanced up and down the street and then entered the shop. The door gave a little silly ping in his face and he found himself in the cheap painted interior. There was a pause and then the proprietor himself appeared in a brown velvet coat. He wore the professional expression of someone so artistic that he would have to go almost into a trance before he could bring himself to release the shutter. But a thick streak of worldly sense evidently lurked somewhere. For as soon as he learned that John Marco actually wanted to *buy* something he whisked back the velvet curtain and produced the photograph. It was while he was standing there with the wedding group in his hand that an idea came into the photographer's mind.

"I've got a separate one of the bride," he said, "if you'd be interested."

John Marco's mouth tightened.

"I'd like to see it," he said quietly.

There in the dim interior of that little studio he realised again how hopelessly and inextricably entangled their lives were, his and Mary's.

"Here it is," said the photographer when he had returned. "Quite one of my successes."

He was holding out the photograph at arm's length and John Marco took it from him. It was more than a photograph, this one: it was Mary herself with her grave eyes smiling at him. But were they smiling? There was that same sadness that he had seen as she had looked up that day in the Tabernacle; it was as though she had been photographed remembering that one moment.

"Just look at the detail in that lace," the photographer urged

262

enthusiastically. "Notice the stalks of those lilies."

John Marco did not answer immediately. Then he turned to the photographer.

"How much is this one?" he asked.

"Cabinet size in best art paper it would be a guinea," he said. "You can choose your own frame."

John Marco drew out his sovereign case and put the money down on the counter.

"I'll take it," he said.

It was then that the velvet jacket got the better of the business man.

"But this is only a rough print," he said. "One of the edges is folded."

"I'll take it as it is," John Marco repeated.

"Very well." The photographer shrugged his shoulders and went to the back of the shop. "I'll try to make up in the mounting," he promised.

Five minutes later John Marco emerged from the shop, the thin, flat parcel under his arm. With this in his possession the future seemed less lonely somehow, less divided. It was something secret, something in a sense that he would share with Mary.

The house in Clarence Gardens by now looked very different from the decayed mansion which had stood there in Mr. Trackett's day. The stucco had been scraped and repainted—it had been like scraping history to strip those walls—and the panels of the front door were newly picked out like coach-work. The whole place under its new coat of cream was undeniably smart; in the evening sunlight it shone like a milky iceberg. There were flowers, too, in the window boxes, bright blood-red geraniums which formed yet one more suspended terrace in those miraculous hanging Gardens of Bayswater which outrivalled Babylon.

John Marco looked and was pleased. He had agreed at last to this re-decorating, this huge expenditure. He had felt that he owed it to his success: it did him no good in business to live in a house which looked as though ghosts inhabited it.

Inside, however, the house was still Mr. Trackett's; John Marco had not agreed to their spending money where no one but themselves would notice. The crimson wall paper, the heavy Axminster carpet with its faded flowers, the bulging mahogany hall stand—it was all the same.

He went straight up to his room and turned the key in the lock. It had become almost instinctive by now, this locking himself away; it was the measure of his separation from the household. Then with clumsy, impatient fingers he undid the string of his parcel—and he was looking into Mary's eyes again. The sad smile which he remembered comforted him; and he saw now that across the forehead the brows were puckered in a little frown.

He sat there for some time holding the portrait in his hand. The frame was smooth and he ran his fingers over it caressingly. At that moment Mary Petter, preparing her husband's supper in the little kitchen over the shop in Harrow Street, and John Marco in his wife's dressing-room in Clarence Gardens, were alone together.

He put the photograph away in one of the drawers of his cabinet and unlocked the door again. Old Mrs. Marco was standing just outside, waiting.

"I thought I heard you, son," she said. She turned and nodded her head mysteriously in the direction of Hesther's bedroom. "You're late," she said. "He's asleep."

It was as she turned that he noticed how old she had become. She was withered. She had looked old enough back in the days in Chapel Villas; as long as he could remember she had been preparing for the end, getting all ready for the day when she and her Maker should suddenly find themselves face to face. After his marriage, however, when she had had someone to wait on her again she had recovered; for a space she had bloomed. But now that her grandchild had been born, now that all the excitement was over, her years had told again. She had cheated only temporarily, and the reckoning looked dangerously close at hand. Her lower jaw nowadays hung downwards a little even while she was awake, and she had moments of forgetfulness, of blankness, which frightened her.

Already she was tugging at his sleeve, pulling him in the direction of the bedroom. It was her special reward of the day to be allowed to go in and stand by the sleeping child, gloating over him. When no one else was about she would smooth out the clothes and rearrange the hangings. In her youth babies had slept higher; and when Hesther was not near she would bunch up the sheet and push a shawl in underneath to give her grandson a proper pillow.

But they were not alone in the bedroom to-night. Hesther was by the cot already. John Marco remained at the door watching. Her face was tired and worn; but at that moment she looked contented. She was smiling. In a world of sorrow and humiliation this cot contained the one reason for existence; while she was nursing the baby or holding him on her knee or simply standing beside him while he slept, she was able to forget that she was not happy and cherished like other wives.

She raised her eyes and caught sight of him. As she did so, the smile vanished. Only the lines in her face remained and she looked ashamed, as though there were something guilty about caring for the child in this way. Before old Mrs. Marco could get any nearer, she had stepped in front of the cot, shielding it.

"We're disturbing him," she said in a whisper. "He's restless."

As she spoke she put her arm through old Mrs. Marco's and led her out of the room; it was obvious that she was jealous and did not want to share her son with anyone. She did not speak as she passed John Marco, and he made no movement; they were within a foot of each other and still separated by an infinite distance.

Then, when the room was empty, John Marco crossed over to the cot himself. Since it had been born he had seen little of the child; it was still a stranger to him. It was lying there, its fists clenched on either side of its face in a pygmy gesture of defiance; it might have been fighting giants. Its hair, dark already like his own, showed dense and black against the shawl.

He bent over it and studied the small, sleeping face. The eyelids looked pearly and transparent, and the lashes were long and sweeping like a girl's. From time to time the corners of the round mouth would twitch as though it were still greedy to be feeding. Still greedy, or was it that already through that tiny, hazy mind the first dreams were passing? he wondered. He took hold of one of the clenched fists and straightened out the fingers; they were reluctant and resisted him—feebly but instinctively. And as he opened the hand he saw the soft deep folds of the knuckles and the pale, dainty nails; and the sight of this flesh of his own flesh for the first time delighted him. The child did not stir when he touched it; it was so drugged and bewildered by sleep; the whole of its body was resting in a placid world of warmth and mandragora. He let go of the fist and watched it re-clench itself. Then, very gently he began passing his hand across the dark hair. It felt polished and smooth like glass, it was so fine. The head beneath it was warm and alive; it throbbed. But as he looked he saw that it was not *his* hair that was black like that: it was Hesther's. H curled upwards from the forehead, and this lay flat upon it. And the shape of the cheek bones too: that was Hesther's. The child was hers; all hers. At the thought, he drew back a little. The child that he had desired was Mary's. He saw it now in the darkness blue-eyed and yellow-haired. The infant in the cot before him was unesteemed and in no way precious; it had no father.

One day perhaps it would realise this, would realise that this was no household into which any child should ever have been born. And then? He shook his head. At the thought of the sorrows and bleaknesses lying somewhere in the path of that sleeping child he found himself loving it again. Perhaps it would be his son after all; it would discover all too early what life was like when love was missing. Perhaps it would suffer as he had suffered. And as John Marco stood there looking down on it as it slept, it seemed that this easy slumber of his son was no more than the last rest before the anguish. Stooping, he kissed the child.

There was a little cry from behind him. It came from Hesther. She had tip-toed back and was already in the room, standing with one hand still on the door.

"So you do love him," she said triumphantly. "You do."

She came forward towards him, her own hands outstretched, and stood waiting for his arms to come round her.

Stood waiting.

Waiting.

Chapter XXI

The photograph of Mary, that unfinished portrait which the photographer claimed as one of his successes, gradually came to be the centre of John Marco's life; it was all he had.

He had not seen Mary face to face since that day in the Tabernacle. For in Mr. Petter, contented and unsuspecting as he was, she had the most jealous of husbands. Whenever John Marco had seen her in the street she had been accompanied by him, his arm protectively round hers, his head held high in sheer pride of possession of this delicious creature.

The pain, however, even of those brief glimpses was still unbearable. Each time he was reminded of what he had lost, he felt deserted and miserable again. But the knowledge that in the privacy of his bedroom he could hold her picture in his hands and stand gazing at it until he grew tired from watching, strangely supported him. For when her picture was before him the gulf that divided them became very narrow; there was a mysterious bridging of what lay between. It was as though Mary herself came to him at those moments. And by the time he had restored the photograph to the drawer and emerged once more into the dark, empty corridor, the world each time had grown calm again.

During the past months Hesther's own sense of loneliness had increased. She would spend long sessions shut away in her room, sewing or reading the literature which Mr. Tuke made a point of leaving, or simply sitting there listening eagerly for the nurse-maid to tell her that the child was awake. Even old Mrs. Marco was no longer a companion. She was all but bed-ridden by now, and lay all day in a huddle of rugs and comforters waiting for her meals to be brought up to her—her appetite even in extremis remained as spectacular as ever.

And left to herself Hesther spent her time planning hopefully, foolishly for the future. The child: he would not be able to resist the child for ever, she told herself; more than once when he had thought that he was not observed she had seen him go over to the cot and stand by it like a father. And once he had admitted that he loved the child, the rest would be natural. He would grow to love her, too, for having given it to him. Then they would come together again and her loneliness would be over. The more she pondered on it the more certain she became; and because of it the child in the cot seemed doubly precious.

But sometimes the mere thought alone seemed insufficient. She needed something to fill the unhappy present. And she would go through into John Marco's room and stand there wondering what she could do to please him. But it was not easy. There seemed to be so little that he needed. His real life began when he reached the shop in the morning and it ceased again after he had locked the big plate glass door behind him at night. This small, shabby room provided him with all that he could want when he was at home; there was the big drawing-room downstairs with the ebony furniture and the silk wallpaper if only he chose to use it. There was her bedroom, too, still waiting for him; she saw now how she had failed in turning him out, and she was sad. If only he would come back to it, if only for one night he would return to her, she would give him, she kept promising herself, all the love that he was now rejecting. At that moment she did not doubt that the whole of their life together could still be re-made.

And so it was that she went through into his room on this shadowy Autumn afternoon. There was surely, something, she felt, that she could do for him, something that would remind him that he was being cared for. But Emmy had already put the room in order; with the lifetime's skill of a London drudge she had whisked round the furniture with a mop and duster. Hesther opened the cupboard door; it was tidy. His suits hung there like a company of ghosts. She turned to the high, old-fashioned chest of drawers and began going through it, methodically straightening the contents. First, the ties and the collars and the handkerchiefs. But even these were not untidy: the drawers might have been one of his own showcases. Then she pulled open the next drawer—it was a large one—and shook out the winter overcoat that he had put away there: it was the black one with the handsome velvet collar that he had been wearing that day he had come to the house when she had first seen him. She ran her finger lovingly over the thick cloth; in a sense this seemed as near as she could ever get to him. And when she had put the coat away again her hands were trembling and she knew that she was weak enough to ask him to come back to her, weak enough to throw away all her pride in asking him. As she went on with her task a new kind of happiness began to fill her. Perhaps she had not so long to wait after all. Perhaps it would be only a matter of days before they were man and wife again.

There remained only one drawer now and she went down on her knees to empty it. It contained nothing that a man might value. There were some tied bundles of papers, an old jacket worn bare at the cuffs and elbows, and a book, *Holy Hours* that he had once read in. She folded the coat as carefully as if it had been new and smoothed down the dog-eared corners of the book. It was as she put it back that her eye caught sight of something thrust away into the corner of the drawer. Only a portion of it was showing; but it was enough. She dropped the book that she was holding and reached out for this other thing. Then she knelt there staring at Mary's picture in front of her.

For a moment she held it in front of her, her lips drawn back in a thin, hard line of anger. Her whole vision of the future had faded in that instant and disappeared. There could be no future for them while this was in the house; it denounced everything on which her hopes were being built. And it was no old photograph either. The wedding dress was proof of the iniquity of the thing; it was something that she had given him after she had become another man's wife. She took one last look at the smiling features that seemed to be mocking her. Then, laying the photograph flat on the floor, she put her heel upon it.

The splintering of the glass and the crack of the expensive frame that the photographer had supplied by way of compensation reminded her abruptly of what she had done; and she paused frightened. The rug at her feet was covered with fragments, and tiny slivers of glass glistened on the oil-cloth. The lower part of the face was broken away now, but the forehead and the veil remained untouched. The eyes, too, were still smiling up at her; and in a sudden rage she crushed her heel down on to the picture again. This time when she looked there was nothing that remained.

For a moment she was glad: she had obliterated this piece of wickedness, and the house was now clean again. But the mood did not last for long. It was succeeded by panic, blind awful panic. She looked again at the drawer and saw that the bundles of papers were not old things thrust away and forgotten. They were Chapel notices and copies of the Synod minutes. John Marco's Amosite Hymnal was among them. It was to this drawer that he went every Sunday before attending the Tabernacle; there would be no time at all before he found that the photograph was destroyed.

The realisation alarmed her still further and she saw that she would have to obliterate her deed. Going down on her hands and knees she began hurriedly gathering up the pieces. Then, when there was nothing left to show what she had done, she closed the drawer again and went out of the room carrying the broken jumble of frame and paper, silk mounting and shattered glass.

At this time every afternoon the rest of the house was deserted; old Mrs. Marco was sleeping in her room and Emmy was upstairs in her attic snatching her last precious minutes of rest before it was time to get tea. Hesther opened the door silently—she felt guilty now, like a criminal—and went downstairs into the dark basement kitchen. There, lifting the iron cover from the range, she thrust her handful of pieces into the flames. There was a sudden flare as the paper and the silk ignited; then the wood began to catch as well and soon only the twisted metal work of the frame remained. The evil picture no longer existed.

When she reached her room again she sat down and covered her face with her hands. Already she doubted the wisdom of what she had done, questioned whether a stronger woman would not have found some other way. The photograph itself was nothing; it was no more than an accusing finger pointing out a sin. The sin itself remained; and she had done nothing to stop its spreading. She sat there rocking herself backwards and forwards on the chair in misery. After a while she went down on her knees and prayed. It was nearly ten minutes later when she rose, exhausted.

Then, when she heard Emmy's door upstairs open and the tired feet begin to descend the stairs towards the kitchen, she went quickly to the cupboard and put on her hat with the high feather and her long black coat.

Her burden at that moment seemed too heavy to bear alone any longer.

Mr. Tuke recognised at once that she had come to lean upon his strength; and he was a pillar. As soon as he heard that Hesther's business was private and urgent, he signalled to Mrs. Tuke to collect her sewing and shoo-ed her out of her own drawing-room as if she had been a servant. Then, after he had helped Hesther to remove her coat, he took her hand in his and pulled his chair up very close beside her.

"Tell me everything, Sister," he said. "I can see that you are troubled."

It was significant that he did not express any surprise at what was told him. The only emotion that he registered was one of anger; as he listened his colour deepened and his breathing became heavier. And when he had heard the whole story he allowed himself only one comment.

"It finally establishes that she *is* his mistress," he said.

"But did I do right to burn it?" Hesther persisted. "Was it the best thing to do?"

"No," Mr. Tuke replied with terrible decisiveness. "It was not. You did wrong. You should have confronted him with it."

"Confronted him?"

"Yes, you should have thrust it in his face. Accused him of it."
Mr. Tuke got up from his chair and began to march about the
room. "It is our duty to expose evil when we find it, not conceal
it. You should have shamed him into confession for the sake of
the child."

"It's too late," Hesther said wearily. "There's nothing that we
can do now."

"It is not too late," Mr. Tuke contradicted her. "Remember
his salvation may be at stake."

Hesther turned towards him.

"But what can we do?" she asked.

"You will tell him."

She drew back and her hands were tightly clenched as if she
were praying.

"I daren't," she said. "I don't know what he would do to me."

"Then if you haven't the courage to tell him, I shall," Mr.
Tuke responded. "I shall challenge him in person."

He felt brave in God's strength as he said it and he was
prepared for Hesther's outburst which followed.

"No. No. You mustn't." She rose in agitation as she said it.
"You don't know him. He might do anything."

Mr. Tuke raised his hand to silence her.

"Then I shall denounce him from the pulpit," he replied. "I
shall strip his soul bare in front of everyone. Do you imagine that
I can allow sin to flourish in the Synod, that I can permit the
house of God to be turned into a brothel?" He dropped his voice
suddenly and came over and put his arm round her shoulder.
"Won't you spare him this humiliation?" he asked gently. "Won't
you make one last effort to save your husband?"

Hesther shook her head.

"I'm not strong enough," she answered.

"Then pray," Mr. Tuke commanded. "Pray and your path will be made clear to you."

When they had prayed, Mr. Tuke was the first to rise. He stood there, towering over her.

"I shall accompany you," he said. "There must be no turning back now."

They had been sitting in the fine drawing-room in Clarence Gardens for nearly half-an-hour before John Marco returned. Ten minutes earlier when Hesther had thought she heard him she had risen hurriedly—too hurriedly, for her head had swum and she had been forced to take a dose of *sal voiatile* to quieten her nerves. But she was calmer now. White-faced and upright, she was waiting for him, quite motionless. On the other side of the fire Mr. Tuke was sitting, the loose folds of his face set into granite.

There was the sound of the front door shutting and Mr. Tuke buttoned up his long frock coat in readiness.

"Remember your resolve," he said firmly. "No weakness."

But John Marco walked past the room without stopping. They heard him mount the stairs and close the door of his room behind him. There was silence.

"Perhaps he's gone to the drawer," said Hesther faintly. "Perhaps he knows already."

Mr. Tuke frowned.

"In that case," he said, "we shall catch him red-handed."

And to show how much he was master of the situation he began to pace up and down the room as though it were his own study. With his square shoulders and his tremendous head set on the thick neck he was like a spiritual wrestler waiting for the bout to begin.

"He's a long time," he observed at last. "A remarkably long time."

Somehow this extra period of waiting was inimical to his whole plan. The first fires of anger were already dying down, and his entire system would now have to be restored before he faced him. Mr. Tuke knew from experience that for a really successful denunciation he should be quivering all over before he even started.

He turned and faced Hesther resentfully.

"Is there no way of summoning him?" he asked. "Can't he be informed of our presence?"

"I . . . suppose we could get Emmy to tell him," Hesther admitted doubtfully.

"Then let us do so," said Mr. Tuke.

He crossed over to the fireplace and tugged angrily at the handle that protruded above the bronze and marble plaque on the wall. There was a scraping of wires, then a jangling like a mad angelus broke out in the basement below them.

"Now," said Mr. Tuke briskly, "we shall *have* to send for him."

The action was precisely what was needed: it got Mr. Tuke into his stride again. And it was he who spoke to Emmy as soon as she came in. Holding up a warning finger to Hesther he addressed Emmy in the voice of someone in command.

"Tell your master that Mrs. Marco and Mr. Tuke wish to speak to him," he said. "Tell him that we are being kept waiting."

Mr. Tuke rubbed his hands and rose up and down once or twice on his toes as though testing his muscles. The quivering that he had been waiting for had started: he was now tingling with rage in every nerve.

When John Marco answered the summons they saw at once how pale he was. He looked tired. The long hours at the shop had left their mark upon him; amid the dark hairs at the temples there were already some which were white. He stood facing them, one eyebrow raised a little questioningly, the corners of his mouth drawn down.

"Come in," Mr. Tuke said bluntly. "We want to talk to you."

John Marco paused for a moment and flushed slightly. Then he crossed over to the fireplace and almost elbowed Mr. Tuke out of the way.

"What is it you want?" he asked when he was facing him again.

"You know what it is," Mr. Tuke answered. "Your heart tells you."

"I know nothing," John Marco replied. "Explain yourself."

Mr. Tuke's voice was grim and colourless as he answered.

"Your wife has told me everything," he said. "I shall expect to hear you make your confession."

There was sudden terror in John Marco's mind as he heard the words: he saw again the dishevelled death-bed with Mr. Trackett lying across it, the piles of bank notes scattered around him; saw himself with the notes that he had stolen; saw Hesther sitting there for the first time in the tiny front parlour of the house in Chapel Villas. That was five years ago now, but it seemed that the past had suddenly come swirling forward and had encircled him; he felt the dark waters rising round him as he stood there. He glanced momentarily towards Hesther, but she was sitting with her eyes cast down to the floor; she avoided him. Then he turned and looked straight at Mr. Tuke.

"I don't understand you," he said.

But Mr. Tuke was not impressed.

"John Marco," he replied, "I am your minister. You have stolen something that belongs to another man."

Stolen: that was what Mr. Tuke had said. The waters of destiny rushed upwards again; they were choking him. He felt them closing over his head. The whole future in an instant was blotted out—the great shop with its many windows that he had planned, the battalion of assistants, his own eminence. His hatred of Hesther suddenly blazed again to think how she had betrayed him. His fists were clenched now and he took a step towards her.

But Hesther was no longer sitting with her eyes downcast. She was looking towards him now: and she was shaking her head as though to deny the meaning in Mr. Tuke's words. There was no hatred in *her* face at all. And as he watched her she made a little movement with her hands as though to hold them out to him. She seemed almost to be protecting him.

He turned to Mr. Tuke again. "I shall want your apology."

And as he uttered them, the falseness of the words rang in his ears. But were they false? Those five years had been long ones. They had changed him. He was a different person now from the one who in that dingy bed-chamber had been laid open to temptation and had fallen.

Already, except for that moment of panic when Mr. Tuke had first spoken, the memory of that night was like looking back on another man's crime; it was sin seen through the wrong end of a telescope.

Mr. Tuke, however, was not to be brow-beaten.

"You have stolen a woman's virtue," he replied slowly. "Why did you hide a portrait of another man's bride in your own bedroom?"

John Marco started. He came forward and gripped the edge of the table in front of him, gripped it hard. But he was angry now, not concealing it. His eyes turned to Hesther.

"So you've been spying on me have you?" he asked. Hesther

shook her head.

"I knew too much already," she said. "I didn't want to find out anything else bad about you."

"But you went to Mr. Tuke and told him," he accused her.

"It was your abominable conduct that drove her," Mr. Tuke replied hotly.

"And are you proud of what you've done?" he asked her.

"I couldn't bear it any longer," she replied. "There was the child to think of."

"Where is the picture now?" he demanded. "What did you do with it?"

Mr. Tuke raised his hand imperiously: this was his moment.

"She destroyed it," he said victoriously. "Destroyed it so that this house might be clean again."

"Is this true?"

John Marco swung round again towards Hesther as he spoke.

"Quite true," she answered without looking at him. "I burnt it."

"She did right," Mr. Tuke interposed. "She was destroying evil."

John Marco turned to him.

"I shall discuss this with her alone," he said. "You have done your work."

At the words Hesther's heart gave a great leap. So he meant to stay with her! He was not so angry that he intended to leave her. That was the one thing that she had feared; that now he knew that she had thrown herself on Mr. Tuke, John Marco's pride would compel him to go away for ever.

Mr. Tuke accepted his dismissal. But he was not surrendering without a fight. He was still both priest and prosecutor.

"Perhaps you will first explain how the picture came into your

279

possession," he said, his whole frame vibrating with anger now. "How you, an Elder, could be so wanton."

"Wanton?"

John Marco repeated the word bitterly.

And Mr. Tuke pounced on it.

"Yes. wanton," he said. "Your own mistress's picture."

The word had slipped out before he was aware of it. And Hesther gave a little cry as she heard it. Even Mr. Tuke at heart was a little frightened. But he folded his arms and stood there, breathing heavily.

John Marco came forward until he was within a few inches of Mr. Tuke.

"Did you mean what you said just now?" he asked.

Mr. Tuke went pale for a moment. But he stood his ground.

"I did," he said. "I have had the evidence of my own eyes."

At that John Marco struck him. It was not a particularly hard blow. It was a contemptuous one, rather. His hand was open all the time. But that only served to increase the sound of it. The white imprint of an extended palm appeared across Mr. Tuke's cheek-bone, and was replaced a moment later, as the blood returned to the spot, by a fiery red one. Mr. Tuke's face now looked as if a vivid naevus disfigured it.

And having struck him, John Marco turned round on Hesther once more.

"This is the end between us," he said. "You can tell Mr. Tuke the real truth if you like. Tell him and be damned to both of you."

He pushed by them as he said it and made towards the door. But as he passed, Hesther suddenly reached out and took him by the hand. She even managed to hold it for a moment.

"Oh, John, John," she said. "You can't mean it."

"I do mean it. Let me go."

"But think of your son."

"He's your son," he said. "Not mine."

And snatching his hand away from her he left them.

A few minutes later there were the sounds of heavy footsteps and then the crash of the massive front door as it slammed behind him. Hesther and Mr. Tuke exchanged glances. They went over to the window together. It was dark outside but a street lamp opposite cast a beam of light up the steps. Down the steps John Marco was descending. He was so muffled up that his face was scarcely to be seen. In his hand was a heavy valise.

At the bottom of the steps he did not pause even to take one last look at the house behind him, but turned rapidly away into the darkness and was lost to sight.

"What have we done?" Hesther asked Mr. Tuke imploringly. "What is it that you've made me do?"

"I only . . . only . . ." Mr. Tuke began.

But standing there amid the ruins of a family, Mr. Tuke, fingering his burning cheek where the blow had fallen, was not really quite sure of what it was that he had done.

Book III

Mary and the Child

Chapter XXII

John Marco woke early in the large front bedroom above the shop and lay listening to the first sounds of traffic in Tredegar Terrace; it was six-thirty and the night had not been long.

But he was, at best, only a short sleeper, and by the time the daily woman came trudging up the stairs to get his breakfast he was usually dressed and in the shop. Often when she arrived she would see him, standing there on that little landing looking over the empty desert of wooden counters and bare oilcloth below him. On those occasions he reminded her of the Captain of a paddle steamer, which had once carried her from Tower Pier to Ramsgate. She had been an impressionable young girl at the time, and the faraway, romantic look in the man's eyes had remained frozen in her imagination. Now, nearly thirty years later, as she passed up the staircase with her string bag and her working shoes in her hand, sometimes getting a "good-morning" and sometimes not, she could almost swear that it was August again, and a fine day with the smell of oranges in the air, and the boat due to leave at ten-thirty.

It was more than a year now since John Marco had slammed the front door behind him and come blindly round to the shop, with the whole world collapsing about his ears. But already that evening, too, was only a faint memory; it had receded somewhere into the dim background of his mind. He had spent the night half upright in the swivel chair in his office. And next morning he had set about refurnishing the suite of rooms which the Old Gentleman had occupied. The rooms themselves had been stripped completely. Miss Foxell had interpreted the clause, ". . . and all the personal effects of which I die possessed," almost too literally: she had cleared out the upstairs rooms even to the china finger-plates on the doors and the ornamental gas-brackets. It had been like rebuilding a sacked and looted city to make those rooms habitable.

And now that he was here, now that there was nothing else in his life besides, he could devote more hours to the business. No matter how early the reformed Mr. Hack-bridge arrived, John Marco was already standing behind the plate glass door ready for him. Such punctuality, indeed, became a kind of nightmare to Mr. Hackbridge; it was like working for a time-machine that never stopped. When the nightmare was really bad he used to imagine John Marco at two or three in the morning still standing there in the abandoned shop, impatiently waiting for his shop-walker to arrive.

The business was bigger by now: and it was still growing. It had absorbed more than Mr. Skewin's primitive establishment. Earlier in the year, when the furrier next door had plunged suddenly and dramatically into liquidation—Special Purchase of Exclusive New Season's Models, one day: bankrupt, and out of business the next—it was John Marco who had bought up the stock and taken over the lease. It had been a gamble, despite the expert valuation, for John Marco knew nothing about furs. On the day after the transfer had been completed he had stood in his

286

new store room surrounded by the stock of seal and pony skin, fox and sable, squirrel and ermine, and had felt like one of the Elizabethan merchant venturers, bewildered in the courts of Muscovy.

The bank that had financed the purchase had raised objections to the loan on the grounds of the borrower's lack of experience in the trade. And John Marco had replied that when he had taken over Mr. Skewin's Gentleman's Outfitting he had known nothing of that trade either; he had not added that six months after he had taken Mr. Skewin's shop away from him, he had searched him out in sheer desperation and had appointed him manager to the business.

This appointment had, in the result, been in the nature of a masterstroke. First, the small nucleus of faithful customers who had been driven away by the new shop-front, returned to him and bought up the remnants. And secondly—and far more important—John Marco now had a new departmental head of the utmost allegiance; for Mr. Skewin had been raised up by the very hand that had struck him down. And he was now, like Mr. Hack-bridge, John Marco's servile slave for life.

These months of violent commercial imperialism, had not gone unnoticed among the other shopkeepers in Paddington and Bayswater. In the Old Gentleman's day, everything about the shop had been austere and respectable; if he had bought up the entire street he would have done so with an air of Bardic benevolence that could have been forgiven. But with John Marco it was all jumpy and disturbing. One rumour grew up that he was going to establish branches; another that he was in financial difficulties already; a third said that a furnishing department (one that would cripple the business opposite) was on the point of opening. On one point were all the rumours agreed: that the rate of growth was too rapid. They all predicted eventual and spectacular collapse. But John Marco only laughed when he heard them. He knew that the people who had started them were jealous; jealous because they had all remained behind the same plate glass window with which they had started. He alone was enlarging and absorbing; it was he alone who was going forward over the heads of other men on this mission of destiny in the tremendous world of retail drapery. . . .

But it was after six-thirty already, and he had work to do. He put on a hat and coat and, raising the shop blinds himself, walked for some minutes up and down the empty pavement outside: he was studying the windows. With a slight frown he noticed that the coquettish wax figure was wearing her guinea hat square on her head like a schoolmistress. He made a note to speak to Mr. Hackbridge about it.

He had repeatedly pointed out that all the ladies of any fashionable pretensions were tilting their hats slightly.

ii

The unusual circumstance of John Marco's living above his shop in Tredegar Terrace, while his wife lived alone amid the stucco magnificence of Clarence Gardens, had not failed to excite some comment. Those who knew no more than the bare outlines of the situation and claimed that he had deserted Hesther, were disconcerted by the fact that he visited Clarence Gardens regularly once a week—they did not know, of course, that it was old Mrs. Marco whom he went to see. And others, whose ear was closer to the ground, whispered that he had gone mad, assaulted his minister and turned Atheist: it was Emmy who had spread this story. The weakness of this variant, however, lay in the fact that he still attended Chapel, even though it was no longer Mr. Tuke's chapel that he attended.

Altogether, the reason for the separate ménage remained a mystery, an outrage and an enigma. But only, of course, among a very tiny circle. In any large town there might be a range of mountains between one street and the next for all the intercourse there is between them. And as Tredegar Terrace was actually just in Bayswater (the line of demarcation was invisible but momentous) it was hardly to be expected that anyone in Paddington should know what was happening in Tredegar Terrace.

Thus Mr. Thomas Petter, Chemist and Druggist, of Harrow Street, in organising his Paddington and Bayswater Master Shopkeepers' Association did not know of any reason why he should not canvass John Marco for membership. He remembered, of course, Mr. Kent's outburst on the night of the Election of the Synod; but Mrs. Kent had made it her business to explain that her husband had opposed Mr. Marco purely on business grounds: she had, indeed, gone out of her way to make that clear. Mary herself had not spoken. And Mr. Tuke after debating fiercely with himself as to whether he should denounce Mary as a sinner of equal blackness, had remembered that one home that he had shattered so irremediably and, at the last moment, had drawn back.

And so it was that Thomas Petter met John Marco by appointment in his own office and shook hands with him as one progressive business man with another.

John Marco sat back in his comfortable arm-chair eyeing him quizzically. This was a meeting that he had been looking forward to; it was one that in his bitterest moments he had even felt tempted to arrange. And now the young man, blissful and unsuspecting, had turned up of his own free will as a kind of voluntary sacrifice on the altar of his curiosity.

Or had he heard something? Like Mr. Tuke, had he come along confident that a word from him would put everything all right? John Marco wondered and waited.

The young man seemed pleasant enough. He was pink and spruce. Once or twice he shifted a trifle awkwardly in his place—the chair reserved for visitors was hard and disconcertingly narrow in the seat—but on the whole he was nicely self-possessed. Behind his shiny rimless glasses, his eyes were blue and direct, and there was nothing but candour in the smooth, clean-shaven chin; altogether, he looked a model minor shopkeeper. John Marco studied him hard and realised that, in other circumstances, he might even have been prepared to like him. And then the absurdity, the grotesqueness of it overcame him. It was this little creature that Mary Kent had got in place of him; this twopenny chemist into whose keeping she had confided body, soul, and fortune, too.

John Marco folded his own hands square on the desk and faced his visitor.

"Yes, Mr. Petter," he said abruptly, "and what can I do for you?"

Now that it was time for him to speak Mr. Petter was eloquent. The Paddington and Bayswater Master Shopkeepers' Association was his own idea, and he spoke with the exuberant enthusiasm of an inventor. His eyes sparkled and his fingers kept clasping and unclasping with excitement.

". . . so if we act together," he wound up, "not only can we safeguard price levels in general but we can pool information about bad debtors. As soon as anyone opens an account with any one of us all the others will know as well and there won't be any more losses to be written off." He paused for a moment as though to review his catechism and then added by way of an afterthought: "Of course there would be certain social differences you'd have to allow for. What would be quite large amounts in one district wouldn't amount to anything very serious in another. For instance your clientele is obviously better class than mine."

"Obviously," John Marco replied.

Now that John Marco knew the object of Mr. Petter's visit, he was simply amused by him. The impudence of the little man was astonishing.

"Are you a large employer of labour yourself?" he asked.

He wanted to hear the colossal egoist before him confess the presumptuous folly of his scheme.

"Oh no," said Mr. Petter engagingly. "I'm just on my own, except for the boy who delivers the medicines. Of course, there's my wife: she helps me at times."

At Mr. Petter's mention of his wife, John Marco felt angry again. For a moment it surprised him to find quite how angry he was. He had tried to put Mary out of his mind, had deliberately suppressed every thought of her as it came to him. He had not even replaced the photograph, and all that remained to remember her by was that half circle of the ring still hanging from his watch-chain. Yet at one mention of her, he found that he had not forgotten her at all; she was the centre of his life again. And he wanted to find out all that he could about her; wanted, if only vicariously, to be beside her once more.

"Does your wife give you much help?" he asked.

"Not now, she doesn't," Mr. Petter replied simply. "You see we've started a family. We've just got a little daughter."

John Marco's heart stopped for a moment, and there was a

blackness before his eyes. He rose and began to walk about the room. But what was the use of reviving this despair? he asked himself; what purpose could it now serve him? So he turned quietly and faced Mr. Petter.

"You're a lucky man," he said. "You should count your blessings while you have them."

"I do," Mr. Petter assured him. He paused for a moment and then added, "Mr. Tuke's god-father to our little daughter. You know him, don't you? You're one of us, I believe."

But John Marco could bear this painful little pantomime no longer. He held out his hand.

"Good day, Mr. Petter," he said. "I've been pleased to make your acquaintance."

"But the Association?" Mr. Petter exclaimed in dismay. "You haven't told me what you think about the Association."

"I'll consider it," John Marco answered. "I'll consider it very carefully."

"Please do," Mr. Petter urged. "I'm sure there's something in it."

He shook John Marco by the hand as he said it and so far as John Marco was concerned the interview was over. But Mr. Petter still hung about expectantly.

"If I haven't made myself clear," he said; "if there's anything else you'd like to know about the Association I'd be very pleased to explain."

"Thank you," John Marco replied. "You made yourself perfectly clear."

He edged Mr. Petter towards the door as he said it; he had a notion that the little man might prove persistent.

And he was right. The other shopkeepers whom he had approached had been smaller fry altogether. John Marco, the rising prince of drapery in those parts, was on a different level. And now that he had established contact with him it would be only very reluctantly that he would leave go.

"Some evening perhaps if you aren't too busy," he said ingratiatingly, "if you'd care to come round and drink a cup of tea with us, I could explain the whole scheme more fully."

John Marco stood motionless: his heart seemed suddenly to be choking him once more. To see Mary again, to be able to sit there looking at her—that was what Mr. Petter was offering him. In his ignorance this fantastic husband of hers had actually *invited* him into the house. He paused, his heart still racing.

"Which afternoon do you close?" he asked.

"Thursdays," said Mr. Petter delightedly. "I'm open again from six to eight, but after that I'm free all the evening. If you could spare the time to come round about eight-thirty we should be all ready for you."

How nice of Mr. Marco he was thinking; how thoughtful of him. There was this great business that was open all the week and closed at one o'clock on Saturdays but he had gone out of his way to remember early closing and make everything comfortable for smaller people like the Petters.

"I . . . I know my wife will look forward to the meeting," he exclaimed in a final flutter of politeness. "I know she will."

"Not more than I shall," John Marco replied.

It was an immensely gratified Mr. Petter who a minute later descended the broad staircase and passed out homewards into the street: he had scored his first big success.

iii

There were three days to kill until Thursday. John Marco woke on the morning after Mr. Petter's departure in a state of suspension in time: he wondered now why he had ever imposed such an intolerable interval upon himself. He could himself have suggested Tuesday just as easily, the little man was so painfully eager for his company. But, no. Tuesday was the evening on which he visited his mother: it was the evening on which, in her own house, Hesther kept out of sight.

The shock of his departure had left old Mrs. Marco sadly unbalanced. She could not grasp the fact that he was not coming back to live there. It seemed instead that he was deliberately keeping away from her. Or being kept away—was that it? It was impossible to say; everything was so strange nowadays. The idea of a weekly visit gradually, however, percolated into her intelligence; and she lay in her big double bed hazily striving to disentangle the muddled sequence of days. If only she could have recalled on which side of Wednesday, Tuesday invariably came, she would have made a special effort each week to be ready to entertain him.

Punctually at nine o'clock John Marco walked round to Clarence Gardens. As he mounted the broad, familiar steps he shivered involuntarily for a moment as though the chill of the big house had already entered into him; the house, each time he entered, seemed colder and less friendly than before. But he did not pause. Searching out the large, old-fashioned key on his ring he let himself into the high dark hall still covered with the heavy blood-red paper, and climbed towards old Mrs. Marco's room.

On these occasions, Emmy spent the entire evening somewhere near the head of the stairs so that she could dart quickly upwards when the time came. It was essential for her peace of mind that she should know how this amazing marriage was prospering. To-night as usual she followed John Marco cautiously up the staircase keeping a flight behind all the time, saw him go into old Mrs. Marco's room, and seated herself on the bottom step to wait.

Inside the bedroom, John Marco walked over to his mother's bed. She appeared at first sight to be asleep, but after a moment she opened her eyes and sat up.

"Why don't you let him come to me?" she asked. "I've never done any harm to him."

He paused.

"Don't you know me?" he asked.

"Of course I do," she said irritably. "I'm not a fool. It's the child I want. They won't let me have him." She leant over and caught John Marco by the arm. "You're out such a lot," she whispered. "You don't know what goes on here. They never let me see him nowadays."

He disengaged the hand that gripped him and laid it gently back on the bed. There seemed to be no real strength in it: it rested limply where he placed it.

"I'll speak to them," he promised.

There was silence for a moment and then the worn cogs in Mrs. Marco's mind began to move again, groping for something for their teeth to catch on.

"Why *are* you out so much?" she asked, with the air of someone who has stumbled unawares on a solution. "Why don't you get married?"

As he did not answer, old Mrs. Marco raised herself a little from the pillow and resumed.

"Why don't you marry Hesther?" she asked. "She's always talking about you."

He placed his hand on his mother's: it felt cold and faintly damp to the touch.

"You're tired," he said. "You're getting confused."

"Am I?" Mrs. Marco asked wearily. "Perhaps you're right. It's time I went to sleep. I could do with a good long sleep."

She closed her eyes and lay back. But at the same moment one of the cogs started whirring again. Inside her brain something or other was happening. Her lips began twitching.

"Have you got married secretly and not told me?" she asked. "You're not in any kind of trouble are you?"

"No," he told her, "I'm not in any trouble."

Mrs. Marco nodded her head dubiously: it was obvious that she was not entirely satisfied with his explanations. Then she beckoned to him in the manner of someone who has a tremendous secret to impart.

"As soon as the child's grown up," she said under her breath, "I'm going away from here."

"You can come away to-night," he answered. "I've told you that before."

"And leave the boy here?" The voice rose almost to a scream. "It's not safe, something might happen to him."

"He's safe enough," John Marco assured her. "You needn't worry."

Mrs. Marco looked at him reproachfully.

"You wouldn't say that if he were your son," she said. "He's such a dear little boy."

Having made her point, the old lady was evidently prepared to let the matter drop. She folded her hands across her chest and closed her eyes again. John Marco sat there in silence until he judged her to be asleep and then he began to move on tiptoe towards the door.

The departure, however, was premature. Old Mrs. Marco was suspended in sleep by only the slenderest of threads; and the disturbance broke it. She woke with a jerk and sat up.

"Don't go," she said. "I was in the middle of telling you something."

He came back and stood at the foot of the bed.

"What is it?" he asked.

But old Mrs. Marco was coy: up among the pillows she simpered.

"Can you keep a secret?" she asked.

John Marco nodded.

"It's something Hesther told me," she said. "She asked me to get you to come back again."

"She asked you that?" John Marco said.

"That's right," old Mrs. Marco answered excitedly. "She wants you back where you belong, same as I do." She paused. "Only that's not the secret," she added.

"Then what is it?"

"The secret," said old Mrs. Marco dropping her voice again, "is that Hesther didn't want you to know that she'd asked me. She wanted you to think that it was just my own idea."

Mrs. Marco gave a sudden little cackle of laughter at the impishness of her disclosure and lay back. John Marco stood there at the end of the bed, waiting for her to continue. But she did not seem disposed to say anything more. Her eyes were closed again and this time she was really sleeping; she slept noisily, fumbling over each mouthful of breath. John Marco went carefully across the room and turning the handle of the door by fractions of an inch opened the door noiselessly and prepared to step out into the dark corridor.

As he did so there was a sudden movement in the blackness in front of him, a swirl of skirts and the squeak of a high heel on the oilcloth. A moment later there was the sound of Hesther's door shutting, and the house was in silence again. The night-light under its patent globe beside old Mrs. Marco's bed sent a faint gleam across the room and illumined an empty corridor.

Down in the front basement, Emmy was almost hugging herself with gratification. No sooner had John Marco gone into his mother's room and she had stationed herself on the second step of the stairs just in case anything should happen, than Hesther herself had emerged from her room and stood in the darkness with her ear close up against old Mrs. Marco's door. While she had been standing there she had repeated her husband's name several times softly to herself, and Emmy had nearly died from excitement when the door had opened and he had appeared: she could still make her heart hammer simply by thinking about it. And what a disclosure! Rather than exchange a single word with her own husband Hesther had darted inside her room again.

Taking up the silver tray that she had been polishing, she aimlessly rubbed it round and round, round and round, round and round with the duster, happily dreaming over this, her private and stupendous revelation.

iv

When he got back to the shop John Marco gathered up the late post which lay at the bottom of the letterbox and made his lonely way upstairs.

The gas was already burning in the sitting-room. The light shone down on the big, red leather chair and the footstool that stood in front of it. His slippers were set out beside it on the Turkey carpet, and there was a fire burning in the grate. The whole room looked male and comfortable and substantial.

When he had taken off his hat and coat he went over and unlocked the cupboard. There was a decanter of whiskey and a syphon. He poured himself a drink, measuring the whiskey carefully against the breadth of his two fingers, and changed into his slippers.

At first when he had drunk a whiskey in the evening he had been conscious of the sin of it: he had remembered Mr. Tuke every time he raised the glass to his lips. But now he never thought of it. It was significant, however, that even in sin he behaved in severe Amosite fashion, allowing himself only one drink each evening and no more. He drank so that he could go on working; not for pleasure.

Settled solidly in his chair, John Marco began to go through the evening's post. But there was one envelope that caught his eye—it was so different from the others. It was a small blue one, written in a rapid, excited hand. It had, moreover, been delivered in person. Pushing the others aside he picked it up and ripped it open.

"Dearest" it ran. *"Thomas has just told me that he has asked you here, but of course he doesn't know anything. And I don't want him to know. He's very good to me and I love him. Please give some excuse so that you needn't come. It'll only make things too difficult for both of us. You know how much I've always loved you and I still do. But we mustn't see each other again"*

The signature was scrawled hurriedly at the bottom and John Marco sat there staring at it. Then he folded it up in its envelope again and thrust it into his pocket.

Mr. Thomas Petter had invited him to his house at eight-thirty on Thursday evening; and at eight-thirty on Thursday evening he would be there.

Chapter XXIII

Mr. Petter's shop stood at the corner of Harrow and Emmanuel Streets. It was small and well-stocked and newly-painted. On either side of the narrow front door stood two enormous coloured bottles that reflected the thoroughfare in giddy sweeping curves and, when the sun shone through them, cast huge blobs of light like prodigious fruit drops.

Mr. Petter, however, had never regarded the bottles merely as ornamental; every time he looked at them he was reminded with a little thrill of pride that the origins of his profession lay buried somewhere in the smoky caves of alchemy—and simply thinking about the antiquity of his calling reconciled him to a lifetime of selling face powders and scented shampoos and other rubbish which he regarded as frivolous. But ornamental, the bottles undoubtedly were. And the whole shop front with its array of sponges and tooth-brushes and elixirs and baby foods, and its neat label "Night Bell" on the side door, might have been a model shop front from a child's toy town.

John Marco arrived punctually at eight-thirty and rang the bell. Almost immediately came the sound of a door shutting somewhere in the flat above and the noise of feet descending the stairs. Then the door opened and Mr. Petter stood there.

He was flushed, but clearly delighted to see his visitor.

"Ah, there you are," he exclaimed. "My wife was afraid that you wouldn't be able to come after all."

"Really," said John Marco as he shook hands with Mr. Petter. "I wonder why that was. I had every intention of coming."

"Then I'll lead the way," said Mr. Petter gaily.

John Marco followed him up the thin strip of carpet which ran up the white-painted stairs. He was breathing deeply. He was very close to Mary now; already he was in the same house with her. Soon he would be holding her by the hand, looking into those clear eyes again. He began mounting faster.

Mr. Petter, for his part, was obviously very proud of the flat into which he was leading him. The white paint on the stairs was only the beginning of it. The doors were white, too. And the window sills and the cupboards of the living room. Nor did the general air of brightness stop there. The walls, instead of being papered, were coloured with an apricot distemper and in place of lace curtains at the windows there were plain casement ones. The whole place, in short, looked gay and modern and abreast of the times. And with so much white about, the air of a bridal suite remained; the silk and wicker bassinet in the hall, looked, indeed almost shockingly premature.

But the room was empty and Mr. Petter looked round it in dismay.

"My wife won't be long," he said reassuringly, "we're just having a little trouble with the child."

"I can wait," John Marco answered. "I'm in no hurry."

He settled himself as deeply as he could manage into a chair that was too small for him and glanced round the room. Despite its newness and its bright up-to-dateness he felt contemptuous towards it. "I could have given you so much better, Mary," he was saying over and over to himself. "So very much better."

But Mr. Petter was busy making conversation.

"It's very moving, sitting up with a sick child," he said. "It does something to you. So helpless, you know."

"So I understand," John Marco replied.

"You've not got any children of your own, then?"

Mr. Petter put the question tentatively as though aware that in cross-examining his important visitor he was exceeding the bounds of good breeding.

And he received his rebuke: John Marco ignored the question.

"How long have you been married now?" he asked.

"Two years," Mr. Petter replied. "We were beginning to wonder whether we'd ever have any children."

Mr. Petter's further matrimonial confessions were interrupted, however. There was a sound in the room above them, and his smooth pink face lit up automatically.

"I can hear her," he said. "She's coming."

John Marco smiled at him.

"How fortunate," he said. "That must mean that the child is asleep again."

But Mary did not appear. After a minute of anxious silence, during which Mr. Petter sat with ears straining for some sign, he rose apologetically.

"I'll just slip upstairs and see what's happened," he said. "That is, if you'll excuse me for a moment."

He was gone for more than a moment and it was evident that there was some hitch. Eventually there was the sound of Mr. Petter's voice raised in remonstrance—and it is difficult to remain discreet in argument in a flat of only four rooms.

"Of course you've got to come down," John Marco heard him saying. "What ever will he think? He particularly wants to meet you."

John Marco re-settled himself in the inadequate armchair and smiled: he felt at that moment as though he held this tiny household balanced on one finger.

It was nearly five minutes later when there was the sound of two people descending the stairs towards the living room. Then the door was thrust open and Mary stood there. Mr. Petter preceded her in the manner of a man exhibiting his most precious possession.

"My wife asks you to excuse her lateness," he said as though even now that he had persuaded her to come he could not guarantee that she would actually say anything. "It was the child. She is teething."

John Marco had risen and was facing her. He held out his hand and, as he did so, he noticed that hers was unsteady.

"I was afraid that I wasn't going to see you," he said.

"I'm sorry," she replied, "but it's not always easy when there's a young child in the house."

She did not raise her eyes to his as she spoke and as soon as he released her hand—even Mr. Petter noticed that he held it a little longer than was usual—she took a chair with her back to the light so that the whole of her face was in shadow. It was her husband who kept the conversation alive.

"I really wonder you didn't know each other already," he observed complacently. "My wife was a Miss Kent before I married her. She was in the Tabernacle, too."

"But I did know her," John Marco replied. "We taught in Sunday School together."

"That was a long while ago," Mary said hurriedly.

Mr. Petter, however, was not to be put off like that. He came over and sat on the arm of Mary's chair. Occasionally his fingers would stray down towards her and begin stroking her arm.

"So you *did* know Mr. Marco all the time," he said, "and you never told me. I call that a very naughty little wife."

He pinched her arm playfully as he said it: it was obvious that he was distractedly in love with her.

But Mary only pulled her arm away: she seemed to resent him anywhere near her. And Mr. Petter after the rebuff did not seem to know what to do. He sat where he was on the arm of her chair, like an injured and unhappy cherub.

John Marco sat staring at them both. It was so manifestly impossible to think of this model druggist as a rival that he did not even feel any jealousy; he had only to raise his finger for the little man to fall over. But, after the first glance, it was not at Mr. Petter that he was looking: it was at Mary. The labour of bearing Mr. Petter's child had rested lightly on her. The only difference between the Mary whom he had begged never to leave him and the Mary who now sat in the chair before him, was that this was a woman; the child who was now sleeping upstairs had somehow completed her. Her eyes when he could see them were the same; and the pure curve of her neck was unaltered. He looked at the pale gold of her hair, brushed up high over the temples and showing almost silvery beneath, and he loved her again.

"It seems strange," Mr. Petter remarked, "that we hadn't met socially before. Of course, I'm new to this Chapel, but I've met most of Mary's friends."

"Perhaps it's because I don't go out very much," John Marco suggested. "I spend most of my evenings working."

"Then we ought to be flattered, oughtn't we, Mary?" Mr. Petter asked. "Really we ought."

There was no opportunity for Mary to reply, for at that moment there came the sound again of a baby's crying. Mary got up and went towards the door.

"You'll have to excuse me," she said. "It's the child."

When she had gone John Marco put his back to the fireplace and faced Mr. Petter. He was jocular now and rather hearty with him, like an employer talking out of business to one of his assistants.

"What about this baby of yours?" he asked. "Aren't I going to be allowed to see her?"

Mr. Petter's face lit up again.

"Would you like to?" he asked eagerly. "Would you really like to?"

John Marco ran the tip of his tongue across his lips. He was doing something to hurt himself in asking to see this child; he knew that. But it was Mary's child and he had to see it. It would be something else he could share with her. It would take him deeper into the pattern of her life again.

"Well I've heard a lot about her, haven't I?" he replied.

"Then come on," said Mr. Petter happily. "We'll pay a surprise visit. She'd never let us get near it if she knew."

They went up the next flight of the staircase—it had become narrower, more intimate and domestic by now—and Mr. Petter threw open the door in front of him. It was then that John Marco saw that it was the Petters' own bedroom that he was in. The big double bed under its pink silk eiderdown was against the wall and, beside it sheltered in a little alcove of screens, was the cot. Mary was bending over it, talking to the bundle in the cot as though it could understand her.

"Mr. Marco wanted to see her," Mr. Petter announced brightly. "So I brought him up."

Mary straightened herself hurriedly and took step between them and the cot. For a moment John Marco thought that she was going to prevent him from approaching the child.

But Mr. Petter had not noticed that anything was amiss. He took Mary by the hand and drew her to one side. Then he turned to John Marco.

"If you stand there," he said, "you can see perfectly. You'll get the light on her little face."

John Marco walked towards the cot and looked down. The child that was lying there had flaxen hair that would one day be gold; its skin was transparent and delicate. John Marco remembered the dark hair of his own son and shuddered. That child was Hesther's; this was Mary's.

He raised his eyes a little, and saw that Mary was looking at him. She did not avoid his gaze any longer. In her pride over the diminutive creature before them, she was smiling. She came up beside him and placed her hand on the side of the cot unable to resist this fascinating infant any longer. John Marco looked again at the child, then turning towards Mary he placed his hand over hers.

From the other side of the cot Mr. Petter observed everything that took place. For a moment he was horrified, he blushed a sudden embarrassed scarlet. Then reason came to him, and he understood. He stepped up and, putting his arm round Mary's waist, he completed the party.

"You're quite right," he said to John Marco. "She is lovely, isn't she?"

It was still quite early when John Marco left them. Mr. Petter came down to the front door to see him off. And as he shook hands he gave a little laugh.

"How funny," he said. "We didn't give you any tea and we haven't spoken a word about the Association."

"Some other time," John Marco answered. "I hope this won't be the last time I shall visit you."

Chapter XXIV

It was very flattering to Mr. Petter's vanity to have John Marco for a friend; for the six months during which he had known him, and his visits had become longer and more frequent. A whole week rarely went past now without his calling on them; and, once he was in the house, it was sometimes as late as eleven-thirty when he left. In particular, Mr. Petter was pleased to observe that Mary had grown to be much more at ease with his new friend. She no longer avoided him and sat by herself in another room while he was in the flat. Mr. Petter, of course, could tell instinctively that she disliked the man; but he was pleased to see how, for his sake, she had overcome her dislike and consented to be one of them. She now joined them quite naturally in the evenings, whenever John Marco was there and, sitting at Mr. Petter's feet, where he liked to have her, continued with her sewing as though the two of them were alone together.

Not until quite recently—a week or so ago, in fact—had Mr. Petter purely by accident discovered the unhappy secret of John Marco's private life.

One of the Chapel Brethren had mentioned it casually as one of those rewarding tit-bits that come the way of men of the world. As Mr. Petter had listened, his mind had suddenly responded. Everything that had been dark before was now lit up, and he understood a lot of things—why John Marco had not answered when he had asked him if he had any children of his own: how terrible, thought Mr. Petter, to have a son and be separated from it; why Mary had not spoken of her acquaintance with him; why John Marco had so self-effacingly resigned from the Synod rather than stir up any kind of scandal within the Chapel. And as he thought of these things his heart went out towards John Marco. For all his fine business and his great company of assistants, the man was lonely and an outcast. Mr. Petter sighed and wished that it were within his power to give him all he wanted.

During all this time John Marco had never managed to see Mary alone. Once or twice in the evening when he had been there, someone had rung the night bell and Mr. Petter had been called away from them. But Mary had always used this as an excuse to leave him; and when Mr. Petter had got back from his dispensary he had always found his visitor sitting alone in the little white and apricot sitting-room, waiting for his return.

But, even though at first, John Marco had been content to abide his time, he realised as the days went past that he could wait no longer. The original solace that he had found in seeing Mary had passed; with Mr. Petter always beside her the pain of these meetings had become unendurable.

He therefore planned his next visit with especial care. He chose for it, four-thirty on a Saturday afternoon. And it was all just as he had expected: the little shop was crowded at the time. He sauntered idly in and stood there waiting for Mr. Petter to emerge from behind the glass partition which cut off his dispensary.

When Mr. Petter appeared, he was surprised and delighted to see his visitor.

"Hello, Marco," he said, holding out over the counter a small pink hand that smelt of ether. "This is an unexpected pleasure."

This dropping of the "Mr." gave Mr. Petter a fresh surge of pleasure every time he became aware of it: it showed how far he had come on since first the friendship had started.

"You can give me something for a headache," John Marco told him. "I've been working too hard lately."

Mr. Petter suppressed his usual reply about needing to find the cause before the effect could be remedied, and took down a bottle of anti-kamnia tablets from one of the loaded shelves.

"I think you'll find that this'll put you on your feet again," he said. "I'll give you a glass of water to drink it with."

"I'd rather drink a cup of tea," John Marco replied, and paused. "Why don't you leave the shop and come upstairs yourself for a moment?" he asked.

"Leave the shop at this time. Oh no, I couldn't do that."

Mr. Petter seemed quite shocked at the suggestion; he evidently felt that it belittled his importance as a shopkeeper. But his face brightened again almost immediately:

"Why don't you have a cup of tea with Mary?" he asked. "She always brings me down a cup about this time."

John Marco regarded Mr. Petter carefully.

"I don't like intruding in this way," he explained. "Especially as you can't join us."

"It wouldn't be intruding," Mr. Petter said reproachfully. "You know that. Besides, Mary'd like it."

"You think so?"

"I'm sure of it," Mr. Petter replied. "Why don't you go up?"

He opened the door of the private stairway that led down into the shop as he said it, and stood back for John Marco to pass. "I'd come up with you," he said, "if it wasn't for the shop. Saturday afternoons are my busy time."

John Marco heard Mr. Petter shut the door behind him and his heart stood still. Somewhere in the flat above him was Mary, and he would be alone with her. He was breathing deeply and his face was flushed when he reached the small landing and called out to her by name.

She came at once. But not in answer to his summons. In her hand she was carrying a cup of tea with two sweet biscuits in the saucer: it was Mr. Petter's afternoon feast being taken to him.

"Your husband has invited me to stay to tea," he said. "That is if you'll have me."

She paused, looking at him incredulously.

"I've got to take this down first," was all she said.

John Marco went into the living-room and sat down on the settee: it was the same settee which he had seen Mary and Mr. Petter buy together on that afternoon when he tried to dismiss Mr. Hackbridge. And at that moment as he sat there and thought of what Mr. Petter had to lose, he felt sorry for the little man so blissfully dispensing in the shop below.

Then Mary came in and began setting out the table. John Marco was the first to speak.

"I've brought you this for the child," he said.

He held out an ivory ring with a silver handle: it was an expensive toy—far more expensive than Mr. Petter would ever have been able to afford.

Mary seemed to hesitate for a moment.

"You're very good to her," she said.

"She's yours," he answered.

She shook her head.

"That's no good reason," she said.

"It's reason enough for me," he told her.

She left him and came back a moment later carrying one of those silver tea pots that have obviously been wedding presents. It amused him to see that she should have brought out for him the best that was in the house: there seemed to be both pride and defiance in it, as though she meant to show him that she had not married so badly after all.

Then, as he watched, he saw her cock her little finger high in the air and began to pour. With her fair head bent forward she might still have been Mr. Kent's unmarried daughter in the family living-room in Abernethy Terrace. It was as though the last three years had run suddenly backwards on their spool, carrying him with them.

It is difficult at any time to recall even the quite immediate past without some feeling of sadness, of misgiving; the years, looked back on from the finish, always seem loaded with regrets. And as John Marco crossed his legs in front of Mr. Petter's fire the thoughts that had been in his mind when he had come there were subdued and replaced by other, gentler ones. In those few minutes the whole strategy of his subtle plan vanished and left him without a purpose. For some time he sat altogether without speaking.

"If we'd been married," he observed almost as though speaking to himself, "it might have been like this."

"I was thinking that too," Mary answered quietly.

At her reply, the reserve, the careful, strenuous reserve, which he had been careful to show ever since these visits had started, left him for a moment. He reached out and grasped her hand. She let him hold it for a moment, even tightening her grip in

312

answer to his urgent, increasing one, and then withdrew it.

"But it's too late now," she said. "We mustn't think about it."

They sat on again in silence. Then John Marco rose slowly and stood with his back to the fireplace. It was easier to be sure of himself when he was away from her to know that nothing he said would betray him.

"I wanted to see you alone to-day," he said. "I've been planning how I could see you."

"I knew you had," she answered. "I knew as soon as you came in."

He paused as though uncertain whether to continue.

"I still love you," he went on at last. "It doesn't grow any less. I've never stopped loving you."

At the words she raised her hands to her face instinctively as though to protect herself.

"You mustn't say that," she told him. "It's wicked."

John Marco shook his head.

"No," he said. "It's not wicked. Not now. I came here to-day because I wanted to make love to you. But I've hurt you enough already. I'm not going to risk hurting you again."

The back of her hand was still raised to her face; he saw her fingers clench themselves involuntarily.

"You don't understand," she said. "I love Thomas now."

He shook his head.

"That's not true," he answered, still in the same quiet voice, "it's me you really love. But you can go on loving your husband just the same. I shan't come between you."

He stopped himself before he said anything further. Even now he had confessed more than he had intended. Already his share of her life, the thin, pitiful share that he had won for himself by cultivating the company of Mr. Petter, had been thrown away. He looked across at her to see if she was angry, if she was going to punish him. But he found instead that she was crying.

Down her cheeks large tears were running. They reminded him of the raindrops that he had seen on her face that first afternoon when he had walked home with her. She covered her eyes with her handkerchief and turned her head away from him.

"Why couldn't you leave me alone?" was all she said. "Why did you have to say all these things?"

He took a step towards her. He wanted to comfort her. And all the time inside his brain a voice was saying, "She hasn't denied that she loves me. She can't deny it. She knows that it's the truth."

But as his arm touched her shoulder she got up and faced him.

"You must go away," she said.

He stepped back and stood regarding her.

"Very well," he answered. "I'll go now. I told you I didn't want to hurt you."

"And you mustn't ever come here again," she said. "We mustn't see each other."

"But I can't live without seeing you," he told her. "I've got to come here. Now that I've told you it'll be easier. You'll understand."

She shook her head.

"No," she said, "it's wrong."

He went slowly over to the door. So this was what it had all come to. Simply because she had crooked her little finger when pouring out a cup of tea, his whole spirit had left him. And in consequence he had ruined everything. She would tell her husband, and it would all be over. In future he would stand on guard over her day and night as if she were in a harem.

But because his shoulders were now drooping, because he no longer held his head as high as when he had entered, she went after him and put her hand over his.

"I can't bear to see you unhappy," she said.

"Then let me come here," he answered. "Still let me see you."

He was very close to her now. He could smell again the scent she was using.

"Later on," she said faintly. "I can't see you at once after this."

"Then I may come again?" he asked. "I needn't stop seeing you?"

She did not move, and he put his arms round her, pulling her to him closer still. She made no resistance. He kissed her while they stood there, her head thrown back and her eyes closed.

There was the sound of the private door from the shop opening, and she pushed him away from her.

"You must go now," she said.

But it was not only Mr. Petter who was coming. There was the sound of two lots of feet and another voice—a rich, resonant voice.

A moment later Mr. Petter confronted them.

"We've got another unexpected visitor who wants some tea," he said. "I didn't tell him who was here. It's Mr. Tuke."

ii

"But I tell you I saw them," Mr. Tuke was saying loudly. "In his own drawing-room, too, while he was downstairs working. They were conniving."

"But how do you know they were conniving?" Mrs. Tuke enquired.

315

"They had a guilty air," Mr. Tuke snapped back at her. "I distinctly saw John Marco flinch as I entered."

"It might not have been anything," Mrs. Tuke assured him in a mild, pacifying kind of voice. "Perhaps he just didn't expect you."

She bent down to find his slippers for him as she said it, and even carried them right over beside the fire. At moments like this when her husband's anger was rising up inside him like a saucepan full of boiling milk she always felt a trifle afraid of him; he boomed so, when he was really angry. And just before his supper, too! He was a man who simply lived on his nerves—even quite tiny things interfered with his digestion—and if he went on like this she would be up all night bringing him glasses of hot water and lumps of sugar soaked in oil of Cajaput.

And she saw to her dismay that her last remark had done nothing whatever to mollify: it had merely irritated.

"Expect me," he shouted. "Of course he didn't expect me. I didn't know myself until the spirit moved me. It simply happened to be tea-time and I dropped in. My footsteps were directed."

"I still think there may be a perfectly innocent explanation," Mrs. Tuke persisted.

"Then why was Mary Petter crying?" Mr. Tuke demanded. "Closeted alone with her lover *and in tears*"

"You didn't tell me that before," Mrs. Tuke replied.

"I wanted to shield her," Mr. Tuke answered. "You dragged it out of me."

"And you don't think Mr. Petter suspected anything."

"Thomas Petter is one of God's pure ones," Mr. Tuke replied. "His eyes must be opened."

"But not by you, please," Mrs. Tuke begged him. "Remember what happened last time."

316

"When?" Mr. Tuke insisted, still in the same threatening voice.

His wife hesitated before answering him: to remind him now of one of his failures seemed an act of the most dangerous folly. But there was no other way round.

"I meant about John Marco's own marriage," she said apologetically. "That was all so dreadful."

"Thomas Petter is a very different cut of man," Mr. Tuke replied. "If he was told he had married one of the frail sisterhood he would remain by her to give her strength. He wouldn't break his vows."

"You can't be too careful," Mrs. Tuke observed.

"I am always careful," Mr. Tuke said abruptly.

"Well it's no use doing anything for the moment," Mrs. Tuke answered in a lighter tone of voice. "Supper's been ready for the last ten minutes. It'll spoil if you don't have it."

"I don't want any supper," Mr. Tuke replied. "I want to go upstairs and pray."

Mrs. Tuke hardly heard the latter half of the sentence: the first half was calamitous enough for her. If Mr. Tuke had really turned against his food she feared that anything might happen.

It was nearly half-an-hour before Mr. Tuke re-appeared. When he came down he was wearing his long, black ecclesiastical overcoat and carried his tall hat in his hand. He was no longer angry, and a kind of terrible calmness seemed to have settled down on him.

"I'm going out," he said shortly.

"Not . . . not to Mr. Petter's," Mrs. Tuke implored him.

"No," Mr. Tuke replied. "Not to Mr. Petter's."

"Then where are you going?" Mrs. Tuke asked hopelessly.

"I'm going about my business," he answered over his shoulder.

317

"God's business."

And before Mrs. Tuke could question him further he had shut the door on her.

Mr. Kent was very pleased to see Mr. Tuke until he heard what he had come about. He had put his coat on again—he spent most of his leisure time comfortably in his shirt sleeves—and was just settling down to an evening's edifying gossip when Mr. Tuke burst his little bombshell. Then Mr. Kent took his coat off again and went over to the door.

"We'd better get Mother in on this," he said. "She'll have to know."

"A mother's feelings . . ." Mr. Tuke began.

But Mr. Kent stopped him.

"She'd never forgive me," he said. "She'll want to handle this herself."

And Mr. Kent was right. Mrs. Kent insisted on hearing everything.

"Him in the house," she said. "Well, why not?"

"Then you knew of it?" asked Mr. Tuke.

"I knew he went there, if that's what you mean," she said. "He never comes *here*"

"But wasn't Mr. Petter warned?" Mr. Tuke asked. "Didn't you tell him?"

Mrs. Kent did not reply immediately. Of course she hadn't warned Mr. Petter. It was scarcely a mother's place to inform her daughter's intended that his fiancée had already been thrown over by another man. And once the marriage was over there had seemed no point in it.

"Well, not exactly," she admitted.

At that Mr. Tuke threw up his hands.

"So the viper was left to flourish," he observed. "The gate was left open for him."

"Not by us, it wasn't," Mrs. Kent said warmly. "She never saw him again while she was still here."

"Then she has deceived you since," Mr. Tuke said sternly.

Mr. Kent dropped his hand across his faded, straggling moustache.

"It certainly looks like it," he admitted.

But Mrs. Kent would have none of this: she gave Mr. Kent a little frown to show that in her opinion he had said too much already.

"After she got married it was Thomas Petter's business to look after her," she replied.

"But how could he look after her if he didn't *know?*" Mr. Tuke insisted.

"Know what?" Mrs. Kent enquired.

"That she had loved another."

"I see your point," Mr. Kent said despondently. "I suppose we ought to have told him."

"Well, I say let sleeping dogs lie," Mrs. Kent retorted.

"And have this thing continue? Allow John Marco to go to the house as though nothing had happened?"

Mrs. Kent tweaked the lace fichu on her bosom, pulling the crumpled, cottony mass into more outstanding and aggressive folds.

"It's for my son-in-law to say who he has to his house, not me," she replied. "He'd stop it soon enough if he saw John Marco getting beyond himself. You may be sure of that."

Mr. Tuke eyed her gravely.

"But suppose that your daughter encouraged it," he said. "Suppose that she led Mr. Marco on?"

"I won't suppose anything of the kind," Mrs. Kent replied promptly. "It isn't like her."

She was sitting bolt upright by now, screwing the heels of her shoe down into the carpet. Mr. Kent began to feel apprehensive and uncomfortable: his wife sat like that only when she was really annoyed about something. He did hope she wasn't going to be rude to Mr. Tuke.

And what was worse was that Mr. Tuke was clearly annoyed, too; he was glowering. He opened his mouth once or twice very wide and then closed it again abruptly as though thinking better of it each time. Finally, he rose and stood over Mrs. Kent's chair.

"I have evidence," he said. "Terrible evidence. I have proof that they're still lovers."

Mrs. Kent ground her heel still deeper into the carpet and went on pulling at the creases of her fichu.

"Explain yourself," she said.

"I will," he replied.

He paused for a moment and sucked in a great rush of air like a swimmer getting ready to dive. Then his lungs full, he plunged.

"I have seen John Marco," he said, "after he was married"— here his voice rose threateningly—"embracing Mary in the street. They were holding each other."

"It couldn't have been Mary," Mrs. Kent interrupted him. "You must have imagined it."

"And did I imagine that she gave him her photograph dressed in her bridal clothes? His own wife found it shut away in his drawer."

"That's only what she said," Mrs. Kent maintained.

Mr. Tuke gave a little gesture of impatience.

"And are you aware that actually at her marriage John Marco was there in the gallery? He blew a kiss as she passed by on her own husband's arm."

"Who says so?"

"Poor Hesther was present. She observed it all."

"We've only got her word for that, too," Mrs. Kent replied.

"And this afternoon," Mr. Tuke resumed, speaking very slowly and distinctly, "I found them closeted alone together. I believe I almost caught them in the act."

Mrs. Kent gave a little gasp and then recovered herself.

"I'm quite sure you didn't," she replied. "And I think it's very unpleasant of you to say so."

"If that's how you take it," Mr. Tuke replied, "I'll bid you good-evening."

"Good evening," Mrs. Kent replied, and turned her back on him.

Mr. Tuke did not wait to shake hands. He simply walked straight out of the room and down the stairs. He let himself out. As he pulled the front door behind him he suddenly felt faint and sick. His stomach seemed to be turning round and round inside him, and he clutched at the railings for support. It was nearly nine o'clock and he had had no tea and no supper.

For the moment it seemed that his Master, on whose business he had been, had utterly deserted him.

Upstairs in the flat Mrs. Kent's self-control had deserted her. She was crying. Her face was half smothered in a cushion and her shoulders were heaving. Mr. Kent was standing over her trying to offer his pocket handkerchief.

"Take it easy, Mother," he was saying. "Take it easy."

When she was a little quieter, he spoke to her again.

"You . . . you . . . don't think there's anything in it, do you?" he asked.

"Of course not," she said. "It's all some horrible mistake."

The mention of it, however, set her crying again. She lay back and moaned.

"My poor darling," he heard her saying. "The things he said about you. The awful things. It isn't true. Oh God, say that it isn't true."

Then words left her and she simply cried.

Chapter XXV

It was not until nearly six months later that John Marco realised that Hesther was watching him.

The indications at first were scanty, but they were sufficient. Once when he went to the window of his office he saw her in broad daylight on the other side of the pavement standing in the shelter of the shop blind looking upwards towards his room; she was dressed entirely in black by now like a widow. The sight shocked him—she looked so old and lonely; shocked him, but left him callous and unmoved because he had never loved her. Then one Sunday after Chapel he happened to glance behind him and, two blocks away, he saw the same black figure, keeping close to the railings, diligently following: her way lay in the opposite direction but she was there urged on by some force within her that was stronger than mere curiosity. And on another occasion when he had been out late, walking alone by himself in the streets, he had stopped and seen her pass the shop several times slowly and lingeringly as if waiting for someone whom she knew would never come.

It was not, however, until one night as he stood outside Mr. Petter's premises in Harrow Street waiting for him to answer the bell—his visits had been resumed uninterrupted and Mary had accepted them—and saw Hesther move away from a doorway opposite that her presence alarmed him. It seemed then as though she were sinister again, as though somehow she were threatening him. But what could she do? He was free of her; it was his life that he was living now. He shook Mr. Petter's hot little hand as it was thrust out delightedly towards him and tried to forget about Hesther.

In a strange, detached fashion he had grown rather to like this cautious prosaic chemist who had become Mary's husband. He was so simple, so dangerously easy to hurt. And his love for Mary was such a reliable, unquestioning thing. Often on evenings when John Marco was there, Mr. Petter would sit perfectly happy just looking at Mary and smiling every time she glanced in his direction. John Marco could not even find it in him to resent him: if he himself had chosen a guardian for Mary, someone who would be ready to lay down his life for her, he could not have selected better.

Mr. Petter was still, of course, as jealous as ever, still as proud of this marriage that he had made; but now that he really knew John Marco, now that he felt that he could trust him, he was generous, too. He was filled with pity for the other man's loneliness and wanted him to feel that here at least he had a home.

As a matter of fact, it was Mr. Petter's kindness—his clumsy, awkward kindness—that first reminded John Marco that he *was* lonely. On that same evening when John Marco had seen Hesther slip away without speaking to him, Mr. Petter, his day's work done, sat comfortably back with his two feet on the fender and counted his blessings.

"Friendship," he said. "That's the grand thing in life. It must be awful to be lonely. Having a friend drop in on one or dropping in on one myself—I don't ask anything better."

But John Marco was not listening to him. He had no friends of his who ever dropped in on him; and this house of Mr. Petter's was the only one that he went inside. On those Tuesday evenings when he called at Clarence Gardens to see old Mrs. Marco—her brain was now more nebulous and diffuse than ever—Hesther still made a point of locking herself away from him, and he spoke to no one.

Now that he came to think of it, he supposed that he was really damnably lonely: his life was without anything behind it. The reason, of course, was the business: it left him with no time to make friends. But were those seven plate glass window panes and the thirty-four assistants—the business had been going forward steadily: its turnover was up again by nearly three thousand pounds—the shadow, or the substance? His eye rested on Mary for a moment and he wondered. If he had married her, it would all have been different, he told himself; friendship would have seemed natural then.

"Not being wanted is the real tragedy," Mr. Petter observed at random. "Think of orphans."

But John Marco was thinking now of Hesther: her spirit still seemed somehow to be pervading the evening. Was that why she had come here to-night, because she was lonely? Because she wasn't wanted? It was, after all, only because she had been so lonely before that she had tried so desperately to draw him into her life.

"We make our own loneliness," John Marco said at last; and as he said it Mary glanced up for a moment from her sewing and they looked into each other's eyes.

Now that he was down in the street once more, he paused. It had

325

been in the doorway opposite that Hesther had been standing. The doorway itself was empty now. But further down the street a four-wheel cab was standing. Against the window of the cab, a face was pressed. It was not a distinct, recognisable face; nothing that he could have named or identified. Across the width of the thoroughfare, it was simply a white smudge with two dark places which were eyes. But apparently his appearance was the signal. For the face at once withdrew; and a hand, a long hand in a black glove like a widow's, tapped on the window.

Immediately the cab began to move away and John Marco stood there looking after it, staring helplessly at that one small window at the back that was blank and non-committal and admitted nothing.

ii

It was the following day that Mr. Petter received the anonymous letter. It arrived innocently enough by the noon delivery. But was that really so innocent? It seemed to Mr. Petter on those innumerable occasions in the future when he dragged the horrible thing out of his pocket and studied it—the message and the hand-writing, and the postmark—that the very hour at which he had received it was suspicious. The letter—it was as The Letter that he subsequently came to think of it—had been posted in Bayswater sometime between midnight and seven-thirty in the morning. It was as though the unknown writer had sat up far into the night composing it, and had then stolen out to the pillar box while the rest of London was asleep.

The text of the message was brief, unsubtle and terrifying. In the middle of a plain sheet of paper—the sort of paper on which a child might write out its exercises: it had obviously been torn from a penny copy-book—the words were inscribed in sharp, angular capitals.

"BEWARE," it ran. "JOHN MARCO IS YOUR WIFE'S LOVER. KEEP HIM FROM THE HOUSE IF YOU RESPECT YOUR MARRIAGE." There was no signature and no address; no date, even. The thing simply existed.

As Mr. Petter read it he felt suddenly sick; it was as though someone had come up close and had spat into his face.

But it is not what an anonymous letter says that does the harm: it is the fear of what else it might have said: What does the writer know? Who is he? Where are the proofs? What evidence is there, can there be? Why was it written? Was it sent to me by someone whom I know, or by a stranger? Is it madness? Or malice? Or——? These were the thoughts that were running wildly and at random through Mr. Petter's mind as he sat down on the stool in his dispensary, his heart jumping and faltering.

To show that letter to Mary and then burn it: that seemed the clean, the common-sense thing to do. But why make her suffer—even if they only laughed about it together afterwards? Why publish this abomination? In any case, perhaps simply to cause anguish had been the unknown writer's intention. If that were so, his object, partially achieved already, would then be complete.

Mr. Petter therefore bravely decided to do nothing. He would burn the letter, unshown; and forget about it. Taking it cautiously from his pocket he read it through once more—for the last time. There was a naked gas-jet in front of him—it was the jet he used for melting the sealing-wax for all his parcels—and his hand moved towards it. But at the last moment he drew back. There was too deep a fascination about this thing that he was holding. It was tangible; it was evidence; it was something with which to go to the police. Without it, the whole incident would become

327

simply like the memory of some dreadful message read in an alarming dream; it would have the new terror of being altogether uncheckable. The writer, too, would surely be delighted that all proof of his guilt had been destroyed.

Thomas Petter therefore folded the letter carefully into its original creases and stowed it safely away in a pocket of his note-book.

It was not until three full days later, during which time he had discovered that to do nothing was impossible, and he had spent whole hours of his time staring senselessly at this single sheet of paper in his hand, that he came to a decision. And once he had come to it he did not question that it was the right one.

He decided that he would take the letter along quite openly and ask Mr. Tuke for his advice.

Chapter XXVI

John Margo was sitting in the handsome gilt and mahogany offices of Bulmer and Urwick, the Issuing House. The cigar which Mr. Bulmer had just given him was between his lips and the air already was thick with sweet blue clouds from Havana. But because John Marco was excited, he was drawing a trifle too hard at his cigar and was causing a little circle of red to dance before his face.

"I'm not interested simply in having the present premises rebuilt," he was saying. "I'm interested in something very much larger—something the whole of Bayswater will come to."

He spread out his hands as he said it, and the vision of a vast shop-front with a battery of windows rose before his eyes again. He saw his own name, JOHN MARCO, JOHN MARCO, JOHN MARCO, repeated in letters of gold—there was going to be no sentimental nonsense about keeping the old name on the frontage—all down the length of the street. The whole thing was so real to him that he could not understand why Mr. Bulmer could not see it just as clearly.

"Then how much have you got in mind?" Mr. Bulmer enquired.

He was a large man with a red carnation in his button-hole, and the points of his butterfly-collar set a trifle too wide. He had a sanguine disposition and cultivated a pleasant talent for assisting money to circulate.

"Five hundred thousand," John Marco answered him. "A straight five hundred."

Mr. Bulmer pursed up his lips for a moment.

"It's a lot of money for a local enterprise," he said at length.

John Marco leant forward and blew out a cloud of the fine helpful smoke.

"I've gone into the figures carefully," he said. "There's no point in starving ourselves before we've started."

Mr. Bulmer began playing with the top of his inkwell.

"I could probably raise it if your results are good enough," he said. "It all depends on the accountants." He sat back and thrust his thumbs into the arm-holes of his waistcoat. "I prefer something I can get my teeth into," he added.

It was a strange place, London, Mr. Bulmer reflected. If you took an office in the right quarter—close beside St. Swithin's Lane, his was—and put out a brass name plate you could get all the money you wanted simply by reaching out your hand for it. Of course you had to have something to offer in exchange. But what? How was he to know, for instance, if a vast new emporium in Bayswater would succeed or not? The answer, of course, was that he didn't know; he didn't even have to know. Once he had got all the particulars down on paper in front of him and had brooded over them he could tell whether he would be able to *sound* as if he knew; and that was all that really mattered. The rest would be up to that simple, childlike, greedy thing, the Public. The Public was always the same: it was comprised of endless numbers of diligent, respectable hard-working little men who had sweated their manhood away working year in and year out from nine o'clock in the morning till seven at night so that they could at last have two or three hundred pounds to call their own and then suddenly—whoosh!—they were prepared to make a paper boat of all their savings and see which way the wind would carry it. It was as though, sometime in the fifties, a second infancy came to them and they began to believe once more in gold mines and perpetual motion and harnessing the sun and god-knows-what besides. A drapery stores would seem gilt edged to those people.

But John Marco was speaking again.

"This is something big," he was saying. "Something big I tell you. There's nothing local about it. We'll show the whole of London. We'll get people out there from Oxford Street and Piccadilly. By the time we're open, the Bon Marché and the rest of them will all be smashed, finished. There'll be people going to my shop from all over the country. . . ."

His eyes were shining as he spoke and he had run his fingers through his hair, ruffling it. During those few minutes, he had felt a mysterious, outside power flowing into him: he had believed. It had been like that in those old days in the Tabernacle. And as he sat there he heard again Mr. Tuke's big voice echoing inside his brain. "The Lord is my Shepherd, I shall not want," the words came back to him. Not to want: that was the great thing: to be secure. And with wealth, everything else would become simple, too. With real wealth, great inexhaustible hoards of it, he would be powerful. And how would a little back-street chemist ever be able to stand against him then?

"With me behind it, it can't fail," he heard himself saying, "it will be tremendous."

But Mr. Bulmer was no longer listening. The golden-paved

square-mile around Threadneedle Street was the mecca of all commercial visionaries, and his mind had grown stale to them. He got up and went over for his hat.

"I am going up West," he said. "Will you come along to my Club for a drink?"

ii

As John Marco and Mr. Bulmer were driving down Ludgate Hill towards Pall Mall, Mr. Petter was just leaving his small shop in Harrow Street on his painful visit to Mr. Tuke.

There was something fugitive and surreptitious about him. He had not told Mary where he was going and he was conscious of the fact that he had deceived her. A moment before as he had kissed her, he had looked into her eyes and resolved that never, never so long as he was alive, should any hint of this terrible letter come to her. Between them, he and Mr. Tuke would protect her from the vicious, nasty world which lay without. He closed the front door behind him silently and almost ran round to the Presbytery.

Mr. Tuke saw him immediately. He stopped writing out in his expert, polished hand the text of the printed announcement for the forthcoming Dorcas and Zenana Mission Tea, and came straight down to his study. In that bleak room of deal bookshelves and upright chairs and views of the Holy Land, he heard Mr. Petter's whole story.

"I'm in trouble," Mr. Petter began. "Dreadful trouble."

"Tell me," said Mr. Tuke rubbing his hands together. "Tell me everything."

As he said it, the picture of Hesther rose suddenly before his eyes; it was in this same room that she had sat, on that calamitous evening when she had come to him. The room was not really like a study at all, he had often told himself: it was much more like a doctor's surgery. And apparently Mr. Petter was proposing to bare himself.

"We're quite alone," he went on encouragingly. "You can begin."

But now that Mr. Petter was actually there he found suddenly that he could tell him nothing. It was one thing to rehearse the words over and over in his head as he lay awake beside Mary in the night—but something very different to hear himself saying them aloud to another man. Instead, he felt in his pocket and dragged out the letter that was haunting him.

"Read this," he said simply.

Mr. Tuke took the letter and inspected it. He handled it gingerly at first as though fearing that it might be infectious; already a faint sickening fear was in his mind as to what this letter might contain. But he subdued this vague, foolish fancy and opened the thing, revealing as he did so that the creases down the back had all been stuck over and mended with stamp paper, the letter had been folded and unfolded so often. His eyes were burning and he began to read.

When he had finished it, Mr. Tuke curled his nostrils.

"Faugh!" he said.

"It came a week ago to-day," Mr. Petter timidly said. "I've shown it to no one."

"To no one at all?" Mr. Tuke exclaimed fastening on the point.

"To no one at all."

"Then we will burn it," said Mr. Tuke decisively. "We will destroy it utterly."

A man of quick action he went down on his knees as he spoke

and held the corner of the letter to the open grate. But Mr. Petter snatched it back from him.

"No," he said. "I may need it. I may want to go to the police with it."

Mr. Tuke eyed him fiercely. This was the last thing in the world that he wanted; at all costs he must prevent another scandal, must prevent one of the brethren from dragging a sister-in-God through the courts. And the whole thing was already dreadfully plain to him. The disguised, printed capitals, the makeshift note-paper, the absence of any signature or any address—these were nothing. But there was something else. He recognised in this letter, as plainly as if the writer had put her name to it, the last pathetic remedy of a desperate and jealous woman.

"It can't do any good," he said, keeping it. "Anything as horrible as that can only go on doing harm."

But Mr. Petter was obstinate.

"I want to keep it," he replied. "I may be able to find out who wrote it."

Mr. Tuke paused.

"Suppose I tell you," he said softly, "that I think I know."

There was silence for a moment as though Mr. Petter could not believe what Mr. Tuke had just told him.

"You know?" he repeated. "You think you know?"

"I believe so," Mr. Tuke replied. "That is why I want you to burn it."

"But tell me who it is," said Mr. Petter eagerly. "Tell me and I'll go and accuse him of it."

Mr. Tuke shook his head.

"It is someone whom you do not know," he answered. "Someone who is very unhappy. Very unhappy and very much

334

misguided. It is someone who needs our prayers, not our accusations."

"But I'm not going to stand for it." Mr. Petter declared. He was so angry that he was trembling; Mr. Tuke was quite startled to see him displaying so much emotion. "I insist on knowing."

"And I refuse to tell you," Mr. Tuke replied. "The person who wrote it is a woman. She has gone through such suffering that her mind is deranged."

"You mean . . . you mean she's mad?" Mr. Petter asked.

Mr. Tuke bowed his head.

"She's not responsible," he replied.

At that answer Mr. Petter temporarily broke down. There were tears in his eyes and his voice, always high, suddenly became childish.

"Oh, I'm so glad," he said. "I can't tell you. There's nothing more to worry about."

"Not from that quarter," Mr. Tuke answered. "I'll make it my business to attend to that."

Mr. Petter got to his feet and steadied himself.

"I'm so thankful I came to see you," he said. "I nearly went round to John Marco himself to see if he knew who it was."

"You were guided here," Mr. Tuke corrected him.

"I must have been," Mr. Petter agreed meekly. "And now no one need ever know. Oh, it's such a weight off my mind."

But Mr. Tuke was paying no attention to him. To avoid scandal was only half the battle: he would be failing in his duties as a Minister if he allowed Mr. Petter to go home like that. The other half of the battle was the difficult part—it was Satan himself, and not a group of idle gossips, that he would be fighting this time.

"There is one thing perhaps that I ought to say," he began

with deliberate deceptive mildness.

"Yes?" asked Mr. Petter: he felt strong enough to face anything now.

"In view of this letter I wonder if it would be fair to Mary to allow Mr. Marco's visits to the house any longer," he said slowly. "There's obviously been some talk about it to set this woman thinking."

"But . . . but John Marco's my great friend," Mr. Petter began.

"I know," Mr. Tuke replied. "And you may have to deny yourself. It is only Mary's good name that I am thinking of."

"But won't she wonder why?" Mr. Petter asked.

"It's better that she should wonder than that she should know," Mr. Tuke replied cryptically.

"Know what?" Mr. Petter enquired: he had a resentful, injured tone as though he felt that Mr. Tuke was being unreasonable.

"That people are talking."

"Only one person—the mad woman," Mr. Petter corrected him.

But Mr. Tuke shook his head.

"Others as well," he said. "I have noticed it myself." Mr. Petter clasped his hands helplessly together.

"Mr. Marco will think it so strange if we suddenly stop seeing him," he said miserably.

"It would be far stranger after this if you did see him," Mr. Tuke retorted.

"But what can be the harm in it?" Mr. Petter asked. "It isn't as if the letter was true."

"I am not saying whether the letter is true or is not true," said Mr. Tuke. "I am saying that I should not have John Marco to the house again."

336

"You mean never?"

Mr. Tuke nodded.

"Never," he said firmly.

"But why?"

Mr. Tuke drew himself to his full height and took hold of the lapels of his coat like a judge.

"I reserve my reasons," he replied.

Mr. Petter was suddenly sitting forward in his chair, his lips trembling and his heart jumping about inside him.

"You . . . you don't mean that you think there is anything in the letter? You don't mean . . ."

"That is a question which I decline to be drawn into," Mr. Tuke answered. "I have already told you that I should keep Mary and John Marco separate. Remember that her honour is in your keeping."

"Then you do . . . *do* believe it!" Mr. Petter said jerkily, "you do. . . ."

But Mr. Tuke was already holding out his hand.

"Good-night, brother," he said. "You can only pray—and watch."

iii

Mr. Petter descended the stone steps of the Presbytery with limbs that were numb and almost useless. He gripped the iron balustrade as he moved and came down slowly, like a child, putting both feet onto one step before he trusted himself to the next. In those last few minutes in Mr. Tuke's study the whole snug world of Mary and Harrow Street and pharmaceutics had gone toppling over into destruction and had left him alone and frightened, groping blindly in the darkness.

For a second or two he stood, undecided, on the pavement and then mechanically began to walk forward. He had no purpose, no direction. The one thing that he wanted was to walk. If only Mr. Tuke had been more definite; if only he had said something. . . . But could he have borne to hear it? Could he have endured it while Mr. Tuke, his own friend and minister, had told him that his wife had been unfaithful? But it was impossible! He didn't believe it. He wouldn't let himself believe it. It couldn't be *his* wife whom he had kissed so fondly half-an-hour before, whom Mr. Tuke had doubted so appallingly. He reviled himself for his momentary weakness in even beginning to believe it, and resolutely held his head up higher. The evening air, it seemed, was reviving him.

By the time he had reached the Edgware Road he was a man again, and a bold plan had come into his head. John Marco, despite everything that Mr. Tuke had said and hinted, was still his friend. He was his best friend; the first person whom Mr. Petter would naturally turn to in time of trouble. And because he was in trouble now, he would go to him and put him to the test. He would show him the letter and tell him the things that people were saying: he would lay this ghost by a single visit. And when he was there he would be able to watch John Marco while he was reading the letter; he could study his face and see if he blenched under it—but no: that wasn't necessary; that was just another scene in the same silly nightmare from which he had now awakened.

When he rang the bell of John Marco's flat he was surprised to find how late it was: it was nearly eleven and Mary would be worrying. But the fact that John Marco was still up, was something: he had seen the light burning in his room as he crossed the street. And already he could hear the sound of footsteps coming down the last flight of stairs. They were slow footsteps, heavy and dragging, as if the man on the stairs were sleepy and tired-out; Mr. Petter felt like apologising for getting him down at all at this time. Then the door opened and John Marco stood there.

He was wearing a dressing-gown and his shirt and trousers were on beneath it. Even his bow-tie was still knotted at his throat, though the collar itself had sprung the stud and was gaping. But it was his hair that Mr. Petter first noticed: it was all ruffled and untidy. Clearly, he must have dropped asleep in front of his fire and then come straight down to open the door.

"What do you want?" John Marco began roughly, and then, seeing who it was standing there, he came forward and put his arm round Mr. Petter's shoulders.

"Come on in," he said. "Come in and keep me company."

His voice, Mr. Petter noticed, sounded muffled and indistinct, and he uttered words as though he were stumbling over them. Mr. Petter felt all the more sorry for having disturbed him, and it was not until he was actually at the foot of the stairs that he realised that John Marco smelt of liquor.

Mr. Petter's first thought was to turn and run: he had the true Amosite's horror of alcohol. But John Marco was beside him and his arm was now through his.

"Come upstairs and talk to me," he was saying. "Proudest day of my life."

And Mr. Petter was helpless. He mounted the stairs hesitatingly, followed by this man who was not quite himself.

Once they had actually reached the flat, it was worse than Mr. Petter ever could have imagined. There was liquor openly displayed there. A decanter nearly full stood on the table beside John Marco's chair; and an empty bottle—the one from which

339

John Marco had just filled the decanter—was standing over on the sideboard. To Mr. Petter's scandalised eyes it seemed, however, that John Marco, having gulped down one bottleful of the fiery spirit was now preparing to do the same with the other.

John Marco brought a second glass and poured out a stiff measure. Then he paused.

"I forget," he said. "You don't drink, do you?"

Mr. Petter drew in his breath.

"No, I don't," he answered. "And I wish you didn't either."

But John Marco only laughed at him. He was in a mood of dangerously good humour.

"Just as you please," he said pleasantly. "Just as you please."

Mr. Petter cleared his throat.

"I wanted to see you," he said. "It's something important."

"Well," John Marco asked him, "and what's it all about?"

"It's about Mary," Mr. Petter replied.

At the mention of her name, John Marco put down the glass that was in his hand and came over towards Mr. Petter. He was frowning.

"Why do you want to see me about *her?*" he asked.

John Marco was not very steady on his feet when he moved, and Mr. Petter became alarmed for himself once more. This wasn't the John Marco he knew; this man who could scarcely stand upright couldn't help him with any good advice.

"It's . . . it's nothing," he said. "I'd rather talk to you some other time."

"No, you won't," John Marco answered, his good humour slipping suddenly from him. "You'll tell me now before you go."

"It's very late," Mr. Petter replied evasively.

But John Marco had grown impatient: he was snapping his fingers at him.

340

"Tell me now," he said.

Mr. Petter regarded him steadily for a moment, rearguing his decision with himself. Then he thrust his hand into his pocket.

"Very well," he said. "Read that."

John Marco stood for a moment looking at the letter without moving, and then almost snatched it out of Mr. Petter's hands. His back was towards Mr. Petter as he read it; all that Mr. Petter could see was his shoulders. They were square and steady enough until suddenly he crumpled the letter up into a tight ball and shot it onto the floor. He turned towards Mr. Petter, turned angrily this time, his face flushed and his eyebrows drawn into a hard line across his forehead.

"Why did you have to show me this?" he demanded.

"I showed it to you because it concerned you," Mr. Petter answered with a calm that astonished him.

"And what do you want me to do?" John Marco asked. "Tell you that it isn't true?"

"I . . .I never doubted you," Mr. Petter replied.

"Then forget you ever read it," John Marco told him.

"But . . . but I've got to decide what to do," Mr. Petter replied.

"Do nothing," said John Marco savagely.

"But that's impossible," Mr. Petter persisted. "I'm afraid that people may begin talking."

"People? What people?"

"I know the person who wrote it is just a poor mad woman," Mr. Petter began, "but . . ."

He was not allowed, however, to get any further. John Marco suddenly turned on him again.

"So you've found out who wrote it, have you?"

"Yes," said Mr. Petter unguardedly. "Mr. Tuke knows her."

He was, as he spoke, quite unprepared for the effect on John

Marco. He knew, of course, that his friend was strange, very strange to-night: he was pursued by the demons of liquor. But for the moment he seemed to go entirely out of his senses. He drew back his lips until the whole extent of his teeth was showing.

"How the devil does Mr. Tuke come to know about this?" he shouted.

Mr. Petter felt frightened by now, and he wanted to get away. He didn't ever want to see again this John Marco who drank and swore. But he stood his ground a moment longer and answered him.

"I only showed him the letter," he replied. "I wanted his advice."

"And what was his advice?" John Marco demanded.

Mr. Petter paused: this needed courage to say to John Marco's face.

"He said I shouldn't have you in the house," he replied quietly.

"He said that, did he?" John Marco answered. "And what do you propose to do about it?"

Mr. Petter squared his shoulders and drew in a deep, unnatural breath.

"I propose to take it," he replied.

His voice, as he said it, rose to a shrill, uncertain squeak; it trembled.

John Marco put down his glass and faced him: he was shaking with anger now.

"You and I have got to understand each other," he said.

"There's nothing else to understand," Mr. Petter replied.

"Oh yes there is," John Marco answered. "When you get away from here you'll understand a lot of things."

He came towards him as he said it; and Mr. Petter instinctively

342

took a step away.

"So Mr. Tuke thinks your wife's in love with me, does he?" he asked.

"He didn't say any such thing," Mr. Petter replied indignantly.

"Well it's true. True, do you hear me? She was in love with me before she ever set eyes on you. And she still is."

"I don't believe it," Mr. Petter managed to reply.

His lips were quivering so uncontrollably that he could scarcely speak the words.

"If you don't believe me, why don't you ask her?" John Marco went on. "Ask her family. Ask Mr. Tuke. Ask anyone. You're the only one who's been blind."

"It's a lie," Mr. Petter jerked out.

"Then why did my wife write that letter?" John Marco demanded. "*Why was she jealous?*"

"So it was your wife who wrote it?"

Mr. Petter's voice was almost inaudible and his hand was raised to his face in a vain gesture of protection.

John Marco nodded.

"You thought that you could keep Mary to yourself simply by turning the key on her," he said. "You thought that she belonged to you. Wait till you find out the truth. Wait till your eyes have been opened. Wait till you've seen something."

The last relics of Mr. Petter's self-control had at last gone from him: he was crying.

"I'm not going to listen to you," he said. "I'm going home."

But John Marco stood in his path, blocking it: his face was thrust forward.

"Why don't you give her up to me now?" he asked. "Why don't you give her up before she's taken from you? If she wants to go, you can't stop her. She'll slip past you. You'll lose her just the same."

"She . . . she loves me, I tell you," Mr. Petter cried out. And pushing his way past John Marco he stumbled blindly out of the room.

John Marco stood where he was staring after him. He did not attempt to follow. His head was aching and his legs were unsteady. He heard Mr. Petter's feet descending into the darkness below, and the flat seemed suddenly to be very quiet. He stood there, swaying.

"It's I who've lost you, Mary," he said aloud. "I'm the one who's lost."

iv

The light in the little pink and white bedroom in Harrow Street was not extinguished until nearly two o'clock that morning; the child—she had been moved into the next room by now—slept on, however, without stirring.

Mary had been asleep when Mr. Petter had got back—she had dropped off for a moment—and started up as she heard his key touch the lock. Putting on a dressing-gown (it was a pretty new one that Mr. Petter in a moment of indulgence had just given her) and with her hair loose about her shoulders she went down to meet him. When she saw him she was startled by his appearance, and a little frightened. Mr. Petter first pushed her violently away, then he kissed her frantically, and finally broke down in her arms. During the next half-hour, still clasped up against her, he had told her everything. . . .

"How could I ever have doubted you?" he said at last. "How

344

could I have been so vile?"

"Don't think about it," Mary told him. "Don't think about it. It was horrible."

She was stroking his head, soothing him, comforting.

"But you do love me, don't you?" he demanded. "You do?"

"What makes you think that I don't?" she asked. "Why do you keep on asking me?"

"Then why don't you tell me," he begged her. "Let me hear you say it."

He had buried his face against her breast by now, his arms folded round her. All the courage which earlier in the evening had supported him had ebbed away again by now, leaving him helpless and afraid.

"Say it," he repeated. "Say it."

"I do love you," she said slowly. "I don't love anyone else."

"Oh, Mary," he said. "You're all I've got. You're everything."

And opening the neck of her pretty dressing-gown he began kissing her again.

Chapter XXVII

John Margo went on the next Tuesday to see his mother; and again on the following Tuesday; but after that there was no point in going any longer.

Old Mrs. Marco's end when it had come, was very sudden. For three brief days she had rallied. She had been able to get about the room and her mind had cleared. She had realised that she was living in Hesther's house, and she was worried because her son was away so much. He was like his father, she said to Hesther—quiet and secretive and in need of watching; and in saying this she allowed herself the first disloyal remark which she had ever made about the departed Mr. Marco. It was as though inside herself old Mrs. Marco was aware that she would be there for only a short time longer and felt that there was no further use in pretending; all her life she had kept up the myth of Mr. Marco's respectability; and then, at one stroke she shattered the whole image of this saturnine, morose man with the high collar and the mutton-chop whiskers. "He wasn't always what he seemed," she said darkly. "He prayed beautifully, but some nights he didn't come home at all." And when Hesther made no reply, old Mrs. Marco told her that it was she, his mother, whom

346

she had to thank for having made John Marco as steady as he was. "He's like a rock, my son is," she observed proudly. "Like a rock."

When Hesther got up, Mrs. Marco was still rambling on about John Marco's childhood; and about revival meetings she had known, when young and old had plunged themselves into the tank unable to restrain themselves; and about the way evil and wickedness were increasing in the world so rapidly that the Second Coming could not be far off. She was still talking to herself when Hesther gently closed the door on her.

And then, next morning, when Emmy took her in a cup of tea, Mrs. Marco was lying there, propped up among the pillows, silent at last.

It had been an untidy finish. The old lady had obviously awakened in the night, because she had started eating again. There was a plate of tea-rusks left beside her and one of these rusks was still fixed between her teeth. After all her years of self-denial and discipline and preparation, when her Maker finally called to her she was sitting up in bed nibbling biscuits like a school-girl.

It was Emmy whom Hesther sent to tell John Marco. Already she saw—indistinct as it was—her opportunity; the very fact of the funeral would bring John Marco beside her at the grave-side. She no longer deluded herself with foolish expectations. But, never for a single moment after that night when he had left her, had she entirely given up hope.

On her return to the house Hesther made Emmy repeat every word, every syllable, that John Marco had uttered. At first, Emmy said, she had been kept waiting; she had been kept waiting so long in fact that she wondered whether he ever intended to see her at all. And when, finally, she had been shown into his room he had treated her as a stranger, as someone whom he had

347

never seen before. But the news of his mother's death had very clearly disturbed him; he had begun walking about the room and he had questioned her closely as to the circumstances. Had it been painless? Had the old lady had any premonition? Why hadn't they sent for him? It was not until Emmy had said diffidently that she expected that they would see him at the cemetery that his aloofness had returned to him.

"I shall not be there," he had said.

"Not be there?" Emmy had repeated. "Not be at your own mother's funeral?"

And John Marco with that terrible deliberation that had always frightened had answered slowly.

"I shall sit with her," he had said. "I shall come to the house to-morrow night as usual. But I shall not be at the funeral."

When Hesther heard this she knew that it was not going to be old Mrs. Marco in death who was to draw them together again. And on the Tuesday evening of the visit she sat in the wicker chair in her bedroom and listened to her own husband's feet pass her door and go into the room opposite.

As John Marco entered the room, his nerve, for a moment, left him; it was very quiet in there and the subtle odour of death pervaded the place. It was like stepping with eyes open into the tomb.

The figure under the sheet looked so small now, so ridiculously small; it was scarcely larger than a big doll and the hand when he touched it was as cold as china. He drew back for a moment, frightened. This thing lying there, as rigid as if in some preposterous fashion it were holding its breath, wasn't his mother; *she* had already slipped out through the mesh and was free. She was up there among the harps and the seven-branched candlesticks, while he was dragging a cane-seated chair across the oil-cloth to sit with the image that she had discarded.

When he at last could bear to do so he folded back the sheet and looked. The face seemed more tranquil than in life he could ever remember it. The lines were still there, running in a close net-work under the eyes and merging with the puckers round her mouth. But somehow she looked younger than he had known her; it was as though in death she had discovered, in part at least, the secret of perpetual youth.

As she lay there she appeared simply to be resting; and perhaps she *was* resting, he reflected. Now that the spark was out, her mind was no longer troubling her; it had ceased casting up those black shadows from the past that had kept deceiving and confusing her. She was as she had been when he was a young man in Chapel Villas. There had been no Hesther in his life when she had looked like that; and no Mary. The Old Gentleman had still been a power in the shop, and Mr. Tuke was his friend. And the years that had changed her into a shapeless, tottery old witch had left their mark on him as well. It was a tired, bitter man who sat there looking at that unmoving face; a man without friends and without a family; someone in the prime of his days who was as cold and alone as she was.

But he halted his thoughts and drove them forward again towards the future; this lingering over his yesterdays was too disturbing. Not to remember, however, was impossible. Everything that he had ever done, or hoped to do, was linked to that silent figure that lay in front of him. And going down on his knees, as he had been trained to do, he started to pray for her.

"Oh Lord," he began, "take this, Thy sister, into Thy fold and protect her for evermore. Let Thy arms be about her and her head on Thy bosom. Let her no longer think of those things which have hurt and injured her. Let her forget this, my marriage, that has been troubling her. Let her . . ." But it was no use. This wasn't the way real Amosites prayed. He had turned his back on it for too long, and the magic of communion had forsaken him. Those words of his reached nowhere; they were simply echoes of what was going on in his own mind. Abruptly, impulsively, he bent forward and kissed the dead face below him, bracing himself against the chill of touching her. Then he gathered up his hat and his gloves and went quickly from the room.

During the last few minutes Hesther had been standing in her room ready for him: her plan was ready and prepared inside her mind. As he emerged, she would go out and meet him and would lay her hand on his arm. Once she was there, once she was touching him again, he could see how much she needed him: and at that one moment more than any other when his mind was purified by contact with the everlasting, he might come to her. Her lips were moving as she stood there in the darkness, waiting; prayer to her seemed every day to grow easier and more natural.

But it all happened so suddenly. Before she had realised even that he had left the room, he had passed in front of her door and was on his way down the stairs. The disaster of it stunned her: her plan, her subtle, brilliant plan, was shattered: and there was nothing left. But wasn't there? She could still catch him, still show him that she belonged. Holding up her skirts, she ran to the top of the stairs, saw his dark figure in the hall below and called after him.

"John! John!" she cried. "Stop. I need you."

For a moment he paused. He half turned his head. Then, as

she called again, he straightened himself again and went forward as though he were alone and had heard nothing.

The front door slammed behind him, rattling the loose fanlight above it, and he was gone.

ii

Mr. Tuke closed his watch with a snap.

"Time we were off," he said. "We don't want to have to rush things."

But Hesther was reluctant to move.

"Let's give him five more minutes," she said. "Just five more minutes in case he's been held up anywhere."

She was standing at the window looking up Clarence Gardens as she said it. Mr. Tuke regarded her sadly and shook his head over the pity of it. He had seen her standing so often at the same window waiting in vain for her husband to return. It seemed heart-breaking to him that anyone should waste her substance in that way.

But he was patient.

"Very well," he said. "We must give him every opportunity. It's not nice to think of a man missing his own mother's funeral."

He was careful to emphasise the last sentence very distinctly as he said it; he wanted to make it quite clear what he really thought of John Marco.

Outside, the mutes—all six of them—were growing restless. They were standing in a small, resentful group on the pavement staring up at the house. Even one of the black horses—chosen by the firm of undertakers for his appearance, and looking like the eldest son of Death himself—was pawing at the roadway like a hackney waiting for the flag to be lowered. And Mr. Tuke,

351

standing beside Hesther with his watch open in his right hand, again might have been the starter.

"It's obvious now," he said with finality as the second hand came upright for the fifth time, "that he doesn't intend to come."

Hesther bowed her head.

"At any rate, not here," she answered. "Perhaps he'll be at the cemetery."

"Perhaps he will," said Mr. Tuke. and he raised his thick black eyebrows as he said it.

The journey to Lower Paddington Cemetery was not long; this twenty-acre park of dissolution lay right in the centre of things. You had, however, to be someone—someone with one foot already in the grave so to speak—to be able to get in there at all; and it was only because Mr. Marco had inherited an impressive granite catacomb (on which during a lean period he had once tried to raise a small loan and failed) that Mrs. Marco was privileged to go there at all. As it was, her party swept through the gates like ticket-holders.

Throughout the ride Mr. Tuke had felt curiously melancholy and depressed. Clarence Gardens by now had become inextricably entangled in his mind with memories of death and disaster; and as he bumped up and down on the hard leather cushions of the coach he could not help remembering the dismal, unattended funeral of Mr. Trackett.

To-day, however, the sunshine was brilliant. As they neared the burial ground and the marble confections of the stonemasons rose into view, it was like stepping into the vanished glories of Greece. But the feeling of uneasiness within Mr. Tuke remained: for all his knowledge of the world and his personal reserves of grace he did not altogether feel at his ease sitting next to a writer of anonymous letters.

The Chapel at Lower Paddington was dingier than at Kensal Rise simply because there was less doing there. The dust rolled out of the hassocks when anyone knelt on them; and it was as much as the light could do to fight its way through the windows. Removing his hat and pulling off his gloves Mr. Tuke took his place on one side of the shining oak coffer, and Hesther in the front pew sat facing him with a handkerchief held to her eyes. The mutes, all wearing their professional countenances of sorrow, stood lined in a row along the back.

For a moment, Hesther raised her head, glanced round the room and then started to cry. At first Mr. Tuke sympathised with her: he approved of women who cry at funerals. But slowly the real significance of that glance came to him. It wasn't old Mrs. Marco she was crying for, it was her husband. And once Mr. Tuke had realised that, he wished that she would stop it. It seemed sheer blasphemy that she should want such a man there at all.

The Marco catacomb when they reached it had been got all ready for them. The big iron gates had been oiled and greased, and a little sand had been sprinkled on the steps. There was an air of homeliness about the threshold. But within, the place still had the undisguisable oppression of the vault. After the bright sunlight outside, the sudden deprivation of warmth and bright-ness seemed physical and personal. Even Mr. Tuke shivered as he stood there. And in the close confines of the cell, Hesther's emotions became still more noticeable, more distressing. Every intake of breath was audible to Mr. Tuke. It was almost as though she were actually in his arms and sobbing there.

Mr. Tuke deliberately shut his ears to it all. He isolated himself. With his eyes closed and his hands folded across his prayer book he was intoning the final passage of the Amosite order of burial . . . *"As we were once purified by water,"* he was declaiming, *"so now, life's pageant over, are we purified by earth. Grant, 0 Lord, that . . ."*, when one of the mutes touched him by the shoulder.

"Excuse me, sir," he said, "the lady's fainted."

Mr. Tuke opened his eyes immediately; opened his eyes and stared. There lying on the stone floor of the catacomb with her legs spread open in vacant, unthinking fashion lay Hesther. She had slid down to the floor silently and unobtrusively just as he had closed his eyes and begun praying.

The fact that she had done such a thing irritated him still further. But in moments such as these he was a man of prompt and effective decision.

"Well, don't stand there doing nothing," he said. "Help me to carry her out."

And because he wanted to do everything he could to preserve the proprieties, he insisted on taking her legs himself. There seemed to him something downright indecent about a handsome stranger in a frockcoat'clasping the unconscious Hesther above the knees.

She was proved to be heavy, however; very heavy. And she kept on slipping. By the time Mr. Tuke had reached the broad gravel highway that ran through the cemetery, he was sweating. His blind, clerical collar had slipped up round his neck and the black shirt-front was creased and puckered. But he struggled on stumbling and slipping—to the contempt of the little cortège behind him who were used to carrying heavy weights without either slipping or stumbling.

The sight of the mourning carriage, when he turned a corner past a handsome granite Parthenon and came suddenly upon it, was so welcome that Mr. Tuke instinctively speeded up. The man in front was quite unprepared for this unexpected acceleration and, for a moment, the unconscious Hesther was folded up between them. Then the undertaker's man recovered himself and they reached the waiting horses almost at the double. The resident chaplain, an old silvery incumbent of the Church of England, stood in the doorway of his little shrine looking on in amazement. He had always disliked Nonconformists, and Amosites more than most of them: there was a kind of devout heartiness about them that grated on him. But to see a minister of God scrambling into a coach with a fainting girl in his arms, like a couple eloping, was more than he could endure. With a final gesture of disgust he went inside and shut the fancy Gothic door behind him.

Hesther began to come round as they got her onto the seat. She made little stirring movements with her hands and began whimpering.

"Take me home," she said feebly. "Take me home. I want to lie down."

The party of mutes had caught up with them by now. They climbed into their places, and the carriage began to move off. Just as they were scrunching rapidly down the gravel past the gates, Mr. Tuke started searching desperately round on the seat beside him. In the rush of departure he found that he had left his top hat behind him.

Letting down the window with a bang he thrust his head out and addressed the driver.

"My hat," he said. "My hat."

But the driver who did not know what he meant, merely nodded: he supposed that Mr. Tuke was airing his feelings and, being a man of God, could not allow himself to say more.

iii

At half-past-six John Marco left Tredegar Terrace and went into the florist's. The girl behind the counter expected him to buy roses or even orchids: there was an expensive look about him that suggested that he might be the sort of gentleman who would put down half-a-sovereign and his card on the counter and so make some fortunate woman happy. But instead, he bought Arum lilies—a great vase-ful of them. And he insisted on carrying them away himself. He left the shop holding the enormous sheaf, with the white, soapy faces of the flowers peering up over his shoulder.

Outside, he hailed a hansom and followed the mourning carriage along the same route that it had taken two hours earlier. The scent of the lilies rose up and made the air sickly and sweet; John Marco's nostrils were full of it. It drugged him. He no longer seemed to belong to this world at all and the hansom trotting smartly up the Edgware Road might have been a balloon cruising in empty space. In this remoteness—even the shop fronts and the people on the pavements seemed shadowy and unreal—his thoughts came and went as they pleased. But a woman standing on the street corner with a small boy beside her remained in his memory long after he had passed her, and he began to think of his own son—Hesther's son. The boy must be almost as tall as that child, he supposed. He was four now—or was it four and a half? Soon he would be going to school, like other boys. He wondered as he sat there with his hands clasping the iron canopy that rose up in front of him, whether the child ever asked after him. And if he asked what did Hesther tell him? Or had the child long since given up asking altogether? Did he even know he had a father? he wondered. The child had always been asleep when

John Marco went to Clarence Gardens; asleep in the small room that led out of Hesther's. Perhaps he did not even know that anyone came to the house; did not know that every week there was a man who went swiftly up the stairs, stayed for an hour in one room and then went as swiftly down the stairs and out of the house again. And now even that would be over.

The cab had just reached the gates when John Marco suddenly realised that he *wanted* to see his son again; if he actually saw him he might, he realised, even find himself loving him. The boy would have grown into a separate human being by now; he would no longer be Hesther's entirely. And to see him, if only for a moment, might help him to fill in some of the lonely places.

But the jolt of the cab as it stopped brought him sharply to his senses. To see the boy would mean that he had to see Hesther, too; would mean that he had to admit her into his life again. And even now he could not trust himself to be brought face to face with the woman who had written that letter which Mr. Petter in his innocence had shown him.

The cemetery by now, was closed, and the big gates padlocked. But the groundsman, for a consideration, opened the little wicket and let John Marco through: he could give just a quarter of an hour, he said. John Marco thanked him and carrying the heavy bundle of flowers that creaked in his arms with every step he took set off down the broad pathway past the silent tombstones. It was dusk, and the cemetery seemed to have a stillness of its own. The sounds of London came washing up to the limits of the high wall that ran round the graveyard and broke themselves there. Inside, it might have been a desert of fallen rocks through which he was walking.

He knew the way to the catacomb well enough; he had been there with his mother to take flowers. And now his mother was

357

there, too; these flowers in his arms were for her. And as he thought of it, his hatred of Hesther grew within him again. If it had not been for her, old Mrs. Marco could have seen him happy like other men; she would have had a grandchild whom she knew was loved.

Inside the catacomb it was almost midnight. He struck a match and groped his way in. The sand on the floor had been trampled, and the trestles on which the coffin had been rested were still there. The coffin itself was up on its stone shelf with only its brass name plate showing. *"Eliza Henrietta Marco,"* he read, "1839-1907": that was what in the end it had come to. All her hopes and expectations and disillusions and disappointments, her marriage and her early widowhood, her poverty and piety and her grief for her son—and the undertaker's engraver had been able to tell the whole story in five words.

On the shelf below was another coffin, not shiny and polished like this one, but old and weather-beaten. John Marco struck another match and peered at the inscription. *"John Augustus Marco"* this one said when he could discern the letters, "1830–1875." Only forty-five years were hidden there: he had left his wife to carry on nearly as long again without him. John Augustus Marco, it seemed, had chosen the easier way.

But the fifteen minutes were running out by now and he did not linger. He laid the sheaf of lilies across the coffin and reached about in the darkness for his hat. Then pulling the iron grille shut behind he stepped out onto the gravel pathway again. It was the first session of evening now, and above him a pale star was shining. Putting his hat on his head he set off towards the gate and the waiting hansom and the world of life.

But the hat on his head did not feel familiar. It rested hard across his forehead. He took it off and screwing up his eyes in the half light he looked inside. There across the lining the words "Eliud Tuke" appeared, carefully inscribed in indelible ink in immaculate, flowing handwriting. John Marco stood staring at the words. Then his anger, his resentment of the man, overcame him. With a great sweep of his arm he flung the hat away. It mounted on an arc into the air, like a large black kite that has lost its string, and sailed off over the crosses and marble tablets into the surrounding dusk.

John Marco stood there looking after it. It seemed to him at that moment that it was the last bit of his old life that he had thrown from him.

Book IV

John Marco, Limited

Chapter XXVIII

Tredegar terrace during the demolition of Morgan and Roberts' presented all the air of desolation of a ruined city: an earthquake might have taken place in its stride. From Lexington Street at one end to Topley Crescent at the other, a huge gash suddenly appeared in the stucco foothills of Bayswater and there were new horizons, new vistas. The glass roof of Paddington Station, like a gigantic potting shed, was temporarily a part of the landscape and the spire of St. Mary's Church was seen for the first time by those who worshipped there. Even those who lived nearest to the demolition and resented the cataclysm most—and the noise of destruction while the housebreakers were actually at work and the row of twelve retail shops were crashing down storey by storey, was simply intolerable—were forced to admit that the sight of so much sky and the sense of freedom that the clearing gave was welcome. It was as though a piece of Salisbury Plain had miraculously been transplanted into the Western purlieus of London.

But the relief of it was to be short-lived. Already the scaffolding was going up in places, and soon there was going to appear something far larger and taller, something vast and frowning in stone amid those residential acres of painted brickwork.

It had not all been easy. Mr. Bulmer, in his office in St. Swithin's Lane, had done his part, of course, with the ineffable ease of the born financier. And the public had behaved exactly as Mr. Bulmer had always been sure they would behave. Just at first they had been shy and diffident. Stray investors, the little people to whom a hundred pounds either way meant the differ-ence between a happy old age and a wretched one, paid their deposits and waited hopefully. But the big money, the important stuff, stayed away. Then a rumour started (it was, of course, Mr. Bulmer himself who had started it) that the issue was already over-subscribed, and the Stock Exchange became first inquisi-tive and then enthusiastic. Rich men advised other rich men to invest their money, and trustees transferred the riches that they were guarding. With the exception of the shares of the little people—an ex-Army man in Cheltenham, a widow in Bournemouth, the rector of some unheard-of village—there probably wasn't a halfpenny that anyone had risked himself. But Mr. Bulmer had not expected that there would be: he was content with things as they were. The cheques that were now flowing across his table, all signed on account of someone else, were simply so many testimonials to his skill in drawing up a prospectus.

John Marco, of course, had had his work to do in preparing things. His experience with Mr. Skewin, who had been so desper-ately anxious to cling to a business that was ruining him, had been a lesson. He did not attempt any more sieges, any more assaults by force. Instead, he went direct to the ground landlord. There were three of the leases that were up that year. When the tenants sought to renew them they found that they were confronted by rentals that would have put a Baring or a Coutts

364

out of business. The tenants expostulated, they reasoned, they begged; they offered bribes; they consulted their lawyers. And they lost. Like early settlers going West, they were forced to emigrate one by one to Hammersmith and Fulham.

Alone among them all, there was the fishmonger at the corner of Lexington Street—one of the key sites to the entire block—who was really obstructionist. An elderly man in a white overall and a straw boater, he stood by the terms of his lease. It had six years to run and he meant to see it through. He had been there for nineteen years already and when he realised in what way things were going he felt like one of the captains of the trawlers which supplied him, when he sees a foreign fishing smack spreading its net over protected waters. If he could have semaphored for a gun-boat he would have done so.

For a time, indeed, it actually looked as if his slanting marble slab, with the corpses of cod and salmon and Dover sole arranged like a flower garden, was going to prove mightier than the City of London: Mr. Bulmer could not move until John Marco had his option on all the sites, and the fishmonger remained piscine in his indifference. But in the end he too came round. In his handsome upstairs drawing-room—even the long velour curtains and the cushions on the couch, John Marco noticed, smelt hauntingly of his profession—it was all concluded. For the remaining years of his lease he was prepared to accept a sum that was between two or three times what it was worth; and John Marco—or rather the ex-Army Captain in Cheltenham and the widow in Bournemouth, and the rest of them—had to pay.

The mass eviction of the tenantry from Tredegar Terrace took in all two years and four months before it was completed. And on the day it was all settled and the last of them had moved out, the housebreakers arrived and started to get their pickaxes into that memorial mass of brickwork.

ii

John Marco stayed on in the rooms which the Old Gentleman had occupied, until the staircase that approached them was scaffolded all down one side and cracks had begun to appear across the ceilings.

During the last months he had been restless and on edge: he had been unable to sleep. It was not the noises that kept him awake, though at night the walls around him groaned and started as though the demolishers were still at work, and the whole place creaked like a ship in heavy weather. It was the sense of excitement, of anticipation, inside him that kept sleep away. As soon as he closed his eyes he saw it—this new building with its high doorways and its long gallery of windows.

And it wasn't simply a dream any longer, something in moonshine that he had scribbled across the pages of his pad. There were drawings, real drawings by now, over in the architect's office in Kensington. He had made many excuses to go there, simply to look at them. The architect hadn't understood; he had thought that John Marco came to criticise. He couldn't believe that all that John Marco wanted was to unroll the big sheet of parchment with its silly clouds and impossible shadows, and stand gazing at this child's picture-book drawing of the stone façade. And quite soon now, this drawing and his own imagination of it would have come true, translated off the parchment into stone and glass and polished metal.

But his impatience every hour was increasing. Half-a-dozen times a day he would go round to the site and stand on the pavement looking up at the men at work above him. From where he was standing they seemed to be working with the ineffectualness of dwarfs up there among the forest of scaffolding.

And during all this time the firm was carrying on among the ruins. Behind windows pasted across with large notices, "BUSINESS AS USUAL DURING REBUILDING," the assistants struggled on, not knowing where to look for things or where to put them when they were found. Mr. Hackbridge, his long frock-coat silvery with the dust that settled everywhere, paraded up and down, a kind of frosted Santa Claus, on a temporary floor that squeaked under his feet like duck boarding.

John Marco himself was the only one who seemed unconcerned. From a make-shift office in one corner he kept an eye on everything. He even bought up the entire bankrupt stock of dresses from a French firm in Brighton, and conducted a special out of season sale amid the turmoil. It was like business in ruined Babylon.

Nevertheless he was glad enough to get away to the quietness of his new lodgings in the evenings. He would stand for a moment at the corner of Lexington Street looking back at the ground layer of the stone-work above which the first shapes of windows were beginning to show themselves; and then would turn and go off with the gratifying, enlarged feeling of a man whose mark is being left on the world.

The house in Windsor Terrace where he now lived was old-fashioned and comfortable. It housed gentlemen. There were barristers and professional men living there. And the landlady was delighted to have John Marco staying with her. He was reserved and well-turned out and so obviously possessed of means; some woman, she often reflected, would be very lucky one day when she got John Marco for a husband.

And in an aloof, bachelor fashion John Marco found himself

beginning to enjoy the ordinary things of life again; he even forgot he was lonely. Sunday mornings were little oases of self-indulgence. He no longer attended an Amosite Tabernacle at all—it was the fashionable St. Luke's Parish Church in Green Street where he now worshipped—and after service he liked to saunter pleasantly off towards the Park.

At those moments with a white slip to his waistcoat and the gold knob of his cane in his hand, he seemed, though still alone, to be stepping into the fullness of things.

iii

It was on one such Sunday morning, a clear shining day with the trees looking as bright as if they had been painted and the frocks of the ladies in the carriages making little splashes of colour against the railings of Park Lane, that he saw Hesther again; saw Hesther and saw his son.

It was not difficult to distinguish her among the Sunday morning crowd. She was heavily veiled and dressed all in black like a nun. It was old shabby stuff that she was wearing, brown in places and bunched together as though by the hand of some back-street dressmaker. Her shoes, too, when they came into sight below the long trailing skirt were shapeless and down at heel. In one hand she was holding a long bulging reticule; her other hand was round the boy's.

John Marco stood and regarded her. This was something that he had not been prepared for, something that had been happening quietly in Clarence Gardens during the years since he had left. There was no excuse for it. She still had the rest of Mr. Trackett's money; she was well provided for. But as he looked he realised that it was not poverty that drove her to this, it was something different, something deep within her that was finding a bleak satisfaction in penury. Out there in those scarecrow clothes in the sunlight of the Park, she was punishing herself by being Mr. Trackett's niece.

It was not, however, at Hesther that he was looking now: it was at the boy. He was shabby, too; unspeakably shabby, in fact. There was a meanness about his clothes, as though they had been bought cheap and then left to wear themselves out utterly. His wrists showed thin and bony beneath the cuffs, and under the long raincoat that he was wearing—it was so long that it fell below his knees—his legs were spindly and quite straight. As he walked the raincoat swung open, and John Marco could see that he was wearing long stockings like a girl's.

John Marco did not move from where he was but stood looking after them when they had passed. And then slowly, so as not to be observed, he followed them. His face was set hard and he was angry. A mad woman—Mr. Tuke had said; and for once Mr. Tuke had been right. She was different from everyone else in the Park, isolated in this fantastic mourning that she was wearing. He noticed that other people, casual cheerful people, nudged each other and looked over their shoulders at her as she passed. And as he followed, he noticed another thing. She and the boy were not speaking. In the midst of all that chatter and noise of voices around them, these two were silent. They walked on hand in hand as though sworn to some mysterious vow of silence.

His feeling of humiliation, as he studied them, increased. There was something so calculated about their drabness. It was as though Hesther were deliberately parading her condition before the whole world. "Perhaps she's revenging herself on the boy," he thought for a moment; "revenging herself on him because he is partly mine."

But she seemed to be loving and solicitous enough. When they reached the roadway at Lancaster Gate she let go of his hand for a moment and put her arm right round him to protect him from the dangers of the traffic. Then having got him safely to the other side she dropped her arm and took hold of him by the hand again. The only remarkable thing was that they still had not spoken.

John Marco did not follow any further. He suddenly wanted them out of his sight, wanted to be able to forget them again. But as he stood there, he knew that he would not be able to forget; something that he had not expected, something from which he had been unable to protect himself, had brought him up close against them.

He took one last glance from the gates of the Park where he was standing, and saw the two figures in the distance, one black and formless and the other, small and silent. And he resolved then, at that moment, that he would get the boy away from her; whether or not she would consent to give him up, he would have to separate them.

A gentleman with a lady on his arm had raised his hat and was bowing to him. John Marco lifted his hat and bowed back. All round him, Sunday morning was going on as usual.

iv

The decision to go round and see Hesther, see her and tell her to her face that he was there to claim his son, had taken possession of him. For two days he pondered over it, counting all other thoughts an interruption. And then in the evening of the third day just as the light was disappearing from the sky and the lamps were being lit down the long sweep of Clarence Gardens, he made his way up the cold familiar steps and pulled at the massive bell handle.

The house itself had deteriorated sadly. The window boxes which in John Marco's day had been as full of flowers as a florist's window, were now empty, and only bare stalks and a handful of withered leaves showed where the blooms had been. Even the brass work on the door was neglected. The knocker, which he remembered as shining, was now something that was black and green.

The jangle of the bell in the basement brought memories of the house crowding back on him; already he felt the chill of it. But the sound of tired feet slopping along the tiled hallway left him no time for recollection. The door opened and there was Emmy standing facing him. She was more wispy and drabbish than ever.

"Is Mrs. Marco in?" he asked. "I want to see her."

Emmy did not attempt to conceal her excitement: this was one of the few big moments—perhaps, for what it might portend, the biggest—of her life.

"I'll wait in the drawing-room," he said. "Tell her I'm here."

As he threw open the door, the musty, disused smell of the room rose up at him. The blinds were half way down already—they were apparently left hanging that way even by day—and he waited while Emmy fumbled at the gas bracket for a light. When the mantle finally popped into life and he could see the room, he noticed that the chairs and sofa were all covered in dust cloths, and that sheets of newspaper had been spread about open on the carpet. It was obvious that he was the first visitor who had gone into the room for months. But there was one thing that ordinary disuse did not explain. The pictures had been taken down and the long mirror over the fireplace was concealed behind a thick curtain. It was as though someone to whom light and brightness were distasteful had gone round the room deliberately subduing it.

He did not have to wait very long for Hesther. He had scarcely sat down—the covers disturbed themselves in fresh clouds of dust as he did so—when he heard her hand faltering on the door handle; and then quietly, almost stealthily it seemed to him, she opened the door and stood there. She was still dressed all in black as he had seen her in the Park. But now she was wearing a close black bonnet as well. It drained the last, thin vestige of colour from her cheeks, leaving her pale and sexless. She seemed magically to have added a generation to her age.

"So you've come," she said, not looking up at him but keeping her eyes to the floor all the time. "My prayers were answered."

He saw as she spoke that her hands—they were long and white and thin-fingered—were pressed against each other as though she were still praying as she stood there.

"I'm not here in answer to your prayers," he said. "I'm here because I want to talk to you."

"You're here because you want to take John away from me," she replied. "You can go away again."

She raised her eyes to his for a moment as she spoke and he saw that hers were deep and burning. There was a new light in them. But she did not seem to be seeing him; it was as though she were looking through him and beyond.

"How did you know I was coming?" he asked.

"I saw you on Sunday," she told him. "You were following us. I knew then that John was in danger. So I prayed."

"To protect him from me?"

"Yes," she said. "I've heard warnings. Voices."

She had not crossed over from where she was standing. Her gaze was still cast down to the floor and her hands remained clasped in front of her. But her head was moving; it was shifting slowly from side to side as though she were listening. Was she even now hearing voices with him there in the room beside her? he wondered. And as he looked at her he saw that she was no longer quite of this world at all. His mind hardened: at all costs he must rescue the boy upstairs; do something for that silent child dressed in his mean clothes with the long stockings like a girl's. He was careful, however, to keep his voice level and steady as he spoke to her.

"Does he go to school yet?" he asked.

"He doesn't need a school," she said. "I teach him myself."

"Has he got any friends?"

"He's got me," she replied. "I'm his mother."

She raised her eyes again for an instant as she said it. There was the same distant look in them, the same suggestion of being fixed on things invisible.

"He'll have to go to school sometime," he said.

"Mr. Tuke will attend to that," she answered. "He'll educate him."

"Does he never go out alone?" he asked.

As he asked the question he saw Hesther's hands suddenly come close sharply together again. The blood was driven from them and the knuckles showed white and papery.

"Never," she said. "There's always someone with him. Always. If you spoke to him he'd only run away. I've warned him about you."

"So you don't even want me to see him?"

"I've got the key of his room here," she said. She raised her hands and brought them up close to her bosom. "You couldn't get in to him if you tried."

He paused and leaning back on the white dust sheet he continued to study her. She was still sitting there as though she were waiting to hear something that only her ears could catch.

"What do your voices say to you?" he asked abruptly.

The question did not seem to surprise her. Evidently the voices were her familiars, she had grown used to them.

"They tell me to do things," she said. "They help."

He rose.

"And do they tell you not to let me see my son?" he asked.

She nodded.

"They tell me that," she said.

They did not speak again as he went towards the front door. Hesther stood behind it in the hall blocking it. It was not until the door was already open that she addressed him.

"Good-night," she said. "I shall pray for you."

Before he had reached the bottom of the steps he heard the sound of the heavy bolts being driven home and the chain being put up. Number twenty-three Clarence Gardens was a fortress that had repelled the invader, and was impregnable again.

v

It was a week later when he returned. They had been tortuous, difficult days, days that did not relate themselves to the ordinary conduct of life at all. He had spent whole hours of them first in the dingy obscurity of Dr. Hanson's surgery in Edgware Road and then in the prosperous magnificence of Dr. Yarberry-Blane's consulting-room in Harley Street. And now all three of them were seated in the Yarberry-Blane carriage and were clopping

374

along through Bayswater.

"I shall go in first," John Marco was saying. "And I shall tell her that you're simply two friends of mine. She'll let you come in as Mr. Tuke will be there."

"Are you sure you can rely on this parson fellow?"

It was Dr. Hanson who spoke: he seemed apprehensive of having brought this aristocrat from Harley Street out to Bayswater for nothing.

"He'll be there," John Marco answered. "I wrote to him myself and sent the note round by hand. He wouldn't miss a thing like this."

"You didn't tell him our real object I hope," Dr. Yarberry-Blane interposed. "I want to see the patient at her most natural."

"I told him nothing," John Marco replied. "Nothing except that I wanted to see him there."

"Because this isn't quite the sort of thing that Dr. Yarberry-Blane is used to." Dr. Hanson said suavely.

"You mustn't expect him to be ready to certify on the strength of one visit. She's not dangerous, remember."

"Judge for yourselves," John Marco answered. "Look into her eyes."

They had reached the corner of Clarence Gardens by now, and the carriage was travelling more slowly as the coachman began searching for the number.

John Marco reached for the speaking tube that dangled against the edge of the seat beside him.

"It's here," he said. "At the next lamp-post."

"I hope that parson won't be late." Dr. Hanson observed.

Mr. Tuke was not late, however. He was standing on the pavement staring up at the house when they got there. As John Marco

dismounted and the others climbed out after him, he saw him—
saw him first, and then saw the house.

But the house was empty and in darkness. The shutters were
fastened and a large notice, "TO BE SOLD," leaned vacantly
over the gateway.

Chapter XXIX

The disappearance of Hesther and the child was final and complete; they had simply and astonishingly vanished.

The estate agent whose board was outside could say nothing except that he had been instructed to put the house on the market and accept any offer over fifteen hundred pounds that he could get. As soon as he had got the money, his instructions were to pass it on to a firm in Clifford's Inn. But the firm in Clifford's Inn did not know anything, they did not even have any address for their client except that of the empty house in Clarence Gardens; in short, they had not been advised. Nor could the bank be of any assistance. The bank manager was obviously disturbed by the whole affair. Mrs. Marco, he said, had called in on the previous Wednesday—the day after John Marco's visit—and had drawn out all she possessed: it was obvious that the man felt that in some obscure fashion he had been slighted.

After the bank manager, John Marco tried the local tradesmen. They knew just as little about the whole affair; so far as they were concerned, it was simply that Hesther had come in and paid off her debts right up to the minute, telling them vaguely that she was moving away somewhere. The milkman was the last to have seen her; his roundsman had been told to pay one more early morning visit and then stop for ever, and he had gone round to the house to find out why. But it was only Emmy he had been able to see. From behind the half-opened door—all transactions with tradesmen at number twenty-three Clarence Gardens were conducted only after the chain had been slipped into position— she had told him that they were going away into the country and not coming back.

It was nearly a week later before John Marco was able to discover the firm of removers who had taken away the stuff. And on the day he found out he went himself over to Clapham to interview them. The visit was wasted, however. They had still got the goods there in their warehouse. The lady, they said, had paid them for a whole year's storage in advance and had told them that they would be hearing from her. They offered, as soon as they got her new address, to forward any letter that John Marco cared to write to them.

John Marco returned to Bayswater, empty and depressed. It was obvious that Hesther had been too clever for him. With only a week in which to arrange everything, she had hidden herself so secretly that he would never be able to find her again. Like all frightened, hunted things, she had covered up her track as she went. And at this moment somewhere behind other locked doors she was guarding the boy that she had rescued so skilfully from the danger that was in pursuit.

But there were other things in John Marco's mind besides the disappearance. There was the Opening. It would not be long now. The whole of the long frontage of the shop was completed; Tredegar Terrace looked already as if it had a palace running down one side of it. Between the cracks in the hoardings could be seen the glitter of plate glass and the gleam of woodwork. And through the gap, where the revolving door, the most up-to-date of its kind was to go, could be seen the vast, shadowy interior. With its pillars and its galleries and its sweeping staircase, it was like looking on the reconstructed glories of Thebes.

John Marco nowadays spent a great part of his time wandering about this emptiness alone. He was like a Bishop, impatient for his Cathedral to be finished. But he was more than a Bishop; in this particular temple he was the little God himself. It was his name, JOHN MARCO, that was repeated in letters of gold two feet high all down the street and round the corner. Everyone who came in to buy a piece of ribbon or a pair of stockings would really be making a suitable offering to this new, retail deity who had just installed himself.

In the whole place, it was the pneumatic change conveyors that pleased John Marco most; the bright brass pipe-work of the apparatus ran everywhere. The class of a shop, he had long considered, could be determined by the way in which it handled the customer's money. In really small establishments, the assistants left their stations and carried the money, spread out on their counter-books, to the cashier somewhere in the background. But in the rush of modern business that sort of thing was unthinkable. And so the overhead system of inclined slipways had been introduced. Along openwork tunnels of flimsy deal the bill and the money went trundling along in a hollow wooden ball like a conjuror's sphere. But to John Marco's mind there had always been something clumsy and rather childish about the system; and it had seemed like a new era in culture when he saw the first spring wire conveyor. All that the assistant had to do there was to pull an elastic cord and the message went tearing away through space like a captive rocket. He dreamed of, and lived for, his own spring wire conveyor until one day in a mammoth store in Oxford Street he saw the first pneumatic tube. And he stood entranced in front of it. The *whoosh* from the intake of air, and the abandon with which the little projectile hit the hanging flap at the end of the tube and fell limply into the reception basket, decided him. He would have been ready at that moment to found his own business simply for that pneumatic conveyor alone.

And in six weeks' time, he reflected, there would be money, real money, pouring along those tubes. The air inside them would be full of it. That bare parquet where he was standing would be scarred and dented under the passage of high, fashionable heels. And the counters, the naked, gleaming counters that at present were piled at one end of the building, would be covered with boxes and lengths of material and books of patterns. The Mayor of Bayswater would cut the ribbon across the central doorway and the crowd—up till then held back by the commissionaire with John Marco's initials on his collar—would be free to surge in and fill the place.

It was strange standing there in the darkness and seeing it all happen in front of him. But he had thought about it so long that it seemed that the day, when it came, would be only the pale shadow of the event; it had already been a reality inside his brain for years. . . .

From nowhere, the image of a boy dressed like an orphan, his hand gripped in the clasp of a woman who did not speak to him, slid into his mind and remained there for a moment. The image startled him. Less than a month ago he had sworn to find that boy and deliver him; and already he had forgotten. But why shouldn't he forget? It was the shop that he had been sent on earth to look after; not Hesther's son.

With a little shrug of his shoulders, as though he were angry almost at the boy for having distracted him, he turned and went up the central gangway to see if the display cases were in position.

ii

John Marco left the engagement of the extra staff to Mr. Hackbridge. And Mr. Hackbridge, still as morbidly afraid as ever of making a mistake under his new master, worked from eight in the morning until nearly ten o'clock at night, interviewing, taking up references, appointing. He was a director now, and not merely a shop-walker. John Marco had insisted on appointing him to the board along with his other appointment, Mr. Skewin: there were five directors in all on the board and John Marco wanted men that he could rely on. He had similarly elevated little Mr. Lyman who was a wizard with the cash. And having listened to the stammered, overwhelmed words of gratitude of the three of them he was careful to treat them even more curtly, more disdainfully, than before: there was to be no nonsense about equality.

Mr. Hackbridge, faced with the unthinkable task of engaging an army of fifty-four assistants, sweated. There was always the terror, the ever-present haunting terror that he might appoint a mischief-maker or a thief. But there was one side of it all that Mr. Hackbridge enjoyed enormously. His old spirit of authority, pent up so long in fear and trepidation, re-asserted itself; and in the temporary office with the words "Staff Manager" on the door he bullied the young ladies unmercifully. They came in their dozens, polite and timid and respectable, drawn from the ends of London by a single advertisement, like moths to a beacon. And once he had got them there, he put them through their paces, making them take their hats off and stand up facing the light where he

381

could see them; criticising their accents—his own on these occasions was full and fruity and over-bearing; taking hold of their hands in his to see if they were properly cared for.

He was in the middle of one such interview when John Marco himself came in and interrupted him. The girl—she did not appear to be more than about eighteen or nineteen—was standing there with her hat in her hand where Mr. Hackbridge had placed her.

"And why do you imagine you should be able to sell lingerie," Mr. Hackbridge was asking sarcastically, "if you haven't got any experience? You're just wasting my time coming here, upon my word you are."

Then he saw John Marco and rose respectfully to his feet.

"What's the matter?" John Marco asked.

He glanced at the girl as he spoke. She was small and dark and her hair was combed up on either side of a pale oval face.

"She'll be good-looking later on," John Marco thought to himself, "when she's come out a bit."

At the moment, however, she looked as if she might be going to cry.

"She's got no experience, sir," Mr. Hackbridge said, flicking her letter of application contemptuously with the back of his hand. "Our advertisement said . . ."

But John Marco had turned towards the girl.

"What's your name?" he asked.

"Eve Harlow, sir."

"How old are you?"

"Nineteen."

"Do you want to learn?"

"Oh yes, sir."

He turned to Mr. Hackbridge.

"Give her a chance," he said. "Fifteen shillings a week. They've all got to learn sometime."

"As you say, sir," said Mr. Hackbridge sadly.

John Marco caught the girl's eye. She smiled at him, and he smiled back at her for a moment. It seemed something to him to have a friend, even a friend at only fifteen bob a week, among that regiment of strangers.

Chapter XXX

The day of the opening was cold but sunny. John Marco looked out of his window and reflected that it was perfect shopping weather. But somehow, now that the day had come round, the first excitement had already gone from it. He was tired, desperately tired. All that he wanted was to settle down to being a shopkeeper again, to put this vast piece of machinery into motion and begin earning money once more. He wished now that he had let the doors be opened at nine o'clock that morning to catch every penny that was going. But, instead of that, the whole place was to be locked up like a prison until half-past-three when the Mayor was coming. He was bringing the Lady Mayoress with him; and the wives of the other Aldermen were coming as well. They were nearly all the wives of trades-men and the big dais in the central hall would contain the cream of the retail aristocracy of Bayswater.

The hall itself was to be filled by specially invited guests drawn from the old customers of Morgan and Roberts. He had sent out five hundred invitations, and one hundred-and-twenty of the best-connected ladies in the neighbourhood had accepted. For a moment after the invitations had gone he had questioned whether anyone would come. But the two words *"AFTERNOON TEA"* at the bottom of the card had proved sufficient. Even without the promise of a mannequin parade they would have been there for their free hot drink and refreshments—he remembered from his old Tabernacle days that there was something about *gratis* beverages and uncharged-for sandwiches that drew people from their homes like the call of the *muezzin*.

He dressed carefully, wearing for the first time a new black silk cravat that he had bought. It was a handsome piece of silk, the sort of thing that a Rajah might put round himself. And into it he thrust a single-pearl tie-pin. His frock coat was new too. He had bought it specially from a tailor in Jeremyn Street instead of from the man in Westbourne Terrace who had always made his clothes. The fit was exemplary. When he had put on his patent leather boots with the suède tops, and stuffed a silk handkerchief into his pocket he stood for a while in front of the cheval glass admiring himself. His hair, which was now grey at the temples, gave an air of authority to him; he might have been an ambassador at the court of St. James, instead of only a draper.

The morning's post was ready for him when he went through for breakfast; it was standing there propped up against the coffee pot. And amid the little huddle of envelopes there was one missive—a postcard—that at once caught his eye. The message on it was printed: in jagged angular letters it ran right across the card. "BEHOLD THESE ARE THE UNGODLY WHO PROSPER IN THE WORLD," it ran. "THEY INCREASE IN RICHES." There was no address and no signature—though no signature of course was needed. He turned it over and looked at the postmark. But the Postmaster-General might have been in league with the sender. There was only a black, half-obliterated smudge.

John Marco stared at it for a moment and then tearing it into tiny fragments threw it into the open grate behind him. But the room did not seem quite the same afterwards. It was as though Hesther herself had been there. He felt himself being watched again. For the rest of the day he would feel that her eyes were on him.

It was four o'clock. The Mayor had blundered through his carefully typewritten speech using the words as if they were great mouthfuls of suet, and the hired mannequin had paraded past the assembled ladies with her hips swaying from side to side in the cultivated manner of her profession. As John Marco looked at her he reflected that it was strange that women who habitually walked like governesses should prefer to select their dresses from someone who glided about like a *houri*. But there was a convention in such things; and as the girl made her last exit with one hand on her waist and the other held stiffly up into the air at a right angle from the elbow as if she were picking a spray of something, everyone who was present felt that Bayswater owed something to John Marco for having brought this breath of the *rue de la Paix* blowing into it.

Then the Mayor, accompanied by the Lady Mayoress, cut the white ribbon that Mr. Hackbridge had fastened across the principal doorway; and John Marco Ltd. was open. The crowd was there all right. The windows, full of special and unrepeatable bargains, had attracted them. It had been John Marco's idea that they should lead off with a sale; and every article in the shop was marked down to half-price as though values had crashed overnight. The uninvited, the ordinary rank and file of the district, had been waiting since two o'clock ready to pounce as soon as the doors had opened. But it was actually two women who had been rather annoyed at having to wait for all this formality who came in first. They sauntered self-consciously into the building where all the assistants were standing ready and between them bought a pair of gloves and a fancy handkerchief. Just as they were taking-out their purses, John Marco bore down on them.

"There will be no charge, madam," he said, "for the first purchase made in the new store."

And taking out his gold pencil he initialed the counter book himself. . . .

By five o'clock the store was full. There were eager, acquisitive women in every department, and Mr. Hack-bridge, who had been awarded the honorary title of Shop Manager, was walking up and down among them like a general on field day. He had got himself up very handsomely for the occasion, and his trousers had the immaculate side crease of King Edward's. His two-inch moustaches were waxed until the ends were like needles, and in his button-hole was a gardenia in a metal holder.

Half-way up the big curved staircase John Marco had found a new pulpit from which he could look down on this bright world of his own invention. With his hand on the polished rail in front of him he stood alone, speaking to no one. In the gangway below him he could see the broad brims and sweeping feathers of the ladies' hats. Their figures of course were square and fore-short-ened like an opera singer's seen from the gallery; and the strains of music were there to complete the illusion. Upstairs in the Old English tea-room where the waitresses wore Puritan aprons and the china on the tables was of cheap willow-pattern, an orchestra of three was fiddling madly away above the clatter of the tea-cups. And down below, the scene of carnival was completed: there were balloons. Two girls stood at the door holding great

387

bunches of them, all printed staringly with his name. Every child who came in was given one. And as they carried them round, held high above their heads for protection, they bobbed up and down in the midst of the crowd like huge soap bubbles.

John Marco did not want to move away from his position. The lights had come on by now and the chandeliers in the ceiling glittered like tiaras, catching the edges of the mirrors, the bright metal balustrades that ran round the galleries, the polished surfaces beneath. The whole place danced and dazzled. *"All these were of costly stones, according to the measure of hewed stones"* he began saying to himself. *"And the foundation was of costly stones, even great stones, stones of ten cubits and stones of eight cubits."* Perhaps, for all his wisdom, Solomon himself had felt just a little like this when he had first looked upon his rising Temple.

But John Marco was dissatisfied: he wanted to be in all the departments at once so that he could watch every purchase being made, be present at every penny that his assistants were taking. There was so much going on around him of which he could never know: that was the trouble. And, for a moment, as he stood there he wondered if he would ever really be able to control this gigantic machine that he had started. The doubt was short-lived, however; this machine had been designed so carefully that it would run itself; if the people came in to feed it, it would run for ever. But the windows! Had Mr. Hackbridge remembered the coloured lights which he had said were to be put on as soon as it grew dusk? Frowning a little he went down the broad staircase and through the busy gangway to inspect the windows.

After the noise and clamour of the shop, it seemed strangely quiet and placid outside on the pavement. The windows, of course, lit up the street. The coloured lights were diving in and out like fishes, and a battery of half-watt lamps was throwing up its glare into people's faces. For a few minutes John Marco walked up and down the frontage pausing one by one in front of the displays, admiring them. Then, just as he was about to go inside again he saw Mary and the child standing there.

It was the toy window, a kind of pre-Christmas bazaar of dolls and stuffed animals and rocking horses that they were looking at; and the child was pointing at something. He could see the faces of both of them as brightly lit as if a photographer had trained his flood lights on them. And at the sight of Mary a sudden weakness, something that had no place in this world of business, ran through him.

For a moment he stood helpless, in the doorway. Then a new feeling of excitement came over him; he went up and stood beside her. This was the nearest that he had been to her since the last night when he had visited Mr. Petter in the little flat in Harrow Street. It was the opportunity for which he had been waiting.

"Mary," he said.

At the sound of his voice, she started. She drew back a little. But he came closer.

"Mary," he said. "It's been so long. . . ."

She turned on him and he found himself looking into those deep eyes again. But they were angry now; there was no tenderness anywhere within them. Without speaking to him she began to move away.

"Don't . . . don't look at me like that, Mary," he began.

But already she was two paces away from him. She was clasping the child by the hand, leading it. Forgetting everything, forgetting even the way in which the other people at the window had turned and were staring at him, he began to follow.

It was because of the little girl who was with her, that he was able to catch them up. She dragged behind, still craning her neck to look at the windows. And an idea came to him.

"Give her anything she wants," he said. "Anything in the whole store. I'll pay for it."

It was as Mary moved away again—though the child by now was staring up at him—that he saw one of the shop-girls standing at the doorway with the last balloons of her bunch in her hand. He took them from her and put them into the child's hand instead. The child took hold of them instinctively.

As soon as he had given them to her, he stopped. It was no use going further; he could not go on forever following someone who would not speak to him. Instead, he stood and watched. Already he was conspicuous; a whole group of people was observing him. But the long street might have been empty, except for the two of them, the mother and the child: they were all he saw. The three balloons with his name on them were swinging out behind and the hand that held them was jerking at the strings, playing with them.

Then at the end of the street, Mary paused: she bent down and said something to the child. He saw her take the balloons away from her and drop them into the gutter. The balloons bounced lightly for a moment and then began to blow gaily back towards him. But Mary, with the child still looking over her shoulder at the bright new present that had been snatched from her, was hurrying on again.

John Marco turned and went back to the shop.

ii

The directors' room when he got there was loud with voices and the chink of glasses. On a table by the window the empty bottles were standing. John Marco opened the door and stood for a moment looking in.

The first person to catch his eye was Mrs. Hackbridge. Her husband had dressed her up for the part of a director's wife, and across the wide brim of her Gainsborough hat a curling ostrich feather now wound like a coiled serpent. Beneath the hat, however, her face showed thin, peaky and unmistakably Hammersmith. She had rolled back her long gloves to the wrist and was over by the buffet eating earnestly. Mrs. Skewin was there beside her. But neither she nor Mr. Skewin had dressed themselves up in the least; there in the midst of affluence they remained as living tokens of unsuccess; unchanged, unnoticed and themselves.

John Marco, however, was not allowed to remain long in the doorway unattended. It was Mr. Bulmer who greeted him. He was sitting on the board table itself with his feet in their elastic-sided boots up on a chair in front of him. He held his cigar jutting out of the corner of his mouth and raised his glass in John Marco's direction.

"The conquering hero," he said, not very distinctly. "Come in and join us."

The Mayor was still there; and the Lady Mayoress. She was still holding the enormous bunch of roses and maiden-hair fern that had been presented to her. They all stopped talking as John Marco entered, and Mr. Hack-bridge, who had slunk upstairs for a moment while the drinks were still going, came forward, a guilty expression on his face, with a glass of champagne for his master.

John Marco took the glass and there, in the midst of all these people who were decently sipping the stuff, he tossed it off. Mr. Bulmer caught his eye approvingly and winked at him. Then

Mr. Hackbridge began backing as inconspicuously as possible towards the door to return to his duties, and the Mayor stepped forward.

"Har you satisfied?" he asked blandly. "Ham I right in supposing that to-day has been a great success?"

John Marco told him that he was; and Mr. Bulmer got down from the table and opened another bottle of champagne.

It was after seven when the party broke up. The Mayor, with the Lady Mayoress on his arm, was the first to go; and then Mr. and Mrs. Skewin; the other directors found the gloves and hand-bags that their wives had mislaid; and last of all Mr. Hackbridge came to collect the uncomely Mrs. Hackbridge.

John Marco was left alone in the room now, the litter of cele-bration all round him. He went over to the sideboard and found a bottle of champagne, half-full, standing there. He poured himself out one glass and then another and drank them in quick succession as he had drunk the first one. He was alone, wasn't he? There was no reason why he shouldn't get drunk if he wanted to. The others had all gone off home with their wives; they weren't left solitary as he was. Even Mr. Hackbridge would find the creature who had worn the picture hat sitting by the fireside when he reached his house. And John Marco would find no one. His fireside and his bed were as unshared as a hermit's. But if he so much as raised his little finger, couldn't he have half the women in London simply for the asking? He could give them everything they wanted, now; they could have their furs and their servants and their town-carriage. At forty, with his hair just silvering a little, he was a catch; he was the most eligible man of his own acquaintance. But he was forgetting; the champagne had blurred things for a moment. He had forgotten the one thing that really mattered. He couldn't offer them anything: that was the whole irony of it. Somewhere or other behind locked doors, with her tracts and her son for company, his help-mate and bed-fellow was waiting for him: in the eyes of God he was not one of the lonely ones.

He set down his wine glass so clumsily that the stem shattered against the bottle and he was left holding the broken fragment in his hand. When he let the piece fall to the table, and heard the silly tinkle that it made, he knew that he was just a little drunk already. And the thought of women, not of any one woman in particular, but the whole sex of them, now came pressing in on him. He remembered faces that he had seen in a crowd long since, and then forgotten; his mind became full of pictures and he surrendered to them. He recalled the way in which women, respectable, well-groomed women, out in the Park with their husbands, had eyed him as he had passed. And other women—less respectable. Weren't the streets full of them? Wouldn't any other man have forgotten his wretchedness that way? At the thought, a wave of coldness and desire ran through him. The evening was still young, and in the darkness outside, the whole Babylon of London lay at his doorstep. For one night at least he could forget everything in life that he had lost.

He looked up and saw Mr. Hackbridge standing there.

"There's something I ought to report, sir," he said hesitatingly. "One of the counterfoils from the Hosiery is missing. I've spoken very severely to the young lady about it. . . ."

But John Marco was not listening. With his hat tilted on the back of his head and with his gold-knobbed cane in his hand, he had gone out of the doorway without answering. His face was flushed and his step on the stairway outside sounded heavy and uncertain.

Out there in the Park, the women who had suddenly filled his mind, were standing in their numbers; and he went among them. Singly, and in twos and threes, they made a moving pattern of invitation. And some instinct seemed to draw them to him. They came close, leaving their cheap heavy scent hanging over him. But he only peered into their strange pale faces and passed on. Somehow, by their openness, their eagerness, they were destroying the very thing that he was seeking hard to find.

And he remembered suddenly that previous night when he had gone alone into the Park. It had been to decide that night; to decide whether at last to break the cords that were still binding him to Mary and unite his life with Hesther's instead. He had made his decision; and the reward, a thousand-fold, had come to him. It was because he had decided, that he was a rich man now, rich and growing richer. His mind clung to the thought and tried to embrace it; to be rich, that was the great adventure. There was nothing on earth now, even this brief space of pleasure that he was seeking, that he could not purchase.

Ahead of him, in the yellow saucer of light that one of the lamps made around it, a woman was standing. He looked at her and his step quickened. She was young, little more than a girl, it seemed, and solitary; she evidently did not consort with the others of her kind. His heart began racing and his lips were dry. The evil, the wickedness, of what he was contemplating momentarily overwhelmed him. *"For of this such are they which creep into houses and lead captive silly women laden with sins, led away by divers lusts:"* The words came into his memory and accused him. He hesitated. But already the figure ahead of him had sauntered idly away into the shadows and he pressed on, following her more urgently, more desperately, than before. The rest of the dark parkland, the rest of London, the rest of his own life even, was blotted out; and only the fascination of the dim form in front remained.

As he drew near, she turned slowly and paused. He spoke to her and she came up and walked beside him, taking hold of his arm as she went. At her touch the desire within him mounted and he thrust his own arm about her roughly. Her body was slight and yielded to his weight; the tenderness of youth still seemed to cling to it.

"This is sin," John Marco told himself. "Sin. But she will help me to forget."

Then as she came into the glow of the next lamp he saw her face. She was glancing sideways and her eyes met his. But her eyes were grey, the heavy gold of her hair was drawn into a coil on the white neck. He started and drew back. It was no longer her face that he was seeing: it was Mary's. But this face was smiling, the red mouth was parted; and he remembered Mary's face as she had turned away from him that afternoon, how cold and bitter it had been. His mind cleared suddenly with the memory, and he saw the woman in front of him as she really was—her loose, stupid lips and the streety simper. "I have lost Mary, to win this," he reflected. "It is this for which I am giving away my soul." And, putting out his arm, he thrust her angrily away from him.

He had left her now: he had put a sovereign into the woman's hand—it had closed over it like a child's—and had gone away leaving her there in the darkness. He was a sane man again, sane and lonely and exhausted. And as he walked his lips were moving.

"Thanks be to God for saving me," he was repeating over and

over again. "Thanks be to God for saving me."

And as he said it, he was aware that the presence—compound of the Reverend Ephraim Sturger, Eliud Tuke and the great Jehovah of old—was still with him.

Still with him, and probably always would be.

Chapter XXXI

The opening sale was over; and the January Sale, too. The windows were discreet and dignified again. There were no more balloons and no free teas. But nevertheless John Marco Limited was still full. For a whole-mile radius around Tredegar Terrace every woman who set out with the light of purchase in her eye turned instinctively in the direction of this mammoth monument of temptation.

And then came away flattered and gratified. Simply to step into the central hall with its brass work and its galleries was to enjoy life on a larger scale. There was intoxication in it. The bright canary-coloured paper in which the parcels were wrapped, the bright canary-coloured vans which delivered the stuff, and the two page boys in their bright canary-coloured uniform, at the main entrance—they were a later idea of John Marco's: he blamed himself bitterly for not having had them there for the opening ceremony—all added to the gaiety of the thing and made the spending of money seem fun, and not something serious. Everything about the place was so wantonly luxurious that it made even quite frugal, economical little women wanton and luxurious, too.

Not, of course, that the shop was cheap to run like that. The yellow vans, the coach-builder had pointed out, would have to be re-painted every twelve months; and the two dwarfish page boys had to change their costumes as often as a diplomat, even though Mr. Hackbridge had instructed them to spread a sheet of newspaper beneath them before they sat down anywhere.

There were other extravagances, too; extravagances that shocked the lean heart of Mr. Skewin and the acid eye of Mr. Lyman in the Counting House. There was the Floristry Department, for example. It occupied one entire bay in the ground floor, like a gaudy, scented sub-colony of Kew. John Marco would not have it filled with chrysanthemums and marguerites and bunches of corn flowers that people could afford to buy. Flowers like that, he argued, could be bought at any street corner. Instead, there were sprays of white lilac out of season, and hot-house mimosa, and orchids that were like sin set in a vase. And naturally half the stock was left unsold every night. It had to be carried away by the bucketful to be disposed of to the staff, and to anyone else who would buy it, at the sheerest rubbish prices. John Marco knew all about this of course. He had a daily report from all the departments put onto his desk at nine o'clock every morning, and it was always the Floristry that was on the wrong side of the sheet. And on the fourth or fifth occasion on which Mr. Lyman's long, thin finger hovered over the Floristry deficit John Marco only laughed at him.

"Put the whole thing down to advertising," he said. "That's what it is really. Brings the women in. That's what's wrong with men like you, Lyman. You don't understand women: you've got no experience of them."

And Mr. Lyman, who had four daughters and supported his wife's sister as well, smiled obediently and said, "Quite so, sir."

But the daily reports were not John Marco's only contact with the business. There was his regular morning tour as well. This began at ten-thirty, as soon as the morning's post had been gone through, and even during those early months it had already assumed a kind of awful significance, like a Captain's inspection on a ship. The sight of John Marco, with Mr. Hackbridge walking beside him like an adjutant, was one of the alarms of living; after he had passed, the assistants began behaving like human beings again.

It was on one of these occasions as he was entering the Millinery Saloon, with his shop manager pounding heavily after him across the thick, pile carpet, that he saw Eve Harlow again. She was very different by now from the girl whom Mr. Hackbridge had enjoyed bullying in those early days when he had been engaging staff. Her dark hair was now piled high on top of her head like a fashionable lady's. And her dress was smarter. She had somehow contrived to make herself a woman about town on fifteen shillings a week. He stood there looking at her and wondered how it was that he had not noticed her before: she had been working for him for over six months and during that time he had never thought of her apart from the eighty or ninety other identical young ladies who streamed into the shop at eight forty-five every morning making it a seraglio, and out of it again at seven-fifteen every night, leaving it like a tomb.

The department was empty at that moment—hats are not the kind of things that are bought in a rush as soon as the stores are open—and, as he watched, he saw Eve Harlow, this assistant from another department, go up to one of the models marked "Exclusive"—it was a piece of black velvet nonsense for which they were asking two guineas—and take it down from the bright nickel stand where it was hanging. She held it for a moment in

her hand, and then, going over to the mirror on the table opposite, she arranged her hair first this way and then that and finally
set the hat on top of it, standing there admiring herself like a lady
in front of her own dressing-table.

Mr. Hackbridge was only half a pace behind John Marco, but
when he saw what was happening he thrust out his chin and
stepped forward.

"Disgryceful!" he said. "Disgryceful!"

But John Marco raised his hand and stopped him. He wanted
that picture in the mirror in front of him to remain. The small
body leaning forwards, the arms that were still lifted to the head,
the slim neck over the black silk dress, the pre-occupation and
eagerness of it all, fascinated him. The abandoned wickedness of
trying on one of the firm's hats was nothing less than sheer revo-
lution; but somehow the way in which she was doing it was at
once feminine and desirable. It reminded him again how womanless his own life seemed sentenced to be.

Then, still with that ridiculous, expensive hat perched on her
head, the girl glanced round for an instant, and saw John Marco
standing there. She did not move, and the three of them stood
looking at each other. It was John Marco who spoke first. He
said something to Mr. Hackbridge and then turned and continued his tour of the other departments.

Mr. Hackbridge advanced majestically towards the girl.

"Take it off," he said. "Take it off at once." He paused deliberately for effect and added quietly but menacingly: "Mr. Marco
wants to see you in his office at closing time."

He thought of saying something biting as well about what
comes of taking on assistants who can't produce references. But
he suppressed the remark. Miss Harlow would understand
perfectly well what that kind of summons implied; and it had

400

been rather clever of Mr. Marco to give her the whole day to think about it.

In any case it was the last two-guinea hat that she was ever likely to handle.

At seven-fifteen Eve Harlow went slowly up the main staircase and stood outside John Marco's door. It seemed strange to be doing so when everyone else was going down the staff staircase at the back. And they would all be climbing up that endless flight of cement steps again to-morrow morning; they were all respectable, reliable young ladies who could be trusted.

She raised a hand that trembled a little and knocked on the door.

John Marco was standing with his back to the fireplace when she entered. He was holding the catalogue of one of the whole-sale firms in his hand.

"Sit down," he said, and went on reading.

Then, when he had finished, he put the catalogue behind him and looked at her. He looked at her so long, in fact, that she stirred a trifle self-consciously. She found herself wishing that he would tell her that she was dismissed and be done with it. But still he went on looking. It was almost as if all the time he were thinking of something else.

"How old did you say you were?" he asked at last.

"Nineteen, sir," she told him.

Nineteen! That was the age which Mary had been when he had first defied convention and walked home with her. He had been a different man then. He wasn't even a man at all any longer, he was a company now, something at the top of note-paper and on the side of vans; and a name in fancy capitals doesn't have any feelings, any emotions. All that a name like that can think about is growing larger and becoming better-known, more talked-about. And all the time that was happening and his name was growing, there would be these girls of nineteen appearing around him. They would be slight like this one, a little timid and uncertain perhaps; and with a gay taste in hats. And he would have to stand back and watch them as they made mistakes and fell in and out of love and finally went off in the arms of other men.

He turned towards her again and let his eyes run up and down her. She seemed so young, so very young, sitting there; the curve of her cheek, her hands folded in her lap, the small close ears that the upward sweep of her hair disclosed—these were the very spirit and essence of her age.

"What made you want that hat?" he asked suddenly.

"I only wanted to see what it looked like," she replied.

"And were you satisfied?" he persisted. "Was it worth it?"

"It was a beautiful hat," she said simply.

He paused. The wall between them seemed higher than ever now. It was as though at nineteen she were ageless and would go on being young for ever, while every year that passed would leave his prime receding from him, till finally he hadn't the strength any longer even to climb the wall and find what lay hidden on the other side.

He left the fireplace and sat down in the big revolving chair.

"Would you like to have that hat?" he asked.

"Why, yes," she said in surprise.

"Then you'd better take it," he said. He was no longer looking at her: he was fiddling with the gold pencil in his hand. "Have it, and wear it Sundays. Wear it when you go out in the Park."

To his surprise she did not answer; and when he looked up at her he saw that she was crying. Not noisily and vulgarly; but like a lady, with her handkerchief close up to her eyes concealing it.

"Thank you," she said at last.

He was brusque again by now.

"Perhaps if you've got a nice hat of your own you won't want to go trying on the firm's property," he said.

"I promise it won't happen again," she answered.

She got up and began to go across the room to the door. But when she reached it, he called her back.

"Just one moment, Miss Harlow," he said.

She turned nervously. Was this then what he had been keeping in store for her? Was he going to dismiss her now that he had made her a present of the detestable hat?

But what he said was quite different.

"What do you get paid?" he asked.

"Fifteen shillings a week, sir," she answered.

He paused.

"Would you like to come out to-night?" he asked. "Somewhere fashionable where people are wearing that kind of hat?"

ii

The Criterion when they got there was noisy and vivacious. There was hubbub in the air, and sparkle; and everyone in the place had that gratified, excited feeling that comes of sitting down to dine in the very centre of the world.

John Marco himself sat at a table in the corner and stared over the cover of the wine-list at his companion.

She looked younger than ever sitting there; she looked, in fact, the youngest thing in the whole room. By comparison most of the other women seemed just a little faded and full-blown. The woman at the next table was a large-bosomed creature all tangled up in white lace: she was being archly fascinating with a little man who was scarcely more than half her size. And beyond her was a lady with a lot of jewellery and dyed hair, philosophically awaiting the inevitable moment of seduction. John Marco let his eyes wander over them and returned to Miss Harlow.

"Tell me something about yourself," he said at last. "Did you always want to go into a shop?"

He sat back in his chair, twirling the stem of his wineglass between his fingers. He liked watching her: she was so obviously happy and flattered by it all; and because she was happy she was pretty, too—prettier than he had ever imagined. Her hands, resting on the table, were clasped, the fingers laced together; he saw how slender they were, how small. "This is someone," he found himself saying, "who could occupy me: someone who could drive out my other thoughts."

But when she had answered, he realised that he had not been listening: he had been looking at her instead. He had heard snatches of what she had been saying, but no more. There was something about a father who had died while she was still quite little and a sister who had thrown away an expensive training— as what, he could not have heard—to get married to a man who had turned out to be a rotter. And now, he gathered, there was only Eve Harlow left out of the lot of them, and the fifteen shillings a week that John Marco Ltd. gave her was the whole of the claim which she had been able to stake out on life.

"But how damn silly it is," he was thinking: "fancy a child with those looks having to spend her time selling petticoats to fat women who want them too tight just to be in fashion." She would realise one day that she could do better for herself than that. And by then, perhaps, he would have lost her: she would have gone the way of the rest of them.

Over coffee, he pushed back the table a little way from them and drew his chair closer up to hers. The small lamp in the centre now seemed to separate them from the rest of London: it left the rest of the room dim and undiscovered. They were as isolated as if they had been on a desert island.

"Aren't you ever lonely?" he asked. "Just living in the hostel with no home of your own?"

"Sometimes," she admitted.

"And haven't you got any plans for the future?"

"Plenty," she said. "Only they don't always come out right."

"Tell me about them," he said.

But the scene around him with the lights and the waiters and the full-blown ladies and the music, and this girl before him, who seemed so young, in the centre of it all, had faded at last and vanished: it had seemed even at the time too good to continue. They had parted politely at the steps of the hostel, and he had given himself back to the shop again with its sales reports and its special display programmes and its tours of inspection. And then ten days later they were back at the Criterion again, at this same table with the same waiter bending over them and the orchestra playing the same pieces. During the interval they had scarcely spoken; but already they were strangers no more. His hand rested longer than it need have done on her shoulder as he helped her out of her coat, and they caught one another's eye and smiled back at each other.

And then that meal, too, slid into limbo and was lost; and once more his life revolved around Mr. Hackbridge and Mr. Lyman and Mr. Skewin. But these dinners together were more frequent now; they were what he lived for. Whenever he was not working, it seemed that he was looking over the top of a wine-glass at his companion.

It was one evening scarcely a month after their first visit to the Criterion as the band was playing just loud enough to drown other conversation than he leant forward and addressed his companion.

"You knew I was married, didn't you?" he said.

She nodded.

"How did you know?" he asked.

"They all know at the shop," she answered.

He paused.

"And do you mind?"

This time it was Miss Harlow who paused.

"No," she said quietly.

But the brightness and liveliness had gone from her face as she spoke.

"I thought you'd say that," he said.

He put his hand over her clasped ones. But her hands, he noticed, felt cold; and after a moment she withdrew them. She sat back without looking at him and began scratching aimless, idle designs on the table cloth with her finger.

Then, because she was silent, he bent forward still closer.

"Are you afraid of what people will say?" he asked.

She shook her head.

"It's not that," she answered.

"Then what is it?"

"I don't know," she replied. "It's only . . . only I wanted things to go on just as they were."

"But they couldn't," he told her. "Don't you ever think of what I feel like every time you leave me?"

"I know," she said. "You needn't tell me."

His eyes were fixed on her now. He saw nothing but the white forehead with the dark shining hair rising above it and the shadowy lines which her eyelashes made against her cheek: her own eyes were still lowered. She had avoided his gaze ever since he had spoken.

"Let's get out of here," he said suddenly. "Let's go somewhere we can talk properly."

iii

It was beneath the silver bow of Eros that they got into a hansom together, and began to drive through the faint blue haze that had descended. The lights of Piccadilly shone out in front of them like the illuminations at a fair, and the pavements were as thronged with people as if a procession were expected. It was one of those moments of early night-time when all cities are beautiful and London itself becomes something ready to dissolve before the sight. A guardsman in red uniform at a street corner was like a figure stuck there by a ballet-master.

John Marco put his arms round her shoulders and drew her to him.

"Do you know," he said, almost under his breath, "I think this is the first time in my life that I've ever really got what I wanted?"

They did not say much, however; and he was content to sit there with all London at his feet. It was not until they had reached the park and were moving along under the shadow of the trees that she spoke to him. She gave a forced little laugh.

"It's funny the way things happen," she said. "Do you know I nearly got married myself three months ago?"

He put his arm closer round her.

"Are you glad you didn't?" he asked.

"I am now," she said.

"Who was it?" he demanded.

"It was someone at the shop," she replied. "I don't expect you'd even know him."

"Did you want to marry him?"

She paused.

"Yes," she said. "I did. A lot."

"Then why didn't you?" he asked.

The thought of how nearly he had lost her, excited him; it seemed that he had been only one move ahead of fate.

"Why didn't you?" he repeated.

"He hadn't got enough money," she answered at last. "He couldn't afford it."

"How much did he earn?" he asked: he had known himself what it was to be cut off from life in this way.

"Thirty-five shillings a week," she said and paused.

"He asked for a rise but you wouldn't give it to him."

"I'm glad I didn't," he replied.

He smiled; and she saw the smile on his face.

"Don't let's talk about it," she said.

"Did you love him much?" he persisted.

"Quite a bit."

"And do you still love him?"

"It wasn't so very long ago, remember," she said quietly.

They were back in his flat now; it was the first time he had taken her there. She looked round the room admiringly, and thought for a moment of her own room. That was comprised of two high, deal partitions with a curtain on a rail to make one side of it. That was life cut down to its limits: this room was life lived the other way.

She had taken her hat and coat off and had thrown them down onto the couch beside her. She was still wearing the plain black dress that she wore every day in the shop and John Marco was standing over by the fireplace looking at her. He came slowly over to her and put out his arms.

"Kiss me," he said. "You haven't kissed me ever since I've known you."

"You do love me, don't you," she said at last. Her voice was young and happy again by now. "Tell me how much you love me."

"I love you so much," he said, "that I want to give you every-thing." And he began kissing her again, on the hair, on her eyes, and on her lips.

The clock on the mantelpiece whirred warningly and then struck: it was eleven. She gave a little laugh.

"I shall have to go," she said. "I'm supposed to be in by eleven."

But he continued to keep his arms around her.

"You can stay here with me," he said.

She shook her head.

"Not to-night," she said.

"Why not?" he asked.

"You've got to give me time to think."

"Time," he repeated. "I've been waiting long enough, haven't I?"

She began stroking his face: it was hard and rough to her hand and the feel of it pleased her.

"You're very difficult to say 'no' to, aren't you?" she said.

He did not answer for a moment. And then taking her face in his two hands he made her look into his eyes.

"Stay here with me," he said. "Say that you'll stop."

"I'll stop," she answered.

But she dropped her eyes as she said it.

The dawn was breaking somewhere over beyond Dalston or Hackney, and the Bayswater chimney pots had come to life again and shone with the light of morning. A flock of pigeons, as white as angels, went wheeling over them, and down in the street below there was the clink of milk cans.

John Marco had lain awake watching the sky change from purple to grey and from grey to the colour of early daylight. Then when the room took shape around him again, he turned on his elbow and looked at the sleeper in the bed beside him. Her dark hair was spread out around her head like a fan and one hand was raised under her cheek, supporting it. He started to bend down and kiss her but he stopped himself. She looked too young somehow; and, in sleep, too helpless. It would have been like disturbing the night-time of a child.

"Let her sleep," he thought. "For her, to-morrow will be a strange world."

And for him? This new life that he had chosen would be strange too. The madness, the desire of last night was over now: it had slid into the dark history of things past. And in its place was left a sadness that threatened to overwhelm him. He was now like any other man who has loved and forgotten and taken his pleasure where he could find it. He had finally destroyed the clear image that he had tried, tried so hard, so uselessly, to keep bright inside his mind; it was in pieces and he had no right to think of Mary now. Even if he were free and Mary able to come to him he could never take her back to him again.

And because of this, because it was the whole of his life that had been demolished, he began to hate that small figure that lay, still sleeping, beside him. It was she—more even than Hesther— because he had loved her, who had broken the image. He closed his eyes for a moment; and, as he did so, he saw Mary's face

410

again close before him. Then he roused himself; and Mary vanished. He was alone again with this girl, this stranger who had tried on a silly hat and had overthrown him. He bent over her once more, staring down at her. But the beauty seemed to have gone from the quiet features. The dark fan of hair repelled him: it was black and thick like Hesther's. And the lips as he watched were moving as though repeating a name that was not his. Quietly, carefully so as not to rouse her, he left the bed and went over to the window.

Then because she was no longer by him, because her breath was not now on his shoulder, his mood changed again, and he grew sorry for her. She had not told him that she loved him; had not denied that previous, defeated lover.

Had not told him that she loved him: he repeated the words over in his mind. Perhaps, after all, she cared nothing, could care nothing so long as the world still contained that other man, the first man she had wanted. And if last night in giving herself she had been treacherous to everything in her own heart, where would their happiness lie, their future? They could never now be like other people, other lovers.

Even in their happy moments, the moments when they should be able to forget everything, they would still be remembering other looks, other voices. They would look into the same fire together and see different faces.

And she was still so young. Her life was not begun yet. "She will grow used to the money I shall give her," he began saying to himself: "and all that she will remember is that man whom she might have had. And if I tire of her, if I no longer want this child beside me because she reminds me too much of what I have lost already, what is there for her then except heartbreak and desolation? She will grow to hate me; hate me as I grew to hate Hesther who took me away from everything that was mine."

The sleeper in bed started and drew one bare white arm across her face. She gave a little sigh, half sigh half whimper, as she felt to-morrow coming to her; and then as though she were not eager for it, as though she were seeking to keep time waiting for her, she drew the clothes closer around her, hiding herself from the bright daylight.

But John Marco went over to her. He looked down at the small face and the shining pattern of her hair.

"Wake up," he said roughly. "I've got to speak to you."

She was still crying, and as she lay there she was trying desperately to fit the pieces of her life in shape again. She was trying to understand this disaster that had overwhelmed her.

"So you didn't love me," she said. "You didn't."

He shook his head.

"That's not true," he said. "You don't understand."

"You only wanted me," she told him. "Just as though I'd been any other woman."

"There's someone else who loves you," he said at last. "Go back to him."

At the words, she began crying again; crying bitterly as she had cried when he had first spoken to her.

"How could I, after this?" she asked.

"But you still love him?"

"I did."

"And he still wants you."

"Yes, he still wants me."

"Then go back: you belong to him."

"Not any longer."

He had gone over to the window and his back was towards

412

her. When he answered it was quietly, almost as though he were speaking to himself.

"On the day you marry him," he said, "I'll give him all the money he wants. There'll be enough for both of you. You're young: I was too old for you. Your future is together." He paused and still more softly so that she scarcely heard it, he added something.

"A man can't live without love," was what he said.

He was standing in front of the fireplace in his living-room. She had gone now, had slipped away without his seeing her again. And in her going his loneliness came back to him. Probably he always would be lonely, he told himself: it was the special punishment that had been prepared for him. He could hope for nothing better. But in a way he was proud, too: it seemed that somehow he had contrived to be faithful again.

The clock on the mantelshelf chimed and he started. The morning was slipping past him. In half-an-hour he should be at the shop. It would be waiting: it couldn't start without him. He didn't belong to himself any longer: he was just the name-piece of John Marco Limited, something that the shareholders had bought and paid for.

Taking down his tall hat from the hat-stand he brushed it carefully: it was most important that when he turned up in the mornings he should set a good example.

Chapter XXXII

The daily tours of inspection went on piling up behind him— he had made over five hundred of them by now.

The whole ritual was exact and invariable. The procession started down in the basement among the ironmongery, and worked up past the general drapery and the dress lengths, through the millinery and lingerie, to the children's section and the restaurant. It was the fact that for nearly a year the whole ceremony had not varied by so much as a single deviation, that made it so astonishing when he suddenly cut out the lingerie altogether and went straight from the perfumery to small woman's as though there had been nothing in between. For an entire week he ignored lingerie as though vests and bodices had not existed.

"Not the lingerie?" Mr. Hackbridge had asked in astonishment on the first morning of the omission. And John Marco had not answered.

After that, Mr. Hackbridge had said nothing. But he had kept his eyes open. It had not of course remained secret for very long that John Marco had been amusing himself with one of the assistants. Someone in the household goods had seen the two of them going into a restaurant together, and the next morning it was all round the building. Mr. Hackbridge put two and two together and pigeon-holed in his mind the fact that it was from the lingerie that the young lady had been chosen.

"So they've had some sort of tiff now, have they?" he mused. "And she's thrown him over. He'll get her back all right."

And at the memory of what his piece of romance, Mrs. Hackbridge, now looked like in the mornings when he slid out of bed in a nightgown that drooped round her like a potato sack, Mr. Hackbridge found himself envying John Marco.

"He's only got to whistle and they come to him," he told himself. "He can have his pick and they daren't say 'no.' He's one of the lucky ones."

But on the following day, still without warning, John Marco had suddenly resumed his accustomed visit: he had walked through the lingerie as though he had never missed it in his life. And the young lady about whom Mr. Hackbridge had his suspicions had given nothing away. She had gone on with her work of sorting out the price tickets without even once looking up. It was not indeed until Mr. Hackbridge had noticed that when John Marco was there she never did look up that his suspicions were confirmed. Only this time he put a different construction on the whole affair.

"He's probably betrayed her," he told himself. "And now he doesn't want to have nothing else to do with her." And he shook his head over the depravity of his employer. "He's a Turk for women," he reflected. "Those dark, thick-set men usually are."

It was nearly a month later that Mr. Hackbridge caught John Marco off his guard: caught him off his guard for the first time since he had known the man. They had just passed through the gloves and were entering the lingerie when John Marco paused and looked back. It was easy enough to see which of the young

415

ladies he was looking at; and this time the young lady did not turn away. She raised her eyes and looked back at him.

Across the whole width of the department they stood staring at each other. But it was not this in itself that was surprising: it was the expression on John Marco's face. It was the saddest thing that Mr. Hackbridge had ever seen; it was the face of a man who has seen his whole life go tumbling into ruins.

He remembered it for days, long after that expression had gone from John Marco's face and the man who remained was simply a machine which occupied the Governor's chair in the inner office, and gave orders and cancelled them, and found fault with everything, and worked for fourteen hours a day and did not seem to have even the smallest kernel of human feeling anywhere inside him.

ii

The annual general meeting—the first of John Marco Limited— was in sight now; and the balance sheet was being prepared.

Except for the daily inspection, the office never saw John Marco. He was there at eight o'clock in the morning and at ten o'clock at night he was still shut away in his room with Mr. Lyman. Little Mr. Lyman wilted under it; his complexion, always rather pale and yellowish, became a kind of blotchy primrose, and deep amber circles appeared under his eyes. When at last he got into bed at night his head was still full of shifting columns of figures that made patterns in front of his eyes; and always in the middle of the pattern he saw the figure of John Marco a cigar between his teeth, like a heathen idol in some mathematical temple built of noughts and digits.

"Nothing to be put to reserve, sir?" he asked wearily on the night of the final session. "Use up every penny we've got?"

"Every penny," John Marco repeated.

"And pay five per cent?"

"Pay five per cent."

"The shareholders won't expect it, you know, sir," Mr. Lyman said diffidently. "Not in the first year, sir."

"But I expect it," John Marco answered. "It's my business."

"Quite so, sir," Mr. Lyman replied hurriedly. "I only meant that it seemed too good to be true."

John Marco crushed out the stump of his cigar in the ash-tray; the butt of the cigar was all ragged and bitten.

"It is too good to be true," he said. "We may have to raise more capital."

iii

It was late one evening as John Marco was passing out through the shop when he saw Mr. Hackbridge coming towards him. Hackbridge was walking very fast, and seemed agitated; he was walking so fast, in fact, that as he dragged his large, heavy feet across the thick pile carpet he left a trail behind him like a tractor's.

"There's a gentleman to see you, sir," he said breathlessly.

John Marco took out his watch and raised his eyebrows.

"At this time?"

"Yes, sir. He said it was urgent."

"What's his name?"

"Mr. Tuke, sir. It's a private matter he wants to see you on."

Mr. Tuke! What did Mr. Tuke want? What right had he to come round to the shop like this after closing time trying to link the old life, the struggling, unpleasant one, onto the new? He

417

would refuse to see him, would snub him bluntly through a second person.

"Tell Mr. Tuke," he replied, "that I am too busy to see him." He paused. "Tell him also," he added, "that I am not aware of any business between us that requires an interview."

Mr. Hackbridge shifted from one leg to the other.

"He told me you would probably give that sort of an answer," he explained, "and he said he wanted you to re-consider it. What he wants to see you about is very private and personal."

For a moment John Marco's heart closed and did not re-open: a little shudder of coldness ran through him. The words sounded sinister and disturbing. But they couldn't mean anything, couldn't mean the one thing that he was alarmed that they might mean: Mr. Tuke didn't know anything about *that*. The words, "very private and personal" remained, however: he stood quite still, frowning, thinking over them.

"Have Mr. Tuke shown up," he said at last. "Have him shown up to my private office."

He broke off and began casting desperately about in his mind for some kind of solution to the mystery of the visit. But seeing that Mr. Hackbridge's eye was on him he controlled himself.

"And have him shown up the main staircase," he added. "I want him to see the sort of place he is in."

Mr. Tuke was standing gazing out of the window when John Marco entered. His hands were clasped behind his back and there was a slip of paper held between them. At the sound that the door made in closing Mr. Tuke swung round and, defiantly lifting the point of his chin above his round collar, he faced John Marco.

It was nearly three years since they had met and John Marco's

418

first impression was that in the interval Mr. Tuke had shrunk somehow; shrunk and grown shoddier. The spell of seeing him in the pulpit every Sunday, had been snapped; and all that remained of that awe-inspiring presence was a large, red-faced man in a shiny clerical suit. His hair was a little longer than it had been, and the silver in it now began to show; it fell in lank, unfrivolous waves about his ears.

But the one thing that had not altered was his voice: that still came resounding out of some deep cavern inside him.

"John Marco," he said gravely, "have you repented? Is your soul ready to be washed?"

"So that's it, is it?" John Marco reflected. "It's my soul he's after."

He did not reply at once. He allowed his eyes to run up and down Mr. Tuke contemptuously. Then he set his feet wide-apart on the rich carpet that was under him and addressed him in the tone of voice which he used sometimes to travellers who were too insistent and could not otherwise be got rid of.

"You're wasting your time, Mr. Tuke," he said. "I'm not interested."

And having said it, he turned deliberately away as though the whole distasteful interview were over.

But Mr. Tuke was not to be put off so easily: he had the consciousness of right on his side. Instead of being abashed, he came forward.

"John Marco," he said, still in the same grave voice, taking hold of the lapels of his coat as though they were the two runners of a stole, "I am come to-night as the bringer of very solemn news."

John Marco turned slowly towards him.

"Very well then," he said. "Tell me."

Mr. Tuke, however, would not allow himself to be hurried.

"I am not satisfied that you are in a state of grace to hear it," he replied.

John Marco drew himself up for a moment as though to say something, but suppressed whatever it was on his lips. Then he came forward, his thumbs under the arm-holes of his waistcoat. His head was a little to one side and he regarded Mr. Tuke through eyes that were more than half closed.

"You're being impertinent, Mr. Tuke," he said. "You're forgetting that I'm no longer of your dispensation."

At the word "impertinent" Mr. Tuke pursed his lips. He could remember clearly the day when John Marco as a young man with too much wrist showing below the cuffs of his jacket had come to him, and asked to be allowed to expound in Sunday School.

"If you choose to show no respect to me," he replied hotly, "at least you owe some to my cloth."

John Marco paused.

"I don't recognise your cloth," he said.

Mr. Tuke still controlled himself.

"Then perhaps you will recognise my years," he answered.

His face was flushed and his breathing came heavily as he said it. He was obviously right on the edge of one of his really spectacular angers.

But John Marco continued to stare at him without moving.

"You came to tell me something, Mr. Tuke," he said.

"I came to give you this," Mr. Tuke replied. "You should purify your soul before you read it." He paused. "It will show how Thomas Petter was prepared to trust you," he added.

As he spoke he handed John Marco the piece of paper that was in his hand.

John Marco hesitated for a moment.

"Did Thomas Petter ask you to come here?" he demanded.
Mr. Tuke shook his head.

"I came," he said, "because it was my duty."

John Marco took the paper and began to read.

"I, Thomas Petter, chemist, of 28 Harrow Street, Paddington" the message ran, *"being of sound mind and under no duress do hereby bequeath to my wife, Mary Ann Petter, all of which I die possessed. As my executors I appoint Mr. Eliud Tuke, of 7 Chapel Walk, Minister of God, and John Marco, of Tredegar Terrace, merchant, and, in the event of the death of the said Mary Ann Petter, to administer my estate for the advantage of my daughter, Mary Elizabeth Petter, infant, until she shall have attained the age of twenty-one years.*

Signed Thomas Petter, May 11th, 1903.

As John Marco held this piece of script in his hand he saw again, clearly, the man who had written those words. There he was, pink and prim and innocent, sitting up at the little fumed-oak desk in the tiny sitting-room, diligently penning this, his own last will and testament. For a moment John Marco felt sorry for him; felt again that queer sensation of pity that Mr. Petter had always provoked. There was something so oddly defenceless, so vulnerable, about him. With all the millions of London to choose from he had deliberately selected for one of his executors the only man who had shown himself to be a peril to him. And having inscribed this foolish document, he had omitted even to have it witnessed; in law the thing might never have existed.

"When did you come by this?" he asked.

"To-day."

"It was written five years ago," John Marco said coldly.

"He was still your friend then, remember," Mr. Tuke replied.

And as he said it, John Marco understood the reason for his visit: Mr. Tuke had seen at last the harm that he had done to Mr. Petter by his foolish warning and was seeking now to make amends for it. He was at one single clumsy stroke trying to repair a breach in a friendship within the Tabernacle and win back the most conspicuous of all his erring Amosites. Between them they had unearthed this old draft of a testimony, and Mr. Tuke had brought it round here in an effort to break John Marco's heart by reminding him of the happy past.

John Marco looked up and saw Mr. Tuke's eyes fixed on him, they were gleaming and moist-looking.

"He shan't have me," John Marco thought bitterly. "I'm free of him."

And folding the paper contemptuously across, he handed it back to Mr. Tuke.

"Take it away," he said. "I've no use for it."

Mr. Tuke almost snatched it from him.

"You're not worthy to touch it," he said. "I debated whether I should even show it to you."

"Then you decided wrong," John Marco answered. He was angry now and his voice was raised to match Mr. Tuke's. "Go back and tell him the truth about me. Tell him that I hated him. Tell him that I tried to seduce his wife. Tell him anything that you like."

Mr. Tuke swallowed hard for a moment and his face took on a deeper colour. Then he turned his back on John Marco and went over to the door. In the doorway he paused for a moment and faced John Marco again.

"I thank God," he said, collecting his dignity about him like a cloak, "that I shall never be able to deliver that message. Our brother is dead."

Chapter XXXIII

It seemed strange to be standing there again in the little doorway in Harrow Street; and as he raised his hand to the bell, John Marco half expected it to be Thomas Petter himself who would come down the stairs in answer to it.

The ride from the shop had been a violent, impetuous one; it seemed that even after all those years every minute was precious. He had hailed a hansom, and by the time he reached Harrow Street he had raised the flap that separated him from the driver half-a-dozen times and had shouted up to him to hurry.

But, now that he had reached the house, there seemed no one to admit him. He had just rung again—it was the third or fourth time that he had rung—when he heard the sound of footsteps descending. They were light footsteps; the footsteps of a woman. But they came down the stairs slowly and wearily. Then the door opened and Mary stood there in front of him.

They stood for a moment looking at each other without speaking.

Then John Marco held out his hand.

"Mary," he said. "I've come to you."

She ignored the hand that was held out to her: her whole

attitude was one of dumb, infinite fatigue.

"There's nothing that you can do," she answered. "It's too late."

"I . . . I thought I might be able to help you," he said.

"I don't need anything," she answered.

She was very calm, he noticed; surprisingly calm. Or was it that she was still dazed by it all and could not yet realise what had happened to her? It would not be until next morning, the first morning in which she woke to a world that did not contain a husband, that she would really understand what it meant.

"Let me come in," John Marco said to her. "I want to talk to you."

She stood back and held the door open for him.

"You can come in," she said.

He followed her up the stairs and into the tiny sitting-room that was full of memories of those evenings when all three of them had been there together. It was not until then that he saw her face. She had recently been crying and her eyes were still wet. Her hair, too, was not brushed smoothly back like pale satin as it usually was: it now fell all about her face, covering up the line of the clear forehead. But the effect of it was somehow to make her look younger. She seemed no different now from the girl who had taught next to him in Mr. Tuke's Sunday School.

"Are you alone here?" he asked.

She shook her head.

"His mother's upstairs," she said. "With him."

"And the child?"

"I sent her back home," she answered. "She doesn't know what's happened yet."

There was something distant and unmoved in the manner in which she answered these questions; it might have been somebody else's tragedy in the midst of which she had found herself.

"What are you going to do?" he asked.

She shook her head.

"I don't know," she answered. "I haven't had time to think."

"Do you know how he left you?" he asked.

Her hand went helplessly to her forehead.

"He never told me," she said. She hesitated for a moment as though other thoughts were filling her mind. "There was always enough for the three of us while he was here," she added.

"Then you don't know whether you're provided for?"

She hesitated again.

"He told me that we might have to go back home again to my people," she answered, and then paused.

"All last night he kept on saying it."

She turned away and went over to the window and he saw she was crying. At first she cried softly, almost silently, as though she were trying to conceal it. Then she gave over the pretence and cried openly. Resting her arm up against the sash she laid her forehead upon it and stood there weeping.

John Marco went towards her and raised his hand to place it on her shoulder. But at the last moment he drew back. Somehow, her grief separated them. They were near to each other, standing side by side, but it was as though her misery had built a wall around her, leaving him on the outer side of it. He felt as he looked at her that, no matter how he tried, he could not reach her. To do something for her, however; to make her feel that at this moment she had never been less alone—that was why he had come.

"You can stay here if you'd rather," he said. "You need never want for money. I'll take care of that."

She did not answer immediately. Instead she kept her face turned away from him. And when she replied her voice was quiet again.

"It's good of you, John," she said. "I always believed in you. But I couldn't take it."

"Why not?" he asked.

"Not after what happened."

He raised his hand again as if to touch her, but he let it fall to his side once more.

"But isn't that over now?" he asked. "Isn't that the past?"

It was here that Mary turned to him. Her face was set hard as she spoke.

"Do you know what my husband said before he died? What his last words were?" she asked.

John Marco dropped his eyes for a moment.

"Tell me," he said.

"That he forgave you," she answered.

He paused.

"There was nothing to forgive," he replied at last.

"You didn't let him think that," she said.

"That was only because I wanted you so much," he answered. "I was desperate that night. Can't you understand?"

"But he wanted me, too. And he wasn't as strong as you are."

John Marco drew in his breath sharply.

"Which of us did you want?" he asked. "Only tell me that."

"I loved you first," she said quietly. "You know that."

"And afterwards?"

"I suppose a woman can't ever give up loving altogether," she replied. "I often used to think about you."

"And did you want me?"

She bowed her head.

"God forgive me, I did."

"Would you have come if I'd asked you?"

"No."

She drew herself up as she said it and the colour came back to her face.

"He was always so good to me," she added. "And he relied on me for everything."

John Marco was no longer standing still beside her. He had begun to pace up and down the room in quick, nervous steps. His eyes were shining and excited.

"Would you come now?" he asked. "Now . . . now that you can't hurt him."

There was a sound from the room above them, the sound of a chair being dragged across the floor. Mary started and looked away from him. It was from her bedroom that the sound had come, from her bedroom that had always looked so pink and white and warm. And now Thomas Petter's mother dressed already in full black, was sitting up there alone.

"You'd better go," she said, passing her hand across her face. "I'd rather be alone to-night."

But John Marco did not move.

"I love you, Mary," he said. "I want you to let me help you."

She shook her head again.

"He wouldn't have wanted it," she told him. "He would have thought it unfaithful of me."

"It's yourself you've got to think of now," he reminded her. "Yourself and the child."

"I can't," she answered simply. "I must do what he would have wanted, always."

She got up and went over to the door.

"I can't bear any more to-night," she said. "Please leave me.

Mr. Tuke's coming back later to try and help me to pray."

John Marco was silent for a moment. Then he came over to her. He put his arms round her for a moment.

"You can come to me whenever you want to," he said. "I shall be waiting."

She remained in his arms without moving. And when he pulled her to him she closed her eyes.

"Kiss me," he said.

She kissed him, still without re-opening her eyes. And then suddenly, as though for the first time realising what she had done, she thrust him away.

"You belong to Hesther," she said. "Not to me. I mustn't see you."

"Never?" he asked.

She bowed her head again.

"Never."

There was a movement in the room above and then footsteps on the stairs outside the door. John Marco walked slowly over to the couch and took up his hat and gloves: he stood there for a moment looking round this room that he knew so well. Then the door of the sitting-room was opened and a small, white-haired woman stood there. It was clear that she had been crying.

"I've just left him," she said. "He looks so peaceful and lovely. He might be asleep."

She spoke in the gentle voice of a mother still able to find something to cherish in her own flesh and handiwork.

Then she saw John Marco.

"Does this gentleman want to see him too?" she asked. "He can go up if he likes. Was he my son's friend?"

Book V

Green Pastures

Chapter XXXIV

It was the day of the Annual General Meeting; the Marble Salon had been cleared for the shareholders; and John Marco was in the middle of his speech.

The shareholders seated in front of him on the rows of little gilt chairs were following every movement he made as if he were a conjurer; and like a conjurer he was playing with them. They had all read about their dividend in the printed report which had been sent to them, and the atmosphere when he started was one of relief even of optimism. But he very soon, and very deliberately destroyed all that. Speaking in a low, emotional voice that touched them, he described the pit-falls and difficulties that every new firm has to contend with; he addressed them as fellow men. And instead of seeing their chairman as a prosperous-looking business man with a flower in his buttonhole, they began to see him as a kind of pilgrim who for their sakes had wandered through the Slough of Despond and the Valley of the Shadow, and had returned with the miraculous flower of five-per-cent attached to his staff. There he was, safe and sound enough for this one afternoon; but to-morrow morning when they were cheerfully spending the interest, he would be setting out again on another twelve months' pilgrimage for their sakes.

When John Marco paused for a moment and allowed himself a sip of water, the whole audience responded; it was as though they had actually seen him just getting to the river before he collapsed. And when he resumed, his tone was lighter: he was dealing now with the dividend that the firm was paying. He attributed none of his success to himself. It was the staff, he said, that they must thank for this; the most loyal, hard-working and conscientious staff in London. A general rustle of applause ran right through the room: it was felt now that as well as being a pilgrim he was also a gentleman. Then, while the feeling of brotherhood was very strong among them all, he came to the real point of the address and told them that the capital was not enough.

The effect of this announcement was immediate and sensational. The timid ones took fright and began scribbling down hasty little notes, and the old hands sat back and pursed up their lips.

"The question we must now ask ourselves," he was saying, "is whether we should be content to remain in the second rank of retail drapery with all the risks of possible extinction from bigger competitors or whether we should ourselves step into the front rank and so be able to snap our fingers at competition. You may ask yourselves why I should even bother to put the alternatives before you as the advantages of the one against the other are so obvious. But the answer to that must be simply that to step into the front rank requires money, a lot of money."

He paused here and the audience became excited again; they felt that in some mysterious way they were being allowed to dabble in high finance. Even the timid ones became infected. And when he resumed, his voice had lost that note of appeal it had taken on before: it became hard and decisive, like that of a

Chancellor announcing a stiff Budget.

"It is because of the fact that competition has now become so desperate and cut-throat in retail commerce," he went on, "that your directors have decided—and I cannot pretend that I disagree with them—that somehow or other we should find the extra money. The sum that we need is another hundred thousand—not a small sum you'll say. But I propose to show our gratitude to those who helped us to find the money in the first place by giving them the opportunity of subscribing the whole of it if they wish, before we let any outsiders into the company."

A quiet, bald man with thick, formidable-looking glasses—a solicitor's managing clerk perhaps—suddenly allowed his report to slip from his fingers and came forward nervously to retrieve it. John Marco pounced on him: if he had been deliberately set down in the audience beforehand he could not have been more useful.

"Please, please," he said addressing the man. "I don't want your money now. In the morning will be time enough."

Someone laughed first and, after that, the rest was easy; John Marco enjoyed himself. He spoke of profits from big undertakings as though they were as easy to gather as apples in a ripe orchard, and began to refer with contempt to the five-per-cent that everyone had been so pleased about earlier in the afternoon. "There are some firms," he said, slowly and with emphasis, "old-established and with a regular patronage who would be proud of the profit which we have announced to-day. But frankly, I am not proud of it. If I had not thought that eventually I could do better, I should not have asked for a penny-piece from any of you. It is because of the five-per-cent this first year that I now ask for your further support so that I may be able to give you ten next year."

433

He sat down and the clapping began. It went on so long in fact that those who asked questions afterwards seemed, alien and dissentient. They were stamped at once as outsiders.

It was just as he had disposed of the last of the questioners— he was a compact, peaky man who expressed an un-swervable belief that any business with proper handling could be run on five hundred thousand pounds—and had sat down again, that he felt his eyes being unaccountably drawn in the direction of one corner of the room: it was as though there were some irre- sistible force attracting him.

At first he could see nothing. There were the familiar ranks of pink faces and, on either side of them, the row of marble columns that supported the roof of the salon. It was then that he saw, half hidden behind one of the columns, the figure of a woman. The figure was dressed all in black; heavy sepulchral stuff that caught the light and swallowed it. The gloves were black. And from the back of her hat hung dense folds of crêpe like a widow's.

John Marco was still staring at her while one of the sharehold- ers, a large, expansive-looking man who seemed to have been born into the world to be the foreman of juries, was proposing a vote of thanks ". . . how grateful we all are for the energy and foresight of our chairman . . ." The words reached John Marco from nowhere, and slid away into limbo again; his gaze was fixed on the long pale face that was now visible against the deathlike ebony of the costume. For a moment, his eyes met Hesther's and the rest of the room, the shareholders, the marble columns and the directors' wives grew faint and vanished.

But the meeting was beginning already to break up. There was the clatter of chairs being bumped against each other and the rustle and movement of people searching for their hats and umbrellas. Half the people had their backs to him now; they

434

were filing slowly out towards the door. There was one person, however, who was not leaving. She remained, composed and impassive, upon her chair.

Then, when the way was clear, she rose and with her long black garments flapping around her, began to advance up the aisle towards him.

He had waited until she was halfway up the hall; and then fled. But now in his own room he felt secure again, at ease. Perhaps she would go away again without troubling him, would return to whatever hiding-place it was from which she had emerged. Up to the very instant when he had seen her it had been his day, his victory; and now she had so nearly destroyed it. Until then he had proved himself cleverer than any of them. They had grasped at their five-per-cent just as he had intended and already they were hungering for more; he had done more than half Mr. Bulmer's job all ready for him. He realised now that he had only to raise his hand for new capital, great shining sack-loads of it, to come pouring in on him, and the whole future suddenly seemed golden. Altogether it had been one of those moments when a man feels as if he were high on a hillside in the landscape of his life with the coming years spread out before him in the sunshine.

The knock of his secretary on the door startled him.

"What is it?" he asked abruptly.

The girl hesitated: she spoke in a hushed, timid voice as though uncertain that she had got the message right.

"Mrs. Marco to see you, sir," she said.

John Marco raised his head.

"Tell her that I'm engaged on important business," he said at last. "Tell her that I can't be disturbed."

The vision of the figure in black rose before him again and he shut his eyes against it.

"She said it was very important," the girl told him. "She said she had to see you."

John Marco sat bolt upright in his chair.

"Tell her that I won't see her," he replied. "Tell her that I've no intention of seeing her."

He picked up one of the papers on his desk and began to read.

The girl turned away obediently. But, as she turned, the door behind her began to open. It opened very slowly as though there were someone on the other side who had been listening to everything that was going on within. Then, at last when it was open to its full width, Hesther stood there. In the clothes that she was wearing she appeared tremendous: she seemed to fill the whole doorway with blackness. The veil around her bonnet was down over her face now, and her eyes were visible only as darker spots amid the darkness.

She came forward.

"I shan't be with you long, John," she said. "When I've got what I came for I shall be going away again."

"Why *are* you here?" he asked as soon as they were alone together. "We've got nothing to talk about."

She settled herself in the chair in front of him and began toying like a coquette with the jet crucifix on her bosom.

"Isn't it natural that I should come to you?" she asked.

John Marco did not move.

"You know we've each gone our own way by now," he answered. "What else is it you've come for?"

Her body straightened itself.

"Money," she said. "That's why I came."

The words seemed to spring out of her. The ultimatum which

436

she had just delivered had evidently been crushed down inside her for years. She stopped playing with the crucifix and clasped her hands together so that the knuckles showed hard and white.

"What money?" he asked.

He was eyeing her narrowly now, his head cocked onto one side.

"God's money," she answered. "I ought to have given it up to Mr. Tuke for the Lord. Not to you for Mammon."

"It's too late to think of that now," he replied. "The bargain's closed."

"Not in God's eyes, it isn't. My voices tell me so."

"And what do your voices tell you to do about it?" he asked.

"Get it back from you," she replied. "Get back God's money and give it to the Tabernacle."

At the mention of God her whole body seemed to have become transformed; it filled. Her eyes were glowing under the veil; they shone. And she had parted her hands as if she were gripping something tangible; the money seemed to be in them already.

"Why don't you give your own money?" he asked. "Your uncle left you plenty."

"I have given it," she answered. "All of it."

He turned away from her.

"I owe you nothing," he said.

He had got up and begun to walk about. She kept her eyes fixed on him, following him round the room as he moved.

"What about the money you stole?" she asked.

He turned abruptly.

"You knew about that when you married me."

"Yes, I sinned too," she said. "That's why I've come here to-night so that we can both be saved."

He made no answer and she went on, speaking rapidly, the

437

words blurring into a long, tangled skein of speech.

"No one can live with my load of sin on their shoulders," she said. "It's the weight of the wickedness that breaks the soul. My voices tell me to get rid of it. I'm going to Mr. Tuke's to-night, and I've come to take you with me. When we leave him our souls will be white again. They'll be like snow. We shall have confessed."

John Marco looked at her incredulously.

"Confessed?" he demanded.

"Yes," she went on. "We must tell him everything. We must lay our sins upon him. Go to him as a repentant thief and cast yourself on the mercy of the Lord." She paused. "My sin is greater because it was carnal. I shall be called to the judgment seat clad in scarlet."

John Marco raised his hand and stopped her.

"Mr. Tuke won't listen to your confession," he said. "He knows you're out of your senses."

"I shall give him proof," she answered. "I shall show him the letter my uncle left me. I shall expose you."

"Then you mean to break your word to me?"

She bowed her head.

"It was a bargain sealed in wickedness," she replied. "My voices tell me to break it."

John Marco went over to the fireplace and stood looking down into the flames. He stood for some time with his back towards her without speaking.

"You came here to ask for money," he said at last. "Don't you think that Mr. Tuke might rather have his money than a confession?"

Hesther drew in a deep breath.

"Yes," she said slowly. "They'll allow that—the voices."

438

"How much do you want?" he asked bluntly.

"You shall bring your offerings of the cattle, even of the herd, and of the flock," Hesther replied. "We must give the Lord all we have."

"Tell me how much you want," he repeated.

"Mr. Tuke needs a thousand pounds," she said. "He's started a fund: it's to build a new Sunday School. It shall be your money that builds it."

John Marco opened the drawer of his desk and took out his cheque book.

"I'll give you a hundred pounds," he said.

Hesther shook her head.

"Your riches will die with you," she said. "You can't deny the Lord. Mr. Tuke needs a thousand pounds, and he must have it."

John Marco threw down his pen.

"Mr. Tuke must make do with less," he said.

Hesther did not remove her eyes from his face.

"It's a thousand pounds that I promised," she told him.

"Promised?"

"I told him that I'd bring it to-night. Mr. Tuke said it would be an answer to his prayer."

"And am I to answer Mr. Tuke's prayers for him?" John Marco asked.

Hesther dropped her eyes and regarded her hands that were folded in her lap.

"You wouldn't want all those shareholders to know you were a thief, would you?" she asked quietly. "It was a lot of money you were asking for this afternoon."

John Marco got up and began walking about the room again. His head was bent forward and he was staring at the floor in front of him. He seemed almost to have forgotten Hesther. And

Hesther was sitting bolt upright, her arms folded and her eyes fixed in front of her.

When he spoke, she started.

"Have you still got that letter?" he asked.

She nodded.

"I've got it here: it doesn't go out of my keeping," she answered. "I carry it about with me."

John Marco paused.

"I'll buy it from you," he told her.

"For a thousand pounds?"

He passed his tongue across his lips.

"For a thousand pounds," he replied.

Hesther opened her bag and drew out a long envelope. Then she seemed to hesitate: she closed the bag again and sat there, the envelope in her hand, her eyes closed as if she were praying. John Marco was leaning forward in his chair regarding her.

Suddenly she opened her eyes again and removed the paper from the envelope.

"The voices tell me you can have it," she said.

The paper that she was holding before him was crumpled and cobwebby with age: it seemed ready to dissolve into fragments. The words written on it looked blurred and indecipherable as he tried to disentangle them. Amid the yellow creases he could faintly see the spidery outlines of figures and Mr. Trackett's own signature.

He put out his hand to take hold of the paper. But she pulled it away from him.

"Give me the money first," she said.

When she had gone he turned in his chair and bending forward held one end of the paper over the fire behind him as if it were a spill. The paper kindled and flared. He held it until his fingers were burning, and then dropped the remains into the open grate.

There was now only a little ash and a trace of smoke to show for the cause of all this havoc of the years.

ii

They were sitting facing each other across the plain deal of Mr. Tuke's table top, and Hesther was smiling at him. She was fastening up her handbag again.

"It's what I promised you," she said. "I've kept faith in the Lord."

Mr. Tuke sat back and folded his hands.

"With prayer everything can be accomplished," he said. "God works in the most surprising way. He chooses the least likely vessels."

441

Chapter XXXV

Even Mr. Skewin and Mr. Hackbridge who had now grown used to seeing money spent on John Marco's lavish scale of things were secretly a little appalled by the way the new capital was devoured. Five thousand pounds of it was consumed in a single reckless gesture: John Marco built a roof garden.

The Board, when the idea was first proposed to them, had voted unanimously against it; but in doing so they were going against their chairman. To John Marco, a roof garden, had suddenly become the first essential of the business; and those who opposed it, opposed him. A roof garden was something which no other store possessed, and he was, therefore, determined that John Marco Ltd. should have it. So the architect was called in to strengthen the roof and the builder's men were about the place once more; and high above the roof tops of Bayswater the contraption of trellis walls and concrete arches and fancy sun-dials and flower boxes was erected.

There was also the acquisition of Louise; she was a special discovery of John Marco's. He had found her in the dress salon of a rival store over in Kensington, and had coveted her. There was an elegance and distinction about her that he felt was

442

needed. But of course she was expensive: she put a good price on herself, and demanded a contract. John Marco gave it to her over lunch one day. And as he watched her sign it—she removed a little silver fountain pen from her silk hand-bag to do so—he found himself admiring her. She was undeniably a pretty woman; and she obviously knew her way about in the world. She was the sort of person who would reward him every time he looked at her.

But reflected over at the end of the year, the roof garden and the new fashion supervisor in the dress salon were no more than adventures—costly ones, admittedly—on the side. There was the installation of the extra lifts; the re-stocking of the principal departments on a scale that was more Oxford Street than Tredegar Terrace; and there were the two electric delivery vans.

Considered objectively these vans were gaunt and ungainly; they were slow; they were hesitating; they were awkward. A horse, on any showing, would have been better. But electric vans were modern: they were a declaration to other and possibly rival shop-keepers that science and John Marco Ltd. were abreast of time.

And there was no denying that John Marco's methods were successful. The shop continued to be crowded; and every day the ledgers of the company grew fuller and fatter, swollen with the endless columns of figures that the Counting House was cease-lessly totting up.

John Marco himself seemed to have become something settled and established like the business; he looked older nowadays, and the wear had begun to show across the grain. Amid his close black hair there was now enough grey, and white even, for it to be apparent; and from the corner of his eyes a little network of lines had begun to spring. No one now seeing him for the first time would possibly think of him any longer as a young man.

He had, too, grown more unapproachable; he was now simply a solitary, uncontradictable figure who ruled everything. Except for Mr. Hackbridge, he barely spoke to anyone, and the words which he did speak to him, were not by any means what in the ordinary way would pass for conversation.

"There's a price ticket fallen off the figure in the corner window," he would remark in his hard clipped voice. "We pay a dresser to look after that kind of thing. And I saw two of the assistants chattering among themselves; I've said before that they should stand apart and not talk except when they're actually serving. The new cambric's very poor quality: tell Mr. Waring to announce it out of stock to any of our regular customers. And while you're in that department ask why they're not pushing that nainsook harder: remember that we've got twenty-five dozen rolls of it."

And so it would go on, with Mr. Hackbridge making notes on his shiny cuffs of the points that John Marco was blurting out at him.

Often at the end of a day Mr. Hackbridge would sit at his own hearthside, exhausted, sweating, wondering how many of the points he had completely forgotten. The strain of these last few years had told on him more heavily even than on his employer; and he used to receive John Marco's summons to go into the room wondering how long it would be before he would collapse, simply collapse, in an ugly, ungainly heap, on the managing director's carpet, under the unnatural pressure of it all.

The hearthside at which John Marco himself sat in the evenings was no longer the modest one in Windsor Terrace. He now lived in a gaunt, towering mansion in Hyde Park Square with a staff of three to look after him and a coach house behind for his carriage. The carriage was a new possession; the lamps

444

and the harness still had their prime glitter. But there was more than glitter alone to the turnout; there was its colour. A broad primrose line—primrose like the paper bags of the firm, and the uniform of the page boys, and the two electric delivery vans—ran right round the middle of it. When John Marco got into it in the mornings, and the horse was whipped up, there was two hundred pounds of advertisement stepping through the streets.

John Marco's solicitor through whom he had bought the house had suggested, tactfully and discreetly, that the place was extravagant for a bachelor establishment. He had tried to persuade him into a new block of fashionable flats in which he had an interest. But John Marco had declined to discuss it and had merely said that he must have room, plenty of it. He had hinted vaguely at dinnerparties and entertaining. And so the place had become his; and his drawing-room, with the long mirrors let into the walls, would comfortably have contained not only the blood-red drawing-room in Clarence Gardens from which he had fled, but also the whole of old Mrs. Marco's shabby villa in Chapel Walk as well.

There was more than one single lady in the neighbourhood, as well as a few married ones besides, who knew John Marco by sight—he was a familiar figure by now: someone to be recognised and pointed out—who tortured themselves to think of this single gentleman with the dark, Italian-looking eyes, shutting himself up every night in the loneliness of this big womanless house.

ii

It was one evening just as he was preparing to return to Hyde Park Square that he was told that one of his assistants wanted to speak to him. The request was clearly unusual: it was Mr. Hackbridge who attended to the staff, and for all John Marco knew about them individually the whole place might have been run by ghosts. But this time Mr. Hackbridge was not sufficient: the demand was to see John Marco personally.

"Very well," John Marco replied at last. "I'll give her a couple of minutes."

"It's not one of the young ladies," Mr. Hackbridge explained. "It's one of the men."

"What does he want?" John Marco asked.

"He wouldn't tell me," Mr. Hackbridge explained apologetically. "He said it was private."

"Very well," John Marco answered. "Bring him in. You may as well stop yourself."

The young man with whom Mr. Hackbridge returned was a familiar enough figure in the drapery. He was thin and smooth-haired, dressed like the rest of them in a shoddy frock coat that suggested that a larger and taller man might have passed it on to him; and his face had the paleness of all things that spend their lives out of the sunlight. John Marco noted that one of his trouser legs was frayed and that his shoes, though they had been polished like a kitchen grate, were cracked and withered across the instep. The young man was clearly more ill at ease than ever when he saw that Mr. Hackbridge was remaining.

"He's probably come to try and borrow money," John Marco reflected. "He's got himself into some kind of trouble."

But the young man made no such request.

"I've come to ask for promotion," he said.

John Marco regarded him coldly.

"Mr. Hackbridge deals with that kind of request, and he doesn't waste my time on it."

446

"But you see, sir, I'm getting married."

"That's no affair of mine," John Marco answered.

He turned his back on the young man as he spoke and took down his hat from the peg behind his desk. It was clear that so far as he was concerned the interview was over.

Mr. Hackbridge caught the young man's eye and jerked his head in the direction of the door.

The young man, however, remained where he was.

"I understood, sir," he said, "that you'd give it to me if I asked you for it."

John Marco looked up again.

"And who gave you to understand that?" he asked.

The young man paused and pressed his hands together against his sides.

"I'd rather tell you alone, sir."

"You'll tell me now," John Marco answered.

He had put his hat down on the desk and was peering at the young man intently.

"It was Miss Harlow, sir," he said.

But John Marco paused.

"She told you that, did she?" he said quietly. "And did she send you along to me?"

"Yes. sir."

"What did she tell you to ask for?"

"Four pounds a week," the young man answered.

He said it in the hushed voice of someone referring to the ultimate goal of things.

"Four pounds a week," John Marco repeated slowly.

But he was not thinking of the words as he said them. The young man and the lumbering figure of Mr. Hack-bridge did not exist any longer. It was early morning and he was back in a room

447

into which first fingers of daylight were gradually piercing. There was a bed in the room and in the bed a young woman was lying. Her dark hair was spread out round her head like a fan and one hand was raised under her cheek, supporting it. She looked too young, somehow, and in sleep, too helpless. . . .

Mr. Hackbridge coughed and the image was broken.

John Marco drew himself up.

"Four pounds a week did you say?" he asked. "That's not a great deal to get married on. Mr. Hackbridge, arrange to have this young man paid two hundred and fifty a year when he marries. Better find a different job for him."

And before Mr. Hackbridge or the young man could reply, John Marco had stuck his hat on his head and had gone out of the room, leaving them staring after him.

He got into his carriage and drew the rug up over him. The night was chilly and he shivered as he sat back against the leather. But he was cold inside himself as well. That young man with the ill-fitting frock coat had stepped suddenly out of the recent past and had taken him back again with him. It had been another of the pieces of his life that he was wanting to forget, another of the fragments which did not fit into the finished pattern.

And now that his mind had started to drift backwards, he saw other scenes, other times as well. The pattern of his life now became more broken and disfigured than ever, and he was back again on the doorstep in Harrow Street on the night when Mr. Petter had died. Then he remembered a second visit as well. He had returned a fortnight later to find the little shop closed and the windows boarded-up. And as he had stood there he had realised that Mr. Petter's death had brought Mary no nearer to him. The years had gone by—were becoming dangerously short in fact—and he was still as lonely as on that first night when he had lost her.

It was because of this that he had tried to find other things that would help him to forget. The house in Hyde Park Square was only a part. But it was a very successful part. It was something after all to be able to go into his house up a broad flight of steps that were flanked by marble, and hand his hat and gloves to a maid in a hall the size of an auditorium. And it was something to have such an address on his notepaper.

To-night the lamp in the hall cast a gleam across the rich mahogany of the furniture and showed the curving staircase with its polished balustrade. There was an air of richness, of opulence, even, about everything around him.

He went up the staircase with the quick, lively tread of an active man. But at the door of his bedroom he paused for a moment; paused with a smile on his lips and then went inside. The curtains had been drawn and the big gas fire was blazing. The air that came into his face was warm and heavy: it was loaded with scent. A silk wrap was lying across the bed and carelessly thrown beside it was a pair of satin slippers. In front of the mirror a woman was sitting, her hand raised to her head stroking down her dark hair.

"You're late, my dear," she said as he entered. "I thought you were never coming."

She turned towards him and smiled.

It was Louise.

The translation of Louise from the dress salon in Tredegar Terrace to the house in Hyde Park Square had been easy, astonishingly easy. From the way she had accepted it, moving in her two suitcases and a dubious-looking cabin-trunk from the single room in Cambridge Gardens where she was lodging, she might have been waiting for this thing to happen; her whole life might have been directed to this single moment when at last she would be able to catch the eye of her employer.

It was a tribute to her intelligence—her shrewd, calculating, Manchester-born intelligence—it was not until some time later that he discovered that she was not Louise Duval at all but Sophie Roseman from Old Trafford—that she learnt her new role so quickly. She was as complete a lady as any in the Square on the first morning when she descended the steps to go shopping in her carriage. Her wide hat, the piece of sable round her neck, the tapering shoes, might all have come from one of Mr. Bradley's fashion drawings. It was only her colouring, a trifle higher than that of most of the other ladies, that was suspect. But no one would have questioned it beneath the flowered mesh of her veil.

And John Marco was content. She kept him amused; she was a handsome companion to be seen about with; and she was a woman. Above all there was no need for any misgivings: she brought with her her own experience of the world. Indeed, for a single woman who had always lived alone, she brought with her quite a surprising amount of experience; so much, in fact, that John Marco was careful not to enquire too closely into her shrouded, mysterious past. It was sufficient that she was there, that she knew why she was there; and it was obvious that she intended to go on being charming enough to remain there.

She was not even extravagant. When she had established what her dress allowance was going to be—it was better, she had said, that they should come to an understanding about that kind of thing straight away—she bought carefully and well. The little pieces of jewellery that she needed, she asked for. And before she

450

put her hair—it was smooth and sleek and blue-black—into the hands of a West End hairdresser, and emerged with a coiffure of curls, she asked for John Marco's permission.

The effect of a woman in the house was immediately discernible. She re-modelled the place. There were flowers in the rooms, and the curtains that had been bought before she came there, were taken down and replaced. The bedroom was transformed. She had asked for single beds as being more modern. But there all restraint in the room ended abruptly. The suite that she chose for herself was of satinwood with mischievous scrolls of gilt on the corners. And she stuck mirrors all about the walls. In the evenings when the candles on the dressing table were lit and the pink silk coverlets were turned down at the corners there was an air of wantonness and luxury that could not have been bettered even in Park Lane.

It was, in a way, the sinful costliness of it all that he enjoyed. By himself he would never have indulged in such an orgy of spending. But now that it was there it served its purpose: it made the break with the past final and complete. The tabernacle of Amos and that bedroom belonged to two different worlds.

The only thing that was missing from the house was friends. But no man who can afford to be hospitable is left unattended for long. And Louise took to issuing the invitations herself. She cultivated the Mayor at first; and then when she had met his friends, she dropped him and asked the richer Aldermen instead. Stray acquaintanceships began to spring up, and city men with large businesses, gentlemen of leisure with private incomes, and professional mixers like Mr. Bulmer, started to come to the house. The whole complexion of their dinner parties gradually changed. There was now usually poker in the evenings afterwards, and the drinks became more liberal. Within six months there was a row of carriages outside the house in Hyde Park Square two or three nights a week

Perhaps it was the open secret about them—for John Marco now openly paraded Louise as his wife—that decided the nature of their friends. The majority of London would not have cared to be seen there; and the Mayor himself was no more eager, after he had learnt the truth about her, to be sitting down with a kept woman than Louise was to have him. And so the circle widened and grew more mixed, and they laid extra places for dinner, and John Marco kept telling himself that he was enjoying it all.

It was during these late evenings—and on nights when there was poker the party did not generally break up until half-past one or two in the mornings—that John Marco began to drink a trifle more than he had been accustomed to. The transition was very gradual; at first he would take simply an extra whiskey when he felt his energy flagging. But later he took more; took more, and took it steadily. There seemed really to be no way out of it. He was at his desk by half-past eight every morning and, when midnight had passed and there were guests still sitting round expecting to be entertained, he had to find a way of keeping level with them. In a sense it was Louise herself who forced him to it: she had her forbears' unexpendable reserves of energy; and she was still smiling and immaculate when the last carriage door outside the house had slammed and she and John Marco were alone again.

The sense of inner fatigue, of nerves stretched taut all the time like wire, was something that he had got used to by now; but it served to remind him that he was on the wrong side of forty—so much on the wrong side, indeed, that he would soon be on the wrong side of fifty, as well. But nevertheless it was the life that he wanted. It was full. It was crowded. And the present moment was always the one that had to be lived in. There was

452

nowhere in it any time for regrets about the past. For all those earlier years now worried him, he might have been born into the middle of this life in Hyde Park Square. He was able to forget the gnarled hands of old Mrs. Marco, the Tabernacle, Mr. Trackett's hoarded money—everything, in fact, that had once seemed sentenced to bear down on him forever.

He was like a man who has escaped handsomely from the darkness of his own shadow.

iii

It was one evening after the ladies had left them and the men were sitting round the table over their port when the maid came close behind John Marco's chair and announced that there was a lady to see him. The lady had seemed distressed, she said, and she had not been able to catch her name.

"What's she like?" John Marco asked.

A faint, almost instinctive, feeling of uneasiness had come over him and he half rose from his chair as he spoke.

"She's all in black, sir."

"Do you mean a widow?"

"Yes, sir, a widow."

"And did you show her in?"

"She's in the morning-room, sir. She said she knew you'd see her."

There was a laugh at this and the guest on his right dug John Marco in the ribs and said something about his sins finding him out.

But John Marco was in no mood for laughing. He should, he supposed, have been prepared for this: it was too much to expect that Hesther should leave him alone altogether. She was like a ghost, whose coming was inescapable and unannounced. But how to be rid of her again? How to clear the house of her without tears and recriminations? He was at her mercy now that she had come there; and she would know it. There was no place for tears and hysterics in this respectable mansion.

"Excuse me, gentlemen," he said. "Business is intruding on pleasure."

He crossed the broad expanse of the hall in trepidation; he was as much afraid as when she had first come to him. But when he opened the door of the morning-room it was not Hesther who was sitting there.

It was Mary.

The past year, however, had lain heavily on her. She seemed much slighter now, thinner even, in the black clothes that she was wearing. The clothes draped themselves about her dejectedly. They seemed to have no substance, no texture, left in them. Her bright hair, too, was hidden under the close hat that she was wearing. But he noticed—and his heart went grey within him as he saw it—that her hair where it was drawn down over her ears was bright no longer. And the hand that she was holding out to him was worn and reddened.

"Mary!" he said and stopped himself.

For, as he looked at her he realised that it was no use any longer. He could only stand there, staring at her, trying to find in her face that secret that had once excited him. The marks of the world were there in its place now, and the face that looked up at him was not the face that he remembered.

As he stood there, his own hand outstretched, he was aware, suddenly aware, of a new truth that dismayed him. It was a truth that cut his life in two. Mary herself, he now realised, was a part of the old life, the other life; she was another figure from the shadows.

There was a mirror behind the chair in which she was sitting and he saw the image of himself in front of him. That was not a young man, either, who was standing there. It was a man whose face beneath the greying hair was lined and heavy. The eyes were still deep and powerful; but the skin beneath them had already puckered into tiny pouches. It was the face of a man in which the spirit is just a little stronger than the flesh; and at that moment John Marco, the unrisen counter-jumper, seemed the happier man.

But Mary was speaking to him and he turned away from the portrait in the mirror.

"I expect you wonder why I've come here," she was saying.

"I told you you could always come," he answered. "I'm glad you remembered."

The words sounded dull and stupid; they were not like real words at all. It wasn't in this way that he talked to Mary.

"There wasn't anything else to do," she said wearily. She paused for a moment as if hesitating to go on any longer and then added suddenly: "I've tried, but it's no use. I can't go on any longer."

He drew another chair up alongside her.

"Tell me," he said.

It was all so pathetic and so obvious when she told him; it was what anyone but a woman must have known would happen. Mr. Petter had left behind him in the bank the round sum of eighty-five pounds as a legacy to his wife and child; and when the manufacturers had been paid and the undertakers had claimed their share of the riches, there remained some twenty-two pounds on which, with the help of Mr. Kent, to face the world. And the twenty-two pounds had vanished, squandered in odd shillings and half crowns to make life more cheerful. And even Mr. Kent at last had been unable to assist any longer. With his eye-sight half gone—he had frittered it away fiddling about with his beloved clockwork in the evenings—he could now do little more than sit behind the counter of his shop waiting for a customer to come in and buy something. But there were no buyers any longer for guinea watches with Swiss movements that wound up with a key, when the market was full of five shilling bits of machinery from America; and the jewellery that he sold was heavy, old-fashioned stuff of the kind that no one wore nowadays. He was going to shut up altogether, Mary said, if things didn't improve somehow.

John Marco leant forward when she had finished. "Don't worry," he said, "I'll help you."

"You're very good," she answered. "I knew I could rely on you."

"Ask for anything you want," he said.

His voice was kind, but as he said it in his heart he was impatient. He wanted the whole transaction to be over, wanted to be able to forget again. The sight of her aroused anger within him as well as pity. This grim, respectable poverty was the price of folly. If she had come to him, when he had offered himself, he could have saved everything. It would have been her house that they were sitting in; her bedroom that looked down on the trees and gardens of the Square.

"I don't want you to give me money," Mary answered. "I want some work to do."

"Work?" he asked. "But you haven't been trained for anything."

"I could serve in the shop," she said. "I'd be careful."

To serve in the shop: to have her by him all day as a reproach! That, least of all, was what he wanted. Besides, people in shops liked the assistants to be young; all the girls in John Marco's were young. A widow with half her mind on her child all the time wasn't the kind of person they employed there.

"No," he said. "I'll pay you what the others get. But I don't want you to have to work for it."

Mary paused.

"It's generous of you and it's kind," she said. "But I couldn't accept it. Thomas wouldn't have liked me to."

The mention of Mr. Petter—it was as though even in death he still stood between them—disturbed him. "So she did love him," he said inside his mind. "She did really love him."

He shook his head.

"There's nothing in the shop," he said. "There won't be anything now until Christmas."

"I see," she replied.

And from the way she said it he knew how often in the past months she had received that kind of answer.

She got up and slowly began buttoning up the neck of her coat.

"If you hear of anything," she said, "will you please tell me?"

John Marco stood there looking at her. It was her hand in particular that he was watching. She was holding her bag—it was a small, cheap one—but her little finger was cocked enchantingly in the air as it had been on that afternoon so long ago now when they had both been young, and both in love, and she had poured tea from her mother's silver tea-pot.

"Don't go," he said under his breath. "I'll find something for you."

"You will?"

For a second her face lit up again as he had known it: her smile had not grown tired like the rest of her.

"Come round to the shop in the morning," he said. "I'll tell Mr. Lyman to find a job for you."

"Thank you, John . . ." she began, but she was interrupted.

The door opened and Louise stood there. She had a new gown on and she looked cool and handsome and well-cared for.

"John," she said, "we've all been waiting."

But when she saw that he was not alone she withdrew again.

"I'm sorry, my dear," she added. "I didn't know you had a visitor."

Mary had gone away again; she had slipped out quietly, scarcely stopping to say good-bye to him. And the guests had gone too by now: it was late. John Marco was standing in the big drawing-room alone with Louise.

"Who was she?" she asked suddenly.

John Marco started.

"Only someone who wanted a job in the shop," he answered.

"And did you give it to her?"

"As a matter of fact, I did."

She came over and sat on the arm of his chair.

"That's all right," she said lightly. "You needn't worry: I'm not jealous. I had a look at her."

Chapter XXXVI

The two little boys in primrose-coloured uniform had at last outgrown their fancy dress and been replaced by two other little boys; and they in turn had been transferred to the packing-room along with their predecessors, and there were now two others who stood there. But in a sense they were still the same little boys: they were simply ageless twins, two diminutive dwarfs dressed like toy soldiers, who stood at attention and opened the big swing doors and bowed when they were spoken to, and defied Time.

And the shop assistants were magically the same, too; they were all of them still young, with gleaming hair and small waists and pretty faces, even though the original ones had long since left to get married, or had gone back to keep house for their fathers, or had fallen out with Mr. Hackbridge. They seemed a separate species, these girls, everlasting and impersonal; a new race of women who never grew any older than twenty-five.

It was John Marco who had altered. In the mornings, the long climb from the front door up the broad, circular staircase to his room, left him panting and exhausted; he now travelled up in the hydraulic lift instead. They were still novelties these lifts;

459

frivolous shoppers used to go up and down in them simply for the prodigious attraction of the thing.

Tired or not, however, John Marco had never for a single day neglected that ritual tour of inspection of his. But he spent less time on it now. He had entirely given up the old, hated business of going behind the counters and seeing whether the boxes themselves were being kept tidy. It was enough, he considered, that the assistants should be reminded that he, the pivot and governing intelligence of everything, was still about among them. And so, every day, the heavy figure of John Marco still went marching through the rooms every forenoon, a symbol to all the truly ambitious young men in the business of the kind of great-ness that retail drapery holds in store for its few and chosen.

His hours at the business were still as long as ever. And while the assistants were passing out light-heartedly down the staff-staircase at the back, the light in that row of windows at the corner of the building was there to remind them that, for one man at least the day's work was not yet over, and the real running of the business was still going on.

There had been a time when the work that John Marco did alone with Mr. Lyman after the others had gone had seemed the most pleasant hours of the day: those columns of figures from the Counting House which every month grew larger and fatter and more complicated, had once appeared to him the reward for the whole day's labours. All his cleverest moves, his best buying, his most astute manoeuvres of salesmanship had been made when the rest of the shop was in darkness. But lately a kind of stale-ness had settled down on him. And when the door opened to admit Mr. Lyman with his charts and ledgers, and he looked across at the corner of his desk and saw the top-heavy trayful of papers all to be read and decided upon and replied to, his heart failed him.

It seemed that in creating this teeming business with its brilliant windows and its brigade of polite assistants and its loaded warehouse, he had somehow built a cage from which escape was impossible. And he was the one man in the whole firm who was trapped in it; that was the nice irony of it all. Anyone else could put his hat on his head and take up his gloves and umbrella and walk out of the front door, singing. But he couldn't do that. He was stuck there forever, getting steadily older and richer and more tired.

On those evenings when he worked late, really late that is, Louise no longer sat at home waiting for him as she had done in the early months of their household. They had been together for more than five years now and the silence and absence of company on these evenings had got on her nerves; she had explained that she was one of those people who must have others around her all the time for her to feel really happy. But now that they had plenty of friends, it was all so easy, so simple. There was a Colonel Carbeth and his wife—he had married an actress from the States—and they kept open, noisy house over on Campden Hill; and the Coughlins who had made all their money in tin and now lived in bright, metallic splendour in Lancaster Gate; and the Burnhams who were Jews and were very busy already getting their money out of theatres and putting it into cinemas; and the Hansells and the Clyde-Dawkins and the Henriques. There were also the various smooth-faced young men with glossy manners— John Marco could never remember their names and even wondered, as they were so much alike, whether they actually had any—who came to the house when they were entertaining and sometimes asked his permission to take Louise out to the theatre—and then on to supper somewhere afterwards. He always let them do it (though he had his suspicions that, with one or two of them at least, it was Louise who generally paid); and in a way he felt rather obliged towards them for their attentions. It was the sort of life that Louise liked and he was not a man who could spend his evenings, even if they were free, sitting night after night in a stall at the theatre.

This evening, in particular, he felt relieved that Louise had someone to occupy her; he had told her earlier in the week how late he would be, and she had simply shrugged her shoulders and said that in that case she supposed that she might as well accept someone-or-other's invitation to take her out to supper. He had asked her who it was, he remembered, and then could not have listened when she told him. But there he was, this anonymous young man, risen up from nowhere to entertain her just when he was wanted.

John Marco had got into the habit of calling the board-meetings in the evening so that the directors could get on with their work by day. At first, when he had started them, Mr. Hackbridge and Mr. Lyman and even Mr. Skewin had raised vague, apologetic objections, saying that their wives and families wanted them at home. But John Marco had brushed that kind of talk aside. And Mr. Hackbridge, and Mr. Skewin, and Mr. Lyman had now put aside all thoughts of whist and music halls and pleasant hours at the fireside, and had agreed to give up the last remaining portion of their leisure.

It was while he was waiting for the other directors to come filing in that John Marco walked across to the big cabinet in the corner and drew out the heavy decanter that he kept there. Strange how reassuring it was simply to feel the hard surface of the glass under his hand and see the shining amber surface of the whiskey ripple and break as he moved it. He knew now as he held the decanter in his hand what he had doubted earlier, that he would be able to sit there for two or three hours longer as the evening unfolded itself, listening to the timid suggestions of Mr. Skewin, and the warnings and cautions of Mr. Lyman and Mr. Hackbridge's forced helpfulness. And he knew, too, that he would as usual be cleverer than the others, turning their pitiful little ideas inside out for them, showing them how business was slipping through their very fingers simply because they weren't smart enough to close on it, putting up his own brilliant proposals.

Mr. Hackbridge was the first to arrive and John Marco observed with irritation that the man looked tired. His whitish, straggling hair was brushed the wrong way and his tie had not been straightened since the afternoon. What was the use, John Marco asked himself, of being inspiring to a man who looked in need of forty-eight hours uninterrupted sleep? He liked people round him to look fresh and energetic, no matter how tired he himself was feeling. But Mr. Hackbridge's fatigue—and, poor man, he had been on those flat shambling feet of his ever since nine o'clock in the morning—was not the least of the evening's irritations. It was Mr. Lyman who was the sore. He entered with one of his stultifying account books under his arm and said in his thin, decayed voice, as soon as they were all seated, that he was afraid the money situation was no better.

John Marco dismissed the point and replied curtly that in October, when they had bought all their Christmas stock and had not yet sold any of it, no one but a fool could expect it to be good.

Mr. Lyman accepted the rebuke, but remained obstinately attached to his original point.

"Quite so, sir," he said. "But what I really meant was that it isn't so satisfactory if you compare it with last year."

"That's because we've bought more for Christmas," John

Marco retorted. "We've bought twenty thousand pounds' worth more."

"I know we have," Mr. Lyman replied; and unbelievably he repeated it. "I know we have," he said again, slowly and distinctly.

John Marco turned sharply towards him.

"What do you mean by that?" he asked.

"I was only wondering about the advisability of it," Mr. Lyman said. It was obvious that he was speaking under strain: he had to screw his courage to utter each word he spoke. "Supposing that we don't get rid of it all, where shall we be then?" he asked.

"Just so," said Mr. Hackbridge. "It *is* rather a lot, you know, sir. I really think . . ."

He was not allowed to get any further, however. John Marco had brought his fist down on the table.

"You don't have to think," he said. "I do that for you. You don't count for anything the whole lot of you. I made the business single-handed. Single-handed I tell you." He was speaking very rapidly by now and the vein in his forehead was throbbing. "If you think that I'm going to draw back," he said, "simply because some of you are frightened, you're mistaken. Do you think that I don't know what the figures are like? Do you think that I haven't sat up all night working on them? But we're going on the way we started. I'm in charge of the buying and if you can't sell what I buy for you, I'll find people who can. If I buy another thousand pounds' worth or another twenty thousand pounds' worth by Christmas it's none of your business. And if you don't like the sort of stuff I buy for you you can get out."

He stopped suddenly—the room for a moment swam in front of his eyes—and there was silence. Mr. Hackbridge coughed nervously but had nothing to say. Mr. Lyman and Mr. Skewin avoided each other's glances.

John Marco turned suddenly to Mr. Lyman.

"Are those the yearly figures you've got there?" he asked.

"Yes, sir," said Mr. Lyman meekly. "You'll find it all set out there. This year's figures are in red."

John Marco held out his hand for the ledger and Mr. Lyman passed it over to him respectfully. With the book open in front of him John Marco appeared oblivious to everything: his head was bent low over the pages and he was jotting down odd figures on the pad beside him. Mr. Hackbridge coughed again and John Marco started. He looked up and then returned to beautiful columns of Mr. Lyman's handwriting.

"You can all go if you want to," he said. "You can leave me here. I understand these figures."

But when the last of them had gone John Marco shut up the book and sat staring emptily into the room in front of him. He had said more than he meant to say, a good deal more. But he had nothing to worry about. There wasn't anything that they could ever do to harm him; they were all three of them too dependent on him for that. And, besides, weren't they all of them still down on their knees to him in sheer gratitude for what he had made them?

It was still early, scarcely more than nine o'clock in fact. But he was tired already—that outburst in the face of Mr. Lyman's stupidity had tired him more than he had realised—and he sat in his chair without moving. Then he went over to the cupboard and poured himself out another drink. He was surprised as he did so to notice how low the level in the decanter had become; he must have drunk more than he remembered.

The thing needed filling nearly every day now.

He put on his great coat and went out through the empty shop into the street. Outside it was cold, very cold. There was a frozen fierceness in the air. He stood on the pavement waiting for a cab, and shivered. Then the cab came into sight, the horse blowing out great festoons of cloudy breath, and he was carried through those silent, winding streets that were simply ravines between the houses, and to-night might have been crevasses in glaciers. The horse's hoofs sounded loud and hollow as if they were falling on ice, and the air that blew in round the corners of the shaky windows was sharp and treacherous. He thought of his leather arm-chair and the fire that would be waiting for him, and drew his great-coat in more closely around him.

When he reached the house and let himself in, the warm protection of the place greeted him like a spell. He stood for a moment in the glow of the chandelier, grateful for the comfort of it all. And as he stood there, he noticed that across one of the chairs in the hall Louise's wrap was lying, carelessly thrown down as though by someone in a hurry.

He went over and smoothed it with his hand—it was velvet, and felt soft and gentle underneath his fingers—folding it carefully across the back of the chair.

"She'll be cold without it," he thought as he passed on up the stairs.

The house was quiet as it always was when Louise was not there; the whole life of it seemed somehow to be missing.

John Marco went into the drawing-room and crossed over to the fireplace. His chair was there, red and soft and yielding, and he sank into it. But as he did so, he heard very distinctly in the silence of the house a sound that he had not expected. It was the noise of someone, a woman probably, rapping urgently with her knuckles on a door. It was not on his door, but on a door somewhere on a floor above. And a moment later the sound of rapping was repeated.

He sat up and listened; and then, rising from his chair, he went and stood in the doorway. He could see the whole sweep of the landing from there. One of the maids was standing there knocking on Louise's bedroom door; her hand in its white cuff was raised ready to rap again. When she heard the sound of John Marco's footsteps on the stairs behind her, she started.

"Is your mistress in?" John Marco demanded.

The girl shook her head.

"No, sir," she said.

"Then why were you knocking?"

The girl did not answer.

For a man of his size John Marco could still move rapidly. He mounted the stairs at a run and pushed the girl aside. Then he turned the handle of the door, ready to walk in. But the door itself was locked.

He was angry again now, flushed and angry as he had been at the board-meeting.

"Who's in there?" he demanded. "Who is it?"

But the girl only pulled out her handkerchief and started crying.

"I don't know, sir," she answered. "Really I don't."

John Marco turned his back on her—it was obvious that she was lying to him—and began pounding on the door with his fists.

"Who's inside?" he shouted, "Let me in."

There was a movement inside the room, and very faint through the thickness of the door, the sound of voices. They were frightened voices, muffled and indistinct. They might have been trying to say something to him. But John Marco did not wait. Stepping back a pace, he ran his shoulder full against the panel. The door seemed for a moment to bend under him and the house shook. But the lock held fast. It was not until he had thrown himself against it twice, three times, four times that something in the woodwork of the lock splintered and the door sprang open.

He was sweating by now and his face was red and furious.

The only sound in the room was the sound of Louise's sobbing.

She was standing over by the dressing-table facing him, her hair dragged back from her head as though it had been pinned hurriedly by shaking fingers. The evening-dress that she was wearing was crumpled and disarranged. Beside her stood a young man, also in evening-dress. He was one of the pale young men whom John Marco dimly remembered. His hair was ruffled and he kept raising his hand to his collar from which his tie was somehow missing.

ii

John Marco went back down the stairs again without speaking; the maid was still there—she had flattened herself against the wall and was staring into the room of the secret—but John Marco did not notice her. He passed her, and went down below out of sight.

His great-coat and hat were down below in the hall where he had left them. He went up to them instinctively; they seemed to be part of him, and not to belong to this house at all. Then swinging the coat roughly onto his shoulders and pulling the hat down onto his head, he slammed the front door after him and was out in the street once more.

The air had grown still colder, and tiny particles of ice that cut into the skin like little frozen spears were being carried on the wind that had now sprung up. But he did not notice them. He was walking blindly, aimlessly and stumbling sometimes; walking in fact as Mr. Petter, miserable and broken, had once walked through the evening streets after hearing the awful warning of Mr. Tuke.

When he turned a corner, and the wind bore down full upon him, he set his head lower and forced his way against it, turning up the collar of his coat still higher. There was only one intention in the walking and that was to separate himself from the bedroom into which he had just looked. The memory of it—and his whole mind was full of nothing else: the room was lit up in his mind as if it had been a stage—made him walk faster. As he blundered along the gas-lit streets, he was almost running. He was not tired any longer, but numb. His legs ached and the cold had seeped into his limbs, drugging them. His head, too, was swimming and he wondered if he were going to faint, to collapse suddenly. The street that he was now in was one that he did not recognise: it stretched bleak and lifeless in front of him like a scenic backcloth, leading into the painted wilderness of Paddington and Maida Vale.

There was a public-house at the corner from which the jangle of mechanical music was coming. The door, as it swung open to admit someone, shot a band of vivid yellow light across the street, and there was the sound of voices and laughter. John Marco walked towards the threshold, his feet dragging as he moved, his lips quivering. Inside, the warmth smote him. The heat rose from the floor in great waves and danced around him. He went over to the bar and called for whiskey.

Not until the drink was in his hand did he look round him. Then he saw that they were cheap premises that he had come into, a place of no repute. Probably the whole neighbourhood was cheap as well—he had blundered right out of his style and class—and was lost in the wild boundaries of the Harrow Road. There was sand on the floor, scraped bare in places by a hundred feet, and below the bar a row of scarred spittoons were standing. He noticed, now, that the others in the bar were staring at him: it was evident that they did not get a gentleman like him with a velvet collar on his coat in the place every night. The house was crowded and as he stood there he felt these scores of eyes pressing in on him.

When his glass was empty—he had drunk quickly—greedily, throwing back his head like a carter—he called for his drink again, and because his knees were weak, he groped his way over towards the couch. At the opposite end of the saloon was another couch set below a large discoloured mirror across which the outlines of ferns and flowers had been stencilled.

This couch was crowded with occupants—all women. There was a tittering sofa-full of them, loud-voiced blowsy women with colouring younger than their figures and large, feathery hats. They were all dressed in bright, rubbishy clothes and they kept taking sips at the glasses in front of them and glancing encouragingly in his direction.

The penny pianola in the corner stopped suddenly and, even with the noise of the voices, the room seemed abruptly to have grown quiet. But already someone was reaching in his pocket and, a moment later, the thing started performing again. John Marco closed his eyes and sat back. But it was not the pianola that he was hearing; it was the sound of Louise's sobbing. He could see her, too; her bare shoulders over the top of the frock showing white and half naked-looking, and her hair, that was all curls now, still half loose about her face. He opened his eyes again trying to forget it all and saw the landlord standing with his

470

arms round his wife's waist. She was a big, clumsy woman with a dull, flattened face and crude, dyed hair. But as he looked he saw her place her red hand over his. "They're happier than I am," thought John Marco. "They're not alone." And when the pot-man drew near him clearing the tables, John Marco called for his glass to be filled again.

It was this drink that overthrew him. The fatigue and then the shock, and now the heat of this stifling parlour, broke him down. His hands felt puffy and unfamiliar and he spilt a little from the glass as he raised it. As though by some inner sympathy among drinkers, the others in the bar recognised him now as one of them, as one of them who no longer was quite himself; and the barriers of class and dress were broken down. They drew in around him.

Before he had been sitting there for long, one of the women from the distant sofa came over and sat beside him. He was aware of her before he looked at her; and when he did look he saw a young woman—she was in her thirties probably—with bright yellow hair and a row of squalid teeth set in a smiling mouth. She moved closer towards him and, after a moment, when he still had made no advances to her, she said good-evening.

The fact that she did so, the fact that he should be sitting there because his big house in the Square was as suddenly shut to him as if it had been barred, and that this drab was now offering to console him in the only way she knew, amused him. After Louise, she was not an attractive companion; her hands which were resting on the table were loaded with rings that seemed to have been forced on them when her fingers had been thinner; the flesh now stood up in little ridges between them. But to have her speak to him, to listen to the tawdry nonsense which was all that she could utter—that would be something. Perhaps for a space

471

she would even enable him to forget again.

"Why don't you drink something?" he asked.

She ordered port, pecking at it politely like a lady, and let her hand rest lightly on his arm. He moved away a little but the hand remained there; it followed his arm. And, now that the others had seen that the gentleman was free with his money, they moved in closer still, and exchanged winks every time John Marco's hand showed itself to be something less than steady. That such a one should drink himself silly in their presence seemed a piece of almost unthinkable entertainment.

The others had all crowded round him by now; they were as close as sheep sheltering. He was aware of the hot, stifling odour of their bodies; but he did not stir. There was one man in partic-ular who fascinated him: he was doing card tricks. In his sordid, dirty fingers the cards melted magically into the air and re-formed themselves again before his eyes, like wonders. The man seemed to have some power over these pieces of pasteboard that was denied to the rest of mankind. He was a Merlin with a broken nose and an almost green bowler set so low on his head that the thing crowned him like a helmet. There were others, too, whom John Marco could not see so plainly—men with red, glistening faces and loud guffaws; leering unpleasant men; and men like himself who could do no more than sit back and undo their waistcoats and fumble for their glasses and laugh a little some-times. And always on his arm was the soft pull of the woman who had come over to him and now sat on the couch beside him, her foot touching his.

When her drink was finished—and even in those dainty lady-like pecks it disappeared—he told her to re-order and because there were so many others near him whose glasses were empty, too, he told them too to call for what they wanted. He drew from his pocket a gold sovereign case and every eye in the room seemed to be mesmerised by it. It was the woman beside him who called out shrilly for the change when the landlord was slow in bringing it; she seemed to have appointed herself his protectress and he did not stop her when her fingers plunged into his pocket pouring in the silver coins.

It was late by now and there were some in the bar who had been drinking all the evening; their heads were full of the fumes. And in that state, tempers and convictions ran high. The trouble started in one corner. There was a big man, hairy and unshaven, who rose suddenly in his place and shot the dregs of his glass into his neighbour's face. The other man jumped to his feet—he was less than half the size of his opponent—and aimed one of those wild silly blows that are as much intended to satisfy honour as to hit anything. But the fact that he had been struck at, that he had been assaulted, was sufficient for the aggressor. He raised his fist—it was large and heavy like a boxer's—and let drive at his assailant's chin. There was a sound like the snapping of a stick, and the man went down. Then, proud and victorious, the unshaven one stepped over his victim and made his way towards the door. He was in the full pride of his blood by now and, coming upon John Marco suddenly, he stopped. The fact that a stranger was in the pub was something that he resented: he was in a mood when people did things only by his permission. Raising his hand again—it was cut and bleeding across the knuckles by now—he knocked John Marco's glass onto the floor and stood there grinning. It was the woman again who attempted to save John Marco. She shot out her little pointed shoe and caught the big man on the shin. He stared at her stupidly for a moment and then caught her across the face with the back of his hand. Immediately she started screaming, and every man in the room

473

who fancied himself came forward. By the time the landlord had scrambled over the bar to save the glasses, the fighting on the sandy floor was general.

John Marco's chair was jerked away from under him—he tried feebly to save himself: he did everything feebly now, he was so blurred—and the next moment he saw the chair being waved wildly in the air and heard it come down on someone's head; then it fell to the ground amid a splinter of glass. He was sprawling now amid the sawdust and dottle that was everywhere, and he pulled himself up onto his knees, clinging to the edge of a table as he did so. But the *tide* of battle surged towards him once more. There was a charge of sweaty bodies, and he was down again. Something struck him on the temple; and when he raised his hand to his face there was blood on it. Then, with the breaking of one of the lamps, the smell of gas filled the room, and the landlord began calling for the police.

It was as John Marco staggered to his feet that he felt a tug—a short, imperious tug this time—at his elbow and saw the woman from the couch standing beside him. She was beckoning him towards the door at the other end of the room. He followed her with faltering, uncertain steps and found that they were in the private bar. There was another door to the bar; and that one led into the street.

They went through it together. Out there in the night, the police whistles were sounding. The woman was supporting him by now.

iii

The room in which John Marco woke was a frowsty little cell of a room with wall-paper that plunged before his eyes in whorls

474

and spirals of gaudy roses. He lay back trying to remember. But his ears were still full of the sound of fighting and the noise of glass being shattered. He recalled dimly the empty street into which he had been led out of all that tumult; recalled also how, at last, he had fallen and how the woman who had been with him had appealed to the loitering gentlemen of those parts to carry him.

His whole body felt bruised and damaged; there were little flames of pain in every part of him. And when he raised his head, the blood drummed and battered on his ears. But suddenly he threw back the cherry-coloured coverlet that was over him and sat up on his elbow. He had remembered suddenly why last night he had gone out at all.

The movement disturbed the other occupant of the room. She was standing over by the dressing-table clad in a dirty wrapper that fell away from her disclosing her faded satin stays, and she came over and stood by him. He recognised her suddenly as the woman who had sat beside him on the couch. She was smiling.

"Feeling better?" she asked brightly.

He stared at her, scarcely comprehending.

"Did you bring me here?" he asked.

She nodded.

"We carried you," she said.

He passed his hand across his forehead.

"Where are my clothes?" he demanded.

"On the chair," she answered. "They undressed you when they brought you here."

She turned back to the dressing-table—there were large photographs of herself all over it—as though she had lost all interest in him, and he slid out of bed. His head reeled as he got onto his feet and his legs felt unsteady. But he pulled his clothes onto him and pushed his feet into his boots.

"I must reward this woman," he was thinking. "She saved me, and I must repay her."

As he stood there, his hand was straying over him—into his waistcoat pocket, his breast pocket, the pocket at his hip. But they were empty. His money, his watch and the watch-chain with the half-ring on it, his pocket-book, had all gone.

"I've been robbed," he said. "Someone's gone over me."

The woman shrugged her shoulders.

"You were drunk last night," she answered.

"You brought me here to rob me," he said.

This time she did not even move.

"The police would have had you if I hadn't," she answered. "You can still go to them. Tell them where you spent the night."

John Marco did not reply. He was dressing quickly, feverishly; dragging the clothes on to him. And the woman on the other side of the room seemed prepared to ignore him again. She was boiling a kettle on a spirit stove and washing up a cup, with an odd saucer with cigarette ash on it, in a hand basin. John Marco knotted his silk cravat round his neck—even the tie-pin was gone too—and went over to the mirror.

It was not a wholesome face that looked back at him; and he stood there peering at it. The stubble of his beard showed grey and harsh, and his forehead where the man's foot had kicked it was stained and angry. A thin dried trickle descended from it.

Taking up his overcoat that was lying across the bed he put it on, turning up the collar around his face. There was no place here where he could wash the wound; the hand basin at which the woman was standing now had a plate and knife and fork in it as well. He turned his back on her and, with his hat in his hand, in the same way in which he walked up the aisle of St.

Mary's Parish Church on Sundays he went towards the door.

The woman reached out her hand towards him.

"Is that all the thanks I get?" she asked. "Is that all you're going to say to me?"

Because he did not answer she came over and leant against the door-post watching him go.

"You look such a pretty gentleman," she said.

John Marco told the doorman to pay the cabby and went straight up in the lift to his private office. From the time he entered until his door had shut behind him had not been more than a couple of minutes; but even so his appearance had been noted and speculated upon. There were whispers. The doorman contended that Mr. Marco had met with an accident. But the lift girl who had actually been closeted with him confessed in the privacy of the lady's rest room that she believed that he had been fighting. The one point of agreement was that something sinister and unusual had happened to the man.

And John Marco did nothing to dispel the rumour. On the contrary, he fed it. He locked himself in. Mr. Hackbridge who knocked on the door once or twice had to go away again, and only the shadow of John Marco as he passed and re-passed the glass panel of his door—he seemed simply to be pacing up and down the room as if trying to make up his mind about something—showed that there was anyone there.

It was not, indeed, until nearly lunch-time when he opened his door and called for his secretary. And from the way he behaved he might have been brazening the whole thing out. He was still unshaven and the broken bruise on his forehead, even after the blood had been washed off it, caught the eye immediately and held it.

But he was still the same John Marco; he might have been awake all night in his study thinking out the flood of instructions which he released—the fresh showcards, the messages of complaint to unlucky members of the staff, new ideas for window dressing, stricter regulations about talking, and the first draft of an ambitious plan for next Christmas. As the girl jotted down the last item she raised her eyebrows a little: Mr. Marco was proposing that every one of the assistants should be put into fancy costume from the beginning of December until Christmas Eve. The silver and gold Christmas tree that had stood in the central hall on the previous year, even the gay balloons at the opening, now seemed no more than trite and obvious pieces of invention.

It was late in the afternoon when the girl took up the last of the papers and left him. And with her departure John Marco Ltd. and all of its million and one affairs deserted him again and he was left once more with the memory of Louise and that locked and desecrated bedroom. He went over to the window and stood gazing down into the street below. The lights were beginning to come on, and the passers-by, as they came for a moment into the circle of each lamp, filled him with a new feeling of his own loneliness; they all seemed so busy, so happy, this race of little people six storeys below him. *They* had homes to go to, wives or husbands waiting for them. From that high window in the corner of the store, they seemed like contented domestic dolls all hurrying back to their own nurseries.

And what was *he* going back to? Not to that fine house of his; there would be no meaning in that now. And for all he knew Louise might have left it already. At this very moment she was probably in the infatuated arms of this young man, who had seemed so young, so much younger than herself, when he had glimpsed at him.

John Marco passed his hand across his forehead: it was wet and sticky. He could no longer think clearly. But through the haze of his own mind he saw the bleak pathway of the future. He would sell the house, of course, that is what he would do, sell it as it stood, with everything that he and Louise had bought still in it. And their friends, their new friends, the Carbeths, and the Henriques and the Clyde-Dawkins, would have to find some other table to dine at. This whole chapter in his life, the only chapter he could remember in which the pages had seemed pleasant as he had turned them, had suddenly been closed on him; and the rest of the book did not now seem worth opening.

Then out of the shadows of his mind, unexpected and uninvited, the memory of his son came springing. There was no clear picture, no portrait of him; only the dim image of a boy making a silent pilgrimage through the sunny park. But the image remained; and the curiosity within him deepened. The boy, of course, would be older by now, different; he must be in his middle teens already. Would he even know him? John Marco wondered. If they met in public they might pass unrecognised, sit opposite staring at each other like strangers. But if that were so, those missing years might have worked otherwise as well; they might have freed the boy. Perhaps he was no longer under Hesther's domination; perhaps already he had begun reaching out towards the world of men that was denied to him. And as the thought came to him John Marco realised that even now he was not left quite alone, that somewhere in the stone forest of London there was another human being who belonged to him.

He stood for a moment longer by the window. But he was impatient by now, drumming on the sill with his fingers. Then he went over to his desk and, sitting down, addressed a letter to

Hesther's solicitors. It was a cold, formal document, one that gave no hint of the feelings that were stirring inside him. It stated merely that as Mr. Marco had never rescinded his rights over the child he now wished to see him, to ascertain whether the boy were being properly cared for and brought up. It also went on to say that if the boy were in need of money for his education, John Marco would be prepared to meet any reasonable demands. When he had finished the letter he signed it with his careful, copper-plate signature, sealed down his envelope and rang for his secretary to collect it.

But when the girl had gone away again, the magic of the idea had departed. He knew that he was still as lonely as he had been before; knew that this unknown schoolboy could do nothing to assist him. And for a moment, because he was tired, miserably tired, he rested his head in his two hands and sat there without moving.

There was a sound behind and he turned round. Over by the door Louise was standing.

Her hand was on the handle; it rested there hesitatingly, as if she expected that she might not be allowed to come any further inside. And the other hand inside the small muff that she was wearing was raised timidly to her chin.

He noticed as she stood there how beautifully made she was, how delicate and distinguished. Her brown eyes seemed even larger than usual; they lit up her whole face.

Then because he did not send her away from him, she came forward.

"My dear," she said in that soft voice of hers, "need we quarrel? We can't all be angels."

Chapter XXXVII

It was the weather, dismal, frozen drenching stuff, that destroyed the Christmas trade. Throughout December, rain alternated with snow so that the streets were always streaming with something; and people who could afford to do so remained indoors; we can wait, they seemed to say to themselves; these blizzards can't go on forever. And then when Christmas week itself arrived, and they realised that they would have to go shopping as usual and make the best of it, the fog came down.

It began quite innocently as an evening mist, pale and gauze-like that wrapped itself around the trees of the Park and made a coloured halo round every lamp post. But the mist thickened and grew darker. The smoke from the chimneys could no longer penetrate it and fell back down into the streets blackening them; and next morning—only three days now to Christmas Eve itself—the fog was so thick that it rose in people's faces like waves of muddy water and circled about them. The Borough Councils produced braziers which they placed at street corners to mitigate the gloom, and businesses tried to carry on as usual with every gas-mantle in the place blazing. But fashionable women do not go shopping by the light of half-a-hundredweight of coke and a little coal gas. And so the shops, especially the big ones, remained empty. People saved their money, and shop-keepers lost theirs.

On the Tuesday before Christmas, John Marco Ltd. had fewer than one hundred customers in at three o'clock in the afternoon. And for all the assistants in their special Christmas uniform attracted people they might have been invisible. Mr. Hackbridge, walking endlessly backwards and forwards through the empty departments, was like a captain who has lost his bearings; through the fog which had penetrated even inside the building and now filled the big central hall he was always expecting to see a crowd and never finding it.

There had been numerous special conferences of directors during those last few days, little meetings of the board without the formality of notice and agenda. And on the second day of the week before Christmas, when the fog had drawn in closer even than before and seemed to be threatening never to lift again, John Marco called them all together and declared that he was going to advertise.

The declaration in itself was sufficiently startling: advertisements of drapery shops in the daily papers were limited as strictly as if by decree to the handful of big shops, the real mammoths of the trade, in Oxford Street and to the one or two in Regent Street and Knightsbridge. The other shops, even quite large ones, confined themselves to their local papers, or did not advertise at all.

But John Marco as he spoke of advertising had that same light in his eye as when he had first spoken of roof-gardens and electric vans: and the others knew that there would be no dissuading him. When he actually mentioned the sum of a thousand pounds, Mr. Lyman swallowed hard for a moment and tried to expostulate: to him a thousand pounds was something sacred. But to John Marco it had suddenly become no more than a piece of bait to be dangled before the noses of the public. He talked Mr. Lyman down as Mr. Tuke might have scourged a back-slider.

And so John Marco Ltd. appeared in print, each line of type having been sifted through the skilful filter of a copy-writer's mind. There was a little block of the shop itself at the head of each advertisement, a small cameo of prosperity. The frontage of the building was drawn in that kind of perspective which is known only to advertiser's block-makers, and the roof sloped away into the background at an angle that suggested something as high as the Monument and as long as Whitehall. The whole two-column spread of the thing, even Mr. Lyman admitted when he saw it, conveyed very temptingly that Bays-water, and Tredegar Terrace in particular, was the home of marvels. And from the moment the first advertisement appeared, everything was set and ready. The assistants had been drilled until a mistake was impossible; the counters were loaded; and all London had been informed; but the fog remained.

At half-past ten on the Wednesday, when the shop was as empty as ever and the streets outside were like midnight, the four directors met again in John Marco's room. They were a hushed and apprehensive body of men by now. Mr. Hackbridge kept shaking his head like a refuted prophet, saying that he had never known such a thing; and Mr. Skewin sat without speaking. He was thinking of bad Christmases which he remembered in the past and was mutely contrasting the kind of ruin with which all his life he had been familiar, with ruin on this new scale of things; and on the whole he had decided that he preferred the old.

Mr. Lyman was silent, too; but his was a gloating, triumphant kind of silence. He had his charts and his day-book with him, and he kept on passing his small hand across the covers as if stroking them. Deep inside him, not entirely smothered by alarm about the business, a little fire of gratification was burning. He had always been timid about John Marco's colossal speculation in the Christmas market; and now this fog had come along just in time to vindicate him. The charts which he now had ready to present to John Marco were like a testimonial to his rejected sagacity.

As for John Marco himself he did not seem worried, only restless. He kept walking about the room, or standing at the window staring up at the sky to see if it were lightening. When he finally came over and took his place at the head of the table he gave a little laugh as though the whole thing did not matter very much either way.

"We might as well give up bothering about the weather," he said. "It's too late now anyway. We've lost."

With that he re-lit the cigar which had gone out between his lips, and settled himself back comfortably, idly almost, in his chair for the conference.

It was only when the others had left him that he called for Mr. Lyman's books and sat there poring over them. It did not need any Mr. Lyman pulling at his elbow to tell him what figures like those in front of him meant.

ii

There was, however, one person whom the advertisements attracted; there was Hesther. They reminded her suddenly of the meeting which John Marco had asked for; reminded her of the letter from his solicitors that she had read and put away and read again, and finally had hidden in the secret drawer of her writing cabinet. The name of Marco, set in staring letters in the columns of the newspaper, awakened her and filled her with fresh resolve. It seemed to her now, after the first terrors that it might be all a plot to steal her child from her had abated, that she was losing a precious opportunity, throwing away something golden that the Lord had provided. Unlocking the writing cabinet she took out the letter and went to her minister for counsel.

It was no longer Mr. Tuke who advised her. Since she had left Paddington and settled down in Stoke Newington—Stoke Newington was where Mr. Sturger's original Tabernacle had been, and was in consequence the Eternal Borough to all good Amosites—it was the Rev. Simon Weelch whom she consulted. A younger man than Mr. Tuke, he was every bit as much God's captain in the earthly fight. In appearance and in elocution he was admittedly a lesser piece of creation, but he had *character*. He was short, almost squat, and above his tangled, jutting eyebrows (they were the one really terrific feature about him) his hair was thin and sleek; and his voice if raised even ever so slightly became reedy and tremulous. He was recognised everywhere, however, as having a wonderfully clear head for figures. It was this latter quality that had promoted him to his present position in the High Synod; and it was this same quality again that made Mr. Tuke regard him with so much disfavour; he saw in him the one jeopardous thing to his own advancement in the fluctuating hierarchy of the Sect. But for Mr. Weelch, Mr. Tuke still did not doubt that he would be one day himself Moderator.

Mr. Weelch, as always, was patient and painstaking. He heard Hesther's long story with interest and dismay. And when it was over, when her long, disjointed catalogue of sorrows was finished, he clasped his hands together and leant forward.

"And exactly how, Sister," he asked, "can I be of service?"

"You can come with us," Hesther answered. "You can be there to give strength."

"Over to Bayswater? In this fog?" Mr. Weelch asked in dismay.

"Yes," Hesther answered. "To Bayswater. To save a soul."

To save a soul! The summons was irresistible: if it had been Buenos Aires instead of Bayswater his minister's vows would not have allowed him to refuse.

"Very well," he replied unenthusiastically. "I'll accompany you."

He got up and held out his hand.

"Send the boy round here first," he added. "It might be as well if I said a few words to him before we go."

They made a conspicuously striking trio—Mr. Weelch, Hesther and the boy—as they set out together, muddling their way through the gloom across the whole width of London, by first one horse bus and then another. Mr. Weelch was wearing his flat, shovel-hat (he wore his tall hat only on Sundays and kept it stored away for the rest of the week for reasons of the strictest economy) and his high-necked frock-coat; and with that sweeping expanse of brim above him and those double rows of buttons running almost to his feet he had the air not of an English minister at all but of a plump oriental mandarin strutting along pavements that were alien. Hesther as usual was clothed in all-enswathing black. When she insisted on paying her fare and the boy's, the money had to be dragged out of some unthinkable pocket hidden deep down beneath layer under layer of stuff. The boy, tall and leggy by now—he was

486

nearly fifteen—was the only one of them who would not excite comment. His thin, pale face, that seemed to mirror the blankness of the day outside, stared moodily out of the window, and he said nothing.

But even so, Mr. Weelch for his part wished that he himself were not with them. The stir caused by Hesther's appearance was considerable and he had the sickening and steadily growing fear that people might take her for his wife. To indicate that he was with, but not of, them Mr Weelch moved a little apart and sat staring at the ceiling. From Stoke Newington High Street to Tredegar Terrace, Bayswater, he read the advertisements that plastered the roof of the bus, and tried to appear at his ease.

Mr. Weelch had not visited John Marco's before; indeed until he had heard Hesther's lavish and excited description he had not even known of it. And now that he saw it, he was amazed; it was so wildly in excess of anything that he could have imagined. He was used to the fantasies of hysterical women, and knew how the size of things often tends to become exaggerated in the telling. But there was no time now for vain reflections: already Hesther was rushing him off his feet. She led the way across the central hall to the main staircase without pausing: she was now in that tense mood of suppressed excitement which comes of putting a much prayed-over plan into operation. Mr. Weelch followed her closely, but the boy stood still once or twice to look round; it was his first glimpse of Babylon and it seemed that already he was tempted.

The first set-back came when Hesther sent in her own name, and was told that John Marco would not see her. But she refused to accept such an answer.

"Tell Mr. Marco that his son is outside," she said to the girl.

The effect of this new message was instantaneous. Hardly

487

had the secretary closed the door behind her than she came out again. There was a new kind of respect in her voice by now.

"Mr. Marco says will you send the boy in, please," she said.

Hesther got up and beckoned to Mr. Weelch to follow.

"Not by himself he doesn't go," she whispered. And taking the boy by the hand she led him in.

John Marco had got up from his desk and was standing in the centre of the room. In the cruel light of the lamp above him his hair showed grey and harsh; in the last few months the grey had spread to the temples and his forehead was now framed in the half-whiteness. But his attitude at that moment was not that of a man whose years are telling on him. He was tense and erect, and there was an eagerness about him; even his arms, now hanging stiffly at his side, seemed ready to be held out for the boy whom he was awaiting.

It was Hesther, however, who came in first, her son behind her. She smoothed back the straggling lock of hair that fell forward across the boy's face, tugged at the creased lapels of his jacket. Then putting her arm about his shoulders she began to push him forward.

"That's your father," she told him in a voice that began trembling as she said it. "Speak to him."

John Marco stood there, staring at him. The boy was taller than he expected; taller and thinner and shabbier. That sad little boy whom he had seen in the Park years ago hand in hand with Hesther, had vanished. He had been shabby, too; but shabbiness is one thing in a child and something else in a youth who reaches to his mother's shoulder. And his shabbiness disgusted him; he wanted to take him down into the shop and re-clothe him, clothe him this time like a man.

But it was not only at the tight Norfolk jacket and deplorable boots that he was looking. He had lifted his eyes and was gazing into the boy's face. And, as he looked, he saw that it was Hesther's face. The jet hair that caught the light and did not reflect it, the deep, incalculable eyes, the heavy mouth that drooped so sharply at the corners—they were all the same. And there was, too, that air half resignation, half resolve, that he remembered.

There *was*, however, something else, something that he couldn't name. It was simply that as he stood there a voice inside him cried out that this boy was his and should be cherished, that every other boy in the world was less to be esteemed. He looked into his face more closely. And as he looked he saw that it was not the face of a child at all; it was the face of someone who has already encountered the first round of life's disappointments.

But the boy, he saw, was holding out his hand to him. He had obediently gone forward and now stood waiting awkwardly for John Marco to say something.

John Marco did not hesitate longer. He held out both hands to him, clasping the boy's thin one in two of his.

"So you've come to see your father at last, have you?" he asked.

His voice in his own ears sounded hollow and unreal as he said it; this wasn't the way he had meant to welcome him, not the way he would have welcomed him if he had been alone.

The boy merely nodded; he had made no attempt to come any nearer.

"And how do you like the look of him now that you have seen him?" he asked. "Is he what you expected?"

There was still the same jocularity in his voice; the same false-ness. But that was because they had a stranger with them, someone to whom this meeting was simply an odd spectacle to

489

be remembered, not something that was of the stuff of a man's own history.

"You can speak to him," Hesther was saying. "Say something."

She addressed the boy in a low voice as though intended for his ears alone; it was obvious that in that instant mother and son were one again, and she was trying to enter into him and fill him with her strength, her courage.

The boy still said nothing. He remained there, awkward and alone.

"Tell your father how pleased you are to see him," Mr. Weelch interposed encouragingly.

John Marco turned away from the boy for a moment and addressed Hesther.

"Who is this man?" he asked. "Why is he here?"

"He's here because he's been looking after your son's soul," Hesther answered. "He's been instructing him."

"Instructing him?" John Marco repeated.

"Certainly. He's going to enter the ministry."

A coldness, a sickness almost, swept over him as he heard the words, and he turned towards the boy again.

"So you're going to be a minister, are you?" he asked. "You're very young to have made up your mind."

"Not too young," Mr. Weelch replied hastily. "The Lord sometimes guides our footsteps early."

John Marco ignored him.

"Do you want to go into orders?" he asked.

His voice had grown natural again by now; it was straight, direct, like the voice of a man talking to his equal.

"Are you sure it's what you want?" he insisted.

"Tell him," said Hesther.

490

"That's right," echoed Mr. Weelch. "Tell him."

There was a pause, a long painful one, and then the boy answered.

"Yes," he said. "I do."

The words were said so quietly that only the movement of his lips showed that he had spoken. But the effect on Hesther and Mr. Weelch of his having spoken at all was strangely apparent. They seemed not only gratified but actually relieved; it was as though someone whom they had trained and re-trained and then trained again had at last been put to the test and had emerged victorious.

"You wouldn't rather come into the business with me?" John Marco asked. "You wouldn't rather make your way in the world?"

Mr. Weelch leaned forward.

"You don't understand the boy's nature," he said. "He's heard the call."

John Marco ignored Mr. Weelch for the second time. He took hold of the boy by the elbow—it was a firm, authoritative grip and the boy did not question it—and led him over to the door.

"Gome outside with me," he said. "Come and look."

The door opened straight out onto the top balcony; and the whole arena of the shop was spread below them. It was only half-a-dozen paces from her, but Hesther started forward nervously. It was evident that she feared that anything might happen once the boy had been taken out of her sight.

But Mr. Weelch subdued her.

"I can see them," he said. "They shan't evade me."

The two of them were alone now, the ageing, heavy-shouldered man and the silent, timid boy. John Marco put his arm around him.

"Do you see that," he was saying. "Do you see all those people moving about down there? I brought them here. They belong to me just as much as those girls behind the counter do. This shop is something that I built out of nothing. There's no one else who knows the secrets of it as I do. There's no one else who could keep it all alive. I've put ten years of my life into it and I want to put the rest into it as well. But when I get too old who am I going to leave it to? Who am I going to trust with it all?" He tightened his grip round the boy's shoulders and dropped his voice a little. "How would you like to have it for your own one day," he asked. "How would you like to be able to order all those assistants about yourself?"

But he was jocular and bantering again by now, and he stopped himself. These words weren't real, they were the kind of thing that all elderly, boastful men say in the presence of shy, unresponsive youngsters who are too self-conscious to reply. Yet within himself he was not joking at all; he was simply waiting for the miracle of seeing the boy beside him turn from Hesther's son into his.

Mr. Weelch, however, was leaning forward watching them anxiously; this conversation had gone on too long altogether, too dangerously long.

"The devil taketh him up into an exceedingly high mountain, and showeth him all the kingdoms of the world, and the glory of them, and saith unto him, all these things will I give thee if thou wilt fall down and worship me," Mr. Weelch was repeating; and as he said it he shook his head over the wisdom of the words.

"Well, do you like it?" John Marco persisted. "Would you like it to be yours one day?"

"It can't be if I'm in the Chapel," the boy replied.

"Then why go into the Chapel?" John Marco asked. "Why

not come here where you belong?"

But the boy shook his head.

"I've promised," he said.

John Marco took him by the arm again, but roughly this time. He was angry by now.

"Who have you promised?" he demanded.

"God," the boy answered.

John Marco bent forward until his face was on a level with the boy's.

"Are you sure it was God?" he asked. "Or was it your mother that you promised? Your mother and that man in there with her now."

But Mr. Weelch was no longer inside the room. In quick, bouncing steps he was advancing towards them

"I'm afraid that time is drawing close," he said. "Mrs. Marco has to be going."

This time John Marco stepped in front of him, so that the whole width of his body separated him from the boy.

"Do you swear it?" he asked. "Do you swear that you want to wear the cloth?"

"I swear it," the boy answered. And he repeated it loudly enough for Mr. Weelch to hear. "I swear that I want to be a minister."

Mr. Weelch's smooth face appeared round John Marco's elbow.

"You see," he said. "The boy's mind is quite made up. I've tried to shake him myself, and failed. He's inflexible."

The three of them went back into the private room, Mr. Weelch with his hand pressed affectionately into the small of the boy's back. Hesther was standing there ready for them, drawing down her black veil as they came in. But before the veil descended

493

John Marco saw the look of victory on her face, the smile that she made no effort to conceal.

"You said that you wanted to do something for your son," she reminded him. "Are you still of the same mind?"

"What is it?" he asked.

"He'll have to go on studying if he's to become a minister," she answered. "There are his fees."

"Only eighty pounds a year," Mr. Weelch put in hurriedly. "Eighty pounds per annum inclusive for five years."

John Marco avoided the eager gaze of Mr. Weelch that was turned in his direction. Then he saw that the boy's eyes were fixed on him, too. They wore that same look, half of resolve, half resignation, that he had noticed when the boy had first stood before him. It was impossible to tell what were the real thoughts behind them.

"Perhaps he's doubting me," he thought. "He doesn't understand why I wanted him to come here."

And turning to Hesther he smiled back at her; there was victory of a kind in his smile, too.

"I'll pay his fees," he said, "if the boy comes to see me from time to time to say how he's getting on. I want him to think of me as his father."

On the following day, the last before Christmas, the fog cleared and Mr. Hackbridge was rushed off his feet again.

494

Chapter XXXVIII

But that one day of sunshine, those nine hours during which people had crowded themselves into the shop like the faithful pouring into Mecca, was not enough; it was lost among all those other blank, abysmal days. Hidden among the losses of that terrible month, the sun clouded over again and the crowds dispersed. And on that morning nearly five months later when Mr. Lyman, in his little glass box of an office in the counting house, drew the last double underline with his ebony ruler to the year's accounts it seemed that for the whole of the past twelve months, and not merely for four weeks of it, they must have been trading in a morass of fog and rain and snow. As Mr. Lyman looked at the final balance he whistled.

Not that the accounts, the final figures, came as any sort of surprise; both he and John Marco had known all the time what they would look like. It was simply that seeing them there set out in his minute feathery hand on the ruled sheet of foolscap gave a finish, an inescapability, to the whole business; it erected a kind of tomb-stone to a melancholy year.

Once the double underline had been drawn, Mr. Lyman read the document over once more very carefully (for nearly six weeks he had been reading and thinking about next to nothing else), and left his office with the thing tucked under his arm. It might have been a certificate of merit, or a prize-poem, from the way he carried it down the long centre gangway of the counting house with the clerks all scribbling away industriously on either side; and when he came to knock on John Marco's door there was the same quiet air of mastery and achievement on his face. His whole manner, pert and mincing and precise, seemed to convey that it was blissfully immaterial to him whether it was a profit or a loss that he was showing. So long as the abstract of figures was correct, his mission was completed; the rest was just the ordinary sordid dog-fight of daily commerce.

John Marco took the balance sheet from him and sat looking at it without speaking; he might have been oblivious of Mr. Lyman's presence. He remained oblivious for so long in fact that Mr. Lyman could endure it no longer: he coughed.

"There is one point, sir," he said. "If I might be allowed to draw your attention to it."

John Marco nodded.

"What is it?"

"It's your own commission, sir."

"Well?"

"It's overdrawn, sir," Mr. Lyman replied. "On those figures it's overdrawn by nearly six thousand pounds."

His voice as he said it rose suddenly. There was just a trace of relish in it as he said it; the sentence ended almost on a note of jubilation.

The words, in the piping voice that had spoken them, remained in John Marco's ears long after Mr. Lyman had returned to his counting house and John Marco had gone over to the cabinet in the corner to pour himself a drink. It was not the overdraft that worried him—six thousand pounds was not a large sum to recover from next year's profits: it was hearing it mentioned on someone else's lips, hearing himself discussed as it were in a way which was both behind his back and to his face. But was six thousand pounds really the kind of sum to be unconcerned about? The house in Hyde Park Square was proving expensive, very expensive; and Louise's tastes had been growing steadily more fastidious, more exacting. She had just refurnished that fine drawing-room of theirs, getting rid of the comfortable chairs and couches of his own choosing and bringing in a lot of costly upright Empire stuff instead. She was planning something of the same kind for the dining-room; and he had told her to have her own way in the matter. But it would all cost money.

Her clothes, too, cost more nowadays; the original allowance no longer covered them, and the bright cardboard boxes from Bond Street were piling up in her boudoir. But he had not the heart to stop her buying the things. She was there to look beautiful; and it would be out of all reason to grudge her a few new clothes if she needed them. Besides, it would mean telling her that he couldn't afford them, would mean confessing to some kind of failure, however temporary. And that was something his nature couldn't expand to. It had been his part of the bargain (a part too obvious for either of them to refer to) when she had agreed to come there, to see that he could always give her anything she asked for. It is only young husbands with wives of the same age as themselves, who can decently admit to being poor.

And somehow the business seemed more difficult to run nowadays, more hazardous. Fashions at the moment were at their most intricate. Ostrich feathers, for example, were at the very height of their boom and were growing scarcer and more costly every day; the alternative was simply to wait and see what happened and possibly to buy at crippling fantastic prices when next Christmas came round again, or to buy now and fill up the store rooms and risk a sudden disastrous feminine swing-over before the stuff had been disposed of. Waists, too, were another thing that was troubling him, they were slipping up and down the figure by as much as two inches. Even a confidential letter from their Paris buyer had failed to fix them. *"Alors, personne n'a pas exactement décidé ,"* the letter had concluded, *"la taille eventuelle de la mode de cette saison angoisseuse."* And with no guidance from abroad, no hint of a superior culture to assist them, English women became awkward and obstinate. At one moment the Spring fashion line in Knightsbridge was three fingers' depth below that of Regent Street and Oxford Circus.

But these were, after all, only the ordinary day by day problems that a retail draper has to face, they were the common round. There was another and far more difficult problem that he had to solve; and that was how to persuade the shareholders of John Marco Ltd., especially those who had put up extra money, that the fact that there would be no dividend this year was simply because nearly five months ago there had been a break in the weather.

ii

For the first time in his life it occurred to John Marco that he was drinking too much; not drinking in wild silly bouts with boisterous companions, but drinking every day in a sober, unecstatic fashion just a little more than was good for him. The vicious circle of the process was already final and complete; there was no gap or loop-hole anywhere. He drank simply because he was tired; and the later into the night he worked, the more he drank. Then, next morning when the elixir that was in the stuff had evaporated and only the dregs remained, silting up his mind inside him, he felt the need sooner and drank earlier.

His eleven o'clock drink when the tour of the shop was over had already become something that was regular and established; he poured the drink out without even thinking about it. And once the back of the morning had been broken he went on working with a glass in his hand, almost unaware of it. In the afternoon it was the same; and in the evening when he finally locked up his desk and hung the key onto his watch chain he was often surprised to notice how low the level of the whiskey in the decanter had become. It was this decanter that provided him with his excuse; and like most drinkers he had felt relieved when he had first thought of the excuse. "If only the decanter were a bottle," he had said to himself, "I should know when it was finished and not trouble to open another one. As it is, it is always refilled for me and I am drinking from something that has no beginning and no ending, and so I never know how much I'm taking."

He had told himself a hundred times that he would have the decanter put away and a bottle set there in its place. But he liked the glittering crystal of the thing and the crisp, hard feel of it beneath his fingers; and somehow the order for its removal was the one order that he never gave.

In a way, too, he did not want to drink any less than he had grown used to: it suited him. Mr. Hackbridge's company in a world without alcohol would have been intolerable; and Mr. Lyman's something not to be contemplated. But with it, he was able to see them both a dozen times a day and forget how tired of each he had become. He suspected, too, that because of it they found him a little easier than they might otherwise have done: it helped to take the sharp edge off his tongue and served to gloss over some of the civilities that were missing.

And without it, probably, he would never have sought again for Mary's friendship, suddenly breaking through the careful, silent reserve with which she had surrounded herself. Perhaps it was, that on that afternoon he had taken a trifle more than usual, had drunk just enough to free himself from the fixed course of things. It was the day of their early closing and the curtains— they were of the new fashionable kind that hung in gay decorative loops—were already down across the windows. Inside the store the assistants were putting the display stuff back into its boxes and hanging white dust-covers over the naked counters.

The public had not been allowed inside the place since one o'clock, and the assistants, if they were fortunate, would be able to leave at about two. The cashiers in the counting house, of course, never enjoyed that particular kind of good fortune; their work on Saturday afternoons went on until three o'clock and sometimes half-past. Long after the aisles and gangways down below had been cleared of people, they were still there checking and crosschecking the innumerable little flimsy sheets of paper with the carbon copy of the order scribbled across it Every desk upstairs in the cash-room had a small printed notice just above the cashier's eye level. "MISTAKES IN CHANGE ARE THE RESPONSIBILITY OF THE CASHIER," it ran. "ANY SHORTAGE WILL BE DEDUCTED FROM WAGES." And the effect of this notice was to root the girls to their high stools. A missing florin—or something really serious like five shillings or seven-and-sixpence that could not be accounted for—would keep a cashier there until the evening lights came on.

It was about two-thirty in the afternoon as John Marco closed the door of his office and began to wander along the empty corridor. There was nothing to go home for: Louise was having one of her bridge parties and the house would be filled with expensive, pre-occupied women who would all chatter shrilly when it came to tea. The only sign of life in the whole store was in the counting house: he could see the tops of the clerks' heads over the glass partition. He went instinctively towards it. And as he opened the door he felt himself surrounded by the close, hushed atmosphere of many people working. The whole room was a silent, busy temple of double-entry and nice balances. Over on the far side, he saw Mary; so far as the others were concerned she was a part of the counting-house by now. It was probably only a trick of light but, for an instant as he stood there, he saw her hair again pale and golden as he had remembered it; and her shoulders in their black dress were like the shoulders of the young Sabbath School teacher. He crossed over and stood beside her.

"Well, Mary," he said.

He was standing there, his legs apart, his hands in his pockets smiling down at her. It was the old, familiar smile that was not often seen on his face nowadays.

She looked up at him and, recognising the smile, she smiled back. Even the voice was as she remembered it. And it seemed for a moment as though they had never been separated, as though they had been looking into each other's eyes for a life-time.

"Are you finished for to-day?" he asked.

She nodded.

"I was just going home," she answered.

"Then I'll take you back there," he said; "it's a long time since we really talked to each other."

He was looking hard at her as he spoke and noticed that her

colour had mounted a little. "It's almost as if she still blushes when she speaks to me," he thought.

She paused, pushing back her hair from her forehead with a little gesture that was half weary, half embarrassed.

"I'm in no hurry," she said. "I've nothing to go home for yet."

"Well, let's drive round the Park together," he suggested. "That's the perfect way for talking."

When she came back to him she was wearing her coat. It was a cheap, thin one, not at all like the coats that Louise had hanging up in her wardrobe. John Marco remembered the heavy rug in the carriage and was glad that it was there to wrap her in.

The air in the Park was cold; and the Park itself had that air of peculiar and even startling sweetness which is to be found in all open spaces in large towns. It was as though, up to its railings, the ordinary grim business of cities went on and then, suddenly, on the other side a new kind of life began, a life in which ladies ride about in carriages, children play together under trees, toy-yachts are sent sailing across ponds, and dogs run barking. John Marco sat back and took his hat off, running his fingers through his hair.

Mary looked towards him.

"You look tired," she said. "You don't give yourself enough rest."

"You've noticed that, have you," he said slowly. "I am tired. Very tired."

"Then why don't you take things more easily?" she asked. "I've been worrying about you for a long time."

"You have?"

Somehow, her admission cheered him; simply by telling him, she had made him feel less alone again. And thrusting his hand under the rug he took hold of hers for a moment and held it.

502

Louise, for her part, seemed never to have thought of him as even possibly being tired; she was so rarely tired herself.

They got out of the carriage and began to walk. A faint breeze, that came and went, kept playing across their faces and the sun was almost warm. Overhead the sky was clear, and the flat acres of the Serpentine, seen through the dark trunks of the elms, showed placid and brilliant. They did not talk much as they walked; they went along side by side in silence like old friends. He held out his arm for her and she took it; to his surprise her touch still pleased him. And as they strolled across the sward he kept glancing sideways down at her.

The warmth had gone out of the air by the time they got back to the carriage and John Marco suggested that they should go somewhere for tea; Gunther's was the best place, he told her.

But Mary answered that she must be getting back again; there was tea to be got for the child who would be coming home from school, she explained. And as she said it, his feeling of loneliness suddenly returned to him; he was aware again of a closed and already complete life that was going on apart from him, something that was self-sufficient and shut-in.

He asked for the address where she was living. But, when he was told, the coachman had not heard of it, and Mary had to direct them when they came to the corner of the street. She had asked him to drop her anywhere so that she could make her way home as usual by bus; but John Marco had refused to hear of it.

The street, when they came to it, was not a pretty one. It was of grey brick, and the houses all had the flattened, lifeless look that comes of windows with curtains that have had all the colour and sparkle washed out of them, and front gardens with nothing brighter or more lively than a privet-hedge inside their borders. It was a street in Paddington and not in Bayswater.

"You will come in, won't you?" Mary asked him as the carriage stopped. "Then I can make us both some tea."

He got down from the carriage and they went in together. Inside, the hall was dark and narrow. It was close, too, as though the air that was imprisoned in it had been breathed a hundred times.

"It's upstairs," she told him. "We live on the second floor."

They mounted the stairs in silence, treading the pattern-less strip of oil cloth that ran up the centre. The paper on the walls was shiny, varnished stuff; it glistened. It had been like that in the house in Chapel Villas where he had been brought up; and perhaps it was because of this, or because he was with Mary again, that his mind began working backwards into the past and old Mrs. Marco was alive once more and he himself was young and keeping up appearances on fifteen shillings a week, and the world was spread out before him.

He started when Mary spoke to him: her voice reached him out of a different level of things.

"This is ours," she said.

She threw open the door in front of him and the fustiness of the house vanished. The room seemed a small oasis of comfort, of civilisation even, amid those deserts of blind windows and sooty brick. There were flowers on the table and pictures that he remembered on the walls. And as he stood there he suddenly saw again that little pink-and-white drawing-room above the chemist's shop in Harrow Street, and he heard the voice of Mr. Petter's mother asking if he had been her son's friend and if he wanted to go upstairs to see him. Everything in the room was just as it had been then. The chair covers were the same, except that the bright dye that had once been so cheerful-looking had faded out of them, leaving them faint and autumnal; and the carpet that had once been new had grown thin and hard to the feet. But there was one difference, he realised; and it was a difference that seemed to mark the whole complexion of the change. Here the paint work was dark; it was something that had been inherited from a succession of shadowy, departed tenants; and in the little flat to which Mary had been taken, it had been all white. John Marco remembered the bridal look that there had been to it.

"Sit down while I put the kettle on," Mary told him. "I shall be back again in a minute."

He seated himself in one of the easy chairs and stretched his legs in front of him. It was very quiet here—the only sound was that of Mary moving about in the other room—and he felt oddly comfortable and at ease. He thought of the tea-party that was going on in Hyde Park Square, and smiled. The maids there would be going around in their lace caps and aprons offering little sugary tit-bits off a silver cake stand; and here he was in an upper back room in a road that his coachman had never even heard of; and he was preferring it. It seemed suddenly, after all those years, so exactly what he wanted, to be there alone with Mary again.

But as he raised his eyes to the mantelpiece he saw that he was not alone. Thomas Petter was there, too; and he was regarding him. His coloured photograph set slantwise upon the shelf was staring full at him; and the eyes, cunningly touched up by the photographer's assistant had more, not less, than the ordinary sparkle of life about them—they hypnotised. At the same moment, John Marco became aware of how much of this room, that had been transported across a score of streets and up three flights of stairs, still belonged to Thomas Petter. His certificate from the Pharmaceutical Society was hanging on the wall in its narrow gilt frame and another photograph of him as a young man, seated amid an Amosite Bible Class that he had been instructing, was opposite. Even the books were his; his Pharmacopoeia was there in the case beside the fireplace in just the spot where a tired man who was interested in his work could stretch out his hand and take it up. If his slippers, too, had been down beside the fender it would not have seemed surprising.

John Marco avoided Thomas Petter's bright, unswerving eyes and sank lower into his chair. Through the window, across the double strip of what had once been gardens, he could see the blank, untidy backs of the houses opposite. There was no pretence about them. No matter what façade the fronts supported, the backs were honest and themselves: they were the backs of tenements.

"So this is what she comes back to at night," he reflected; "this is her life now." But it had been about *him* that she had said she had been worrying. She had spoken as though *her* existence were the one which was secure and sheltered, and *his* the bleak, arduous one. It was evident that the other life, the streety one that went on around her, had not touched her at all; inside these four walls she was shut away. "Perhaps she can afford to keep alive her memories," he thought.

She came in carrying the tea tray and set it down on the small table beside him.

"We'll have it like this," she said. "It's easier."

He lay back looking at her.

"It seems strange seeing you do this," he said slowly. She paused.

"Then you must come again so that it won't be strange," she told him.

"I'd like to," he replied simply.

And as he said it he realised that, if they were to see each other again like this, it would have to be here that they met. He hadn't got a house of his own now, a house that he could bring her to. It was Louise's house; her house, and he lived in it. The people they entertained were her friends, not his.

"You don't ever go to the Tabernacle now, do you?" she asked.

John Marco shook his head

"I haven't been there since I saw you get married," he answered quietly.

Mary did not reply immediately: she glanced for a moment at the picture on the mantelshelf and then dropped her eyes again.

"I still go," she went on. "But the people are different mostly. It doesn't seem like the same chapel nowadays."

John Marco had closed his eyes: he was sitting back with his hand across his face.

"How long is it?" he asked suddenly, "since the night when you were baptised?"

She hesitated.

"I was eighteen then," she said. "I'm thirty-nine now."

She saw the fingers of his hand tighten for a moment.

"Twenty-one years," he said slowly. "The best years." He paused. "I wonder what they would have been like if we'd been together."

"I think we should have been very happy," she replied.

"Yes," he said. "We shouldn't have been like this then. We wouldn't either of us have known what it was to be lonely."

"It's not too late," she told him. "We can still be with each other sometimes."

"What has happened to that other woman," she wondered; "the dark-haired woman who came into the room when I was there. Has he left her, too. Is it this that's added to his bitterness?"

507

She wanted to go over and put her arms round him and comfort him; and she wanted his arms to go round her too, holding her as he had held her that night at the bottom of the staircase in Abernethy Terrace when her mother had allowed them to go as far as the front door together.

But there was too much between them now; the years had separated them. It wouldn't be the same person who went over to him, and it was not the same man who was sitting there. Could she make them both the same again? That was what she wondered. Had she the strength in her to wind back the years that were wasted, to re-set the hour that was on them both? Then she remembered Hesther; and she remembered the vows that the Chapel imposed on marriage. But what right had Hesther still got to him? Where was her title after those years of separation? He had never loved her; they had never really belonged to each other. It was Hesther's touch that had changed him and made him cold; like the Snow Queen she had taken him away and frozen up his heart. And now at last, when she had not expected it, had come the chance to release him. Like Gerda she could make him free again. But she looked at her hands that were resting in her lap and she saw that they were worn and red; and she remembered the age she was and the way no one ever looked at her now; and the hope inside her slid away into the litter of all other vain, silly things. She was suddenly nearly forty again; and it was five o'clock, and the fire was dying out.

She got up and began clearing away the tea things.

"I've got to make fresh tea for Ann," she said. "She'll be in any moment now."

The words roused him and he dropped his hand from his face. A moment before it had seemed that their two lives had joined mysteriously again; he had waited there with eyes closed to feel her hand on his shoulder and know how she needed him, too. But now that she had spoken, it was not of him at all that she was thinking, it was of that other life of hers, the life that centred on the child which Thomas Petter had given her.

"I must go," he said roughly. "I shall be getting in the way."

Mary put down the tray she was holding and came over to him.

"But you must stay and see Ann," she said. "She's grown so, I'm very proud of her."

He shook his head.

"No," he said. "It's late. I must be getting back again."

"I had hoped you'd have seen her," Mary said slowly. "She's very like I was at her age."

But John Marco was already buttoning up his coat.

"No," he said again. "She's part of your life, I don't belong in there at all."

He held out his hand and they said good-bye quietly, unemotionally, like people who mean nothing to each other.

"I'll come down with you," Mary said. "It may be dark on those stairs."

"I can find my way," he answered.

His back was already towards her as he spoke.

At the door, however, he turned to look back and saw that she was crying. She was standing there with her arms to her side as he had left her and her face was still towards him. He stood for a moment at the door and then came over and put his arms round her.

"I'm sorry, Mary," he said. "I shouldn't have come here. I'm still jealous. I can't help it."

Then he kissed her.

But the kiss, when Mary remembered it after he had gone,

seemed the last tragic humiliation of that meeting. She had been in his arms again as she had dreamed that sometime she would be, and the kiss which he had given her had been faint and cold and passionless.

It had been a kiss between two people who were unhappy, not in love.

As John Marco drove back round the Park which was dark and sunless by now, and the cold air of the evening blew into his face he shivered, and drew the heavy rug more closely round him. His face was set again into the hard, angry lines that it wore so often; it was the face of a bitter, disappointed man.

But it was not of Mary that he was now thinking: he was wondering how to face a roomful of waiting shareholders, people who had trusted him, and tell them that he had failed; wondering how long the bank would remain smiling and polite in the face of the overdraft; wondering how long it would be before the spring inside him snapped and he hadn't the strength to go on juggling with all the bits of the business any longer.

Louise was waiting for him in the drawing-room when he got back there. She was wearing a new dress which he had not seen before: it was a costly affair sprinkled all over with sequins. There was a diamond clip in her hair.

"My dear," she said, "you'll have to hurry. You're late. We've got a lot of people dining at the house to-night."

Book VI

The Cracks Widen

Chapter XXXIX

When a business begins to go to pieces, the cracks appear everywhere. The process is not immediate; it is slow and scarcely discernible at first. But it seems to advance irresistibly according to certain pre-determined laws.

Some of the cracks start as tiny, thread-like things, but they run down into the heart of the organisation: they divide it. Mistakes, for example, occur in the buying, and disputes arise with the manufacturers. Heads of departments make miraculous, unaccountable blunders and blame their seconds-in-command for the consequences, and junior assistants offend important customers. Then the network of small fissures widens and other pieces become unstuck as well. People arrive late for no particular reason or stay away altogether without warning. Lunch-time becomes an hour and five minutes, and illicit tea is drunk in the afternoon and is lingered over. Stock is mislaid, and articles that are lying in bales in the store room downstairs are reported up in the shop as unobtainable. In short, though the business continues to look as if the whole city of London depended on it, there is not a department or sub-department in the place but has gone quietly and successfully to blazes.

When a business is in this state, it needs a man with energy bursting out of him to put things right again. John Marco had been full of that kind of energy once. He had bullied and worn down Mr. Hackbridge, and Mr. Hackbridge had bullied and worn down the heads of each department and they in turn had bullied and worn down the assistants that were under them until there was not a person in the shop who was not jumpy and on his toes in case someone else just a little above him should notice that, even for a second, he was resting.

But for the last eighteen months or so, John Marco had left the ordinary, everyday supervision of the shop, the poking about into corners to see that the dust hadn't been allowed to settle there, more and more to Mr. Hackbridge; and Mr. Hackbridge, exhausted and frayed by years of working for John Marco, had left it more and more to itself. Mr. Hackbridge still made the same morning tour in the place of his master, visiting the same departments in the same order; but the old spirit was missing. The assistants scarcely even looked in his direction as he passed.

John Marco himself was seen less than ever. He shut himself away in his room, guarding his soul and Mr. Lyman's financial statements in solitude. On the rare occasions when he did emerge, it was usually to make trouble. There were sudden furious sallies when he would stamp through the shop at his old speed, his face dark and angry, on his way to annihilate some employee or other who had displeased him. The pretext for these excursions were sometimes slight—a mistake in cutting, a colour that did not match the rolls that were already in stock, or a letter of complaint from a customer. But at those moments it was the original John Marco who was there again, the man whom his assistants were afraid of; and Mr. Hackbridge, hearing John Marco's voice raised, even though it was someone else that he was shouting at, used to feel the pit of his stomach grow cold on these occasions and the tips of his fingers begin to tremble.

There were some people who said that John Marco's temper was shorter than it had been because he was drinking too much—the fact that he kept spirits in his room had not passed without comment in the house. And others, the very knowing ones, said that it was because the lady in Hyde Park Square, their own mysterious ex-colleague, was unfaithful and extravagant. And though both these reasons were perhaps true they were only a part, a small part, of it all.

The real trouble lay outside the business, somewhere five or six miles away down in the heart of London. It was there that the ugliest of rumours of all were circulating; it was in the offices of brokers and half-commission men that people shook their heads and said that the business of John Marco Ltd. itself was shaky.

They were right too: that was the grim point. John Marco knew perfectly well that they were right; and he knew why. That enormous palace of Portland stone and plate glass was too expensive to be lived in. It wasn't that the public didn't come there: he could still fill the shop by one of his advertisements whenever he had been able to buy at the right place. But even when the gangways were blocked, and the stuff was passing in waves over the counters, there was still that marble court with the Pompeian pillars to be paid for, still the cost of that building that he had dreamed about, to be snatched back somehow out of thin air above his head.

Alone in his room, he had grown to hate the splendour that he had insisted upon; the fact that he was surrounded by it, oppressed him. He had only to go outside and look at the majestic sweep of the staircase to know that you can't pay for that sort of thing out of a yard or so of ribbon and stray reels of cotton; it

515

was a lifetime's work for one man to recover what he had paid for his crystal chandeliers. And it all meant that the whole time, without daring to pause even for a single moment, he had to be just that bit cleverer than every other draper in London over everything he bought and over every price that he charged. "Without it all," he had said to himself a hundred times—and the yellow uniforms of the page boys, and the floristry department stocked with lilac out of season, and the fancy dresses for the assistants at Christmas time, had long since disappeared and had even ceased to be talked about—"I should be making my profit: the gold would have piled itself up inside the bank by now. But with it all, it means that I must spend my whole day from eight-thirty in the morning until I go to bed at night juggling about with fractions of halfpennies and decimals of farthings, and I can't even pay a dividend."

And on those occasions as he sat alone in his room with the reports of the various departments spread out on the desk in front of him, like a bewildering patch-work table-cloth, there was a strange, recurrent nightmare, a kind of inner panic, that infected him: it seemed at those moments as though, if he stopped thinking about the business even for a single instant, he would see the whole carefully-oiled mechanism of buying and selling go to pieces before his eyes, as though his brain were the dynamo that was driving everything, and if that stopped, everything else in the shop would have to stop at exactly the same moment. And the nightmare, the panic, always developed along exactly the same lines until finally it had enveloped him. First of all, there was the terrible fear of what would happen if he did stop; and then there was the even more terrible fear that he would *have* to stop.

"I can't go on," he had heard himself saying aloud when the

516

panic was at its worst and he had been there alone, working late. "I can't go on." And then he would go over to the cupboard and place the decanter on the table beside him, and run his fingers through his hair and start working again, with every bit in his brain red hot and the figures, huge, silly piles of them, forming and reforming themselves before his eyes.

For some time now Mr. Skewin and Mr. Hackbridge had both been keeping a very careful eye on John Marco: they had been observing him. And they had been talking him over together pretty thoroughly, dissecting him coldly and dispassionately like a specimen under the glass.

"He'll be dead inside a year if he isn't careful," Mr. Hackbridge volunteered with a kind of sagacious cheerfulness.

Mr. Hackbridge was a man who set great store on taking care; his whole life was one of mufflers and throat-pastilles and judicious night-caps.

"But the *business*" Mr. Lyman's thinner voice put in. "Think of what's happening to the business."

And as they both had a plan—it was Mr. Lyman's plan—and as they needed support for it, they went and lobbied Mr. Skewin. He was dim and adaptable as usual. He expressed himself entirely captured by the whole idea, and even went so far as to say that he thought that John Marco would appreciate it to know that they were thinking about him.

So the three of them went up to John Marco's office on the following evening. It was just as they had expected. In answer to the bark from within that greeted Mr. Hack-bridge's somewhat timid knock on the door, they filed in and found John Marco working there—the sheets of figures stretched out around him, and the decanter standing in the middle with the half empty glass beside it. The rest of the room was in darkness and the lamp in front of him spread a bright pool of light over the papers like sunshine. When he looked up and the rays caught his face, sharpening every feature and etching in the shadows under his eyes more deeply, they saw how grey and lined he was. He was like a general in the thick of a campaign, poring over maps that seemed set against him.

"We were wondering if we might see you for a moment?" Mr. Lyman began.

John Marco started: he moved abruptly with the jerkiness of a man whose nerves are unprotected.

"What is it?" he asked. "Has anything gone wrong?"

"No, no," Mr. Lyman assured him. "It isn't that. It's simply something that we wanted to discuss with you."

"Now?" John Marco asked.

The figures on the desk were staring up at him accusingly; they seemed to have a hundred small eyes which were regarding him.

"We thought it might be the best time," Mr. Lyman went on. It was noticeable, now that they were actually in John Marco's presence, that the others did not appear to be at all eager to say anything. "No interruptions you know," Mr. Lyman added.

John Marco had half risen from his chair and had then sat down again. He passed his hand across his eyes and told Mr. Lyman to continue.

The room was silent, quite silent, as Mr. Lyman started to speak.

"We've been rather anxious about you for some time, sir," he began in a modest, diffident kind of manner. "We know the great strain the business imposes on you and we can't help feeling worried about your health."

"You've been worried about my health," John Marco repeated.

518

The corners of his mouth were drawn down and the vein in his forehead was standing out, throbbing. "You interrupted me to tell me that?"

"We did, sir," Mr. Lyman explained, "because we thought we'd found the solution."

He was being very careful, very tactful; a great deal depended on the right inflexion and intonation of every word he was uttering.

"And might I ask what it is?" John Marco demanded. He was drumming his fingers impatiently on the desk as he spoke to them. "Might I ask why I should be bothered in this way?"

"What we had thought," Mr. Lyman continued, feeling his way daintily step by step, like a cat, as he went along, "was that perhaps you might care to take a holiday. We know how little rest you give yourself and we thought that if we suggested it you might consider the idea."

John Marco started.

"Whose idea was this?" he demanded. His voice was coarse and rough as he said it; he was almost shouting.

He was breathing heavily by now.

Mr. Lyman rather shame-facedly took the lead again.

"We often feel the strain ourselves, sir," he said tactfully. "We often get a bit under the weather. And with everything that you have to think about, it's too much without a holiday."

"That's right, sir," Mr. Hackbridge put in, as though to show that his word in conference counted for something. "We often get tired ourselves, sir. Very tired."

John Marco did not reply immediately. The blood was hammering inside his head and his heart was pounding. They wanted to get rid of him for a time—that much was obvious. They had been plotting, and he would have to destroy their designs. But he would have to be careful: exceedingly careful. He had been drinking—a lot to drink in fact: the whiskey had disappeared from the decanter faster even than usual—and he could not afford to make any mistake just now. He got up and walked slowly over to the mantelpiece and set his shoulders against it.

"You were saying, Mr. Hackbridge, I believe," he replied, his voice deliberately kept level and under control, "that you find your work very tiring. I'm not surprised. It's usual to get a little tired if you work. But I can do nothing for you. If you find it's too much for you, you have your remedy, you know: you can resign." He turned slowly away from Mr. Hackbridge and addressed Mr. Lyman again. "And so can you, Mr. Lyman. If you wish to resign I shan't hinder you; there's only one person in this firm whom I regard as indispensable." He paused long enough for it to become apparent whom he meant, and then approached his desk again. "If that is all, gentlemen, I will say good-night. I have work to do."

He had taken up the ruler that lay on his desk and sat there gripping it after they had gone, staring across the width of the room in front of him. His hands were clasped so tightly round the ruler that the bones of the knuckles showed; the ruler itself was bent into a steep arc like a bow.

"I'll show them that they can't treat me like this," he said, speaking aloud to the empty room: this speaking aloud had now become a habit. "I'll show them their mistake. I'll make them sorry."

There was a report so loud and near that it made him jump, and the heavy ruler that he had been holding broke in two in his face. He threw the pieces into the basket beside him and reached out for the decanter again.

But his hand was trembling so much that the whiskey went spilling everywhere.

ii

"You're very quiet to-night, my dear," Louise said to him.

John Marco looked up at her as though her words had surprised him, as though he had not known that she was there. He shook his head.

"It's nothing," he answered. "Nothing at all."

The corners of his mouth twisted downwards again as he said it. Those three men whom he had raised up from street level to be directors of a great firm had been conspiring together to get rid of him; and he called it nothing. But it would be nothing, after he had done with them; they could have no picture as yet of the trouble they had brought down upon themselves, no hint at all of what was coming.

Louise had got up and crossed over to him. She sat herself down on the arm of his chair.

"Don't go and make yourself ill," she said.

"I'm not ill," he answered.

But did he look ill? he wondered. Could other people really see in his face what state his mind was inside him?

"Remember, you're not so young as you were," she went on; she was stroking the side of his face with her hand as she said it.

He shook her hand clear of him, however, and got up and moved away from her. His feet seemed to drag a little across the carpet as he walked.

"So you don't find me so young as you did," he said bitterly. "Is that what you came over to tell me?"

But Louise only laughed at him.

"You're young enough for me," she answered. "That's what I came over to say."

She was smiling and holding out her hand towards him again. From where he was standing he noticed how perfect she looked, how beautiful, and elegant. With that beauty and elegance belonging to him, it seemed foolish to quarrel with it. The lines in his face softened.

"Come over here," he said.

He put his arms round her and, as he breathed in the perfume that she was using, all his senses seemed to come alive again. Her body was soft and warm, and he could feel her hair against his cheek.

"You're worth everything," he said.

She closed her eyes for a moment.

"I'm so happy, my dear." She gave a little tremor as she spoke. "I almost thought you'd given up loving me in this kind of way."

"You did?"

"I often lie awake for you," she answered, "but you're always working."

"Not always," he said, putting his face down to hers again. "Not to-night."

Chapter XL

The night was still early when he left her. He drew the coverlet up round her shoulders so that she should not stir and
closed the door behind him softly. Then he went down to his
study and put on the lights. It was strange sitting down at his
desk when the rest of London was sleeping. But he had work to
do. He took out a piece of paper and began covering it with
figures—the same grim accusing figures that had been surrounding him at the shop: he knew them by heart by now and knew
what was wrong with them. He knew also how to put them right.
He heard three o'clock strike from St. Mary's clock and then
four; and still he went on working. Towards five o'clock his hand
had grown heavy on the paper and his eyes began to close.
Finally, he folded his arms on the desk and rested his head on it.
He slept.

Scarcely more than two hours afterwards he woke again,
woke suddenly and sat up. His back was rigid and his shoulders
ached. Inside his head the pulses were drumming and as he
straightened himself a cloud of blackness passed for a moment
in front of his eyes. But once he was on his feet again he was
wide-awake; wideawake and ready for the day that was in front

of him. At eight-thirty his carriage drew up in front of the shop and he went inside.

It was in this flushed, sleepless state, with his eyes still hot and burning inside his head, that he started his campaign of terror and economy. It was ruthless and unrelenting. There was not a department or an employee which escaped. By the time the campaign was over and the victims, both those who had been dismissed and those who remained, had recovered themselves, John Marco's name was one of the unprettiest and least esteemed in the cut-throat annals of retail shopkeeping.

It began with a conference. John Marco called the three plotters, the men who had betrayed him, into his office. He began speaking before the last of them had had time to sit down, and spoke rapidly in the manner of a man whose mind is ready set like a gun.

"We employ too many people," he said abruptly. "We must get rid of half of them."

"Half!" Mr. Hackbridge exclaimed in astonishment. "Half!"

"That's what I said," John Marco replied. "Half. And I shall leave it to you, Mr. Hackbridge, to arrange for the dismissals. It had better be the older ones who. go: we don't have to pay the young ones so much."

"But do you think we can carry on the business with half the staff? "Mr. Skewin asked in the slow, half apologetic way of his. "Don't you think it may be too much for them?"

"Then if it's too much they must go too," John Marco answered. "You must find people, Mr. Hackbridge, who are prepared to work a little harder."

"Quite so," said Mr. Lyman approvingly. "They're certainly very well paid."

"I was coming to that," John Marco interrupted. "They won't be so well paid in future. I want you to inform the staff, Mr. Hackbridge, that all salaries are being reduced. The larger salaries are being reduced most. I've got the scale here."

He passed over a sheet of paper covered with his handwriting as he said it.

"It'll be very discouraging," said Mr. Hackbridge bravely. "It'll make it all the more difficult to get the best out of them."

"I've told you before," John Marco answered, "that if they're not satisfactory they must be replaced."

"I quite approve," volunteered Mr. Lyman.

His voice as he said it seemed thinner and more knife-like than ever.

John Marco turned to him. He eyed him steadily for a moment and then addressed him very slowly.

"I'm glad you do, Mr. Lyman," he said. "Because this affects all of us. I'm proposing that directors' salaries should be cut by half."

There was silence after he had spoken and then Mr. Lyman replied for them all.

"I hardly think that the Board would agree to that," he said.

John Marco smiled; it was a cold, unhumorous smile that drew in the corners of his mouth and left the eyes steady and unchanged.

"The Board will have no alternative," he replied. "At the next General Meeting I myself will propose it. I do not imagine that any director who opposes it will be re-elected."

There was silence again.

"Are you proposing to halve your own salary, might I ask?" Mr. Lyman enquired.

He was leaning forward in his seat as he said it, his eyes,

behind their thick glasses, thrusting forward at his chairman.

The smile returned for a moment to John Marco's face.

He paused and defiantly poured himself out a drink under their very noses.

"I am," he said.

"And in the eyes of the shareholders," he went on, "it would be better for your future if you were to make your sacrifice ungrudgingly as Mr. Hackbridge and Mr. Skewin are doing. I had hoped you would second my proposal. Otherwise we may find ourselves without you." He paused again and sat back in his chair. "That is all, gentlemen," he said.

He did not add that all the previous night while these others who were now around him had been sleeping, he had been awake—very much awake in fact. He had been calculating carefully and exactly how many times his halved salary would come back to him as commission out of the profits which these murderous economies would bring.

But dismissing people—simply writing them off the firm's books as not wanted—is not so easy as it appears on paper. There are always some difficult ones who will not accept the pink slip in the weekly pay envelope, awkward natures, apparently bent on making trouble. The worst of these, some twenty or so, demanded interviews with John Marco; and he refused them. It was Mr. Hackbridge who had to see them all. And during the week of the cutting-down, he returned every night to his home in Hammersmith, with his soul loaded down with tears and petitions and confidences and recriminations and ugly scenes. He was not a young man any longer: he was fifty-nine. And the strain of it all had told on him. "He's wearing me down, and when I'm no good any more, he'll get rid of me," he kept on saying to himself. "I don't trust him." And on the Wednesday night when he woke with palpitations after a particularly unpleasant encounter with a man of his own age who protested that there was nothing for him but the workhouse, he lay there with the bed-clothes pulled up to his chin, and his heart fluttering about inside him like a dying bird, and cried out so loudly that Mrs. Hackbridge woke too and sat up with her hair all tangled and her cotton nightgown sliding untidily off one shoulder.

"He didn't ought to expect it of me. He's not a man, he's a wolf. Cutting me down to three-ten a week again: it's a bloody crime."

This cry in the night by a man who for the moment thought himself to be dying was the first that Mrs. Hack-bridge had heard of the alarming turn of things . . .

But next morning Mr. Hackbridge was back on duty again and they were all in John Marco's room once more. It was John Marco who was talking. And there was a kind of unnatural jocularity about him, a false heartiness that he seemed to be forcing out of himself. He was sitting in his chair with his cigar set jauntily in his mouth and his hands clasped together across his waistcoat.

"Well," he said, "can we now start doing some business again? Have we cleared out all the waste?"

Mr. Hackbridge pulled nervously at his tie.

"There are one or two special cases I'd like you to consider, sir," he said.

But John Marco waved him aside.

"I don't want to hear them," he said.

"There's real hardship," Mr. Hackbridge went on.

His own recent reduction had made him suddenly very

sensitive to the sufferings of others; the fact that his heart was going back on him and that in nine months' time he would be sixty kept rising up in his mind.

But John Marco apparently suffered no such misgivings.

"Of course there's hardship," he said. "There's bound to be hardship. You can't dismiss people without it."

He reached out his hand towards Mr. Hackbridge.

"Give me the salaries list," he said. "I want to look over it."

The three men were watching him closely as he took it. It was one of those moments when he seemed somehow to be removed and different from the rest of them; removed and different even from Mr. Lyman, who, too, seemed to suffer no misgivings about the dismissals. As John Marco sat there motionless, the smoke of his cigar rising above him in blue spirals, staring down at the ruled sheets in front of him where every other name was struck through in red he seemed not like a fellow human being at all but like some robust heathen idol gloating over the day's sacrifices.

Then he looked up, and there was a smooth, ingratiating smile upon his face.

"This is more like it," he said. "This must be right: it comes to exactly what I wanted it."

The smile, however, had vanished as instantly as it had come. There was a name that had caught his eye, caught it, and held it there.

"There's one mistake," he said. "I don't want you to cut Mrs. Petter's salary. Leave it just as it was."

Mr. Lyman leaned forward.

"Don't you think it may cause disaffection if one person is specially singled out?" he asked.

"They won't know about it," John Marco replied. "Mrs. Petter won't talk. She's not a fool. Besides, I wish it."

There was a finality about his voice that dissuaded the others from questioning him further. And John Marco was already engrossed in those sheets of names and salaries again; he was scanning the columns anxiously for one other name which he could not remember. And as he ran his finger down them, he saw not names and figures any longer but a bedroom with dawn breaking into it and the figure of a girl lying sleeping with her hair spread around her head like a soft dark fan. "I'll keep my word to her," he was saying inside his mind. "Nothing shall prevent that."

And when his eye alighted on the name that he had been searching for his face lit up again.

"There's one other that I don't wish you to reduce," he said. "You may keep this salary as it is."

He marked the name with a cross and handed the paper back to Mr. Hackbridge. Then he surveyed his brother directors with a kind of half smile upon his face.

"Has anyone got any remarks to make?" he asked.

He was looking full at Mr. Lyman as he spoke.

But Mr. Lyman was silent. It was Mr. Skewin who answered.

"There's just one thing I wondered," Mr. Skewin began in his pleading, flattened voice that echoed defeat in every syllable. "It's my nephew. I wonder if you could make an exception there."

"Why should I?" John Marco asked.

"He's a very reliable young man," Mr. Skewin assured him. "Very reliable indeed."

Mr. Skewin had removed the list from Mr. Hackbridge's hand and set his finger against the name of his nephew.

"That's him," he said proudly.

John Marco took the paper impatiently. Then he re-creased it and handed it back again.

"He may be very reliable, Mr. Skewin," he said. "But he's also very expensive. I'm afraid that I cannot allow the company to spend over sixty pounds a year on a man simply because he's a nephew of one of the directors."

He sat back and lit his cigar again. The meeting of the directors was over.

Chapter XLI

Because of the way in which he had cut his own salary, dividing it clean through the middle in a gesture which was to be admired by the shareholders, and because of the way in which Louise was finding it difficult to keep inside the allowance that they had agreed on, John Marco discovered himself to be acutely short of money as this awkward, unfriendly year proceeded.

It was not the kind of sudden poverty, in which maids are given notice, unnecessary rooms are closed up and frantic economies are effected downstairs in the kitchen. On the contrary, it was the much more dangerous kind in which everything goes on exactly as before and champagne is still drunk at dinner-parties and there are lilies in the drawing-room as before, and each month brings in its own little cascade of old, unreceipted bills.

By June, John Marco recognised that he would have to do something about it. He had thought at first that the bank, when he put it to them, would be ready to accommodate him a little further. But the manager had been hesitant and difficult. He made it clear that for his part John Marco was welcome to the entire reserves of the company; but he drew a picture of the inspectors of the bank as a race of men dedicated to hounding down branch managers who showed any tendency to be open-handed. In short he refused; and John Marco with nearly three thousand pounds worth of debts on his shoulders had simply to smile back at him and say something about supposing that he would have to sell some securities or lodge a few bonds. Then, setting his top hat a little sideways upon his head and toying with the flower in his buttonhole, he had walked grandly out past the cash-counters to his black and yellow carriage that was waiting outside. But there were, of course, no bonds or securities. They had all gone on that fine house of his; and now that was mortgaged, too. It was so thoroughly mortgaged in fact that there was not another penny to be squeezed out of it.

John Marco now spent whole evenings pacing up and down his study not thinking of the business but of himself; half London seemed to be his creditor and the money would have to come from somewhere. "I've got to play for time," he kept repeating to himself. "I've got to play for time." And then with a sudden lightening of the load that was on him he remembered the costly furniture which Louise had chosen, the suites and pieces which the dealers had purred over and had seemed reluctant to part with; and he decided that he would raise money on these too. He would make them, as it were, lend him temporarily some of the gold that he had invested in them.

This mortgage, however, was more difficult to arrange than the one on the house had been. He did not go to his solicitors this time, but paid visits himself to shady little firms of auctioneers in back streets. The details were complicated by the fact that Louise was to know nothing of it, just as she knew nothing about the mortgage on the house. This meant that the inventory had to be taken when she was away from home. And one fine Saturday, as she sat beside John Marco in the carriage and was driven down to Richmond, the little man whom John Marco had sent for was going from room to room, sizing up the furniture, casting his eyes over the silver, fingering the fabric of the curtains. It was all over by the time Louise returned—the maids did not mention the visit; John Marco had forbidden it—and a week later the papers were signed and John Marco was richer by eight hundred pounds.

It was not a great deal of money; but, on the other hand, John Marco told himself it had not got a great time to last. The golden year that was before the company had only another six months to run and then the mortgages and the debts would vanish like dew in the sunlight. As soon as the miraculous economy inside the store had been vouchsafed to the shareholders and there was a dividend again, he would be a rich man once more and able to sit again at a fireside that was really his. In the meantime, it gave him a kind of subtle pleasure, a feeling of victory over Mr. Lyman and the others, to let them see him still enjoying the fullness of life while they themselves were eking out and paring.

But perhaps because he was working too hard, because he was cheating himself out of sleep and drinking heavily because his body needed it, those stray moments of panic kept returning to him. He would be sitting late in his study after Louise had gone to bed and would remember suddenly that the house around him and even the chair that he was sitting on were no longer his: that he had thrown his dice into the future and must wait to see how they would fall.

At those moments he would reach out more urgently than ever for the decanter that was always beside him, and take a deep drink and sit back and tell himself that everything would be all right, and that only time was needed.

But the sense of strain was with him all the time, the

consciousness of having to wait for those six months to consume themselves. He became too restless to remain indoors, and sometimes in the evenings he would make vague, transparent excuses to Louise and wander off through the streets by himself, trying to solve the riddles that his mind was full of. Louise did not attempt to stop him. There were generally enough people in the house to amuse her, and the rooms would be full of laughter and the sound of talk while the host who might have been there in the midst of it all was walking in the night by himself, sometimes pausing at a corner because one way meant no more than another in his present mood; sometimes repeating out loud little sentences that came into his head and would not be banished; always telling himself that it is the courageous gambler who wins the largest stakes.

It was on one of these melancholy perambulations that he found himself in Chapel Walk again. The small, squat houses stretched in front of him in shabby double-row and, at the end, the Tabernacle loomed vast and black like a Roman ruin. The street oppressed him, it was too full of memories, and he began to walk faster. As he passed the house where he had been brought up he looked away from it: it seemed somehow by the alchemy of time to have been transmuted into something that was too happy even to be gazed upon, this inferior little villa with the stairs leading straight off the living room. He set his head lower and hurried on. But as he drew near to the Tabernacle itself his curiosity overcame him. It was nearly ten years now since he had been inside it, and a sudden longing to see those sweeping ranks of pews again, to hurt himself deliberately by looking once more on something that was part, so big a part, of his boyhood, took possession of him. Glancing over his shoulder to see if he were observed he began to mount the familiar flight of steps beneath the teeming notice boards. "GOD REJOICETH OVER THE LOST LAMB," one of the placards proclaimed above him.

It was as he pushed open the green baize door inside that he heard the organ and realised that there was some kind of service going on. He became cautious and slid into one of the back benches behind a pillar. But the congregation was on its knees praying and his entrance seemed to have excited no comment from anyone; he was one more unnoticed soul among hundreds.

He looked around him and noticed that in places the plaster was peeling from the walls and that the organ needed regilding. The only other people beside him in the pew were an elderly man and a thin, depressed-looking woman. He did not know them; and he remembered that Mary had said that the faces were different now and that the whole place seemed altered.

But there was one thing that remained: constant and unchangeable: the voice of Mr. Tuke. He could hear it raised above everything, leading the devout like a trumpet. "O God of mercy and infinite pity," it was saying, "spare thou the wicked who repent. Grant that through Thy Son the evil may be washed clean again. Give them strength in their hearts to confess their sins. Let them declare their evils and be saved."

Then the praying ceased and the congregation got back onto their wooden seats again. John Marco could see Mr. Tuke by now. He had marched onto the front of the platform, ready to lead them in a hymn. His right arm was already beginning to beat time with the organ.

Sweep on avenging sword
Whose chastisement is death.
Subdue with steely breath
The traitors to the Lord.

The whole congregation all began singing, but John Marco did not listen. There had been a time when he had joined in these warlike hymns himself, but those days had gone; the words of terror had no meaning for him now.

He did not listen again until Mr. Tuke mounted the pulpit to deliver his short, evening address. It was not a sermon (the hour was too late for that) and Mr. Tuke kept all his talents hidden. He appealed gently, hopelessly, it seemed, for more forgiveness and an unhardening of hearts. It was simple, like the tired, forlorn advice of an old man. And John Marco realised suddenly that Mr. Tuke *was* an old man, that he was no longer young himself, and that the Tabernacle was older than either of them. And then somehow Mr. Tuke's words became lost to him and he remembered only a young man, someone crushed but not yet utterly broken, who had thrown a kiss from the gallery down to a bride who had been passing underneath.

Mr. Tuke descended the steps of the pulpit again and stood ready to conduct the last hymn that closed everything. The organ threw out a quavering reminiscent chord and John Marco found the words astonishingly flowing back into his mind. They were naïve, foolish lines, but they came charged with childhood and the memory of things. They weren't ordinary words at all, they were scenes from the past, his past, that had escaped somehow into the present and were being sung by other people.

The prayers that I learnt at my fond mother's knee,
Their echoes still linger, they still comfort me.
The things that she taught me, the words that she said,
Are a cloak in the tempest, a tent o'er my head.

He looked at Mr. Tuke's face as he stood there in front of them all, singing. The expression of the priest militant had now vanished; his eyes were closed and he had folded his hands on his stomach. His whole face seemed to have slipped into a gentle, unconcerned repose not far removed from sleep.

Another verse of the hymn was just beginning:

> *As a child I was sinless and happy and free*
> *Till life's snares and perils encompassèd me.*

But John Marco had slipped out of the pew and was making quietly for the door. In a moment, while the last verse was proceeding, Mr. Tuke would be walking down from the aisle, still singing, ready to shake hands with his flock as they filed out through the porch. That was something that John Marco could not wait for; he was gone before Mr. Tuke had even moved.

And as he went on down the street, reluctant still to go back to the house where Louise's friends would be seated about in the drawing-room and everything would be so gay and bright and noisy he found himself almost envying Mr. Tuke his crumbling Tabernacle and the silly, sleepy hymns that people still sang there.

But there were other occasions, dark sinister ones that did not bear looking back on, when these evening wanderings did not always end in so seemly, so innocent a fashion. When he had drunk too much already before he left the house, he would often drink more as soon as he was outside, pushing open one gilt-and-frosted saloon door after another. And a moment would come on these evenings when suddenly the fire in the liquor would be released inside him and he would laugh at all his stupid fears and feel the earth beneath his feet again and grow reckless. At such times he became his own victim, drifting helplessly into company that sober men would have shunned, mixing easily and on common terms with the night-time population that frequent the streets.

"It won't always be like this," he would tell himself as he made his way back stumblingly to the magnificence of the square he lived in. "Once this year is over, once I *know* that everything is all right, I shall settle down again, Louise and I will take a holiday together, a long holiday, the kind of holiday that Mr. Lyman was talking about. Then I shall feel easier in my mind again. I shall stop drinking."

And a week later would find him making the same resolve with the same fixed intention as he turned unsteadily up the broad sweep of Sussex Gardens and searched out the way towards his house.

He had been drinking heavily one evening, squandering the spirits upon himself, when he resolved abruptly to have no more of it. Through the first mists of alcohol that had begun mercifully to cloud across his brain, the old panic, the urgent alarm that things were getting out of his control at the shop and that he was needed there to look after them, came back to him. He pulled out his watch and sat staring at it for a moment, his mind unable to register the hour that it showed. Then shifting himself awkwardly to his feet he quitted the saloon where he had been sitting and began to blunder through the lamp-lit streets towards the shop. The air on his face was cool; it blew soothingly. But it seemed only to increase the headiness of the drink that he had taken, and once or twice he swayed and had to raise his hand as if he were about to fall.

But the shop had no use for him at that time of night. It turned a blank face to him, black and forbidding; and he lacked the courage to ring for the night-watchman to let him in. The large building with its unlighted windows seemed some sort of tomb, a monument erected to things long dead. He would be back there soon enough—the morning could be only seven or eight hours away—by the time it had come to life again; and until then its stones would have to content themselves without him. He turned and began to walk slowly away.

He had walked for perhaps a hundred yards when his eyes suddenly caught his own name shining in the darkness in front of him. The letters, scrolled elaborate things, were etched across a brass plate on a door that caught the light of a solitary street lamp. He paused. This was something else of his, the hostel where the young ladies lived, some forty of them. He had never been inside the place; it was a chaste and separate harem ruled over by a grey-haired housekeeper of Mr. Hackbridge's appointment. And then as he stood there he remembered that it was to this doorway that he had first showed Eve Harlow home; it was from this cheap dormitory that he had sought to take her and give her everything in life that could have made her happy. Why hadn't he taken her? he asked himself. What was it that had prevented him when she at last had been so willing and so precious? But his mind was dim and indistinct to-night, and the mystery of the tragedy remained unsolved. He passed his hand across his forehead and to steady himself he rested his shoulder against the pillar of the door.

Then the idea came to him that he would see inside the place, would find out what kind of dwelling it was that Eve Harlow had known before he had cherished her. For a second he hesitated: it was late and the young ladies would be asleep refreshing themselves for their long hours of standing to attention on the morrow. But it was *his*, all *his*, he told himself; if he wanted to go inside he had only to give the order to the caretaker. Raising his hand, he set the bell pealing and waited impatiently for the man to answer.

The caretaker was clearly surprised to see him; surprised but respectful. He touched his forelock when he saw who it was and, when he heard that John Marco wanted to come in, he stepped aside and held the door politely back. He made a strange, dishevelled figure in his flannel nightgown tucked clumsily down into the top of his trousers, and John Marco threw back his head and laughed at him. He was still laughing as he crossed the hall and began to stumble up the high staircase.

The caretaker followed wonderingly, padding up the stairs in his felt slippers. Should he call the lady housekeeper? he asked.

But John Marco shook his head.

"Tour of inspection," he said in a low, slurred voice. "Making sure that everything's in order. No need to disturb anybody."

There were two doors opening out from the landing in front of him. John Marco hesitated and then walked awkwardly towards the further one. It was the voice of the caretaker behind him that stopped him suddenly and made him turn.

"Not in there, sir." The man said in horror. "That's where the young ladies sleep."

John Marco turned his back on him.

"That's what I want to see," he said over his shoulder. "That's what I came here to see."

He threw the door open and peered inside. It was a long room with a narrow aisle down the centre between a double row of curtains; at the far end a lamp, turned so low that it was a glow merely, was hanging.

"So this is the kind of life she knew," he said, speaking aloud to himself. "This is what she came back to when she left me."

And for no reason he began to laugh again.

The caretaker came nearer and dropped his voice.

"You'll wake them, sir," he said. "There's ten of them in here."

"Go away," John Marco told him. "Go back and mind the door. I shan't wake anyone."

He tiptoed forward as he said it and stood for a moment waiting. It was strange standing there in that quiet, polished room with only the sound of breathing, the heavy, regular breathing of sleep, in the air. Then he raised his hand and slid one of the curtains back along its runners. Within, he could see the faint outline of a bed, a chair and a long cupboard.

"Like a cell," he thought. "Like a nun's bloody cell."

But there was a movement from the bed. The sleeper stirred and then raised herself suddenly on one elbow. At the sight of the heavy form standing there, blotting out what small glimmer the lamp provided, she screamed.

John Marco did not remember how long after the scream he stood there. He recalled only that all round him behind those curtains there were sudden frightened movements; and the atmosphere of sleep was shattered. Then there were hands, strong angry hands, that seized him and dragged him out back onto the landing again. But they were not the hands of the caretaker, because he remained over by the door. They belonged instead to the grey-haired woman whose dressing-gown was belted across her like a uniform.

"Not while I'm in charge here you don't," she was saying. "You try and get at my girls again and I'll send for the police."

John Marco was silent for a moment and then he laughed again.

"Do you imagine," he said, "that I came here to do mischief?

Do you think that I wanted to ravish all forty of them?"

And leaning against the top column of the balustrade he went on laughing, louder this time; laughed until the whole staircase echoed with it and doors on the other landings began to open as well.

"He's drunk," he heard the woman saying. "We must fetch a cab. None of the girls must know that it was Mr. Marco."

Chapter XLII

But of course the girls knew soon enough; everyone in the shop knew in fact. The incident, discreditable as it was, was enlarged upon and distorted. John Marco, the rumour went, had entered the ladies' hostel, had attempted to abduct one of their number forcibly and had finally been ejected after a terrible scene of violence. The police, rumour had it, had been called: John Marco had been arrested, and had been released again.

Mr. Lyman and Mr. Hackbridge took careful notes of the whole affair; and they compared them. In the end there was nothing that they did not know about it. They interviewed the lady-housekeeper and the door-keeper, and they sent for the girl into whose cubicle John Marco had intruded. Her part of the story was slight and unconvincing at the start; she was diffident and nervous. But under cross-examination she improved. As she went on she recalled that it was not until he was actually beside her bed that she had wakened and as she had started up she had felt his hand upon her shoulder pressing her down, his reeking breath upon her cheek. Put that way it was a pretty horrifying indictment, and Mr. Lyman and Mr. Hackbridge pored over it together.

"It can't go on," said Mr. Hackbridge lugubriously when the girl had gone. "He's riding for a fall. He ought to be warned."

But Mr. Lyman only shook his head.

"It suits us better that things should go on exactly as they are," he said. "Just exactly as they are."

And all through the autumn, almost as though unconsciously obeying Mr. Lyman, John Marco continued with his drinking. Under the influence of it he grew steadily more despotic and unapproachable; nowadays even tiny differences of opinion, put forward hesitatingly and with due politeness, produced rages that silenced all opposition. They left him a lonely, isolated figure, surrounded by men who hated and were afraid of him. The fear had always been there; there had never been an assistant in the place who would have answered him back to his face. But it was the hatred that was something new. So long as the weekly pay envelope had not been tampered with, the assistants had quaked and been contented. But men with families who have been earning three pounds ten a week and then find themselves reduced to thirty-five shillings are not of the stuff that loyal bodyguards are made. And there was not an employee in the store who would not have walked out and gone round to the Bon Marché for an extra half-a-crown a week if only the Bon Marché had offered it.

There was, too, another effect that the drinking was having on him: he was growing careless and untidy in his dress, slovenly even. His cravats were no longer the perfectly tied things they had once been; they hung round his neck nowadays, and there were stains and spots on the front of them. During the last year or so he had come to stoop a little and his clothes, his expensively cut clothes, hung from him awkwardly. As he usually wore his coat unbuttoned, he seemed at times to be shambling along like

544

a man older than his years.

But in his own mind, he was, in fact, a little easier: he saw the position improving itself every day in front of his own eyes. The figures that Mr. Lyman brought to him showed entries in solid, reassuring black where there had been red before. And he knew that thanks to those endless unsleeping nights spent pacing up and down his study, thanks to his cleverness and sagacity and his courage in putting a knife through everyone's salary including his own, John Marco Ltd. was now turning up on the right side again.

It was only the matter of ready money in his pocket that still troubled him. The eight hundred pounds that the little auctioneer had given him was almost exhausted; some of it had gone to pay the interest on the mortgage on the house, and some of it, of course, had gone back into the pockets of the little auctioneer himself. But it was November already and John Marco could see daylight breaking on the road ahead of him. And simply to ensure that he could go down the road decently and in style until the dawn was really there, he decided that he must raise some more money somehow.

This time there were only money-lenders to turn to. He found them in their hidden offices in dark courtyards and dubious alley ways. He bargained with them, matching his skill at figures against theirs, and he signed his name to pieces of paper that gave him what he wanted. "It's only for three months or perhaps four," he said to himself, "then I can tear up those documents in their faces. I can scatter the pieces over them." And in the meantime, it was pleasant enough to feel his wallet bulging inside his coat again, to draw from his pocket a crackling, watermarked fiver with all the gold in the Bank of England behind it when he went to pay for something.

And when the Christmas trade was really upon them—it was a good shopping Christmas this year—and he saw the assistants breaking themselves in their efforts to serve the customers who were massed along the counters, he stood on his high balcony looking down on it all, and laughed to think of the despair that he had struggled through. Even when two of the young ladies who had been on their feet since nine o'clock in the morning fainted as seven o'clock came round—the shop remained open an hour later as Christmas approached—John Marco did not reproach himself when Mr. Hackbridge told him.

"Young girls often faint," he said. "It's their nature. I only hope that they didn't upset the customers."

And he waved Mr. Hackbridge aside and poured himself out a drink and went on adding and re-adding those sheets of golden figures that the counting house kept sending down to him.

But the tiredness, the sense of driving the machine that was himself harder than any machine ever should be driven, continued; his hand was unsteady as he opened his letters in the mornings and there were times as he sat quietly in his chair when his heart without warning would start pounding angrily as if he had been running, and he would begin gasping as if his breath were imprisoned inside him. After these attacks—and they lasted sometimes for minutes on end—his face would go ashen and he would feel the sweat breaking out along his forehead. But there was no one else in the room to see. And as soon as he could breathe again he would turn back to his desk and go on working.

The climax, the moment when his heart without warning refused altogether for the time being to work for him, came one night as he was at dinner with Louise. It was nearly nine o'clock before the meal had started, and they were alone. John Marco had not changed his clothes: he was still wearing the frock coat that he had worn all day at the shop. It was a handsome, well-cut garment and only the facing which had worn a little shiny on the lapels showed that it was not altogether new. But there was a flower in the button-hole and the shoulders were full and rounded with the weight of man inside them.

"He looks important," Louise thought. "Someone that you would notice in a crowd."

And then as she was watching him, he suddenly did not look important any longer. She saw him pull at his collar and falter for an instant as though someone had spoken to him; and then, quite slowly, he folded forward onto the table, his arms sprawling, and his head down on the cloth across which the purple stain of the wine from the overturned glass was spreading. And before either Louise or the maid who was waiting on them could reach him, he had slid off his chair and collapsed on the floor, lying there on his back with one hand tugging at his collar. Only it was a limp, clammy hand that fell away aimlessly as they moved him.

By the time the doctor had arrived, they had carried John Marco upstairs and laid him along the wide couch in the drawing-room.

The house now had the deep hush of disaster hanging over it. The maids were going about on tiptoe and the doctor's heavy tread on the stairs seemed callous and unthinking. The doctor himself was slow and unconcerned, like a man who expects death to wait for him; he opened his bag as unhurriedly as a pedlar. And all this time, John Marco, with his collar pulled open and his neck swollen and suffused, was lying with his head on one of the ivory silk cushions and his legs in their striped trousers lounging across the upholstery. He was breathing ponderously, as if the air around him were drowning him.

Then the doctor bent down and applied his stethoscope. He was on his knees beside the unconscious man for nearly five minutes. When he got to his feet again he was grave and silent like the rest of them.

"He must have rest," he said. "Absolute rest. He's been killing himself."

"Is he in danger?" Louise asked him.

The doctor shrugged his shoulders.

"Yes, if he goes on drinking," he said quietly.

It was nearly midnight when John Marco awoke. He was in his bed by then and there was a nurse standing by him. She was mixing something coloured in a glass. For a moment he lay there, the pieces of his mind grating against each other, and then he sat up on his elbow, staring in front of him.

"What's the matter," he asked. "What's happened to me?"

Out of the shadows by the fireplace Louise appeared.

"You're ill, my dear," she said. "You're not to worry." She forced his shoulders back down onto the pillow and began stroking his forehead. And because he had no strength in him he obeyed her, lying back staring up emptily at the ceiling.

"You'll be in bed a long time," she remarked quietly. "You've got to rest."

To rest! She was right, how right she was she would never guess. It had been more than one man could do to build up that business out of nothing; and then, because the seasons and the fashions had been difficult, to break it all up again and start building it anew. It was something that no one else could ever have done; and Louise in the security of that fine house of theirs had never known what he had suffered. But he had succeeded, too. The shop was minting its own gold again; Mr. Lyman's ledgers

548

were full of it. He could afford to rest for a while in the half light of this bedroom with only the soft voice of Louise to tell him things.

But these dreams disappeared abruptly, and his mind became clear again. He remembered that Mr. Lyman and Mr. Hackbridge were plotting against him, that the house wasn't his really, that he had given his signature on notes to men whom he should never in his senses have trusted, and that the very bed that he was lying on belonged to a shabby little auctioneer who had visited the house one day when he had taken Louise out driving.

He sat up on his elbow again and pointed at the nurse with a hand that was shaking and unsteady.

"Send her away," he said. "I don't need her. I shall be getting up. I shall be back at the shop to-morrow. I've got to be there. Got to be there, I tell you."

And next morning, at his usual time, his face greyer than ever and his collar turned up high round his cheeks, he was climbing out of his carriage in Tredegar Terrace. Louise was with him: she had insisted on coming. And he leant heavily on her arm as he went inside.

Mr. Hackbridge was there and bowed politely to both of them. When they had passed him, however, he stood looking after them, and nodded his head slowly, pursing his lips as he did so.

"He must have had a wet night," he said to himself knowingly. "A very wet one."

ii

It was after Christmas now; the battle between the thin ranks of the assistants and the massed hordes of West London was over

549

and won, and the merciful armistice of Boxing Day, when all the girls were able at last to rest their feet, had intervened. After Christmas; and the doctor had been proved wrong. That was the delicious irony of it. Louise had told John Marco what the doctor had said, and he had laughed at it. But, at the time, he had laughed a little diffidently as though fearing that somehow his heart and the doctor might be in league together. It was only now that he could afford to open his mouth really wide and say what a fool the man was, what fools all doctors always were. It was only now that he could raise his glass to his lips again without expecting to be struck down as a punishment. And he needed the stuff more than ever he had done; it was the mainspring that kept him going.

During those five weeks when he ought to have been dead, he had spent ten hours a day at the shop; he had lived there. And now, instead of getting himself ready for the mutes and the lilies, he was preparing for the January Sales, getting the pieces in shape for something that would shake the plate glass palaces of Oxford Street.

Of that last attack which had so nearly done away with him, only a kind of treacherous weakness still remained. When a new plan came to him, and his head was still full of them—there was now a reluctance inside his brain, a sort of drowsiness that did not want to be disturbed. It was as though one part of his mind was protecting his life from the rest of him. But this did not make him spare other people. "Let *them* get tired," he said. "Let *them* see what it's like to fall asleep at their desks and wake themselves up again and still go on working." And so poor Mr. Hackbridge and the uncomplaining Mr. Skewin were kept on the run like page-boys, and Mr. Lyman was everlastingly being given new sets of figures to prepare, ingenious fresh sums that all added up to the brave new total.

It was into this world of pressure and urgency, this frantic, rushed world of profits and competition, that Hesther suddenly appeared again. He no longer even thought about her; and each time when his son had presented himself—he came obediently like an overgrown schoolboy accustomed to authority: it was a tribute to her faith in him that Hesther now allowed him to come alone—they had not spoken of her. On these occasions, John Marco had been curt with the youth: he had wanted to get him out of his sight again. It was hard to find anything admirable in this shy young man who wore heavy boots and the round collar of an Amosite deacon. In him, he had seen the last of his dreams dissolving; had known that, after he was gone, there would be someone else, a stranger, giving the orders in John Marco Ltd.; had realised that his name on the shop-front would one day be all that was left of him.

It was the first day of the January Sales and the gangways of the store were crowded like sheep pens, when Hesther came into the shop. John Marco had gone out onto his balcony a dozen times that afternoon, and each time he had returned satisfied. Below him, as he had looked, he had been able to see nothing but the shifting sea of ladies' hats, with the bald head of Mr. Hackbridge appearing in the midst of it like a floating iceberg. And because the weariness that he had been fighting was creeping over him again, he drained the last glass out of the decanter and put on his hat and coat ready to leave.

It was only when he stepped out onto the balcony again and saw the bright, blurred lights of the chandeliers above his head, and felt his feet unsteady beneath him as he moved, that he acknowledged to himself how much he must have drunk. But it was six o'clock already and his day was over. He could afford now to have things a little blurred and unsteady until to-morrow morning. And he went down the curving staircase slowly and carefully, keeping close to the balustrade. All round him there rose the drone and vibration of the great shop in action; it seemed the very hum of life itself.

Down on the ground floor he had to push and jostle with the shoppers that crowded in on him. He was one of them now, caught up in this mob that he had enticed there. It was hot, very hot, down here; and his head was swimming. His thoughts came to him, indiscriminate and confused. But there was one central thread running right through them. "We're making money, coining it," he kept repeating; "We're bankers, not drapers. Everything around me is turning into gold." And for a moment his tiredness vanished, and only the exhilaration of success remained.

Then through a gap in the crowd he saw the tall, black figure of Hesther. She seemed busy and preoccupied, moving about among the other shoppers as though oblivious to them. In her hand she was carrying a sheaf of tracts.

He stood still, his eyes kept close on her unable at first to bring his mind full circle properly to comprehend what he saw. "She is nothing of mine," he told himself; "this woman does not belong to me. She is out of the shadows, out of the past. My life is the bright, glittering one of the shop that is all around her. Why does she still come here? Can't she see that our ways are divided?"

And as he watched her he saw her go over to one of the assistants and hand her one of the tracts. The assistant took it politely, and then smiled. John Marco could see the words on it. Printed in heavy type as though to terrify the indifferent was the message "REPENT YE, THE LORD": the rest of the admonition was lost in a fold of the paper.

John Marco watched Hesther move away in search of other souls to save, and went over to the girl. He took the piece of paper away from her, and threw it angrily onto the floor.

"Get on with your work," he said.

His hands were trembling by now and there was a red mist in front of his eyes. It was his shop, his sale, his life in fact; and Hesther had suddenly broken into the midst of it all, destroying everything. His heart was pounding and the vein in his temple was standing out as he made his way through the crowd to stop her.

And then as he reached her, Hesther paused and saw him. Her face lit up with a new exaltation at the sight.

"Sinner," she said. "Read the Lord's warning. Take heed before it is too late."

And she thrust one of the printed handbills at him.

He crumpled it up and threw it down on the floor as he had thrown down the other one.

"Get back outside into the street," he said. "Don't bring this rubbish here."

His voice was louder than he had intended, and he saw several of the shoppers pause and look in their direction.

But Hesther's voice was raised louder than his: it was now full and carrying like Mr. Tuke's.

"The Lord's word can never be rubbish," she answered. "It is written in blood for man's salvation."

A crowd, a separate crowd from that at the counters began to form round them by now: Hesther and John Marco were the centre of a group of silly, frightened women who could only open their eyes and stare.

"Get outside," John Marco repeated.

He had dropped his voice by now, and was speaking through

teeth that were almost closed.

"Not until I have delivered the message," Hesther replied defiantly. "Not until the Lord's work is done."

It was Mr. Hackbridge who, seeing the unusual obstruction in the middle of one of the main thoroughfares of the shop, stepped forward. When he saw Mr. Marco and the black figure of Hesther he stopped. But John Marco called him forward. His face was flushed and he was breathing heavily.

"Remove this woman," he said. "Put her outside."

Mr. Hackbridge was very tactful about it. He laid his hand on Hesther's arm without even allowing his fingers to close round it. The whole gesture was delicate and considerate: it was as though he were trying to brush the whole incident aside without offending anyone.

"This way, please," he said.

But Hesther did not move. She turned towards John Marco again.

"You're my husband," she said. "I have a right to stay. I demand in God's name that I remain; I am needed. This whole shop is tainted."

The red mist in front of John Marco's eyes thickened: in the centre of it he saw Hesther's face, the lips drawn back from the large white teeth like a man's. He forgot Mr. Hackbridge and the circle of Bayswater ladies, forgot about the shop and the sale and everything, and struck at the face in front of him; struck and struck again.

He remembered the rest of the scene only dimly. There was Mr. Hackbridge's shocked voice saying, "Take it easy, sir, take it easy"; there was the harsh rustle of Hesther's dress as she fell and the screams of the ladies who were standing near; there was the pain in his knuckles where he had struck. And then he was blundering forward, pushing the other people aside, trying to make his way towards the door, trying to get away somewhere among strangers who would not know what had happened.

Chapter XLIII

The day had come. They were all seated round the long board room table with John Marco at their head. He was wearing an orchid, a gaudy fleshy affair, in his buttonhole, and his silk cravat was new and gorgeous-looking. Altogether, there was something of the old magnificence about him, the same sense of fullness and well-being. His face over the high points of his collar had lost some of its greyness and only the heavy pockets under his eyes, the loose pouches where the skin hung limply, remained. His head was cocked on one side in the manner of someone who knows that all the cards, and the joker too perhaps, are in his hand. He alone knew how tired he was.

It was an unusually full board meeting; the whole eight of them, including the solemn, silver-haired nominee of the bank, had assembled. John Marco sat back and smiled on them. It was his day, the day on which they were going to announce a dividend again—ten per cent if they wanted it—and so wipe out the shame and the disgrace of the preceding years. His soul ran over at the thought of it and, as he sat there, he felt as Joshua must have felt when he had brought them dry-footed over Jordan. Besides, he had his own little surprise to spring on them; it was something that he was saving up until the rest of the business of the meeting had been completed, something that would make every man around him sit up pretty straight when he heard it.

But Mr. Lyman in that thin, skeleton voice of his was already reading the minutes of the last board meeting; and everyone, especially those directors who were not usually present, was sitting very upright on his chair, listening with a fixed, polite attention. John Marco was the only one who was not listening. He was sitting back with his hands tucked into the armholes of his waistcoat, waiting impatiently for Mr. Lyman to stop. The minutes which Mr. Lyman was reading were mostly concerned with the sacrifices of the directors in halving their salaries, and now John Marco was proposing to restore them again. He had taught Mr. Lyman and Mr. Hackbridge their lesson, and he could afford to be generous once more. In a way he now felt rather sorry for them.

His speech from the chair was a deliberately fulsome, over-generous affair; it was intended very largely for the ears of the bank's nominee to show what a happy, united family they were. John Marco spoke of Mr. Hackbridge's efforts and of Mr. Lyman's as the kind of things that go down in the hagiology of commercial history, and he explained why he was so anxious to see that they should be adequately rewarded. It was just after he had referred to Mr. Lyman, as "my brilliant colleague to whom I am always pleased to turn for advice and guidance," that he glanced for a moment in Mr. Lyman's direction. But Mr. Lyman was looking down unswervingly at the pad before him; it was as though he had not heard the words that John Marco had just uttered. And even Mr. Hack-bridge seemed embarrassed rather than pleased by the tributes to himself. He shifted uncomfortably in his chair every time John Marco referred to him.

557

John Marco left the discussion of the dividend for a moment and led straight on to the little surprise that he had been storing-up for them.

"My own contract comes up for renewal this year," he said blandly, "and it will be for you gentlemen to vote upon it. If it is your pleasure that I should continue to manage the company that I founded"—here John Marco paused and smiled conde-scendingly upon them all—"I shall endeavour to serve your interests and those of the shareholders as faithfully as I have served them in the past. Only there is one condition that I shall have to make. As a result of certain economies which have been made we are about to enter a new period of prosperity. And as there will be money to spare again I'm afraid that the company may find me a little more expensive than it has done in the past. In fact, quite a bit more expensive. In view of the services which I have rendered I feel justified in asking for twenty per cent of the profits instead of only ten."

He paused again, and regarded them humorously.

"Well, gentlemen," he said, "let us dispose of this motion so that we can get on with other business. Perhaps Mr. Lyman will propose and Mr. Hackbridge will second it."

He sat down again; and, as he did so, the weakness that had been in the background all the time crept over him: he had exhausted himself more than he had realised. There was no strength left anywhere in him; even his heart was pounding. He closed his eyes for a moment and held his hand over them.

And as he did so he heard the pale voice of Mr. Lyman say very slowly and distinctly: "I regret that I have to oppose the motion."

John Marco did not even trouble to look at him.

"So *you* think that twenty per cent is too much, do you?" he asked. "You don't think I earn it."

His voice, though quiet, was dangerous.

But Mr. Lyman only shook his head.

"I mean that I oppose the re-election of Mr. Marco," he replied to the room at large.

There was scarcely any pause at all before Mr. Hack-bridge's thicker, clumsier voice, which faltered a little as he spoke, joined in.

"I second that motion," he said.

The two speeches came out glib and pat, like a lesson that had been carefully learnt and practised beforehand.

The board meeting had become hushed now. There were simply eight silent figures sitting there. John Marco himself had not moved. His hand was still over his eyes, but the blackness that was suddenly before them was darker than any shadow that his hand could give. He felt the blood rise inside his head, beating, drumming; yet his body had grown cold. His face was grey again. But he sat up and faced Mr. Lyman squarely.

"May I ask your reasons?"

His voice was cold and hard as he spoke to him.

Mr. Lyman did not raise his eyes from the pad.

"Mightn't that lead to unpleasantness?" he replied.

But John Marco continued to regard him so fixedly that Mr. Lyman shifted uncomfortably in his chair as he sat there.

"Why, pray?" he asked in that same iron, icy voice.

Mr. Lyman lifted his eyes for a moment, met John Marco's, and dropped them again.

"I'm afraid it's all connected with your drinking," he said.

"That's a lie," John Marco shouted. He was leaning forward right over the table by now. "How much I drink is my own concern."

"But unfortunately other people see the results," Mr. Lyman replied. "The whole staff is talking. First there was the affair in the young ladies' hostel which Mr. Hack-bridge and I tried to suppress. And then the episode with Mrs. Marco in the shop. That sort of thing can't be kept dark, you know."

"Show me what harm it's done," John Marco answered. "Show me how it's ever cost the company a penny."

"Very well," Mr. Lyman replied. "If you insist on it."

He removed a folder from under the mass of papers that was in front of him, and opened it.

"I have here three letters from customers who removed their accounts elsewhere after the unfortunate affair with Mrs. Marco. They were all three most excellent accounts."

"Why wasn't I shown them?" John Marco demanded. "What right had you to keep them back?"

He raised his hand to his forehead as he spoke. The blood was still throbbing against his ear-drums and waves of faintness that threatened to overthrow his balance were passing through him.

"They were given to Mr. Hackbridge personally," Mr. Lyman replied. "And he preferred that they should be brought up in the proper quarter."

Mr. Hackbridge added something faint and inaudible under his breath, and began pulling at his tie.

"You and Hackbridge forged these between you," John Marco answered.

"Then please examine the names," Mr. Lyman replied. He half rose in his chair and pushed the papers towards John Marco.

It was noticeable that John Marco's hand trembled as he put it out to take them; the pieces of paper fluttered. But he read them carefully, slowly, as he always read every letter. Then with the corners of his mouth turned down into a kind of crooked smile, he creased the letters and tore them; tore them until they were only tiny shreds.

"That's how much attention I pay to them," he said.

Mr. Lyman coughed.

"I've kept sworn copies," he answered.

"And have you anything to show these gentlemen?" John Marco enquired. "Anything else that reflects on me?"

"Only this," Mr. Lyman replied.

It was a piece of paper with some forty names on it.

"This document contains the signatures of the young ladies who live in the hostel," Mr. Lyman said quietly. "They wish to register their protest against Mr. Marco's behaviour. They are apprehensive for their safety."

"You made them sign it," John Marco answered. His voice was suddenly raised; he was shouting at Mr. Lyman again.

"On the contrary," Mr. Lyman answered. "It was the lady housekeeper. She brought it round herself."

"And is that all?"

"There are also the errors in buying. Some of them are very grave ones. I've kept a record of them."

There was silence for a moment.

"But aren't we losing sight of our main object?"

It was the bank's nominee who had spoken: they were the first words that he had said.

"I understood that you gentlemen had some kind of offer to make to Mr. Marco."

"An offer?" John Marco repeated.

"The offer I had mentioned to me," the nominee went on as gently as before, "was that you should retire from the management and receive an annuity." He paused and pressed the tips of his fingers together. "If left to the board of directors," he added,

561

"I have no doubt that the annuity would be a very generous one."

But John Marco had risen now and was holding on to the table for support.

"Gentlemen," he said. "I won't listen to you. I prefer to fight you. Fight you, I tell you. Fight the whole bloody lot of you. I'll fight you at the General Meeting, and I'll win."

He stepped back, hotly, clumsily, and the chair behind him crashed over onto the floor. Then without speaking again, without even looking in their direction, he walked past them towards the door.

He was alone now; one man against seven. But the vigour seemed to have gone out of him and his feet were dragging across the thick carpet as he moved. His face was quite bloodless and his hands which were clenched beside him were twitching. He swayed for a moment at the door, as though the faintness had overcome him, and Mr. Skewin half rose to save him.

But John Marco recovered himself: he swung the door open in Mr. Skewin's face and then slammed it after him. They could hear those jerking, dragging feet retreating down the corridor.

The board room was silent again; a charged, unnatural kind of silence. The bank's nominee opened his handkerchief and coughed discreetly into it.

"It's all most unfortunate," he said. "I had wanted to raise the question of the dividend. I'm really afraid that the bank must be shown some consideration first."

ii

There were still five weeks before the General Meeting, and for

562

that month and a quarter John Marco abruptly ceased drinking. The cut-glass decanter on its silver tray remained locked inside the cupboard, and there was no one who saw John Marco with even a trace of spirits upon him. No one at the shop that is; at home it was different. He would go straight to his study in the evenings and would emerge again, faltering and uncertain of himself. At first Louise was patient with him, trying to help him out of the slough into which he had fallen. She was careful to bring to the house only those friends whom he liked, the people who might interest him. But he ignored them. He would leave the company without explanation when they went upstairs to the drawing-room, and she would find him later when she went up to bed, sprawling in his chair, the bottle three-quarters empty on the table and his eyes glazed and stupid.

And it was not only her friends that he ignored: it was Louise as well. He seemed oblivious of her presence in the house at all. It was nearly six months since that night when he had gone into her room; he apparently never thought of her. And he looked a different man now. His clothes hung still more loosely on him and his face had lost its hard, firm lines: the outlines of it blurred and sunken. There was age in the face; age and also the breaking down of everything inside him. He was no longer even the kind of man whom she wanted for a lover. She locked her door after her at nights.

Twice during that last month Mr. Lyman and Mr. Hackbridge had asked if they could see him; and each time he had refused. There was no kind of intercourse at all between them. John Marco no longer spoke to them, and what messages were sent were carried by his secretary. He still saw all the important travellers himself; still sorted through the vast, untidy heap of the morning mail, watching every movement inside the machine that he still governed. Since the board-meeting, moreover, he had returned to his tours of inspection. Only, he went alone now, without Mr. Hackbridge shambling after him. And out of the corner of his eye he watched the expression on the faces of the assistants, pondering whether when the last fight really came he could still count on them.

iii

The Annual General Meeting was close now; only two days away in fact. But the young man in sombre, respectable black and the round, narrow collar of the Amosite deaconry, who walked rapidly through the shop and up the broad staircase towards John Marco's room, knew nothing of this. His mind was centred on himself. There was a resolve about him, a fixed certainty of purpose, that separated him from the idle shoppers in the aisles. He walked like a man whose mind is made up about something.

The secretary's room was empty when he got there and he stood for a moment tapping his heels together impatiently. Then, setting back his shoulders, he walked across the room and swung open the door of John Marco's office.

"I've come," he said.

From the desk at the end of the room, John Marco looked up at him. And, as he looked up, the young man noticed how ill he seemed, how wasted and shrunken. And he was more glad than ever that he had not waited, that he had come now when he was wanted.

"I've come," he said, "I've changed my mind."

John Marco still did not answer. He was staring up at the young man in front of him. The youth had grown up suddenly, breaking through the mould that Hesther had imposed on him. There was independence in the way he held himself. And as John Marco looked at him what he saw was himself standing there, with the Old Gentleman somewhere in the background and the Sunday School, and Mary ready to walk home with him. He got up and came towards him incredulously.

"Why have you come here?" he asked. "I didn't send for you."

"I want you to take me into the firm," the other John Marco answered. "You offered it to me once."

John Marco paused and regarded him; he ran his eyes up and down his figure as if he were measuring him.

"Are you serious?" he asked. "Do you really want to be here with me?"

The young man nodded: his mouth was drawn down at the corners as John Marco's so often was.

"I've made up my mind," he said simply.

"But aren't you a minister by now?" John Marco asked. "Haven't you been ordained?"

"I'm not fitted for it," he answered. "I see now that I haven't got the grace. I must get out into the world."

John Marco suddenly put out his hand and laid it on the young man's shoulder. He could feel hard bone there, bone of his bone; his touch rested at last on something that belonged to him. And for a moment the weight on his mind lifted and the young man's strength seemed to become his. But then he remembered the board meeting and his debts, and the mortgages, and how Mr. Lyman and Mr. Hackbridge—all of them in fact— were ranged against him, and how the General Meeting was coming on the day after to-morrow. His heart froze up within him and he turned away.

"It's no use," he said. "It's too late now."

"You mean you don't want me?"

The young man was looking him full in the face and John Marco met his gaze. He started: he had seen the fierce darkness of those eyes before, in Hesther; they were a part of his heritage that the young man would never be able to disown. But now that he was angry he seemed somehow more like John Marco than ever; there was no longer even the division of the years between them. And because it was too much like admitting his own failure to himself, John Marco was hard and abrupt.

"Stay where you are in the Chapel," he said. "I've nothing for you here."

There was silence for a moment.

"Is that your final answer?" the young man demanded.

John Marco drew his hand across his eyes. His head was dizzy once more. But what else was there to say to him? What other answer could he give when in two days' time this whole business might have been voted away from him? But no: that couldn't happen: that sort of thought was simply panic. The shareholders would never be such fools after all that he had done for them, all that he was going to do. In three days' time he'd be master in his own house again; he would have broken Mr. Lyman and Mr. Hackbridge, broken them for the last time and discarded them.

"I asked if that was your final answer," the young man repeated.

John Marco's back was still towards him as he spoke.

"It is," he said. "You chose the cloth. You must stick to it."

The faintness and the dizziness had increased, and he began groping his way back to his chair. When the young man answered, the words came to him faint and from a distance.

"My mother was right about you," he was saying. "She told me you'd got no heart anywhere inside you, and I didn't believe her. I believe her now. There's nothing human about you."

By the time John Marco had reached his chair the young man had already left him; the glass door had slammed to after him and he was gone. John Marco sat down and remained there without moving. He wanted to go after the young man and call him back; call him back and make him understand; wanted to make him realise. He wanted in fact to explain that when a man in the middle of a tight rope sees his long-lost son he cannot be expected to throw his arms around him.

He tried feebly to get up, but his heart was fluttering too much. His breath was choking him again and he sank back. "He came and I sent him away again," he said over and over again. Then at last his lips ceased moving and he sat waiting—waiting as he had waited for those last five weeks for the hour of the General Meeting that it seemed would never come.

Chapter XLIV

But it had come; it was over and finished by now. The meeting had broken up a quarter of an hour ago, and he was back in his room again.

He was still trembling from the strain of it, still trembling and sick. He gripped the front edge of the mantelpiece for support and tried to collect himself. But he was too much shaken, too much bruised and trampled on, for any thoughts to come to him. And his ears were still full of what they had been saying to him, about him, against him. He saw now how wide-spread the plot had been, wider than he had ever imagined; even the speakers from the centre of the hall had exchanged glances before addressing him.

Mr. Lyman's duplicity, it appeared, had reached right back through the years; even in those days when he had still seemed so negligible and contemptible and John Marco had bullied and shouted at him, he had been keeping a record of everything, faithfully writing down the hostile evidence in that dainty hand of his. It was a supplementary and uncensored minute book that he possessed. There was nothing that had escaped him, and he had evidently primed his confederates in the body of the hall. First one man rose to ask about the loss on the Floristry Department and the five thousand pounds that had been spent on the roof garden. Then another man, three seats away, raised the question of the extravagance of putting the assistants into costume at Christmas time, and the fatal overstocks against which the other directors had advised. And there had been another and more sinister side to these revelations. A stranger got up and asked why John Marco had suddenly promoted a young man with no especial talent and made him the head of a department at a time when there were other and senior men who should have been considered; and dropping his voice a little he had added that he understood that when the ruthless economies, the halving of incomes had come, their chairman had refused to allow this particular assistant's salary to be tampered with. And just at this point another outsider, someone who, but for Mr. Lyman's treachery, could not have known, had risen and asked if it were true that there had been only one other exception to the economies in the whole firm—a woman: he had left it at that, and had allowed the shareholders to draw their own conclusions.

And John Marco had been forced to sit beside him and listen to it all. This had been the one meeting from which he could not walk out: they could say what they liked to him and he had to remain there and listen to them. They had howled down his speech, simply because a pale, forlorn-looking man, whose voice was mean and vindictive, had asked whether it was true that John Marco had proposed that his own commission should be doubled. And there had been boos and cat-calls from all over the hall. John Marco had faced these rows of chairs and seen hundreds of angry eyes all staring in his direction. "They don't know how I've worked for them," he had told himself, "they don't know what I've done." But the meeting had taken on a power and momentum of its own: it had ridden over him. There had been cries of "Resign! Resign!" and he had seen a score of fingers all pointing at him at once. He was the target, the bull's-eye, at which they were all firing: it was like facing an execution squad without being blind-folded. And when the nominee of a large block of shares called for a committee of shareholders it was as though the volley had been fired already and he was nicely dead and disposed of.

It had been when this motion was put to the meeting that John Marco had realised that he had failed; that he no longer counted. He was in the chair and it was in his power to conclude the meeting: the chairman's hammer was on the table at his side. But he had not the strength to use it; his mind was numb and dazed. He let a stranger stand up in front of him and wave his copy of the printed prospectus in his face like a banner of insurrection.

It had been during the voting that John Marco had seen Hesther. She had chosen her usual place behind one of the pillars where she could observe everything without being seen. And it was only now that she had emerged. John Marco could picture the gloating there would be inside her, the way her long hands would be rubbing together over this retribution called down from heaven. And then suddenly he had been glad that she was there. She would repeat it all to her son, would tell him how God punished the evil even upon earth; and the boy would under-stand then why he had driven him away again, why he had refused the first friendly hand for years that had been held out to him.

It was of the boy that he had been thinking as he had watched Hesther's dark glove raised in the voting against him; and when he had turned his head for a moment he had seen nearly every other hand in the room raised as well. And still he had sat there. Then when the same men who had proposed the committee of shareholders had proposed that they should call upon Mr. Lyman to head the committee John Marco had got up, holding himself as erect as his pounding heart would allow him, and had descended the steps from the platform, walking past the front row of the shareholders without even turning his head to look at them, back to his own room where he could be alone again.

Only it wasn't his room any longer. It would be Mr. Lyman who would be occupying that chair to-morrow; Mr. Lyman who would be ringing the bell and asking for Mr. Hackbridge—his friend, Mr. Hackbridge—to step upstairs for a moment; Mr. Lyman who would be signing the letters on notepaper with the name of a discarded man across the top of it.

Still holding onto the edge of the mantelshelf to steady himself, John Marco surveyed the room once more. During the last few years he had often come to hate it, this handsome, silent office where he had sat beating his brains trying to earn a dividend for fools. But now it looked familiar and congenial; there were years of his life locked in it.

But the meeting was over: Mr. Lyman might actually come into the room, his room, at any moment. John Marco went over to the desk and with a hand that shook a little extinguished the standard lamp that stood there. Then he put on his hat and coat, and took from the stand the umbrella with the thick gold band round it. Those three things were all there were that belonged to him; everything else was Mr. Lyman's now.

He took one last look round the room and then went outside setting the Yale catch so that the door would lock itself after him;

it had a private key this one, even the watchman did not possess a duplicate.

If Mr. Lyman wanted to get in now he would have to send for someone to break down the door for him.

ii

The house in Hyde Park Square seemed strangely empty when he reached it, and the maid who took his hat and coat from him kept glancing sideways at him as he stood there. "Can she have heard anything?" he began wondering. "Is the news of my defeat all over London already?" "But this is panic," he answered himself. "This is what I must guard against. No one knows yet: not even Louise." And at the thought of telling Louise his mind faltered again. "Later," he said, "I will break it to her after I have rested. I will have something to drink: then perhaps I can bring myself to face her with the news."

His study was warm and comforting, the table pulled up beside his chair in readiness. He sat down wearily, so wearily that he lay there for a time with his legs thrust out in front of him and his arms hanging limply over the side. Then, when some strength had come back to him, he poured himself a drink; and another; and another.

He ate dinner alone, not even asking where Louise was—he was used to these lonely dinners nowadays—and then groped his way back to his study. The decanter still stood there and, by the time he went upstairs to his bedroom, he had mercifully blotted out everything, his defeat, the blackness of the future that lay ahead of him; everything.

He could not even understand what it meant when he saw the note in Louise's handwriting that was lying on his dressing table.

He just stood there, with the blurred image of himself in the mirror in front of him, reading and re-reading the message that it contained. Then his eyes fastened on the last page and remained there. *"If you'd wanted me I'd have stayed,"* the words ran. *"But I have seen for months now that I don't mean anything to you, and I've decided to go away. You'll still have the shop: it's all that interests you and I shall be happier somewhere else. In the memory of earlier times, your still affectionate Louise."*

Then his mind cleared a little and the emptiness of the house frightened him. He ran from the room calling for Louise by name.

Book VII

John Marco Reaches Jordan

Chapter XLV

It was nearly three months since Louise had gone away—with whom, he still wondered.

He was alone now; the servants had given their notice and he had let them go. No one ever came to the house and when he went from one room to another, the dust rose out of the carpets and there were echoes behind him in the silent hall.

Some of Louise's friends had been sorry for him at first; they had sent him invitations and had tried to see him. But he had avoided the lot of them, clinging closely to his own company. And when he met anyone in the street he walked on, either not recognising or not wanting to be recognised. People said, too, that he was behaving queerly. He went about unshaven nowadays; his clothes untidy and his shoes unpolished. But for the most part he remained inside the house; he was seen standing at the windows that were always fastened, staring blankly across the street as if waiting for someone. No one knew what meals he had.

His store of ready money had been less than a hundred pounds when Louise had left him. The company had not parted with a penny of the commission that was due to him; Mr. Lyman had punctiliously set it against John Marco's over-draft with the firm. And the bank had refused to accommodate him further; he had seen his own cheques come back dishonoured, and the bills now lay littering the hall; he walked over them on the rare occasions when he went outside. The tradesmen had all learned, that same night it seemed, of what had happened; and their collectors waited, smoking innumerable cigarettes at the top of the area steps, for someone to come out. And then finding that the massive front door would never be opened to them, there had been summonses. John Marco had had one such paper served on him nearly at midnight by a solicitor's clerk who did not conceal the victory that it was to him. John Marco had thrust the summons into his pocket and had walked on: he had not looked at it since.

The terror that he had was not of the tradesmen and the petty creditors who surrounded him, but of the mortgagees. "When they throw me out of the house, where shall I go?" he asked himself. "Who is there to take me in?" And he sweated, reflecting that there was not a single friend to turn to, not a single door that he could expect to be opened to him. "I'm too old," he kept repeating, "no one wants me. And I haven't got the strength to start again." These terrors became worst at night: he would lie on the bed—he rarely undressed completely—with the waking nightmare upon him, and at those moments it seemed that the whole of London was united against him, waiting for the moment when they could break in and over-run him. For the last week he had even given up attempting to sleep at night. He dozed on and off in his chair by day, and sat on through the evening and the small hours reading. It was always the same book that he read, and often the same page. He read it sometimes aloud to himself, mouthing out the Scriptures as Mr. Tuke himself might have done, so that the room no longer seemed empty and he forgot that he was alone. And while he was reading it the mists for a moment retreated and he was in the light again.

There were times now when his mind was no longer clear within him. He would ring the bell impatiently for the maid to come to him, or turn his head thinking that it was Louise's voice that he had heard. Once it was the white-haired Mr. Morgan whom he thought he saw before him and he half rose respectfully, as though ashamed that the Old Gentleman should have caught him resting.

During the last month Hesther came often to the house. On the last occasion, she stood on the doorstep for nearly an hour, in her copious black that was like an advertisement of the tomb, ringing at the bell and waiting. Finally she thrust a handful of tracts and exhortations through the letter box, on top of the accumulated bills, and went away again, glancing hopefully over her shoulder to see if there were any movement. From behind the shutters in the drawing-room, John Marco watched her as she went back down the street. He stood there, his eyes fixed on those trailing, sepulchral skirts.

And when she had left him, he had not moved away at once but had stayed where he was in the darkness, his eyes still fixed on the deserted street before him.

The delusions that came to him in the empty house gradually grew wider and more varied. At times it seemed to him that there were other people, strangers whom he had not seen before, around him, or that the other rooms were full of his friends, Louise's friends, and that they were waiting for him. On these occasions he would wander all round the house, standing about on the dusty landings, peering and listening. And only when he had satisfied himself that there was no one there would he go

579

back to his room and lock the door behind him and settle down to his reading again. He usually turned the key in the lock behind him nowadays, because of the sense of safety, of security, that it gave; he found comfort in it. "They can't get me here," he kept re-assuring himself; "even if they force their way in they won't be able to reach me here." He had never attempted to define within his mind who "They" were. "They" remained something shadowy in the background, a vague, malevolent influence that was seeking to destroy him. And as the sense of persecution grew within him he went, not once a night, but a dozen times to see that the doors were fastened and that the bars were set firmly across the shutters. Then the house would seem a fortress to him, something unassailable and impregnable. "If they try to break in," he told himself, "I shall defend myself. I shall stand at the head of the stairs and keep them back."

But he knew in his own heart that he was not strong enough to defend himself from anyone; he could scarcely creep up the high staircase without pausing on every step. And on the day when the little auctioneer's men did break in—they did it very politely and discreetly for the sake of the neighbourhood, forcing open one of the lower windows, while a policeman in plain clothes stood by to drive away the inquisitive errand boys—and John Marco heard footsteps, real footsteps, on the stairs and knew that the hour had come, he could only advance towards them, trembling all over, asking in the weak, querulous voice of an old man why they were there, what was it that they had come for.

And when they had told him that they were there to take away the furniture, that the house would be stripped in a few hours, he had offered no resistance. The terrifying blackness, that had descended on him for a moment, had cleared away again when he had realised that it was not him that they had come for. And he had stood by and let them enter one room after another, had seen them going even into Louise's bedroom, into his bedroom, and he had done nothing to prevent it. He had watched the drawing-room being dismantled, himself sitting in one of the big easy chairs by the fireplace, until that, too, was wanted and he was turned out of it, and was driven into another room where already the carpet was turned back and the pictures were down off the walls. They worked with a horrid and a silent efficiency, these men; they were like executioners. He saw his whole private world as he had known it, torn to pieces and destroyed. But he no longer minded: it seemed to him that it was not his home that they were destroying, but Louise's. And Louise had no further use for it. She had gone away and left it. Nothing that the men could do could hurt either of them now.

When the men had gone down the stairs for the last time and the echo of their steps had gone from the house again, the foreman, a grey elderly man, had gone back up the steps once more and had sought out John Marco where he was standing.

"You oughtn't to stop here all alone," he had said. "You'll be doing some mischief to yourself."

But John Marco had only shaken his head and remained where he was, amid the litter of the emptied rooms.

"I can't go yet," he had answered. "I'm not ready."

And that night John Marco began to pray. The prayers were not those that any Amosite minister would have recognised, though there were whole sentences of Mr. Sturger's Devotionary included in them. The words came out in a rush from the turmoil of the present and from the lost places of the memory. And as John Marco prayed, going down on his knees on the bare boards that were all that had been left to him, he was in the Presence again and the room was filled with light and power. There were the rushing of wings about his head and the tongues of serpents; there were great blinding waters and bright cataracts of stars. And because it was nearly two days since he had eaten, he was faint and his mind became released from his body and spanned the heights and the depths. "Call down your vengeance, O Lord, on those that have deceived me and done me wrong," he prayed at one moment; and, at the next, the tears were running down his face and he was contrite: "Miserable I am that I have sinned and betrayed Thy name. Make me whole again so that I may truly repent. Let His precious blood redeem and wipe away my stains." And the prayers became mingled and confused, and he repeated verses of hymns that he had sung as a child and snatches of other confessions that he had heard made in Tabernacle, and words that had reached him from the Bible. He had been praying so long that all sense of time had left him, and even his weakness seemed to have departed too; and still the Presence was there, and the light and the power. And suddenly, in a voice not like that of a man praying, but in a quiet low voice as though he were uttering a confidence to another man, he said aloud: "It wasn't stealing the money that was the sin. The thief were forgiven on the cross. My sin was in betraying Mary. If I had taken my punishment then, she would have been there, waiting; and I should have been clean again. I could have lived. Now I am alone. My sin was turning away from life. For that, God, I ask forgiveness." And he added a private, selfish prayer of his own; something that he did not utter aloud but merely repeated within himself; repeated, time and time again.

It was some hours later—it must have been—because the light had gone out of the sky and the room was in darkness—when he roused himself and listened. There a bell clanging

582

somewhere in the basement of the house. As he listened, it pealed again. He began to tremble, and started to grope his way down-stairs and through the blackness of the hall towards the door. "I must hurry," he kept telling himself; "I must hurry or it will be too late. She will have gone away again." And at last he found the handle of the front door and drew back the bolt that he had fastened there and swung open the heavy door. He could feel the night air on his face again.

It was Mary's voice that spoke to him.

He went away with her so naturally that he did not even remember leaving the dark house behind him; he simply rested his weight upon her arm that seemed so strong beside his weakness, and set out with her.

In front of him the street flickered and grew mysterious and there were forms around him whose faces he could not see. But a new feeling of happiness was filling him; the nightmares that had been surrounding him seemed suddenly to have dissolved. "I am with Mary," his whole body told him, "and there is nothing to fear." And as he walked he found himself in the street that he and Mary had gone down together on the first day when he had walked back with her to the shop in Abernethy Terrace. And the years joined and fused together, and Mary was young and a little shy again; and he was proud and excited and wondered what the Kents would think of him when he had made his introduction. And then he remembered the crime of stealing Mr. Tuke's umbrella and wondered if he would be able to replace it before Mr. Tuke discovered that it was missing. "The rain's come on very suddenly," he observed abruptly, and he glanced down again to catch sight of the rain-drops on her hair; but he saw now that the night was dry and rainless, and he grew confused and bewildered and could not understand.

And as they went his pace became slower; he rested more heavily on her arm at every step. She grew anxious and asked him if he were ill, if she should get help for him. But he did not listen to her, and replied instead: "I wasn't thinking about the lecture, I was thinking about you." And he began to walk faster, swaying on his legs as he did so.

It was when they were nearly home that his knees collapsed under him and he nearly fell. His face was quite grey again by now and he seemed to have stopped breathing altogether. But when he recovered himself he managed, even though the words were no more than a whisper, to say: "It was the miracle before Capernaum that I taught them about to-day"; and he added as if there were a third person beside them: "I shan't ask her to marry me until I can give her everything that she deserves. It may mean one year or it may mean two."

And then he was silent again.

They had reached the house by now—it was the house to which he had driven up that afternoon in his carriage—and Mary was helping him up the steps that mounted to the door. His feet were dragging and his body sagged against her at every movement.

"I shall be all right," he persisted. "I shall be all right. I'm strong."

It was as they reached the second landing, that the door in front of them opened and a girl stood there. The glow from the room caught her for a moment as if she were suspended in light and the pale gold of her hair was shining. Her body was young and slender, and the white neck seemed too slight to support the heavy coil of hair that was piled upon it.

"This is my daughter," said Mary proudly. "You wouldn't wait to see her before."

But John Marco had not advanced any further. He stood still gazing at the girl, even though he was unable to breathe any longer and his blood was ebbing away inside him. He held out his arms towards her.

"Mary," he said. "Mary."

Then another cloud descended on him as he stood there, and he could no longer see. It was as though veils, each one thicker and more dense than the last, were being drawn across his eyes. He thrust out his hands to force them apart. But they remained there. Yet somehow he was not alarmed: she was there, and he had seen her. In the midst of this strange darkness the new feeling of happiness that had come was still with him; only stronger and indestructible by now. He was inside the pattern once more, the true one this time, and life was still there, waiting. Then the last veil of all, the black final curtain descended, and he slid forward gently onto the floor at their feet.

Mary ran forward, shielding him from the girl's eyes. But she need not have troubled: there was nothing in his face that would have distressed her.

John Marco, without a penny to his name, was lying there at his ease, smiling.

A NOTE ON THE AUTHOR

Norman Richard Collins was born in Beaconsfield, Buckinghamshire, on October 3, 1907. By the time he was nine years old, at the William Ellis School in Hampstead, he displayed a talent for both writing and publishing. In January 1933, when he was twenty-five, he became assistant managing director in the publishing house run by Victor Gollancz. In 1941 Collins was forced to move to the BBC due to increasingly poor relationship with Gollancz, who resented Collins' talent and saw him as a rival. During this time he became known for his innovative programming which included *Woman's Hour*, which still airs today on BBC Radio Four. He rose to Controller of the BBC Television Service, later leaving to co-found what is now ITV after deciding a competitor to the BBC's monopoly was needed.

Alongside his busy career, Collins wrote fourteen novels and one work of non-fiction in his lifetime, most of which were popular successes, published begrudgingly by Gollancz. Collins also became well known for his innovative programming at the British Broadcasting Corporation during the late 1940s, and later for advocating and leading the movement toward commercial television broadcasting in Great Britain.

An unmistakable mark of Collins' power of application and creative energy was that he continued to write fiction throughout such an active working life. Although never a full-time writer he was a fluent and prolific author with sixteen titles and two plays to his credit between 1934 and 1981. An autographed edition of twelve of his novels was published during the 1960s.